Valley of of Chaya

TRACEY HOFFMANN

de
publishing

Cover photo by Tim & Trev Gainey
Cover design by INH Graphix
Edited by Susan Lohrer & Annamaria Grafas

Scriptures taken from the Holy Bible, New International Version ®, NIV®
Copyright © 1973, 1978, 1984, 2011 by Biblica, Inc.™
Used by permission. All rights reserved worldwide.

ISBN-13: 978-1478106715 Createspace
ISBN-10: 1478106719 Createspace
ISBN 978-0-9871824-1-8 Edition 1
Published by Dawn Esmond Publishing, Australia

National Library of Australia Cataloguing-in-Publication entry

Author:	Hoffmann, Tracey.
Title:	Valley of Chaya / Tracey Hoffmann.
ISBN:	978-0-9871824-1-8 (pbk.)
Dewey Number:	A823.4

God
may you use these words
to encourage freedom

Allan the love of my life
you taught me the discipline of time

Sarah and Denise my daughters
for the love and grace you extended to your mother
through good times and bad

Annamaria my sister and friend
you encouraged every word and believe in me

Susan thank you
for polishing this book to completion
you are a true gift.

Chapter 1

Ashok loved Shanti. His eyebrows drew together as he watched Shanti play in the dirt, a piece of broken plastic, her toy. He was her brother, and it was his job to look after her and keep her safe. The responsibility weighed heavily on his ten-year-old shoulders. It had always been only the two of them. They must have had parents, but as he tried to visualize his mother's face, no memory came to mind. Shanti depended on him for everything. Her chocolate-brown eyes mirrored her trust and lack of concern for the things he worried about. Yesterday Ashok noticed some men watching Shanti, his stomach churned at the danger she could be in. He'd heard of young girls disappearing off the streets, and he'd tried to explain to her about being careful, but she didn't understand. Shanti was only little.

Looking at the dirt under his fingernails, he wondered what it'd be like to have smooth, clean hands like the white children he sometimes saw. He was tired, hungry, and needed to find a place for them to sleep before it got dark. He pulled the well-worn card from his pocket and looked at the words, wishing he could read them. The card was creased through the middle where he'd repeatedly folded it and pushed it into his pocket.

Shanti dropped the piece of plastic she was playing with and scurried across to him. "Ashok, are you reading the card? Can you tell me about it again?" She squatted beside him, her face alight with anticipation.

"No, Shanti. You know what it says. I have told you many times."

"Please. It makes me feel happy." Shanti placed her hand on his elbow.

Sighing, Ashok circled her thin shoulders with his arm. Maybe hearing the story again would take her mind off her hunger. "You remember when the man gave me this card?"

Shanti nodded, and Ashok placed the card in her hand. She ran a dirty finger over the picture, and a tiny smile lifted her lips.

"The picture is Jesus holding a little lamb. The lamb is us, Shanti— we are his children. Jesus loves us. The card says Jesus will keep you in happiness, if you trust him."

"Who is Jesus, Ashok? Tell me again who he is," she pleaded, pawing at his skin with her fingers.

"He's God's Son and he knows your name, Shanti." Ashok breathed deeply at the thought.

"Why does he love us?" Shanti whispered.

"I don't know, he just does. You know how you trust me to look after you? Well, I trust Jesus to look after me." Ashok shrugged, hoping his answer explained something he himself struggled to understand.

"I'm hungry. Do you think Jesus will help us find food?" She rubbed her flat, hollow stomach.

"He has so far, hasn't he?" Doubt gnawed at Ashok's chest and he avoided her eyes.

~~~

The smell of rotting garbage was almost unbearable. Ashok arched his back to release the ache from bending over. He glanced at Shanti and saw her pick up a ripped piece of rag. She turned to show him, waving the material in the air.

Ashok hated the rubbish dump the most. Shoving his hair back from his forehead, he gritted his teeth. He knew Shanti was waiting for him to acknowledge her find. He lifted his hand and forced a smile to his lips.

Every day people congregated to pick through the stinking household rubbish. Men and women lined up behind the trucks and got first nabs at it. Some people had been pickers all their lives. He hated the thought of this being his lot. He shook his head as he thought of the people who discarded so much.

His fingers touched something sticky, and he knelt down to look, hope rising in his throat and his stomach moved at the thought of food. But someone had fouled the area. He pulled his hand away and hollered in disgust.

Shaking his hand frantically, he moved away to look for water. He came across an empty tin that had captured rainwater. He dunked his fingers into the rusty tin, and then dusted dirt over them. He repeated the action three times before he was satisfied.

Tentatively Ashok lifted his fingers to his nose and sniffed. He screwed up his face and slapped his hand against his pants. Everything smelled bad at the dump. He'd signal Shanti and call it a day.

She was bent over and had her head close to the ground. Her fingers moved quickly through the debris. His eye's narrowed as he saw the stray dog head towards her. The animal shouldn't bother Shanti, he thought, and he waited for it to walk past her.

Shanti jumped up, waving a piece of moldy bread in her hand.

Ashok's heart raced as he watched the dog growl and bare its teeth at her. He saw his sister freeze for a minute, before she spun around and took off. Shanti raced across the rubbish as the dog sped after her.

"Throw it at him, Shanti," Ashok shouted as he scurried towards her.

Shanti swerved to the right, letting go of the piece of bread, which sailed through the air towards the dog. Her foot caught on some unseen obstacle, and she lunged forward, landing on her hands and knees. Her scream sent shivers through Ashok as he reached her. Bending down, he helped her sit up.

"You okay?" He rubbed her arms trying to comfort her. Shanti was inconsolable. Tears streaked down her cheeks, leaving a smudged trail on her dirty face.

"Stop crying Shanti, please." Ashok looked around for help, but no one was interested in them. Shanti pulled her right knee up, and when he saw the steady stream of blood oozing from a deep cut, he gasped.

"Cry onto your knee, Shanti," Ashok ordered, his own tears joining hers. He shakily ripped the dirty material of his shirt and dabbed at her knee.

Shanti leant forward to do as he said. When the rough material scraped across the gash, she closed her eyes tight. Her head snapped up and she pushed at him, anger twisting her face.

"Why did you tell me to give the stupid dog my bread? I could have outrun him."

"I don't think so, Shanti. I'm sorry you hurt yourself." He reached out to her.

She shoved him away. "Why are the dogs here, Ashok? It's not fair—this is our place."

Ashok cringed at her words. He didn't want this to be their place. "The dogs have to eat too, and you need to keep away from them," he said sternly.

Shanti nodded, got up, and hobbled away from him.

Chapter 2

The noise in the church hall was deafening. Charlotte smiled as she gathered her group of teenage girls in a huddle.

"Quick, girls—here's our chance to win."

A petite girl picked up a balloon and placed it between her legs. The others helped her hop to the starting line.

Charlotte laughed at the concentration on her face.

In unison her team shouted, "Go!" Nine voices yelled encouragement as she raced her friends across the hall. Laughter and shouts mingled together. The balloon popped out from between her legs, and groans of disappointment could be heard from her team.

Clapping her hands, Charlotte called out, "Well done." Her girls followed suit and raced to hug their friend.

She looked across at Pamela Benton and caught her nod. Pamela had been Charlotte's youth leader and still helped out every Tuesday and Friday night. Charlotte thought of her own family and marveled that they'd been attending Rosewood Baptist Church, in Sydney, for three generations. Her grandmother still made one service a week and loved to join in the women's Bible study on a Wednesday afternoon.

Smiling, she thought of her Nan and mentally planned to help her with some gardening on the weekend.

After the girls had been picked up by their parents, Charlotte stayed behind to help clean up. She manned a large broom and charged across the hall in a manner that showed she'd done it many times.

"Charlie, we've finished cleaning the kitchen." Her friend Ruth dusted her hands on her jeans. "Are you nearly done here?"

Charlotte turned to her and smiled. "I'm just about finished. You go. I want to have a word with Pamela before I leave."

Ruth nodded and waved as she left.

Securing a loose strand of hair behind her ear, Charlotte bent and picked up the dust, dumped it in the trash, put the broom away, and hurried to help Pamela load her car. She had a lot of respect for Pamela Benton and her commitment to the young people in Baulkham Hills.

After placing a box of folders on the backseat of Pamela's car, Charlotte straightened and closed the door.

Pamela rubbed her back. "I can always rely on you to stay to the end. Thanks, honey."

Shrugged away her thanks, Charlotte smiled.

"How are your plans coming along for your trip?"

Charlotte's brow furrowed slightly, and she pushed her hair out of her face. "Ruth isn't sure she'll have enough money saved. I suggested we have a garage sale to help her." She heard the doubt in her voice.

"Don't give up. If God wants you to go to India before you start university, then it'll happen."

Moving restlessly on her feet, Charlotte nodded. It had been her dream since she was fifteen to visit India, and she'd thought Ruth shared the dream. But Ruth was always spending her money on clothes and outings, and was now saying she wasn't sure she wanted to go. Charlotte was disappointed her friend was having second thoughts and wondered if her parents would let her go on her own.

"I can't help on Friday night. My boss's sister isn't too well. I volunteered to work for him so he could go visit her." She hated letting people down, but Mr. Grey needed her help. Her heart ached when she remembered the look on his face as he told her they didn't expect his sister to be with them much longer. He trusted her at the restaurant; if he was called away, she often filled in for him.

"That's fine, dear." Pamela patted Charlotte's hand and got into her car. "Give Wilbert my regards and tell him to call me if there's anything I can do."

Charlotte watched her drive off and stood staring at the church. The old building had seen better days, but the grounds were well cared for and a new lick of paint graced the wooden partitions around the entrance. She squinted as the last rays of sunshine bounced off the stained-glass windows. Two weeks ago, on her birthday, the church had hummed with people celebrating with her. Someone had made a banner and hung it across the hall's entrance. 'Charlotte Rose Turner— eighteen today!' It had been a great night, and Charlotte smiled at the memory.

She glanced at her watch and then trotted to her car; her parents would be waiting for her to get home so they could have dinner together.

Things would work out, she thought. She'd convince her parents it was okay to go to India on her own. Charlotte was determined, she wasn't a child, and they'd have to accept this.

~~~

Tonight Ashok and Shanti would share the pavement with the Chander family. Bashaar Chander was Ashok's friend. He'd been born on the pavement of Masjid Road as had his father and grandfather.

Bashaar's mother smiled at Ashok as he walked towards them.

Ashok nodded back and glanced down at Shanti. Her eyes were downcast and she hadn't spoken since they'd left the rubbish dump.

"You can lie next to Bashaar, Ashok." Mrs. Chander reached for an empty-looking bag at her feet. It couldn't contain more than a few crusts, and she'd need it to feed her family tomorrow. "Have you had any food today?"

"Thank you—yes," Ashok answered.

He turned away from her knowing eyes and led his sister towards Bashaar. Shanti lay on the hard concrete and turned her back to Ashok. He sucked in a sad breath as he worried about her knee. He'd tried to wipe it clean, but Shanti cried every time he touched it. Ashok patted her back and bent to kiss her cheek.

"You'll be all right, Shanti. I'm proud of how fast you ran to get away from the dog." He felt Shanti pull away, and his eyes burned. Ashok wanted to close his eyes and sleep, but he didn't know when he'd see his friend again. Sighing, he lowered himself down beside her and turned to talk to Bashaar.

"How have you been?" Ashok raised his eyebrows.

"I have forgotten what it's like to smile, Ashok. Yesterday I followed some rich people with the hope of some rupee, maybe a paise or two. The women wouldn't look at us, and a man pushed me to the ground and trampled over me. We are like rats to them." Bashaar closed his eyes dramatically. "My family has high standing on this street. Yet if I were gone tomorrow, who would remember my name?"

"I would, Bashaar Chander. You had a bad day, tomorrow will be better." Ashok tilted his head to watch Bashaar's family settling for the night. Each person seemed to cup the next for warmth. Ashok's heart swelled, and he smiled. He waved his hand expressively. "Look at your family—you are rich indeed, my friend."

Ashok turned and pulled Shanti close to him. Her body relaxed as his arm became a pillow for her head. He knew he'd be stiff in the morning, but it was worth it to see her relax. As he closed his eyes, he became aware of the sounds of the street. Cars drove past, close to their bodies, with only a broken kerbing protecting them from the speeding wheels. How many feet had walked this pavement during the day? How much dirt had been stamped into the broken crevices where he now lay his head? He shivered and moved his head off the ground momentarily. He could hear the shuffling sound of Bashaar's family getting comfortable. He would never be comfortable sleeping here.

Jesus, is it wrong to want more for Shanti and me? I want to be able to read the words on my card. To be able to care for her as a brother should. Can you help me know what to do tomorrow? I can't take her back to the dump.

His eyes became heavy, and he willed his arm to relax. At least tonight he would sleep. The Chander family would wake him if any danger approached.

~~~

Shanti woke to the sound of a car horn. Her knee rubbed the material of her pants, and she caught her breath. As she sat up, she heard Ashok moan. He pulled his arm from under her, and Shanti's eyes widened. His arm must hurt; she'd kept her head on it all night. Tears stung her eyes, and her mouth wobbled. It wasn't Ashok's fault the nasty dog had chased her, yet she'd blamed him and screamed when he tried to clean her knee. Shanti tentatively touched her wound. It could be worse; at least the dog had moved away once it had her bread. She'd have to say sorry to Ashok for not talking to him. Maybe she could find him some food to eat as a surprise.

Carefully she moved between the sleeping forms sandwiched together all around her. She pushed her hand through her hair, twisting it away from her face. The tangles pulled, and she wished she had a hair band. Ashok didn't like her going off on her own, but if she kept him in sight she'd be okay.

As she moved down the street, she looked back to see if Ashok was still sleeping. She'd found nothing and sighed in disappointment.

Shanti remembered seeing a *vada pav* stand around the corner and her mouth watered as she thought of the fried potato stuffed in bread. Surely it wouldn't hurt to take a quick look. As she approached the vendor, Shanti's eyes narrowed. Ashok would not let her steal, he said Jesus would not like it. As the smell of spices tantalized her nostrils, her stomach growled.

Her eyes grew wider as she watched a tall, smartly dressed man drop coin into the vendor's hand. Turning abruptly, the man bumped into Shanti knocking her knee. A small sob escaped as her eyes flooded with tears.

The man looked down at her from a great height.

She'd never seen such a scary face; dark, mean eyes set in deep grooves seemed to look right through her. She quickly scrambled up. Ashok told her not to talk to strangers, and now she wished she hadn't left his side.

The man reached down and grabbed her arm. Shanti's breath escaped her, and a silent scream rose in her throat.

~~~

Ashok moved slowly and felt stiff in every part of his body. He flexed his arm to get the blood circulating. He tipped his head from side to side to stretch his neck as his eyes scanned for Shanti among the people moving on the pavement. Perhaps she had gone to relieve herself.

Standing, he said good morning to Bashaar and asked if he'd seen Shanti.

"No, my friend. She was gone when I woke up." Bashaar shrugged and walked away.

He spun around looking in every direction. He was fully awake now and his stomach twisted in fear. Where was she? He called good-bye to the Chander family and hurried down the street. His pace increased to a run as he turned the corner, frantically looking for his sister. He had to find her. His heart pumped wildly and hot tears streaked down his cheeks.

~~~

"Hush, girl. I'm sorry I knocked you. Are you hungry?"

Shanti nodded and stifled a sob. The man pushed his purchase into her hands and ordered another. Her mouth dropped open as she looked up at him.

The large man handed more money to the vendor then turned

14

towards her. "You need to get that knee seen to. Have you any money?"

His eyes squinted as he looked over her appearance, taking in her tattered clothes and filthy hair. His hand dug in his pocket and he dropped some coin into her outstretched hand.

"Thank you, *saab*, thank you." Shanti backed away and she hobbled down the street laughing as she thought of her good fortune. As she turned the corner she saw Ashok running towards her. He'd be happy with her, and they could eat together.

"Shanti," he puffed. "Do you know how frightened I was when I woke up and you were gone?" Ashok scolded. His arms circled her and held on tight.

"I'm sorry, Ashok—but look what I have." Shanti pushed away from him and held out the bread. She laughed as his eyes widened. "A man bumped into me and my knee started to bleed again, so he gave me this and these coins." She held out the coins to him with her other hand.

Quickly taking the money, he pushed it into his pocket. He grabbed the top of her arm and moved away from the corner. "Where is this man? Did he want anything from you?"

"No. Once he gave me the coins, I ran off," she said with a beaming smile. "Please don't be angry with me. I wanted to get you some food." Shanti tried to ignore the throb in her knee and she lowered her eyes as she noticed the tears on Ashok's face. "Can we eat?" she asked in a small voice.

"Yes. Thank you, Shanti, God is good to us." Ashok mumbled. He brushed his cheek and gave a watery smile as he split the bread in two.

Sitting beside her brother, Shanti ran her tongue over the top of her lips in anticipation. She stretched her legs out in front of her, with her right knee slightly raised.

Ashok shuffled down beside her. Turning, he looked closely at her knee as he dabbed at the blood with the corner of his shirt.

Shanti raised her eyes to his. "Ashok, please leave it until later."

Ashok nodded and closed his eyes as he chewed.

She finished her last bite of bread and giggled as she licked her fingers. "That was sooo good. Did you enjoy it, Ashok?"

"Yes, very much." Ashok crossed his legs and turned towards her. "I need to see your knee—can you keep still for me?" His gaze gentled, and she nodded.

The material of her pants had stuck to the wound, and Ashok puckered his lips in indecision. He pulled at the fabric, fumbling though she could tell he was trying to be careful. When he finally tore the cloth from the wound, she could see the gash had reddened and her knee had swollen.

"Shanti, I don't know what to do. How does it feel?"

"It burns, Ashok. When I walk, it hurts." Her shoulders shook as she raised watery eyes to his face.

He patted her shoulder. "Jesus will help us. We have eaten well this morning and have a pocket full of rupee—now we find a doctor to look at your knee."

Chapter 3

Charlotte smiled at the girl in the photo. When Nan gave her the child sponsorship as a birthday gift two years ago, her heart had been drawn to the dark-skinned, pretty Indian girl. A seed was planted. Charlotte believed God wanted her to go to India. She placed the photo back on the shelf and then flicked through her folder. Picking up a pen, she scribbled, "India, a land of many contrasts. Old, new, great, small, utter poverty and extreme wealth."

She had to go.

Rubbing her forehead, she tensed at the thought of telling her parents she intended to continue with her plans without Ruth. Maybe she could talk Eli into going with her. Her brother was her hero. Their relationship had always been special. He'd taken the role of big brother seriously from the minute they'd placed her in his arms. He'd been the one to shorten her name to Charlie Rose or Bud, as he affectionately called her at times. If she could convince him to take three weeks off work and go with her, then her parents would agree. Her mood felt lighter with the idea and a grin teased her mouth.

~~~

Eli knew she was up to something. She had that look on her face that said I'm your little sister and you love me. He stifled a laugh and tried to appear unsuspecting.

"Eli, I've missed you. You haven't been here for ages. What excuse do you have?" Charlotte hugged her brother and stepped back to study his face.

"I have been around, Bud—but you're never here." He cocked his head to the side and surveyed her. When had she grown up? Her golden hair hung loose down her back, and her cream complexion highlighted large hazel eyes. She was beautiful. His eyes widened at the thought. It wouldn't be long before she was fighting off the boys. Maybe she already was. Would she tell him if this became a problem?

"Where have you been every time I visit Mum and Dad?" He reached out and ruffled her hair. He knew he'd get a reaction to this and laughed as she pushed his hand away.

"Don't do that. You know I don't like it." She screwed up her nose. "I've been helping out at the restaurant more now school's over." Charlotte cocked her head, and her eyes bore into his. "How come you don't call in there anymore to see me?"

"I'm seeing someone, Charlie." He grinned as he watched her mouth open and close.

"Who? How long? Do Mum and Dad know?" Charlotte sat forward and grabbed his arm.

Laughing, he tangled his fingers with hers. "Not long." He lifted his eyebrows as she laughed. "Her name's Tina and I met her on Hamilton Island."

"That's three months ago."

"I only asked her out three weeks ago. Mum and Dad know. I asked them not to tell you—I wanted to." He watched the slideshow of emotion flash across her face. She'd know he was serious about Tina, because he never asked girls out. Lately he'd seen his friends get married and he'd felt an emptiness in his heart. He wanted a family of his own. A wife to share his life with, children to love and treasure.

"When can I meet her, Eli? Have you got her photo on your phone?" Charlotte held her hand out in expectation.

Handing the phone over, Eli watched her frown as she looked at Tina's photo. A smile tugged at his mouth, and he reached over and kissed Charlotte's cheek. "You'll like her, Charlie. She's sweet like you."

"Is she a Christian?"

"That's a dumb question coming from you. Of course she is." Shaking his head, Eli reclaimed his phone and pocketed it. Eli was aware that life was uncomplicated for Charlie. She'd been brought up sheltered and protected. Tina hadn't.

Thoughts of Tina caused his heart to flip. He wanted to spend all his spare time with her. She attracted him as no other woman had. Eli shook his head again. He was with Charlie and she deserved his full attention.

"What about you, Charlie? How are you?" Because of her petite frame and delicate hands, many people made the mistake in thinking Charlie was fragile, weak. Her determination and stamina often surprised him.

"I'm trying to work out my trip." Charlotte spoke slowly. "Ruth doesn't seem to want to come anymore."

"That could be a problem. Mum and Dad won't let you go on your own."

"I was hoping you might come with me." Her eyes locked on his and he lifted his brow in surprise.

Charlotte tucked a stray strand of hair behind her ear. "It's only three weeks, and you haven't had a holiday for a while," she playfully stabbed her finger into his arm. "Come on Eli, you know you want to, otherwise why have you learnt to speak Marathi with me over the last two years?"

Eli knew he couldn't go and felt a moment of regret. "I attended those classes because I wanted to spend time with you, and because I will get to India one day," pausing he rubbed his chin. "What made

19

Ruth change her mind?" he asked, stalling for time.

"Truthfully, I don't know. She said she doesn't think it's what God wants her to do, and I have to accept this." Charlotte tilted her head and gave a sad smile. "I wish she'd told me earlier, that's all."

"I can't go with you, Charlie. I can't afford the time or money right now. I'm sorry." Eli felt a gut-wrenching pull in his stomach as he took in her disappointed shrug. He couldn't always solve her problems. He squared his shoulders, looked her in the eye and smiled.

Charlotte nodded. Her head lifted, a sparkle of determination in her eyes made them dance. "It was worth a try. I am going though, Eli."

~~~

Wiping her hands on the towel, Charlotte sighed. She walked across the restaurant to pour Mrs. Davenport another coffee. She enjoyed her job; people like this dear old lady made the time go so quickly.

"Can you sit for a while, Charlotte?"

Charlotte smiled and eased into the chair beside her. "Yes, it's still early and we're not too busy." Charlotte's eyes lowered to take in Mrs. Davenport's swollen knuckles and joints. "How have your hands been this week?"

Mrs. Davenport had been married three times, and each of her husbands had died. Some of the girls at school had joked about her cooking. Charlotte didn't like the insinuations and knew Mrs. Davenport was lonely and had a sweet heart.

"Stiff, I have to say. Still, no good complaining. I have a little something for you, Charlotte. You've been a good friend to me over the last two years, dear. I wanted to give you something to help with your trip."

"That's not necessary. I enjoy spending time with you. Please you don't have to give me anything." Charlotte's face heated and she twisted her hands. What if she couldn't go?

"I know that. Not many young women your age want to visit an oldie like me. I know I don't go to your church, dear—but I've been thinking lately that I might call in one of these days. Maybe your grandmother would pick me up?"

"I'm sure she would. She'd enjoy your company. I'll ask her for you." Charlotte flicked her plait over her shoulder and looked towards the kitchen. She'd need to get back there and help before things piled up. She watched as Mrs. Davenport placed an envelope on the table.

"Open it later, dear. Bless you." Mrs. Davenport dabbed at the corner of her eye and shooed Charlotte away. Impulsively she bent and kissed the wrinkled old cheek before she turned and raced to the kitchen.

She pushed the envelope into her back pocket as she rushed over to help unpack the dishwasher. She couldn't keep the smile off her face. Surely God had confirmed her decision to go to India on her own. Tonight she would talk to her parents.

Chapter 4

Hand in hand they walked into the hospital. Ashok tightened his fingers around Shanti's. His gaze swept the foyer and his shoulders slumped. The place was crawling with people; they leaned against walls or sat on the floor. He saw families congregated together eating food as if they'd been there for a long time. He screwed up his nose at the smell of sickness.

It felt like the inside of his chest was trembling. He wished he were bigger so he wouldn't feel so invisible. He moved across to a counter surrounded by people. The confined noise of everyone talking at once was deafening, and his head began to thump. As he waited in line he glanced down at Shanti. Her hand felt sticky and she had her eyes closed.

His feet ached from standing, but he could now see the counter. He was just about to step up and ask for help when a fat man pushed him away. Ashok pushed back and tried to regain his place. The man scowled at him and Ashok stepped back. A nurse walked past, and Ashok ran and grabbed her hand.

"Please, miss, can you help my sister?"

Ashok's hand was slapped away and the woman glared at him. She beckoned a man dressed in a dark blue uniform. He sauntered over to Ashok, grabbed his hair, and dragged him to the door. Ashok struggled to get free of the man's hand; his scalp stung and he fought the tears that threatened to fall. His face burned with shame as people stopped talking and watched what was happening with uncaring eyes.

As the man shoved him out the door, Ashok lost his balance and toppled down the steps, the hard edges biting into his back. He scrambled to his feet. He needed to get Shanti.

"We don't let dogs in here, boy. If you know what's good for you, you'll keep away." The man turned and entered the building.

Shanti limped towards him and held out her hand. "You're not a dog, Ashok, but that man looked like a monkey." Her face crinkled as she giggled hysterically.

Ashok placed his hand in hers and looked at her glassy eyes. He touched her forehead, and heat radiated from her skin. He'd seen a cut turn black before, and the smell had made him vomit.

"Boy, wait, wait. Is the little girl okay?" A woman called out as she hurried down the steps. "My husband's a doctor and may be able to help."

Turning, Ashok squinted at her. A man dressed in a business suit slowly followed her down the steps. The tall, pale woman touched the man's arm and pointed to them. The man glanced at them and shook his head. The woman said something and walked towards them. Ashok watched as the man looked at his watch and followed her. Ashok stood in front of Shanti, shielding her body from them.

The man's eyes softened and his face looked kind.

"A doctor?" Ashok's gaze locked on the man. "Please, saab, my sister has a cut knee. I have money if you can help her." Ashok held out the coin Shanti had given him and offered it to the man.

Sighing with resignation, the man knelt beside Shanti. "Hello, little girl. My name is Paul Simmons, and this is my wife Wendy. Can I take a look at your knee?"

Shanti nodded. The man gently removed the material of her pants, and he inhaled a deep breath. Ashok's stomach tightened.

"That's a nasty gash you have there. I'll need to clean it up for you." He looked at Wendy, his forehead wrinkling, then back at Ashok. "Put your money away, boy. What's your name?"

"Ashok, saab." Ashok felt warm inside. "My sister is Shanti," he stated firmly.

Paul pointed across the street. "We're staying over there. I don't think it's a good idea to go back into the hospital. I think it's best if you come over to our hotel with us. Will you do that?"

Tears spiked Ashok's eyelashes and he nodded, unable to speak. He helped Shanti up and stumbled as she placed her arm around him. The woman named Wendy smiled at him and took Shanti's hand.

As they walked into the foyer of the big hotel, Ashok felt eyes on him. He pretended not to notice and lifted his chin. *Jesus, you sent these people to help us—I know you did.* His heart fluttered at the thought. His mind saying over and over again, *Jesus knows my name.*

The lady helped Shanti shower. Ashok could hear her giggling, and a smile touched his lips at the sound. The man was foraging around in a brown satchel, pulling out bandages, bottles, and a small knife. Ashok's lips tightened at the thought of the knife touching his sister's skin.

He walked over to the man. "Saab, is my sister going to be all right?" He straightened his back and stood tall. He tried to stop his voice from shaking, but he felt wobbly inside.

"I'm sure she'll be okay. Let's see how the knee looks once it's clean." Paul patted Ashok on the shoulder and cleared the table. "Where are your parents, Ashok?" he asked gently.

Ashok shrugged. His stomach hummed with nerves. Would the man call the police and have them arrested? Did he think he had stolen the money? Ashok stepped back from him and gauged the distance to the door.

"You look after your sister? It's just the two of you, isn't it?" Paul's kind voice encouraged Ashok to nod.

"I do not remember parents, saab."

Wendy and Shanti came into the room, and Ashok turned to check his sister. She was wearing new clothes. A blue T-shirt and shorts. Her hair was brushed and tied back in a band. She looked beautiful. His eyebrows rose in question. Where had the clothes come from?

"We have a son and daughter back home, about the same age as you two," Wendy informed him. "I have some clothes that will fit you, Ashok. Would you like to have a shower too?" Ashok lowered his eyes and nodded. These people were too kind. The thought of clean water and new clothes excited him. He followed Wendy to the bathroom, where she gave him a towel. A pile of folded clothes waited on a stool.

"Take as long as you like. When you're ready, come out and Paul will look at Shanti's knee." Wendy left the room and Ashok did a little skip. He touched the new clothes in awe. Ripping off his soiled shirt and pants, he kicked them away and stepped into the shower where he let the water stream down his back. His eyes closed and a small gurgle escaped his throat. Ashok cried in happiness.

~~~

Shanti closed her eyes tight and tried not to cry. She gripped the edge of the table with her hands to stop herself from moving. The kind doctor was helping her. Ashok had whispered that Jesus had brought them to fix her knee. As pain screamed up her leg, a small noise escaped her lips. Her eyes snapped open and searched for Ashok. Shanti had to lift her head off the table to see him. He sat bent over with his head in his hands. His shoulders shook and Shanti wanted to know if he was okay. "Ashok?" She glanced at the lady standing beside her.

Wendy smiled. "Ashok was feeling a little faint, honey. So I suggested he sit down until Paul finishes stitching your knee."

Pushing up on her elbows, Shanti looked at her knee. The man named Paul had scraped some of the skin off and stitched the gash. It looked better already. The beginning of a smile tugged at her face. "Thank you," she said shyly.

25

Paul nodded. "You are a very brave little girl. I would have cried my eyes out. You're going to be fine in a few days." He stepped back to allow Wendy the space to put an adhesive strip over the stitching.

"Ashok, I want to tell you and Shanti how to look after the knee."

She watched her brother carefully as he came to stand beside her. His eyes took in the neat stitching and he expelled a heavy sigh from his chest.

Paul placed his hand on Ashok's shoulder. "You did well, Ashok. I used to get woozy when I saw blood too." Ashok looked up at him in admiration. "Now, you two, you need to keep the knee clean and dry. I have a bag here with adhesive strips in it. Change the Band-Aid, every day. Shanti, you need to rest your knee. I'm also going to give you a tetanus shot, just to be on the safe side, and I have these tablets I'd like you to take for ten days." Paul rattled the pills in the small plastic bottle. He dropped them into Ashok's hand. "It's your job to remember to give them to her Ashok—one a day."

Ashok nodded. He gripped the bottle and squinted at the unfamiliar words.

"Thank you, Mr. Paul. Shanti and I, we are very thankful." Ashok bowed in respect.

Wendy's hand cupped Shanti's face. "There are a few things we need to go and do now. But I'd like you to stay the night with us. That way Paul can check your knee in the morning, Shanti. I've ordered room service—food—which will be up shortly for you. We'll be back in about an hour."

~~~

Paul and Wendy didn't speak as they took the lift to the foyer. He knew Wendy was trying to work out a way to help the children. India's children always broke their hearts. "You can't have them, Wendy. We've done all we can. You know we're leaving tomorrow."

"I know, honey. Did you see the way Ashok looks at his sister? I don't think I've met a more serious little boy. How old do you think they are?"

"No more than eight and ten, I'd say. If we call the authorities, what will they do with them?"

"They'll end up in an institution of some sort. They could even be separated. I don't want that." Tears glistened in Wendy's eyes. "I want to buy them some clothes, soap, water, a bag each—just a few things. Do you want to come with me, Paul?"

Paul's throat grew tight with his love for her compassion. "No. I'll meet you back here in an hour. There are a few things I want to get for them too."

~~~

Ashok and Shanti slept on the deep, soft couch covered by a fluffy rug. When the sun's rays pushed through the window, Ashok stretched and remembered. He was stunned at their good fortune. He reached over and picked up his card from the small table. The man Paul and Wendy were like Jesus, helping little children. Perhaps they could stay with them—always. Should he ask? What if he didn't ask and they were waiting for him to? Wendy had returned on her own yesterday with gifts for them. She'd given them each a bag. She called them backpacks. They had waterproof jackets, long pants, a hairbrush and bands for Shanti, and shoes. The shoes and socks were what surprised Ashok. He'd never had shoes and felt tingly thinking about them. Slipping out from under the cover, he crept over to his new clothing. He silently got dressed in his new pants and shirt and sat to put on his socks. The shoes had Velcro straps on them. Wendy said she thought it would be easier for them than laces, and he had nodded as if he understood about laces. Standing, Ashok ran his hand down his pants and moved to look at himself in the mirror. His head tilted slightly as he stood staring at the image of a boy he barely recognized. He knew he was only ten, but his reflection surprised him. He'd thought he was bigger, taller. Shanti came and stood beside him. He hadn't heard her moving and tilted his head to look at her. Her hair was ruffled from sleep, but she smelled good. He wanted this for her; warmth, food, and care. He would ask Mr. Paul if they could be his children and stay with them forever.

Chapter 5

"Absolutely—no—way." Bill Turner's voice didn't encourage discussion. Charlotte looked at her father, her heart twisting at the look of concern on his face. She licked her lips and set her shoulders. She'd prayed, asking God to give her wisdom on how to broach the subject of travelling alone.

"Dad, I'm sorry, but I've made up my mind. I'm going." Her voice was soft and firm. Her eyes locked with his, and she refused to be intimidated by his stance.

"Charlie, it's not safe travelling on your own. I wouldn't sleep a wink." Her father reached over and took her hand. He gently rubbed his thumb over the knuckles. "Sweetheart, we love you and only want what's best for you."

"I know that, Dad. Look at it from my perspective—I've planned this trip for two years. Worked, saved, and dreamed about it nonstop. Every minute is organized. Do you know how much time it took me to map it all out?" Charlotte lifted her hand as her father went to speak. "I understand how you feel. You still see me as your little girl and want to keep me safe. I love you for that—but I'm eighteen now. You can't wrap me in cotton wool all my life. I believe God wants me to take this trip."

"Charlotte, you're not listening to me. I'm telling you, you're not going to India alone."

Charlotte diverted her eyes and blinked to stop the tears. She hated defying her father, but this was important.

"The way I see it, Dad, is that you have two options. One, you accept that I'm going with or without your blessing, or two, you come with me." Her eyes narrowed as his eyebrows rose.

"You'd love it, I know you would," Charlotte said excitedly. She flashed her parents a dazzling smile. "Mum, imagine the fun we'd have. You're always talking about creating memories together, and here's our chance."

"No, Charlotte. Your mother and I will not go to India with you. Not everything revolves around you. Once you accept the timing's out for this trip, we will all be much happier. I'm not prepared to discuss it any further." Bill rose and ignored Macy's icy glare.

"Mum?" Charlotte felt sick to her stomach. She loved her father and had never had to disobey him before. If she weren't living at home, would she still be having this conversation?

Macy Turner shook her head. "I agree with your father, honey. It's not a good idea to go on your own. Why don't we go out to the movies tonight? I'm sure in the morning you'll see things clearly. You will get to India, Charlie. Maybe in a year or two when you have a group of people wanting to go."

Charlotte felt betrayed. Didn't anyone know her heart? Why did she have such an urgency in her heart to go now? The thing was, she couldn't see a good reason to cancel her trip, and she'd lose money on the ticket this close to departure.

"I don't want to go to the movies. I'm going to my room." Charlotte spoke in a small voice.

"Charlotte Rose, I don't want you going to your room to sulk. You know we love you—I expect you down for dinner." Macy turned away and missed the hurt look on Charlotte's face.

Closing her bedroom door, Charlotte collapsed on her bed. Did her mother think she'd change her personality because things weren't going her way? When had she ever sulked?

"Lord Jesus, your word says the path of the righteous is level, that you make the way of the righteous smooth. It doesn't feel smooth, Lord. I've committed this trip to you, planned every step with you. I've investigated mission stations and orphanages. You've placed this love for the people of India in my heart, and it's not about me, but about what you have for my life." Falling to her knees, Charlotte spread out on the carpet. Her arms stretched above her head. "Lord, if you don't want me to go, take away my burden. Give me deep inner peace that will help me step in confidence, I pray."

The tears began softly. Her eyes squeezed tight as her shoulders shook with sobs. She grieved the argument with her parents and what was to come.

~~~

The sun warmed Charlotte's back. Her Nan would be out with ice water soon. As she scratched the fork through the freshly turned soil, her mind was in turmoil. It had been a week since the argument with her parents, and both her mother and father acted like the issue was resolved. Her eyebrows drew together as she acknowledged that the unspoken words were always the most painful. She saw her Nan out of the corner of her eye, stood, brushed the dirt off her knees, and moved to join her.

"Thank you, Charlie. The flower beds look amazing." Her Nan's smile lifted Charlotte's mood, and she reached over and kissed her before sitting on the iron patio chair. Charlotte picked up the glass and took a long drink.

"Your mother told me about your trip being cancelled," her Nan said with an empathetic tone. "You can talk to me about it, honey."

Charlotte averted her eyes and pulled the band out of her hair. Silky blonde strands surrounded her face, and she pushed it behind her ears.

"Dad won't listen to anything I have to say. It's black-and-white for him—end of discussion. Do you think God would put such a passion in my heart for India and then squash it?"

"No, dear. Not squash it, but maybe delay it?" her Nan said gently.

"I love my parents, and I know they don't want anything to happen to me. But isn't that living in fear? I'm eighteen and an adult. I can drive a car, vote, work—leave home." Charlotte stood and paced the lawn. "If it was Eli wanting to go, they wouldn't hesitate to encourage him."

"That's not fair, Charlotte. It's different for a girl, there are dangers that Eli wouldn't have to face."

"I can take care of myself, Nan. I've done everything to prepare for this trip." Charlotte flexed her arm. "I've had injections for hepatitis, typhoid, tablets for malaria. I completed a self-defense course—and I'm fit." Charlotte plopped back into her seat. "Bad things happen here. Do you listen to the news?"

"I choose not to watch the news these days. I prefer to fill my mind with happy things. I would miss you if you went to India right now. Who would help me with my garden and brighten my day with her beautiful smile?"

Charlotte grinned at her Nan and let her think the subject was dropped. Where was faith in all this? Her eyes rose, and she spied a wood pigeon on Nan's clothesline. The bird cooed, and Charlotte inhaled as the verse filled her mind. She glanced at her Nan. She would speak the words, declare them, and walk where God would take her. "It says in Deuteronomy, Nan, that the Lord himself goes before me and is with me. He will never leave me. He tells me not to be afraid, not to be discouraged."

Nan frowned, her skin creased down her cheeks. "You're a good girl, Charlie. I'm proud of the way you're handling this."

~~~

Macy watched the television with blank eyes. Tomorrow would have been the day Charlotte left to go on her trip. She glanced over at Bill and scowled. Didn't he care that their daughter was upset? Macy wanted to blame Bill for Charlotte's quiet mood and headache, but she knew she should have tried to talk to her. How could she tell her daughter she was sorry her trip was cancelled when in truth she wasn't? She'd tried to broach the subject with Bill, but he refused to talk about it. Charlotte needed her father to hold her right now, not distance himself from her. Macy rose to her feet. Her eyes snapped at him. "I'm going to bed."

"She'll be okay. Macy, trust me in this." Standing, he pulled her into his arms. Macy sighed and let her body relax. Her arms rose and circled his shoulders. Everything would look different in the morning.

"I'm going to stay up for a while," Bill said. "Are you okay?"

Nodding, Macy kissed his cheek, and moved away.

~~~

The television murmured in the background as Bill slumped in his chair. Charlotte had been an easy child. Her gentle nature made it a pleasure to teach her. She'd always loved God. Right from the moment she could talk, she babbled away to Jesus as if she could see him. Charlotte never questioned what he told her; she trusted her daddy. He remembered when she excitedly told him Jesus died for her. His eyes watered as he recalled her shining face.

They'd never had words; she never pushed the boundaries like Eli had. His gut wrenched. He thought of the hurt on her face when he'd closed the door to further discussion on her trip. Whenever he'd said no in the past she hadn't argued, believing he had her best interest at heart. Why hadn't he been able to explain his fear to her? Explain that he loved her so much, that the thought of her alone in India would kill him.

Pushing to his feet, he turned the television off and flicked out the lights. His steps stopped outside Charlotte's bedroom. A beam of light shone from under the door. She was still awake. His hand cupped the door handle, but he hesitated. What could he say to her that would make her feel better?

Shrugging, he silently moved on down the hall.

Chapter 6

The silence in the room was heavy. Paul had pulled the bags out of the bedroom and left them by the door. Wendy couldn't look at him. How could they walk away from these two desperate children?

The boy moved towards her. He looked adorable in his new clothes, and his hair was swept back off his forehead.

"Please—Shanti and I want to live with you. We are strong and will do anything you ask of us. We will be good servants to you. Please, saab—I'm sure your children will like us," Ashok said in a small, grave voice.

Paul shook his head. "I'm sorry, Ashok. We're flying to America today. I have a surprise for you, though." Squatting down in front of Ashok, Paul pulled out a plastic bag filled with notes.

When Ashok looked at the money and burst into tears, Wendy felt her throat clog up. She heard her husband clear his throat.

"Don't cry, lad. There's 50,000 rupee in there. You should be able to find a place to stay with that. I've paid for you to stay here for two more days—food will also be sent up to you. Shanti will be able to rest her leg." Paul looked over at her, and his eyes beseeched her for help. She nodded and pulled out some tissues.

"Dry your eyes, Ashok. Look what I have for you." She held up a packet of candy and grinned. She handed a small wooden doll to the little girl.

Shanti's eyes looked sad, but a tiny smile lifted her lips. "Thank you, Miss. Wendy."

Wendy caught her breath at the beauty in the child's smile, and her heart ached. Stiffening her shoulders, she picked up her carry bag. "Take care. It's been lovely getting to know you." She hugged Shanti and rubbed Ashok's arm.

"Good-bye, children," Paul said gruffly. He reached out to shake Ashok's hand. Ashok looked at the outstretched hand and threw himself at Paul.

"Thank you, saab. You saved Shanti. God bless you."

Paul coughed as he pulled away from the little arms holding him tight. "Yes, yes. You're welcome. Come on, Wendy, we need to go."

Tears streamed down Wendy's face as she walked away from the children.

As they sat in the moving taxi she looked across at her husband. Words froze in her throat. She couldn't condemn him; she too wanted her comfortable life back in the States. Ashok and Shanti would be all right—hadn't Paul seen to that by giving them all that money?

~~~

Ashok stiffened his shoulders. He had to be thankful. He pulled out his shirt and stuffed the money into his underwear. He looked across at his sister and smiled. They had two more days in this big room, and they had it all to themselves. "Shanti, we need to keep our bags packed, ready to go. Keep your shoes on, even when you're sleeping."

Shanti nodded and hugged the doll to her chest. "Why didn't they want us, Ashok? I tried not to cry when Mr. Paul cut my knee. I tried to be good." Her voice was muffled against the doll.

"You are good. They already have children." Ashok clapped his hands. "Let's watch television." As he pressed the button, his sister's eyes sparkled. He looked down at his new shoes, and happiness filled him. He wouldn't think about tomorrow—there was too much fun to be had in this room. He grabbed a banana, peeled back the skin, and jumped onto the couch, laughing. He scoffed the banana down and reached for some grapes. He'd never watched television before, and now he wanted to stay here forever, glued to the screen.

Shanti hopped to the bedroom. She stretched out on the massive bed and giggled. "Two televisions, Ashok," she called. "One for you and one for me." Shanti pressed the buttons on the remote until she got to the nature channel. "Ashok, come look. It's a forest. I didn't know about forests. The trees are so big and there's so many of them. Look at the river, Ashok, it's beautiful, the water is so clear," she exclaimed in wonder.

Ashok jumped up and down on the couch and bounced off onto the floor. He raced into the bedroom and tickled Shanti.

She pushed his hands away, laughing. "Stop, stop."

Collapsing back onto the fluffy white pillow Ashok closed his eyes. He patted his full tummy and wiggled his hands in the air. "See, Shanti, Jesus loves us." He touched the fluffy, soft pillow and sunk his head into its depth.

The hour was late and Ashok yawned as he returned from the toilet. He'd drunk too much lemonade. He wanted to kick off his shoes as they were rubbing his heels, but he decided against it. Shanti was asleep and breathing deeply. He rolled over and looked at her relaxed face. Her knee wasn't hurting as much, she'd told him. He smiled as he thought of all the apples she'd stuffed into her bag. He'd started to tell her not to, as they had another day and night in the big room, but stopped himself. What did it matter? Yawning again, he moved onto his back and closed his eyes.

He heard a click in the door, and his head snapped up. He covered Shanti's mouth as he shook her. Her eyes opened and gazed up at him sleepily.

"Get up," he whispered. "No noise."

Shanti's eyes widened in fear.

Ashok tiptoed to the bedroom door and peeped out. The apartment door opened and a tall, skinny man in a uniform entered the room and turned on the light.

Moving through the door, Ashok jutted his chin out for courage. "This is our room. What do you want?" he demanded.

"Wrong. This is my hotel and I say you leave. Get your stuff—you're going now." The man stepped towards Ashok.

"Mr. Paul said he paid for us to stay here two more days. You can't kick us out."

The man snarled at him, and his hands fisted. "Your Mr. Paul has gone, and I can get good money for this room. Did you think I would let scum like you stay in my hotel? Out!" he shouted.

Ashok grabbed his bag and slung it on his back. He moved across to help Shanti with hers. He squinted at the man. "Please, saab, we will go quietly in the morning. Let us stay tonight?"

"No, I want you gone before my guests wake up. I don't want anyone to see you." He seized Ashok's ear and twisted it.

"Oww. Let go." Ashok kicked out, and his shoe contacted with the man's shin, causing him to let go of Ashok's ear. "Quick, Shanti, run."

As they ran out of the room Ashok slammed the door as loudly as he could. "You are a bad man," he shouted, using his loudest voice.

The man raced after them and lunged at Ashok, grabbing his foot. Ashok fell and kicked frantically to get free. Shanti stopped, and he yelled at her to keep going. His foot slipped out of his shoe, and he scrambled up, spun around, and charged after Shanti. They made it to the door of the hotel as the man appeared.

He bared his teeth and hissed at them.

Ashok flung the door open and stepped onto the dark street. He pulled at Shanti, and they moved away from the front of the building. Looking down at his feet, he felt anger burn inside him.

He'd lost one shoe. He pulled off the remaining shoe and flung it across the pavement at the hotel window, hoping it would smash. It bounced off onto the ground, landing with a dull thud.

Ashok dropped to the ground and pulled off his socks. His chin quivered as the ground chilled his bare feet.

Chapter 7

Macy stirred the pancake mixture determined to help Charlotte feel better. She glanced at her watch and sighed. Charlotte never slept this late. Saturday mornings usually found her out running, eager to make the most of the day. If she didn't come down soon, she'd have to go and get her.

Bill entered the kitchen, his hair wet from a shower. He came up behind her, circled her waist with his arms, and gently kissed her head before he stepped away. He smelt of soap and aftershave. She smiled.

"Morning, Macy. Yum, pancakes." Bill dipped his finger in the pancake mix. "Where's Charlie?" he asked.

"She's not up yet." Placing the spatula in his hand, she pushed him gently towards the hot plate. "Can you flip these for me—I'll go wake her for breakfast." As she turned, he grabbed her arm.

"She loves your pancakes, honey. You're a good mother—I love you."

Tears pricked her eyes. He knew her so well. "I hate to see her upset."

Macy hurried out of the kitchen. She stood outside Charlotte's door and gently knocked. Several seconds slipped by before she slowly opened the door. "Charlie, honey, wake up." Her eyes snapped to the made-up bed and the envelope on the pillow. A chill ran down her back as she looked frantically around the room and realized her daughter was gone. Grabbing the letter, she turned to speed down the stairs. Puffing, she burst into the kitchen. "Bill, she's not there."

"Maybe she's gone for a run?" he replied calmly. He flicked his wrist, sending a golden pancake through the air.

"Turn that off," Macy snapped.

Bill swiveled to look at her, and his hand dropped. He moved the pan and turned off the element.

"This was on her pillow. Bill, she's gone." Macy sunk to a kitchen chair and dropped her head into her hands. Bill joined her and took the letter. He tore it open, his eyebrows drawing together.

"She's gone to India," he thundered. "How dare she disobey me."

Snatching the letter from his hand, she looked down at her daughter's handwriting. The words blurred for a moment, and then she silently read what Charlotte had written.

Mum, Dad, I love you. I'm going to India as planned. I will phone once I arrive. Please forgive me for sneaking out—I felt I had no choice. Don't worry, God is with me.

xxx Charlotte

Macy stiffened her shoulders and spun around to face Bill. "If you'd talked to her instead of laying down the law, this would never have happened."

"Don't blame me for this—you could have talked her out of it, but you chose to remain silent." He slung his anger at her. "You always take the middle ground and make me look like the bad guy."

"What are we going to do?" Macy's voice caught in her throat.

"Do we have a copy of her travel plans? What time was her flight?" Bill asked. "Maybe there's still time to stop her."

"I think her flight left at six. She'd be on her way by now. It's a fourteen-hour flight direct to Mumbai."

Bill reached over and took her hand. She forced herself not to pull away, and she closed her eyes to block out his searching gaze. He was right, she could have talked to Charlotte, but she'd chosen to avoid upsetting her daughter further.

~~~

The Chattrapathi Shivaji International Airport was like an up market shopping mall with duty-free shops trying to entice you to buy things you didn't need. Charlotte stopped and caught her breath. The bustle of people thrilled her, and she turned slowly on the spot to take it all in. She'd moved through customs easily, explaining she had only a backpack because she planned to move around a lot while in India.

Stepping onto the travelator, she moved between borders of tall palm trees with fairy lights gracing their trunks. Today she planned to book into the hotel and then spend the day at Juhu Beach. Charlotte wished Ruth were here to share the excitement she felt. She stepped off the belt and stumbled when a man bumped into her.

He stopped. "Sorry, Miss. I help with bag? I take you taxi—yes?" He grabbed at her backpack.

Charlotte slapped his hand away. "No! Move back," she growled at him. He stepped back and bowed at the waist as he moved away from her. She was sure she heard him curse under his breath. She gripped the shoulder straps of her backpack and hurried her steps, grateful for the self-defense lessons she'd taken.

As she moved out of the air-conditioned building, the heat assailed her like a wave. Sweat broke out on her back and she wiped a hand over her forehead. For early in the morning, the humidity seemed dense already. Her heart hammered as she approached the line of taxis. Men stared at her, and she felt tension tighten her shoulders. She lifted her chin and stepped up to a small skinny man leaning against a yellow-and-black taxi.

"Ramee Guestline Hotel, Juhu, please."

"Ramee. Yes, Miss." He nodded, moved to the boot of his car, and flicked it open, gesturing for her bag.

"Thank you. It's only a ten-minute drive to the hotel, isn't it?" Charlotte slipped the backpack off her shoulders and allowed him to hoist it into the car.

"Yes, Miss." He nodded several times.

As the car moved away from the curb Charlotte exhaled a deep breath. Maybe *yes, miss* was the only English he knew. Charlotte's mouth lifted at the corners, and her eyes widened as she gazed out the window, devouring her first tastes of India. She took in the bustle of people wandering the streets and all the vibrant colors. Sucking in her breath, she let the tension drift from her shoulders. She'd made it.

~~~

Eli pounded on his computer. He raked a hand through his hair and frowned. He'd been feeling uneasy all morning, as if he'd missed something. He normally didn't work on a Saturday, but he wanted to get a jump on the end-of-month reporting. His mobile phone shrilled beside him and he picked it up, seeing his father's number come up.

"Eli, Charlie's gone to India."

"How'd she manage to talk you around, Dad?" Eli sat back in his chair, stunned his father had agreed on her travelling alone.

"She snuck out last night without telling us."

Eli grimaced.

"She left a brief letter saying she'd phone when she arrived. I thought you'd want to know."

"Thanks, Dad. Can you call me after you hear from her?" Eli listened for a few more minutes before ending the call. He walked over to the window and stared out at the clear blue sky. Charlie was out there, somewhere, alone. She'd told him she was going to go, and he'd shrugged it off, believing his father would stop her. He'd not taken her seriously, and now dread clawed at his stomach.

~~~

Charlotte collapsed on the bed in satisfaction. What a marvelous day.

She'd met interesting people, taken lots of photos, and loved every diverse minute. She had deliberately put off her call home until after the tour so she would have something to talk about. Pressing the speed dial on her phone, she waited.

"Mum, it's Charlotte." She nervously twirled her finger in her hair, closing her eyes briefly.

"Oh, Charlotte." Macy's voice faltered. "Where are you, honey?"

"Mumbai. I am staying at the Ramee Guestline Hotel, at Juhu Beach."

"I'm sorry, Charlie. I wish you could have told me you planned to—"

"You would have tried to talk me out of it." Charlotte swallowed. Tears welled up in her eyes. She wanted to ask how her father was but stopped herself. What good was it hearing he was angry with her?

"Mum, I spent the day on Juhu beach—people watching. There are outdoor markets and bazaars. I risked trying some *chaats* and *pani puri* from a food vendor." Charlotte paused. "Tasty. I think I could get used to Indian food."

"Be careful of the food, Charlotte. You don't want to get an upset stomach."

"I'm fine. There were a lot of tourists buying food from the vendor, so I took that as a sign to be adventurous. I snapped some photos to capture the color. I'll try and e-mail them tomorrow."

"I miss you, honey. Your father's indicating he wants to say hello."

Charlotte sucked in her bottom lip as she waited for her father to speak.

"How's my little girl? Was the flight okay?" His gentle voice caused her tears to spill out.

"Daddy, I'm sorry." Emotion clogged her throat.

"Charlie, you're there now—I want you to have a great time. Keep in touch and make sure you keep in a crowd. Think about where you're going, and if you change your plans at the last minute, text us. Can you do that for me?"

"Yes," she answered in a small voice.

"I've worked out the time difference, and we're four hours ahead of you. So we'll phone you at eight your time each evening."

"You don't need to do that, Dad." Charlotte sat up and brushed her hair out of her eyes. Her father never made a step unless he knew all the variances. Her heart warmed at the care she'd had all her life. What would it hurt to let him call her? If it brought him peace of mind, it was the least she could do.

"It'll be great talking to you every day, telling you what I've been doing. Thanks for being such a great father—I love you," she said brightly. "Daddy, it's so colorful here. I brought Mum a sari today and will post it tomorrow. Tell her she has to wear it to church." Laughing, Charlotte talked to both her parents for half an hour before she said her good-byes.

She picked up the printout of information on Hope Mumbai as she snuggled into bed. She could hardly wait until tomorrow; this was what her trip was all about—the children of India. As she closed her eyes, she tried to think of things to say to the little children she hoped to meet.

~~~

Ashok desperately pulled Shanti's hand. The air around them seemed to thicken, and his knees felt weak. A sharp loose stone stabbed his heel, and he tried to ignore the rough texture of the street pushing into his hurting foot. If he could get them to the corner, he felt sure they'd be safe. "Come on, Shanti, you have to run." Looking over his shoulder, he listened.

"I can't, I'm tired. Stop—pulling—me." Shanti stopped walking and sat on the dusty, broken road.

The darkened sky sent a chill down his spine, and he shivered. He felt an urgency to leave the alley. He'd spotted a man in dark glasses and a baggy coat, watching them earlier today. He'd raced Shanti from street to street, ducking into this alley as a last precaution.

Shuffling at the corner made his head snap up. Tension tightened his shoulders, and his mouth dropped open as two burly men entered the alley. One was the same man he'd seen earlier.

"Get up now!" Ashok shouted. He had no choice but to pull hard on her hand. Ashok started to run, dragging Shanti behind him.

Scrambling to her feet, Shanti looked behind her. Her feet sped after him, and her fingers tightened on his. He wished he was magic and could fly. Ashok's breath was labored, coming in quick, painful, gulps. Heavy footsteps thudded behind them. He could feel the sweat on Shanti's hand and squeezed to secure a better grip. If only someone else would enter the alley.

Shanti screamed.

The stranger jerked Shanti away and hoisted her up over his shoulder. Ashok lunged at Shanti, grabbing her arms.

"Kick, Shanti—fight him." His heart throbbed as he took in the white terror on her face.

The man looked down at him and gave a cold laugh. He nodded.

Ashok twisted his head in time to see the other man bend towards him. He screamed as two hands roughly picked him up and flung him away. His arms flapped wildly in panic as his body sailed through the air. The air was sucked from his lungs, as he crashed to the ground in a messy heap.

"Ashok!" Shanti screamed. She kicked crazily at the man's back.

Pulling himself up he tried to move, but his head ached and his eyes blurred. He had to get to her. The men were walking away with his sister. He had to stop them. He tried to stand, but his legs crumbled beneath him.

Crying, he crawled along the ground like a dog. "Shanti, I'll find you," he promised in a broken voice.

Shanti reached out to him, her fingers spread wide in despair. The men turned the corner and she was gone.

Ashok drew his knees to his chest, his whole body convulsing in deep, heart-wrenching sobs.

"Shanti!" His cry echoed off the tin walls around him and bounced back to haunt him.

"Shanti!" He hollered, his battered body numb compared to the pain he felt in his heart.

Chapter 8

Eli raked his hand through his hair and briefly closed his eyes. What time would it be in India?

"Are you even here with me, Eli?" Tina put her hand on her hip.

"I'm sorry. I can't get Charlie out of my mind."

"Eli, she made a decision and you have to let her grow up. I'm sure she's fine."

He didn't like the tone of Tina's voice. A tightness formed between his eyebrows as he studied her. "I wouldn't like the idea of you travelling alone in India either," he said quietly.

Tina's eyes smiled at him, and she laid her hand on top of his. "Let's not talk about Charlotte. Can you please focus on us?"

Eli had grown up in a family who talked about how they felt, and Tina closing the subject of Charlotte confused him. He nodded and tried to concentrate on what she said.

Time sped by and he enjoyed her company. The car trip to her house was made in silence, and Eli recalled his mother's words— *Son, you don't have to fill the gaps in conversation. Rest in them. True friendship doesn't need words.* As he walked Tina to the door he picked up her hand and gently teased her fingers with his.

She turned at the door and gave him a radiant smile. "Eli, this was a special night." She touched his face with her fingers and tiptoed up to lightly kiss his lips.

Surprise gripped his chest. He stepped back and looked down at his shoes.

An overwhelming need consumed Eli. It snapped his head up and darkened his eyes as he reached out to cup the back of her head. He pulled her towards him.

~~~

Much later, Eli rested his head on the steering wheel. How had passion grown so quickly? One minute he'd planned to walk her to the door and ask her out again, then he was crazily kissing her, his hands roaming unchecked over her body. He slapped his palm against his forehead and opened the car door. Tina hadn't stopped him, or seemed to want him to stop. Where had his principles gone? He'd felt like something had pulled loose inside of him, drowning all he believed in. He'd wanted to make love to her—he'd not even thought of what God said on the subject. His face flamed at what he'd done. His body was reacting to thoughts of Tina even now. His heart beat wildly in his chest as he thought of the struggle it would be to control his need for this woman.

~~~

Charlotte checked her bag, picked up her camera, and left the hotel. Excitement had her skipping down the steps towards the waiting taxi. Her heart pummeled in her chest as she got into the car, thinking of the children she'd meet today. She planned to spend two days with Hope Mumbai, a mission station that reached out to street children in numerous ways.

She rummaged through her bag as the taxi sped along the crowded streets and then slowed to a stop. Charlotte pulled out her sunglasses, put them on, and leaned forward to thank the driver. As she alighted from the taxi, children asking for money swamped her. She smiled, lightly touching their heads with her hand. "No, no." Her softly spoken words brought huge smiles to their faces. Charlotte knew she must look strange to them with her pale skin that didn't seem to brown, even with days in the sun.

They followed her to the door of the mission and touched her clothes with grubby little fingers. Charlotte didn't care about the dirt—she wanted to hug them all.

"Charlotte Turner?" An attractive middle-aged woman strode towards her with her hand extended.

"Yes, hello. Ms. Cloudy?" Charlotte shyly took her hand and flashed an excited smile.

"Yes, that's me. But call me Bernie." Bernie stared openly at Charlotte. "Gosh, you're a pretty wee thing. Are you on your own or is your friend with you?"

"Unfortunately my friend couldn't make it at the last moment, so I came alone," Charlotte explained.

"I see." The woman squinted and then led Charlotte into her office. "You said in your e-mail you have two days with us, is that correct?"

"Yes. Thank you for allowing me to see what you do. I don't want to be in the way at all."

"Oh, you won't be. The children will love you. You're going out with Phil. Dr. Phillip Mangan. He volunteers here for six months of the year. Great guy." She shuffled through her desk, creating more mess, until she picked up some loose paper. "Can you fill out these forms for me, Charlotte? You can leave your bag and camera here for safekeeping. I'd prefer you didn't take photos when you're working—I don't want the children to feel like they're a tourist attraction when we're with them."

Heat scorched her face and Charlotte lifted the strap of her camera over her head. "Oh, I'm sorry. I didn't think." She placed her camera and bag on the desk.

Bernie rounded the desk, patted her shoulder, and laughed. "Don't worry, I'm sure you have the best motives for volunteering. I'll leave you to fill out those forms. When you're finished, come through to the supply room and meet Phil." Bernie indicated where the supply room was and left Charlotte alone.

Charlotte nervously picked up a pen and completed the task. As she moved from the room, she surveyed her surroundings. Neatly stacked boxes lined every wall. There seemed to be order in the chaos. A small kitchen table stood in one corner with an urn, cups, and tea makings. She imagined the place turning into a hive of activity. She arrived at the door of the supply room, but heard a conversation that obviously wasn't meant for her ears, so she paused, unsure she should proceed.

"I don't have time to babysit another tourist out to earn brownie points." The man's voice sounded tense and annoyed.

"Come on, Phil. I have a good feeling about this one. The e-mails we've exchanged have shown genuine interest. Give her a chance."

"She'll only be in the way. Why can't she stay here and help you?"

Stepping back from the door, Charlotte hesitated. Her parents had treated her like a child, and now this man thought she was helpless, without even meeting her. Squaring her shoulders, she entered the room.

"I'd be happy to help you here, Bernie." She glared at the man before swinging around to look at Bernie. "If Dr. Mangan is going to judge me as a nuisance before he even knows me, then I'd prefer to spend my time here with someone else."

"Charlotte, my dear. Please forgive Phillip—he's a bit lacking in the social-skills department. Say you're sorry, Phillip." Bernie turned her head to Phillip and widened her eyes in demand.

"Please forgive me, Miss. Turner. Obviously my comments weren't for your ears. However, since you heard them, I apologise." He stared hard into her eyes, challenging her to back down.

Charlotte managed a smile. It would be so easy to walk away, but she hadn't come all this way to give up now. Why should she let his attitude sabotage her dream of helping these beautiful children?

"Apology accepted. I'm looking forward to going out with you, Dr. Mangan. I haven't needed a babysitter for some years now. I'm sure I won't be in your way."

"We'll just have to wait and see, won't we." He pointed his finger towards two heavy-looking bags. "Right, let's go. Charlotte, can you grab those."

"Have fun you two, see you tomorrow." Bernie moved away as the phone in the office began to ring.

Charlotte hefted one bag. It was as heavy as it looked, but she managed to pick it up easily. Grabbing the other bag, she raced after Phillip. He had his arms full of water bottles.

She watched Phillip as he drove and thought he'd be good looking if he stopped scowling.

Phillip stopped the car and turned to her. "Ready?" His eyes creased around the corners. "Expect bedlam. The children have been waiting days for our van to show up. We try and call into each centre once a month, but sometimes we get held up."

"What brings the children to the clinic?" Charlotte asked.

"It's not only children we see. It's hard to turn anyone away. They come with infected wounds, fevers, burns," his hand waved expressively. "Some have tuberculosis or malaria. Many don't get enough to eat. A lot of the children have been abused, and many are traumatized." His mouth lifted slightly. "What I want you to do is just mill around talking to the children—help make them feel relaxed. Do you think you can do that?"

"Yes. Anything to help." Charlotte's eyes widened as she stepped out of the van. There were sick children lying on the street, moaning. Her eyes welled up and she bent down to touch a little girl.

Phillip grabbed her arm and pulled her after him.

She twisted her arm out of his grip and stopped. "I thought you said for me to talk to the children." She stood her ground, resting her hands on her hips.

"That's right. But before you jump in the deep end, how about we get you some gloves. The last thing I want on my conscience is you getting sick."

Charlotte flared a heated look back at him. What was it about this man that got to her? "You could have told me earlier that I'd need gloves. Where are they?"

"In the bag you've left in the van." He gave her a condescending smile, and she spun on her heels and stormed back to the van. Charlotte fumed under her breath as she pulled the bags out of the van. She lugged them towards the rusted tin shed, which was to host the clinic for the day. Just as Phillip had warned her, the clinic blended in with the other makeshift buildings around it.

She glanced at Phillip and saw him smiling at a small child. She watched the gentle way he lifted the child's arm and was startled by the compassion she saw in his eyes. He looked up and caught her staring. She quickly averted her glance and unzipped the bag to look for the gloves.

~~~

Phillip wearily lifted his shoulders. The children's needs pressed heavily upon him; he knew they'd leave with many unseen. This was what kept bringing him back. The little ones with their huge, trusting eyes. Back home in the States, his friends said he didn't have a life— that he'd given it away. But when had it ever been his? God had picked him up out of nothing and placed him with his foster family, who loved him. At the age of six he'd watched his father die of an overdose. His mother had tried to look after him for a few months, but her drinking got worse, and she often forgot to feed him. He became a ward of the state at seven and he never saw his mother again. He was told she had died when he was ten, but that's all he knew. Both his foster parents were doctors and strong Christians. Growing up, Phil went on mission trips to Africa, where he learnt of a different type of hardship. One of poverty and courage.

Sighing, he dried his hands and went to look for Charlotte. He hadn't seen her for a couple of hours; he smiled as he pictured her annoyance at being ignored. He could always pick the ones who just wanted to feel good about themselves. She'd go home and tell her friends some story about making a difference. She'd then get on with her life, forgetting the pain that travelled daily with these children. What would two days do? She was probably sitting by the van, waiting to go. His mouth lifted in a smile as he thought of her pristine designer jeans and soft pink top.

"Dr. Phillip, saab." A frail Indian woman bowed before him at the door. Phillip frowned. His instinct was to turn her away. How often would she come back asking for medicine to make her well? Surely she had a choice. Every time she sold her body for money she knew the risks. Hadn't he tried to talk to her about this time and time again. He crossed his arms and nodded in response.

"I not well. Please help me. Sores, pain here." She clutched her stomach. "I sick," she whispered with downcast eyes.

"You need to help yourself," he said, not caring that his voice sounded hard. Many women came to the clinic expecting him to be sympathetic to their symptoms. Anger boiled within him that they continued to ignore his advice, expected him to clean them up so they could go back out and continue their lifestyles of immorality.

"This is the last time I will give you anything," he stated firmly and indicated for her to come in.

He looked at his watch later and sighed. Time to go and still many people unseen. Shaking his head, he stepped out of the clinic onto the dusty street and stopped. All the children were grouped around Charlotte. She was sitting crossed-legged in the dirt with a small girl on her lap. Her hands were moving in action to the song she sang. The simple words of "Jesus Loves the Little Children" reached his ears. Some of the older children were doing the actions and laughing.

Phillip leaned back against the building and closed his eyes as he listened to the sweet sound of children singing to Jesus. As the song finished, Charlotte clapped and the children cheered. He noticed she'd taken her gloves off. Her hand rested on the arm of the little girl she held, and her fingers gently stroked the dry, scaly skin. Charlotte dipped her head to listen to a boy sitting beside her in the dirt.

He ran a hand through his hair and frowned as she smiled in response to the words he could not hear. She was beautiful.

Pushing off the wall, he ambled over to join her. As she looked up, their eyes locked and he couldn't look away. Her gaze searched his for reprimand, and he grimaced. He noticed her mouth straighten as she gently lifted the child off her knee and stood up.

"Hi. Are you ready to go?" Two children on either side of Charlotte had slipped their hands into hers, and she'd automatically closed her fingers.

"Dr. Phil, Charlie taught us how to play knucklebones. She's given us five sets to leave here."

Phillip turned his head to see who was talking to him. The young boy had his hand extended with a set of grey knucklebones proudly displayed in his palm. His grin split his face, and Phillip smiled in response.

His eyebrows lifted in question. "Charlie?"

"Yes. That's what my friends call me." She turned to the children and reached over to hug them. "Thank you for looking after me. I had a great time playing with you all." Charlotte's voice wobbled slightly, and Phillip frowned as his chest constricted.

The children moved with Charlotte to the van and watched as she opened the door. He couldn't look away as she ran her tongue over her lips and sucked in her bottom lip. She waved as they drove off, then her eyes dropped to her hands, folded neatly in her lap.

"You did well today. Thank you for entertaining the children." Phillip tried to break the spell of her enchantment over him. She'd be gone in a day.

"I enjoyed it," she said quietly.

"It's not easy walking away, is it?" He gentled his voice, and Charlotte looked up in surprise.

She shook her head and frowned. "How do you do this? I mean— you never get to see all the children."

"That's what keeps bringing me back. I'm addicted to their smiles."

"I can understand that. I wish I had more time here." Charlotte looked out the window, her eyes swimming with tears.

Phillip reached out and touched her arm, "Charlie, are you okay?"

Charlotte nodded without turning.

"Maybe you can come back sometime." But Phillip hardened his heart to her. Surely if she wanted to, she could stay longer.

"Yes, maybe," Charlotte answered softly.

Chapter 9

The clear blue sky mocked Macy as she pegged out the washing. Outwardly she appeared relaxed and at peace with her world, yet inwardly her mood darkened as the day progressed. Each day that Charlotte was in India alone, Macy worried. She blamed Bill. She'd begged him to go and join Charlotte, but he refused. Macy stepped back and knocked over the peg basket and frowned. The pegs scattered on the grass, and she stared blankly at them. Her lower lip puckered as she thought of how badly she'd been treating Bill. It wasn't his fault that Charlotte had snuck off in the night. Why did she feel so fearful when all her life she'd believed that perfect love, God's love, drove out fear? When had she slipped into this habit of imagining the worst possible scenario? And when had she become this bad-tempered, moody woman? Bill must be sick of her whining. She decided to apologize to him and put a smile on her face. She squared her shoulders, practiced a smile, and went to find her husband.

Bill looked up from the newspaper as she entered the kitchen, gave her a fleeting smile, and went back to reading.

"Bill, I need to talk to you." Macy lowered herself into a kitchen chair and leaned on the table.

"What have I done wrong now?" Bill's voice held a laugh in it, and Macy found herself smiling for the first time since Charlotte had left.

"It's been a bit like that, hasn't it? I'm sorry, honey." She grinned and reached for his hand. "Instead of owning up to the truth about how I felt about Charlotte being in India on her own, I've been blaming you—for everything."

Bill nodded, and his eyes sparkled with humor and relief.

She sat on his knee and chuckled. "I love you. Thanks for being patient with me."

"I know you've been worried about Charlie, and so have I." His eyes softened as he leaned his head on hers. "How about we phone her and see what her day's been like?"

Macy jumped off his knee and smiled at the thought of talking to Charlotte. "Let's use the phone in the office, that way we can put her on speaker phone."

As they sat and waited for a connection, Macy watched her husband's face and loved the excitement she saw sparkling from his eyes. He looked relaxed. He'd had some shortness of breath lately and she'd been concerned.

"Hello, Dad?" Charlotte's voice came through clearly, and Macy smiled broadly.

"Sweetheart, Dad and I have you on speaker phone. How are you?"

"I've had the greatest day. I went out with Dr. Phillip Mangan, from Hope Mumbai, and met some amazing children."

"That's nice, dear." Macy missed Charlotte so much that she had to swallow past the lump in her throat.

"Mum, they're so sweet and trusting. They have literally only the clothes on their backs, yet their smiles are genuine and melt my heart." Macy heard the sweetness in her daughter's voice and knew exactly how Charlotte felt.

"What did you do with the children?" Bill asked.

"Sang songs, played knucklebones, and just sat around talking. I only have one more day here. I wish I could stay longer and build better relationships with them." Charlotte paused and cleared her throat. "Phillip is amazing with the children. He's so gentle and kind. I'm thinking of—"

"We miss you, sweetheart," Macy interrupted. "I'm counting the days until you get home. Your brother and Tina are coming over for dinner tonight." Macy knew she'd cut Charlotte off, but the thought of her staying longer in India and putting herself at risk was beyond thinking about.

"Say hi for me. Daddy, are you cooking?"

"Mmm. I'm going to get Eli to barbeque the steaks. Charlie, thanks for the photos. Keep them coming, honey. What are your plans for tomorrow?" Bill asked.

"I'm spending the day with Dr. Phillip. I need to get up early and meet him at the clinic. Can you get Eli to call me? This time tomorrow would be good."

"Okay. You sound tired. Get to bed and sleep tight, sweetheart." Macy smiled at the thought of Charlotte tucked safe in bed for the night. She could feel Bill glaring at her as she hung up the phone and turned to face him. She knew what he was going to say and didn't want to hear it. Crossing her arms, she lifted her chin in defense as she looked into his annoyed eyes.

"Macy, you shouldn't cut Charlie off like that. Now we don't know what she was thinking, and it could have been important."

"You don't want her over there any more than I do," she snapped, "so don't condemn me for not encouraging her to make new plans." Macy left the room, hot tears burning her eyes. She wanted her daughter back home, now!

~~~

By the time Eli pulled into his parents' driveway, he wanted to turn the car around and take Tina home. She hadn't wanted to come. She insisted they go somewhere alone and spend quality time together. He'd tried to explain that it was important to him that she get to know his parents. Tina didn't like the idea of having dinner with them once a week. She was becoming more demanding by the day; surely this wasn't the way a relationship should be? He frowned as he stepped out of the car and waited for her to join him. Her face was sulky and her lips pouted, showing her displeasure. What would his parents think of her attitude?

"Come on, Tina, at least try and look happy to be here."

"Why should I? We always do what you want," she sneered.

The door opened, and Tina's face changed instantly. She smiled at his mother and gushed hello. He followed her into the house, confused, angry, and tired of the games she played.

Chapter 10

Shanti's arm burned and she shivered in fear. The scary man had twisted it to stop her screaming. They had stuffed her into a smelly sack like a piece of rubbish. She knew she was in the boot of a car, and her body bounced as the car bumped along a rough road. Shanti sobbed as she wondered how Ashok was going to find her. Her skin itched against the rough fabric of the sack, and she tried to free her hands from the rope around her wrists. Her eyes closed tight and her lips moved as she mumbled a prayer to Jesus. Had she been a bad girl by not hurrying like Ashok had told her to? It was her fault the man had hurt Ashok. She chewed her lip as she remembered Ashok falling to the ground. She'd heard him call out her name. He'd tried to get up but had stumbled and fell. Her heart fluttered. Would she ever see him again? Did he know she loved him? Time stretched and Shanti longed for the car to stop. Her body felt bruised and weary. She kept her eyes closed, and the motion of the car lulled her to sleep.

When she opened her eyes, she was confused for a moment and wondered where she was. The dim light from the car boot infiltrated the sack she lay in. As she remembered, a sob of anguish caught in her throat.

The car stopped and the boot opened, letting in a gush of air. She heard voices and her nerves jumped. Her throat locked in fear. What was happening to her? Invisible hands grabbed her, pulling her roughly from the car. Her shoulder banged against something hard and pain shot up her neck. Shanti screamed. Her body tensed as the sack was slung over someone's shoulder. A hand squeezed her legs tightly, and a harsh voice told her to be quiet if she knew what was good for her.

Shanti held her breath and kept very still. She didn't want to make the men angry again. She heard them open a door and talk to someone. She tried to listen but the words seemed muffled. A huge hand reached in and forcibly hauled her out of the sack and dropped her on the ground. She tried to stand and yelped with pain as a tingly, prickly feeling attacked her feet. Blood pounded through her body as she looked frantically around. A third man was in the room. Shanti cowered back from him. He stepped towards her and she had to tilt her head back to see his face. He had a raised red scar running down one side of his face, from his eyebrow to his mouth. Shanti shuddered as he grabbed her chin with dirty, tight fingers and tilted her head.

"Yes, good," he stated. He pulled out a large knife and Shanti's eyes widened. Was he going to kill her? Her heart beat wildly and she held her breath. Fear tightened her muscles ready to spring. He ran the knife down her chest and then flicked it through the rope holding her hands together. His mouth opened and he smiled a toothless grin. "He will like her. Take her to Padma to get her ready."

The trembling started in her stomach, and she thought she was going to vomit. Her eyes darted around the room looking for a way to escape. The place was creepy, too quiet, and she couldn't guess what time of day it was. Her shoulder was shoved from behind and she stumbled. She took tentative steps forward, but everything in her wanted to run in the other direction. Nervously she pushed her hand through her tangled hair and glanced at door. The burly man scowled at her and gave a throaty laugh.

"No escape for you, scab." He grasped her arm. His long strides made Shanti run to keep up with him. They walked down a dark corridor and into a circular courtyard that had a solitary tree with a bench under it. Sunlight filtered from above, and Shanti longed to spring into the tree's branches, to gain freedom from what lay ahead of her. Her heart pummeled as she was led across the courtyard into a dimly lit room. She'd never been separated from Ashok before, and she wondered if she could survive the pain of waiting for him to find her. When she'd cut her knee, Ashok had told her to be brave. He'd assured her that Jesus would help them. Shanti lifted her chin in determination, and her mouth tightened in resolve. Ashok would find her, and Jesus would bring them together again and bring them happiness, wasn't that what the card said?

The man shoved her forward, and she stumbled and fell to the ground. Pain shot through her knee and she gasped. He laughed as he turned from her. "Padma," he called.

A woman moved towards them from the shadows. She stopped and glanced down at Shanti, her features smooth and unmoving. Shanti had never seen such a beautiful woman, and her eyes watered in hope of being saved. She scrambled to her feet and stepped towards the woman.

"Please, help me." She reached out and touched the woman's tunic in desperation. Hard, cold eyes look down at her, and Shanti dropped her hand.

"Get her ready," the man snapped, and he left them.

The woman named Padma squinted, looked down at Shanti, and said, "Come."

As Shanti followed Padma, she noticed other women lounging on mats. They watched her with blank faces and tight mouths. Their eyes followed her as she moved through the room. She felt like a fly caught in a spider web. A chill ran down her back, and the silence in the room caused her to hurry after Padma. What was this place? Who were all these people?

"Please, why am I here? What do you want with me?" Shanti

stopped. Tears spilled down her cheeks, and she sobbed. "I want my brother."

Padma turned and grabbed her face in tight fingers. She pulled her forward and hissed at Shanti's face. Shanti could smell a sweet fragrance that came off Padma's skin.

"You will not talk. Do you understand?"

Shanti's eyes widened and she had difficulty swallowing. She nodded and then blinked furiously to stop the tears.

"Good. Follow me." Padma opened a door and stepped into a large bathroom. She turned on the tap over a large bath and tipped some liquid into the water.

The smell that rose from the water was like nothing Shanti had ever smelled before, and it made her feel slightly sick.

"Strip and get into the bath," Padma demanded.

"I don't want to. The water smells bad."

The slap across her face stunned Shanti, and she staggered back. Her hand went to her cheek as fresh tears stung her eyes. Fear gripped her stomach, and Shanti curled up into a tight ball on the floor.

Padma sat on the edge of the bath and waited. Her eyes narrowed. "What's your name, child?"

Lifting her head slightly, Shanti peeped out at Padma. She didn't want to upset her again and feel the sting of her hand. "Shanti," she whispered.

"I'm sorry I hit you, Shanti. You need to learn fast here if you're going to survive. Can you get in the tub and then we can talk."

Shanti slowly got up and eyed the big tub. She looked down at her grubby fingers and gave a deep sigh. She slipped out of her clothes and stepped into the warm water. Padma started to wipe her back with soap, and Shanti let her shoulders relax.

"This is your home now, Shanti. You must do as you are told, without arguing."

"No. My home is with Ashok. I need to find him, he'll be so worried about me."

The sharp tug on Shanti's hair pulled her head back and her face went under the water. She came up spluttering and gasping for breath.

"I said—you must not argue," Padma snapped.

Rubbing the water out of her eyes, Shanti sucked in the sob that was been building in her throat. Why did Padma hate her so much? Her head dropped until her chin rested on her chest, and she shut her eyes tight. Padma scrubbed her skin until it burned and then told her to get out of the tub. After she was dried off, Padma rubbed cream, which smelled like jasmine, into her skin. She wrapped Shanti in a beautiful sari, and Shanti touched the soft material in wonder. As Padma brushed her hair, she talked.

"Shanti, you must listen to me. Tonight you meet your new master. You must not talk when you are with him—not one word. If you talk, he will beat you until you die. Do not talk and do not cry. Crying makes him mad, and you don't want to see him mad." Padma stroked Shanti's hair, and her words sent shivers down Shanti's back.

"No, Padma. Please, I want to stay with you. I don't want to have a marter."

"Not *marter*, child, master." Padma sighed and moved away from Shanti. "You don't have a choice. He owns you. He will hurt you in a way you have never experience before, but if you want to live, you must keep silent." Padma's face screwed up and she avoided Shanti's eyes.

"I want Asho-o-ok," Shanti screamed.

The smack on her face stilled her scream, and Shanti's fists hit out at Padma. Padma easily grasped her hands and shook her.

"I'm trying to help you, Shanti. The choice is yours." Padma took Shanti by the hand and led her back into the room with all the other women. A large pot rested on a table, and bowls of rice were scattered around the room.

"Eat, Shanti. Then I want you to lie down over there until you are called."

"I don't want to eat, I feel sick. Please, can I go now?" Shanti begged.

Padma's hand snaked out and gripped the lobe of Shanti's ear. Shanti hollered as the tight fingers twisted, burning her skin. Her eyes flooded with unshed tears.

"You will do as I tell you! Eat." Padma let go of her and turned and walked away.

Shanti looked around and saw that other woman and girls were eating. No one was talking, and the room felt so filled with tension that Shanti wanted to scream.

When a girl walked past her and helped herself to a bowl of rice, Shanti tentatively followed her. Her hand shook as she spooned rice into her bowl. She went across to where Padma had indicated and sat down. Her stomach rumbled with hunger as she gazed down at the puffy rice. How long had it been since she'd eaten? Using her fingers, she ate the rice and tried not to cry.

After a while there was a quiet murmur of conversations in the room, and it looked like some were getting ready to leave. Shanti finished her rice and leaned back against the wall. It was the first moment she'd had when she could look around without someone watching her. The room seemed to be a sleeping space for all the girls. Mats lay scattered across the floor, but there were no chairs or any other sign of furniture. Clothes hung from nails protruding from the walls. Shanti closed her eyes and tried to visualize Ashok bursting into the room to rescue her.

A hush came over the room, and Shanti opened her eyes. All the women were looking at a man who had entered the room. It was the man with the ugly scar, and Shanti hoped he couldn't see her in the corner. As if controlled by a switch, all the women turned to look at Shanti. Shanti knew in an instant that the man had come for her.

She scurried to her feet and ran to the door in the corner. Her fists pounded the solid wood as she yelled for help.

As he grabbed her, she remembered what Padma had said. If she wanted to live, she needed to be quiet. All sound froze in her throat, and she imagined a muzzle over her mouth.

The man turned her around and laughed. "Come on, scab, it's time to meet the boss."

Chapter 11

Macy absently wiped dust off Charlotte's dresser with her hand. She picked up the small porcelain doll Charlotte kept on a stand beside her mirror, and gently removed dust from its face. Her hand stilled as she remembered the awe on Charlie's face when she'd opened her tenth birthday gift and discovered the doll. Where had the years gone? She tried to picture her precious daughter wandering the streets of India on her own, and a shudder rippled through her.

Placing the doll back on its stand Macy went to sit on Charlotte's bed. She closed her eyes and drew in a long, deep breath. Why did she worry so? When Charlotte was a little child, Macy had been very protective. If it looked like Charlie was going to fall and skin her knee, Macy physically felt a shiver run through her body in response.

She loved both her children. As her eyes wandered around the room, she acknowledged for the first time that she had a special place in her heart for her only daughter. Charlotte still came and curled up beside her on the couch and talked openly about her feelings. They were best friends as well as mother and daughter. Some of Macy's friends envied her relationship with her daughter. This trip to India was the first time Charlotte had ever disobeyed them.

She'd blamed Bill for not going with Charlie to India, but Macy knew she too could have taken the trip, or tried to support Charlotte in her decision to go. She would apologize to her once she returned. Nothing could get in the way of their relationship returning to how it was.   She smoothed over the bedcover and smiled. Only one more week before Charlotte boarded the plane home. Macy started to plan what she would cook as a welcome-home meal. She'd need to get flowers, chocolates, invite Eli and Tina over. She'd get Bill to cook a barbeque. Charlie loved eating outdoors.

Standing with purpose, Macy moved out of the room and allowed the excitement of Charlotte's coming home to push away any worry from her mind. As she bustled around the kitchen, she pictured her family sitting around the table, loving each other and celebrating all that God had done for them.

Tina's exuberance the other night entered her mind. There was something about that young lady that didn't quite sit right with her.

Glancing at her watch, Macy decided to give Eli a call. He was a good son, never minded her interrupting him at work or anytime for that matter. Yes, God had certainly blessed them with special children.

"Hi, Mum." Eli's voice sounded tense to Macy.

"I'm not getting you at a bad time, am I?"

"No, it's all right. How are you?" he replied.

"Fine, darling. I was just tidying up the kitchen and thinking about Tina. How is she?"

Eli didn't answer straightaway. The long pause caused a frown to tighten Macy's forehead.

"Tina is—how should I say? Annoyed with me at the moment."

Macy rolled her eyes. Didn't the girl know what an amazing man her son was? She was lucky he was interested in her.

"I'm sure she won't stay annoyed at you long, Eli. Do you want to talk about it?" A smile tugged at her lips; she knew he would refuse her offer. He'd always been a bit of a loner. She knew that he talked to Bill about some things, but he often treated her like a treasure to be taken care of. Not that she was complaining—she loved who Eli had become.

"Thanks, Mum. It's nothing much. I didn't agree with her about something, and she got annoyed. She'll get over it."

"Maybe you should have agreed with her," she said in a slightly amused voice.

"I don't think so," he said gruffly.

"I would love you to be here when Charlotte gets home. I thought I'd get your father to light the barbeque. Have a bit of a celebration."

"I don't think we should pamper Charlie. She acted irresponsibly in taking off like that," he pointed out.

"That aside, Eli, I want her to know we forgive her and are glad to have her home. Is that too much to ask?"

"Can I think about it?"

Macy felt her heart fall like an autumn leaf from a tree. He'd never acted like this before. He always supported and encouraged Charlotte at every opportunity. Macy licked her lips before she answered.

"Yes, of course, dear. I'll let you get back to work now."

Wearily rubbing her forehead, Macy ended the call. Surely Eli wouldn't hold a grudge against Charlotte for following her heart? They'd always been so close, and the thought of Eli distancing himself from Charlotte was unthinkable.

~~~

Shanti's eyes moved nervously around the room. A metal bed took up the majority of the space. It had no blankets but was covered with a single faded sheet. There was a basin in the corner of the room, with a solitary rusting tap protruding from the wall. Her heart thumped so loudly in her chest that she thought it would explode.

A tall, dark man stood with his back to the window. It was difficult to see his face, as his body blocked out the light. Shanti wanted to scream at him, explain that this was all a big mistake, that he had the wrong girl. She was Ashok's sister, and he needed to let her go to find him.

As the man approached her, she stepped back until her back was pushing against the door. His pupils and irises were totally black. Shanti thought she would drown in the evil she saw there. Her eyes widened as he stopped in front of her. Her instinct said run, but she was like a caged bird. She dropped her head to her chest to avoid the scrutiny in his eyes.

His finger traced a line from her forehead to her lips and then tilted her head up to look at him.

"You call me Boss. Do you know what that means?" His voice was laced with steel, and Shanti's stomach roiled with fear. She was too frightened to answer.

"You and I will get along just fine if you do as I say. Come here." He stepped back and moved towards the bed.

Shanti stepped tentatively forward, and her chin wobbled. "Please—"

His fist struck her face and knocked her across the room. Pain erupted in her temple. Spots danced before her eyes, and Shanti shook her head to clear her vision.

He yanked her towards him, picked her up and threw her across the bed. His fingers tore at her clothes, and the need to escape screamed within her. His body blocked out the light as he forced himself inside her.

Closing her eyes tight, Shanti tried to escape the pain of what was happening. If she lived another day, it would be one day too many. Darkness cloaked her mind, and she slipped into oblivion.

~~~

Padma paced. Would the girl survive the boss? She stopped and picked up a soft cloth. Her mouth tightened, and she hardened her heart. She gathered surgical sutures, sterilized needles, a small bowl, and a clean sheet. How many times had she done this? Maybe this time the child would survive.

She remembered the first time she'd been called to tidy up his mess; she'd vomited and paid the price of her actions by being denied food for ten days. Now she at least had some privileges. Her own room allowed her some privacy from the other women. The women were expected to service around fifty men a day, and being the cleaner, as they described her, cut back her numbers by half. Yes, it was better to distance yourself and do as you were told.

When her door opened, Padma jumped. Scarface entered the room with a smirk on his ugly face.

"Ready?" His eyes challenged her.

Padma lifted her chin and nodded. There were no words wasted between them. In a strange way they had a relationship; he controlled them all for the boss. He reveled in it. He was a sadist and enjoyed seeing them cower before him. He took any opportunity to inflict pain upon them. It had been five years since he brought her here and demanded she call him Scarface. She liked it that way and hoped one day to be free of this place and forget he ever existed.

She refused to give him the satisfaction of seeing fear in her eyes. Stiffening her back, she picked up her things and followed him. As soon as he opened the door to the room, Padma stalked past him. She wanted her back to him when she saw the child. Her chest tightened at the blood spilled on the sheet.

"Looks like the boss had fun in here," he stated. He lifted Shanti's arm, felt for a pulse, nodded, and then let the arm flop lifeless to the bed. "Maybe she'll make it." His voice was devoid of feeling.

She waited until she heard the door close behind him before she took a breath. Her stomach churned, and she forced herself to step to the bed.

Shanti lay naked, and her body seemed twisted, broken.

Licking her lips, Padma leant forward. "Shanti, it's Padma. I'm going to clean you up."

Padma moved to the basin and filled the bowl with water. She saturated a cloth, squeezed it out, and sponged Shanti's small face.

72

What was it about this child? Usually she didn't refer to the children by name—it helped her keep an emotional distance from them. The boss hadn't touched Shanti's face, apart from a small cut at the side of her mouth. It looked like it might swell up.

Shrugging, Padma allowed her eyes to move down Shanti's body. She gently pulled her towards the edge of the bed. Spreading Shanti's legs apart, Padma surveyed for tearing. Squinting, she marveled at what she saw. There was a lot of blood but not much damage. Padma readied the needle and suture and carefully fixed what evil had torn.

Shanti moaned, and Padma placed her hand on the girl's thigh to stop her from moving. She whispered soft words of comfort, hoping Shanti could hear her. Once she felt she'd done all she could, she rolled Shanti to one side of the bed and pulled up the sheet, then repeated the action, stripping the soiled sheet from the mattress. Quickly, with expert hands, she replaced the clean sheet and moved Shanti to rest on it.

Sighing, she carried the bowl to the basin and rinsed her hands. She hated watching the blood fill the basin as she wrung out the cloth.

"Padma," Shanti whispered.

Padma spun around and hurried to the bed. Her hand cupped the child's face in wonder.

Shanti's eyes watered and tears spilled down her cheeks. "I didn't talk, Padma. I wanted to scream, but I cried inside like you told me to. Did I do good?"

"Yes, child—" Padma caught her breath. Her heart hammered at the pain etched on Shanti's face, and she felt ashamed. "You did good, Shanti, I'm proud of you."

"Is it over? Can I go now?" Shanti's eyes beseeched her.

How could she tell Shanti it wasn't over, that her nightmare had only just began?

Chapter 12

Charlotte walked down the side alley towards her hotel, her mind on Phillip. When he'd said good-bye, he'd taken her hand and gently squeezed it. He told her he hoped she'd return one day. Her hand still burned from the touch of his firm fingers holding hers. She respected him so much; he was the sort of man she could easily fall in love with.

Stopping mid-step, Charlotte laughed. She'd known the man only a few days, and already she was marrying him. Her mother would have a fit.

She needed to focus on the next few days and then the trip back to Australia. If she had her way, she'd stay here longer, but once she got back home she could start saving for her next trip. India was definitely a big part of her future.

Something made Charlotte look behind her, and she drew a sharp breath. Was someone following her? The alley seemed empty, and she quickened her step. As she rounded the corner, she heard a shuffle and spun around to look.

Her eyes locked on the stranger's face. Fear rippled through her body.

He looked directly at her and nodded.

Charlotte spun around and sprinted towards the entrance of the hotel.

Once inside her room, she locked the door and sat puffing on her bed. Pulling out her mobile phone, she dialed Eli's number. He would know what to do.

~~~

Touching the connect button on his phone, Eli said, "Hello, Charlie."

"Eli, I didn't know who else to call. I don't know what to do."

"What, no hello Eli, how are you?" Eli knew he was being sarcastic but didn't care. Things with Tina had gone too far last night, and he felt guilty. He'd slept with her, and now Charlotte was getting the brunt of his anger. In a way she deserved it. Hadn't she been selfish in her decision to fly off to India and not care about how it affected her family?

"Eli, I've been followed. Whoever it is, is outside the hotel. What should I do?"

He could hear the breathlessness in her voice and sat up straighter in his chair. Could she be in danger? The need to protect her rose up in him, and he slowed down his speech in an attempt to calm her. "Can you tell me where you are, Charlie? What's the name of your hotel? What street is it on and what town are you in?"

She continued as if he hadn't spoken. "Eli, when I came back yesterday, my hotel door wasn't locked. It looked like everything was in my room, so I thought maybe the hotel cleaning staff had forgot to lock it. I called the manager and he said not to worry—it was a mistake."

"Charlie, you need to focus. Can you tell me where you are?"

"Yes, of course. I am staying at Fari Hotel on Veer Savarkar Marg. Mum and Dad have all my details."

Eli wrote down the address. "Have you locked your door?"

"Yes. I locked it the moment I came in. Eli, I'm frightened," she exclaimed.

"Tell me why you think you were being followed," he said.

"At first I thought it was my imagination and that I was being paranoid. I had to stop to cross the road when I noticed this man watching me. When he saw me looking at him, he turned away and walked off. I forgot all about it until I saw him again ten minutes later. As I hurried to increase the distance between us, he seemed to drop all pretense of not following me and began to catch up to me. Eli, I ran. I was terrified he was going to catch me."

He spoke her name softly. "Bud, listen to me—we need to call the police. Is there a phone in your room?"

"No. You have to go down to the office, and then it's right by the front door. Often there's no one manning the desk. Shall I call them on my cell?" Charlotte's voice echoed over the line. She sounded close to tears.

"I don't want you to hang up. Have you got the phone number of the police station?"

"No."

"I'll look it up from here." Eli booted up his computer as he talked and he began to search Google for the correct phone number.

"I'm sorry you've been angry with me for leaving the way I did. I didn't know what else to do. Please don't tell Mum and Dad about this. I'll be home soon, and they'll only worry."

"I've got the number, Charlie. It shouldn't take long to go through. I'll use the landline, that way we can stay connected." Eli thought she was probably overreacting, but better to be safe than sorry. A small smile lifted the corner of his mouth. At least they were talking; it wasn't really her fault that she had followed her heart to India. He'd tell her that once they had alerted the police about her being followed.

"Eli." Charlotte whispered, and he had difficulty hearing her. Her voice was full of tension. "Someone's trying the door handle. Eli, there's someone outside my door."

He could hear banging in the background, like someone trying to shoulder a door. Whoever was there was serious about getting into the room and didn't seem to care about how much noise he made.

"Charlie, quick, is there another way out of the room?"

"No."

Eli thumped his fist down on the table. He'd never felt so helpless. Listening to what was happening in the room and being powerless to help her enraged him. If anyone hurt her, they would answer to him. He pressed both phones harder against his ears and tried to regulate his breathing. He needed to stay in control for Charlie.

Someone answered the other phone, and he screamed into the handset. "This is an urgent call, you have to send a car around to Fari Hotel immediately. My sister has got someone breaking into her room as we speak."

"Please hold and I will get someone to help you."

Eli heard music, and cursed. They'd put him on hold.

"Eli, they're trying to force the door! Eli, I—"

Sweat formed on his forehead, and his heart pounded in his chest. "Stay calm, Bud. If they take you, I'll find you. I promise, I won't give up!"

He heard the crash of the door giving way, and for a moment there was silence. He tried to visualize the scene his sister was in and shuddered. Charlie must have flicked her phone onto loudspeaker and dropped it to the ground, because he could hear what was happening.

"Who are you? Get out of my room?" The distress in Charlie's voice came through clearly.

"Do not talk and you will not be harmed." Eli could hear the shuffle of feet and things being thrown around. What did they want with his sister? Adrenaline pumped though his body, with no outlet for release.

"You're the man I saw on the street, I recognize you because of the scar on your right cheek—let me go—"

She screamed and then Eli heard a sickening thump; he shouted her name into the phone. There was no reply, and then the line was disconnected. The sound of Charlotte's heart-rending shriek and then the sound of a fist hitting flesh would be forever etched in his mind.

He pulled at his hair and howled. How could this have happened inside her hotel room? Where was the hotel security? If someone didn't come on the phone from the police soon, there would be hell to pay.

"Good day. You want to report a crime. Please give me the details," a heavily accented voice enquired.

Eli paced as he told them the address and his name. "You need to get someone over there straightaway! You may still be able to track whoever's has taken her. Please hurry." Desperation made Eli's voice sound panicked.

"Mr. Turner, I have indicated to have a car sent around to investigate," the man said with infuriating calmness. "Now if you would be so kind as to give me your details, and everything you know about what has happened?"

Chapter 13

Dinner was ruined. Macy sighed as she turned off the oven. How could she have been so absentminded? Bill would laugh at her when she explained she'd been absorbed in her book and forgotten the time. Smiling, she went to find him, to explain the dilemma.

Bill was snoozing on the couch, his chest rising and falling in a relaxed rhythm. Macy felt her heart turn over. Thirty years they'd been married this September, and still she loved to stand and look at him. He must have sensed her staring, because his eyes opened.

Stretching his arms high above his head, Bill yawned. "How long have I been asleep?" he asked in a contented voice.

"I'm not sure, darling. Maybe twenty minutes or so. Do you feel refreshed?" Macy perched on the edge of the couch and rubbed her hand through his hair, massaging his head.

"Mmm. Something smells interesting. I'm guessing pizza for dinner?" He laughed as he hoisted himself up to hug her.

The front door banged open, and Macy jerked to see who was there.

Eli burst into the room. The distraught look on his face caused Macy's hand to flutter over her heart. What on earth could have happened? She flew across the room to him and grabbed his arm.

"Eli, come and sit down. Are you all right?"

"Mum, Dad. Please—can you sit down? I have some bad news." The desperate tone of Eli's voice alerted Macy to the seriousness of his statement. Her heart flipped over and she glanced at Bill. He took her hand and they resumed their seat on the couch.

"What is it, Son?" Bill's hand tightened on Macy's fingers, and she grimaced.

Her heart caught in her throat as she watched her son collapse into a chair and stare at them. His eyes seemed lost, empty. Macy straightened her back and wanted to yell at him to hurry up and tell them. Knowing would be better than this deafening silence that had taken over the room.

"I'm sorry, there isn't any easy way to say this—Charlie has been—abducted."

Macy jumped up. "What are you talking about, Eli? How can you say such a thing?" she demanded.

Bill's face went a pasty grey. Macy looked from her husband to her son. A hundred questions crashed through her mind. She needed answers. She reached down and grabbed Eli's shirt, pulling him to his feet.

"Tell me what you mean. How do you know this?" She scrutinized his face, hoping it was all a bad joke.

"I was talking to her when it happened. I felt so helpless. There was nothing I could do. I've called the police and they went to Charlie's hotel room. It was completely stripped of all her things. There was, evidence of a—struggle." Eli dropped his head and raked a hand through his hair. His shoulders slumped, as though he carried a heavy load.

Her mouth fell open. Was this real? Why couldn't she feel anything?

Bill cleared his throat. "Are you telling us that Charlotte has been— that someone has—has taken my baby?" Tears flooded his eyes.

"Yes. There was nothing I could do." Eli's eyes flicked from his father to her.

"No, Eli, you must be mistaken," Macy said urgently.

"She's gone, Mum." He looked down to avoid her eyes.

Everything in her wanted to pretend it wasn't true. She wanted to deny what her mind was telling her, but the look on Eli's face and the defeated way he stood confirmed the horror welling up within her.

"Noooooooo." A soul-wrenching wail rose up from the depth of her being. Her knees wobbled and gave way, and she collapsed to the floor.

Bill turned and pulled her up into his arms. Macy thrashed at him. She screamed, unable to curtail the pain that was overtaking her. She fought him, seeing the hands of men who had snatched her daughter. She saw the horrendous, violent things that could happen to her little girl and scratched Bill as if he were the enemy. Was Charlotte alive? Would they ever see her again? Macy felt paralyzed with fear. This couldn't be happening to them. Everything went blurry, and it felt like all the blood had been sucked out of her face. Macy fought her body's need to pass out. Her baby needed her, she had to get a grip on herself.

~~~

Ashok struggled to walk. The dull throb in his left ankle wouldn't let up. Every time he placed his foot on the ground, he felt woozy. It was hopeless; he couldn't walk another step. He leaned over and carefully touched the puffiness around his ankle. His breath caught at the sharp pain. His foot looked twice its normal size. A small part of him liked the pain; it was something he could see and feel. Not like the great gaping hole in his heart.

Turning onto his hands and knees, with his left foot elevated off the ground, Ashok began to crawl. The ground scratched his knees, but it was better than the pain in his ankle. His face tightened with displeasure and he hoped he wouldn't see anyone he knew. News of Shanti being taken had rippled through the streets. Ashok hated the looks of pity he got from everyone. No one talked about what had happened, and when he'd tried to get help, his so-called friends walked away from him.

Why did these things happen? Was it fair to love someone and then have her ripped away from him? Ashok stopped as his knee felt a prick of a sharp stone. He couldn't keep crawling like this. He needed help. Anger over took him and he screamed his frustration. The noise turned the heads of the people walking the street, but no one came to his aid.

Did no one care? Was his pain invisible to them? Where was Jesus? How could he promise to bring Ashok happiness when he was so silent? He stood and leaned against the side of a building. He closed his eyes to the feeling of abandonment.

His mind recalled the look of sheer terror on Shanti's face as they pulled her away from him. Shanti, screaming his name, would be forever burnt into his brain. His stomach churned and he moaned as horrific thoughts of torture entered his mind. What would they do to his little sister? He clutched his stomach and bent over in agony. He'd let her down. It was his job to look after her and he'd failed. Bile rose from the pit of his stomach, and he gagged at the foul taste. A gut-wrenching sob shook his body. He bent over, cupping the back of his head in his hands, and he rocked back and forth. Despair gripped him as he wept uncontrollably.

He'd never felt this tired before. His eyes felt heavy and sore from crying. He lay on the dusty ground as the light dimmed from the sky. Shadows started to merge together as the air cooled.

Slowly he sat up. Looking after his sister had given his senseless life meaning. He pulled the tattered card from his pocket and stared at the picture. He licked his lips, and a tear escaped his eye. He needed Jesus, more than anything, now. Jesus needed to take care of Shanti, while he couldn't.

His eyes misted over, and he held the card to his heart. He hoped Shanti would remember to trust in Jesus. Ashok squeezed his eyes tight, ignored the darkness crowding in on him, and bowed his head.

"Jesus, please look after Shanti until I find her. I need your help not to give up. Help me, Jesus. Carry me, like in the picture."

Maybe he'd spend the night here. Curling onto his side, he rested his head on his hand. Things would look better in the morning. He believed the card; maybe things didn't look so good now, but he would find his sister. Everything would work out for them. He imagined Shanti's face when she saw him. It would light up and she would sing with joy. He closed his eyes and sighed heavily. The tension in Ashok's shoulders eased, and he relaxed into sleep.

"Ashok. Wake up." Bashaar pushed Ashok's shoulder to wake him.

"No, go away. Leave me be, Bashaar," Ashok grumbled.

"Look what I have found you, my friend."

Ashok sat up and rubbed his eyes. He carefully flexed his ankle to see if it still hurt and gasped. Bashaar proudly held out a buckled piece of wood. Ashok looked at him with blank eyes.

"Give me your hand, Ashok." The smile on Bashaar's face was contagious, and Ashok grasped his hand.

Last night he'd complained that no one cared. Yet here was Bashaar, his friend, offering him a stick. Ashok laughed as he reached for the stick.

"See, it is a great walking stick. I rubbed the end on the road to smooth the edges for you. Try it, Ashok, does it help you walk?"

His fingers ran over the wood, smoothed by his friend, and a huge smile widened his mouth. He took a step, using the stick as a leg, and kept his sore foot off the ground. He would be able to move much quicker this way. His eyes sparkled, and he turned and hugged his friend.

"Thank you, Bashaar. It is a very good stick."

"I've heard of a good doctor who helps sick children for free. I don't feel like working the street today, and Appa said I could help you. Come, Ashok. The sooner we get to the clinic, the sooner you can get in line."

Chapter 14

The noise of Macy moving around downstairs was somehow comforting to Bill. He glanced at the bedside clock. He'd closed his eyes for only twenty minutes, and now he felt worse than he had before he lay down. His baby was missing. The lump in his throat thickened, and he turned over onto his side. His body felt heavy, and the thought of getting out of bed seemed insurmountable. He rubbed the overnight growth on his chin and wondered how he was going to manage to shave today. Charlotte was—lost. Bill's hand went to his chest, and he pressed the ache that grew there. *Lord Jesus, be with her. Wherever she is, be with her.*

Closing his eyes, he sighed. Macy would need him; he had to be strong for her. Slowly he sat on the side of the bed; his hands gripped the mattress and his head drooped. He felt like an old, old man. Bill knew he couldn't get through the day without the Lord's strength. The fear inside him for his daughter was like a gigantic hand, tightly squeezing his heart muscle of all blood. He felt drained of life.

Every time he visualized Charlotte's precious little face, he pictured her as a small child with her arms outstretched to him. Last night he'd dreamed she was running towards him. She'd laughed and called out,

"Daddy," in her musical voice. He smiled, waved at her, and ambled towards her. A dark chasm opened up under her feet and she screamed as she plunged uncontrollably downward. He lunged for her hand but missed her fingers by a fraction of an inch. He watched helplessly as she sailed through the air, her head flung back and her eyes locked with his. It was only seconds before the darkness swallowed her from his sight.

He'd woken trembling, with sweat pouring down his face. If only he'd run towards her and not walked. If only he'd been able to reach her fingers and pull her back up out of the chasm. Why hadn't he gone to India after her? Sobs vibrated through his body, his hands fisting as he dropped to the floor. Prostrate before God he reached his arms above his head. His fingers spread on the carpet and he imagined the hand of Almighty God grasping his. He was but a man, minute, frail, hopeless.

"I call on your name, Almighty God. I put my trust in you—for you, my Lord and God, have not forsaken me." Bill opened his heart to hope. He'd go to India and bring his daughter back.

~~~

Macy knew her face looked drawn, distraught. She'd been up all night praying and writing a list of people to call. All her life she'd been the one praying for others; now she needed a miracle and fast. She knew word would spread and that her church family would rise up in petition for Charlotte's safe return.

Bill had contacted the Australian Federal Police yesterday to see what they could do to help, and they had talked about partner relationships and explained that the responsibility for conducting searches overseas rests with the local police force abroad. In other words, nothing, Macy thought. How could the world carry on as if nothing had happened?

Eli had scribbled down information he found about contacting local charitable and voluntary organizations specializing in tracing missing persons. But Charlotte wasn't just missing, she was abducted!

She'd already found flights that left for India tomorrow and needed to confirm her booking, after talking to Bill. No matter how long it took, she would stay in India until they found Charlotte.

Closing her eyes Macy leaned heavily on the kitchen bench. What was it Bill had told her the police from Mumbai had said? More than fifty people a day go missing in their city. Now her girl, oh God, not her little girl. She wouldn't allow herself to think about what could happen to Charlotte, she would focus her mind on the search to find her.

"Morning, Macy." Bill's voice sound dull, forced.

"Bill, I've checked and we can leave tomorrow. The flight is at 6:00 a.m., what do you think?" Her eyes searched his, and a frown plucked her brow. She noticed the nick on his chin from shaving and wondered how he could do something so mundane as shave, when there was so much to organize.

"Is it the same flight Charlie took?" His eyes watered and he looked away.

"Yes. Eli wants to come too."

Bill nodded. He stood at the entrance to the room, and Macy wished he'd come in and stop staring at her.

"I should have gone to India with her. I'm sorry."

"It's too late to think about what we should have done. Sit down, I'll get you breakfast." Macy knew in her heart she should release him from blame, that it wasn't his fault. What did he expect from her? Couldn't he see it was too late for words? She had her own regrets to live with, without carrying his.

"We will find her, Macy."

"God willing." Her tone sharpened and she turned her back on him.

Bill staggered to the dining room table, his hand pressed his chest. His legs wobbled and gave way as he collapsed on the floor.

Macy spun around and gasped. The skin on his face seemed transparent, and his breathing was labored. His hand was pressed to the centre of his chest, and his eyes widened, locking with hers.

"Macy—" Bill slumped to the floor, closing his eyes.

Macy raced to him. "Bill, what's wrong?" Her heart thumped so loudly, she could hardly think straight. She gently touched his face with her fingers.

"Hospital," he whispered.

She sped across the room, made the call and hurried back to his side. His eyes were closed and his arms hung lifeless beside him.

"Bill. Wake up! Don't you dare leave me!" Tears flowed down her cheeks, and she gripped his arms in desperation.

~~~

Charlotte sat on the floor hugging her knees. Two days they'd left her in here, alone. A tall, thickset man had opened the door twice and stood looking at her. The ugly scar on his face had shocked her, and her heart had filled with compassion. His eyes had hardened and devoured her like she was a piece of merchandise in a shop window. Charlotte shivered and ran her hands up and down her arms. Her stomach growled, reminding her she needed food. Her efforts to moisten her lips with her tongue only deepened her need for water. Charlotte tried to remember what had happened after they had grabbed her, but her mind was foggy on the details.

She stood and paced around the small room. There was only one door, and the window was barred. She pulled at the window's latch, hoping she could call for help. Thick, rusty nails stopped it from budging. Rubbing at the dirty glass pane, she peered out at a closed courtyard.

She caught at her hair and tried to twist it into a knot. She felt dirty, and her skin itched from sleeping on the soiled floor. How much longer would they keep her in here without food or water?

Surely you will rescue me, Lord, from the fowler's snare. Charlotte closed her eyes as the words sunk into her soul. *I will say of the Lord, he is my refuge and my fortress, my God in whom I trust.*

The sound of a key clanking in the lock stopped Charlotte's movements. She moved to the back of the room. Every nerve in her body tensed like a coil ready to spring.

The door opened. Charlotte recognized the big man, and her eyes quickly swung to the stranger beside him. His eyes were the color of night and he seemed to not blink. Her gaze felt glued to his, caught in the evil that reflected back at her. As he stepped towards her, she sucked in a breath.

"You are very beautiful. Pale, like a *devas*—shining one. You will be very popular."

Charlotte lifted her head and took a step forward. She would not cower in the corner like a frightened child. "Who are you? What do you want with me?"

"Arr. I see you have spirit. Good. You are now my property. Do you understand?" His cold voice mocked her.

"No. I'm not your property. How can you say that? You have to let me go!" she screamed.

The man's lips twisted in a cruel smile. He nodded.

The scarred man beside him stepped towards her, grabbed her hair, and jerked her forward until she stumbled to her knees. He yanked back and up, hard, forcing her to look up at the man who had spoken. Her eyes watered, and she blinked several times to stop from crying.

"I am the Boss." His thin lips narrowed, making his mouth look like a slit. "I own you—you will do as I say, or die. The choice is yours."

Charlotte's eyes widened at his words. The pressure on her skull tightened, and she let out a soft moan.

"You will use your body to please high-paying clients, and do so willingly, with a smile on that pale face of yours. Or—our friend here will teach you to obey me."

"No. I won't! I would rather die," Charlotte screamed.

The large man shoved her backward and planted his foot on her stomach.

Softly, his master laughed. "Don't mark her face. I want her ready and compliant by the end of the week."

"Yes, Boss."

Charlotte heard the door lock behind the boss, leaving her in the room with her captor. She'd never felt so helpless. Fear crawled up her spine and made her shake.

The man with the scar laughed as he flexed his fingers. The size of his hands terrified Charlotte. She lunged for the door, banging her hands loudly on the panels as she screamed for help.

He lifted her from behind and threw her across the room.

"This is your life now. There is no escape, no rescue. Step out of line and you answer to me. Get up!"

Moving carefully, Charlotte braced herself for further attack. Her eyes met her enforcer's, and she shuddered.

"Take off your clothes."

Shaking her head, Charlotte lifted her chin and stared defiantly at him.

He reached out and grabbed the front of her dress, ripping the material as he pulled.

She swatted at his hand and he laughed and punched her in the stomach. She buckled over, gasping for breath. He yanked her arm and pulled her to standing and stepped back.

"I said, take—off—your—clothes." His voice, his eyes, his raised fists, challenged her to disobey.

Charlotte knew she had no choice. It was either comply or be beaten. She realized he wanted her to fight him, wanted her to give him cause to hurt her.

"Please, don't do this. You don't have to listen to the boss. I have money. Help me escape and I will pay you. Please, help me," she begged him.

His fist landed in her rib cage. She heard the crack before she felt the sharp pain. Charlotte crawled onto her hands and knees and gasped as pain stabbed her. She could see his feet beside her and knew she had to stop him from hitting her rib again. Struggling to stand, she pulled her dress down over her hips and looked at the wall behind him. Humiliation turned her skin red.

"All of it," he sneered.

Tears streamed down her face as she did as he said. The shaking started deep within her and she couldn't control it. She tried to cover her chest with her hands. He glared at her as if he hated who she was. She closed her eyes to block him from sight.

"Open your eyes and walk around me."

How could he torture her like this? Didn't he have any feelings? Charlotte caught a sob in her throat and swallowed it. He was the first man to see her naked. Her dream of one day being an innocent bride vanished. This was only the beginning; how would she ever survive this?

Remember Me, Charlotte.

The inner voice beckoned her, and a small smile touched her lips.

"He will cover me with his feathers, and under his wings I will find refuge." Her voice rang out with assurance in the quiet room.

"There's no refuge for you, girl," the man with the ugly scar mocked. His hard fingers dug into her shoulder, and he laughed as his fist smacked into her stomach.

Charlotte gasped and buckled over as the air left her lungs.

Chapter 15

Eli groaned at the thumping in his temples. Too much whiskey last night had only dulled his senses; he'd hoped it would knock him out. How had he allowed his life to get so out of control? He'd left his parents late last night and gone straight to Tina's. He couldn't blame Tina for the things he'd done. She'd been a part of it, but he knew he had to take responsibility. He'd turned to her for comfort, wanting her to dull the pain of losing Charlie.

Rubbing the back of his neck, Eli longed for relief from his thoughts. He didn't like the type of man he'd become over the last two weeks. How could such a short time seem like a lifetime? Everything he'd held sacred, he'd thrown away. He'd slept with Tina numerous times and told her he wanted to marry her to make things right. She believed it was important to find out if they were compatible in passion before they talked marriage. Tina had boasted of two previous lovers. At first he'd been disappointed, but in the heat of the moment, he'd stopped caring. He'd missed two dinners with his parents to appease Tina and used alcohol to wash away his guilt. When his father asked him why he hadn't been in church the last couple of weeks, he'd lied, saying he had to work. How had he thrown away so easily, all he believed in and lived for?

His head drooped in shame, and he gave an anguished cry. Would he ever see his sister again? She'd always loved and believed in him. What would she think about what he'd been doing? Would he see disappointment in her eyes?

Tina hadn't understood his need to go to India. She'd been furious and told him to let his parents go. For the first time, Eli began to see clearly that Tina wasn't the girl for him, that he needed to get his life back on a solid foundation.

He sighed and closed his eyes. *Lord Jesus, forgive me. I've messed up big-time. I let lust sweep me away. I can't get back what I've lost, but I can try to walk upright with you again.*

The relief of his confession caused him to relax. It felt like he'd lifted the lid off a pressure cooker and the reassurance of God's grace, and mercy flooded his heart. His headache lifted, and he longed to talk to his father about what had happened. Going to India with his parents would help distance him from Tina.

The shrilling of the phone woke him, it felt like he'd just closed his eyes. Turning on his side, he pulled his mobile phone to his ear as he checked the time on the bedside clock—8:30 a.m.

"Eli, your father's had a heart attack," his mother spluttered through sobs. "They're operating on him now. Can you come to the hospital?"

"No!" he exploded, then cursed. Silence greeted his outburst. Eli flung the blankets off and stood up. "Sorry, Mum. I'm on my way."

Slamming the car door didn't relieve any of his tension. Was he now going to lose his father as well as his sister? How could God allow that to happen? Hadn't he just asked God to forgive him? Eli gripped the steering wheel so tightly that his knuckles turned white. A violent rage boiled within him. His anger focused on the unseen enemy who was trying to destroy his family. He would not back down now; he would stand firm on the promises in the Bible. He would fight for his family, even if it meant sacrificing all he had.

Lord Jesus, protect my father. Give the surgeons wisdom to operate

on his heart. Heal my Dad, Lord. I can't lose him. Please, Lord, oh—
my—God, don't take him from us. Not yet, not now!

~~~

Macy sat with her hands in her lap. Why hadn't she noticed Bill wasn't well? In hindsight, she'd been aware of his shortness of breath but put it down to his getting older, being slightly overweight and unfit. He wasn't the sort to complain if he was feeling a little under the weather.

Her hand fluttered to her neck, and she sucked in her lips. Telling Eli his father was in hospital had just about done her in. She'd been surprised by how calm he was once he arrived at the hospital. He'd handed her a coffee and prayed. She'd been concerned about him the last little while, but right now, as she looked across at him in the waiting room, she felt like she had her son back.

"Shouldn't be long now, Mum."

His smile brought tears to her eyes. The thought of losing her husband had never entered her mind. They weren't even grandparents yet, and surely God wouldn't take Bill from her before they got Charlotte back. She needed him, his consistent strength; he grounded her. *Please, Lord.* Further words weren't necessary for Macy. She knew God heard her and knew her heart.

The doctor entered the room and smiled. "It went well. We've performed a triple bypass, and I'm very happy with the results."

Her hand fluttered to her mouth and she turned to Eli. Tears streamed down her face and the tension in her shoulders eased.

Eli pulled her into his arms. "It's okay, Mum. Dad's going to be fine," he assured her.

Sitting back, she sniffed and grabbed a tissue off the table. "Thank you, Doctor, thank you so much."

"How long will Dad be in hospital, Doctor?"

"The average postoperative is five days, maybe less if he picks up quickly. I've arranged for a nurse to come and explain the recovery process to you, Mrs. Turner."

"Thank you."

After the doctor left them, Eli slumped down beside Macy and picked up her hand. Words couldn't explain the way she felt. Bill would be okay, but would Charlotte? She felt torn between her husband and daughter, and a sob escaped her.

"Dad's going to be fine, you heard the doctor," Eli reassured her.

Straightening her back in the chair, Macy spun around to face her son. Her eyes teared up at the decision she had to make. How could she leave Bill? Would he see it as abandonment? What if something happened to him while she was in India? How would she cope if he relapsed and she wasn't here with him? Her stomach knotted and she closed her eyes. If she didn't go to India, would Charlie understand? Macy anguished over her decision. Her heart felt snapped in two. She clutched Eli's hand tightly and expelled a deep breath. The tightness in her throat made it difficult to swallow.

"Mum, I'm here. Talk to me," Eli said gently.

Moistening her lips, Macy nodded. "Eli, you'll have to go to India on your own. I can't leave Bill—it'll take weeks for him to recover from this."

"I know. You take care of Dad for me, and I'll go get Charlotte. I won't come back until I find her."

"Thank you, darling." Standing, Macy took his face in her hands and kissed both cheeks. "Please be careful. I couldn't stand losing you too. I love you, Eli."

~~~

Waiting to board the aircraft only accentuated the length of time it would take to fly from Sydney to India. Eli knew he'd have lots of thinking time once he was seated and in a way this worried him. The line was moving now, and he took his passport and boarding pass out of his pocket in preparation.

"Good morning, sir, please move through to the left aisle." Eli nodded and moved to his seat. He hoped no one would take the seat next to him. How many times had he crossed oceans to exotic destinations and enjoyed the excitement of travel. This time, worry clouded his mind. Where was she? What sort of trouble had she walked into?

"Hello there."

Eli opened his eyes to see a hand proffered out in front of him. Without moving his head, he allowed his eyes to move to the man's face. The expression of excitement couldn't be missed. This man was keen to start up a conversation, and Eli grimaced at the thought of sitting next to him.

Shuffling in his seat, he turned towards the window, and closed his eyes. As he feigned sleep, his mind got busy. He and Tina were over. She'd surprised him by agreeing they weren't suited and thanked him for a good time. No hard feelings, she'd said. She'd taken it all so lightly that he'd felt stunned, hurt somehow.

Shrugging, he moved slightly and sighed. He needed to focus on Charlotte. She'd been missing five days now and could be anywhere. Giving up the pretense of sleep, he sat up and pulled his satchel from under his seat.

"Can't sleep?" the man asked. "My name's Ted."

Eli opened his satchel and pulled out some papers. Maybe if he continued to ignore the man . . . He thumbed through the papers until he found what he wanted. He rubbed his forehead and squinted. The stats on human trafficking astounded him. How was it people became so engrossed in their own lives that they stopped caring about what was happening to people around them?

"You've got a frown on your face bigger than the Grand Canyon, friend," Ted said in a friendly American voice.

Lowering the paper Eli turned towards Ted. "Guess I have. Did you know that approximately 12.3 million people are in forced labor or sexual servitude at any given time?"

"Can't say I did. That's an awful lot of people. You some kind of human-rights activist?"

"No," Eli answered flatly.

"Hard to believe that sort of thing is happening in the world today. I thought slavery was a thing of the past."

"Well, it's not. My sister refused to eat the Easter egg I brought her last year because it wasn't made from fair trade cocoa. I laughed it off at the time. Never gave any thought to what she was really saying."

"So it's your sister who's got you interested in this stuff?"

"In a way, yes." Eli's eyes welled up and he blinked. Charlie was passionate about injustice, and he'd preferred to throw her a few dollars rather than get involved.

"I love India," Ted stated. "Finally got the wife and kids to move there a couple of years ago, so we're just one, big, happy family. I manage a large hotel chain. What about you, Eli? What brings you to India?"

Eli hesitated. Maybe verbalizing what had happened would help him get his head around it. "My sister, Charlotte, was abducted five days ago. I was talking to her on the phone when it happened. They broke into her hotel room and—" Eli stopped. What more was there to say?

Ted touched Eli's arm. "I'm sorry."

Eli cleared his throat and nodded. The compassion he saw etched on Ted's face caused him to suck in a breath.

"What are the police doing to find her?"

"That's just it, the police searched the hotel room and asked around, but it's like she's gone and that's it. It's as if she wasn't even there." Eli rubbed his eyes and sighed. "My parents have contacted an organization that supports people who've had a family member go missing abroad. They're setting up a twenty-four-hour hotline, posters, media releases, and, well—"

"Surely someone saw something? I mean, she was there—you said you were talking to her when they took her. Did you hear anything that would, I don't know, help at all?"

"I've been going over and over my conversation with Charlie, and what happened once she dropped the phone. She tried to describe a man to me before—" Eli cleared his throat and turned his head to look out the plane window to hide his emotion.

"That's something, I suppose," Ted encouraged.

"Yes. Although from what I've researched, there are all sorts of people doing this. It could be gangs, organizations, locals setting up brothels for themselves." Eli pounded his hand on his knee. "God will help me find her, I believe that."

"Not too sure about the God stuff myself, but if I can help you at all—here's my card."

Eli took the card, glanced at it, and pushed it into his wallet. A leading in his heart prompted him to speak. "Thanks. You got another one of those?"

Ted raised his eyebrows in question, but handed another card over. Eli scribbled his name and phone number on the back and held it out.

Chapter 16

The line of children seemed to get longer each day. Phillip flexed his
shoulders and began unloading the van. He couldn't stop thinking
about Charlotte; just knowing she'd been outside with the children
had lifted his spirits. It was like sharing the burden. Although she'd
only spent a short time with him, he'd been impressed by who she
was. At first he was ticked off about having to take her with him; it
was hard enough getting through all his work without a hanger-on. But
Charlie hadn't been like that, she'd genuinely cared.

Their last conversation pulled on his mind. She'd told him that
she wanted to be a doctor like him and was planning on going back
to Australia to study. Part of him wanted to encourage her to stay and
support him. He'd been drawn to her. A smile tugged on his mouth as
he recalled her sweet voice singing songs to the children. He could
sure use her here today.

He scanned the line, looking to see if anyone needed urgent
attention. Out of the corner of his eye he saw two boys laboriously
walking towards him. One had his arm slung around the other's
shoulder, and he hopped on one foot. Something about the boys drew
him. He liked it when he saw people helping each other. Walking to

meet them, he squatted down to say hello.

"Looks like you have a good friend here, young man." He smiled at the boys.

"Yes, Doctor, my friend Bashaar made me a walking stick. It broke and he's helped me walk the rest of the way."

Phillip rested his hand on Bashaar's shoulder. "Well done, lad." Turning his head to the other boy, Phillip asked his name.

"Ashok, Doctor." Ashok smiled a wide smile. Phillip lifted him in his arms and told Bashaar to follow. Once he had him up on the cot, he gently pressed at Ashok's swollen ankle.

"You certainly did a good job spraining your ankle. This is going to hurt, lad. I think the swelling is a good thing. I can see the bruising coming out." His expert fingers moved over the outside of the ankle.

"How did you do this, Ashok?" he asked to distract the boy from the pain he was inflicting.

"I was thrown and landed badly on my foot," the boy replied in a sad voice.

"What do you mean by *thrown?*" Phillip knew there were many sad stories. Usually he didn't ask, as he didn't have time to become too involved.

As the boy's deep brown eyes stared back at him, Phillip's mouth tightened at the pain reflected there.

"I was with my sister, Doctor, Shanti. Two men came and took her from me, and I tried to stop them. One of the men picked me up and threw me into a wall."

Phillip's hand stopped moving on Ashok's ankle. He grasped the boy's thin shoulder and squatted down to look in his eyes. "Have you notified the police about this?"

"The police don't care about us, Doctor. They tell us to go away."

Phillip knew numerous children went missing or were found dead. No one claimed the bodies or seemed to grieve their loss. A chill moved through him and he touched Ashok's arm.

"Ashok, you've damaged the ligaments on the outside of your

ankle. You must have turned over, so the side of your foot faced inwards. The good news is, that I don't think it's broken."

"How long before I can walk on it, Doctor?"

"I'll strap it for you now. You need to elevate it and keep off it to let the swelling go down."

Ashok's head bowed. His lips quivered and he shook his head. "I need to find my sister."

Phillip leaned over and rubbed Ashok's back. "How about you stay here for a few days? You can sleep in the shelter with the other children who need to stay put. The clinic brings food here once a day. Give your foot a week to heal, and then you will be able to go look for your sister."

Bashaar grinned at Ashok. "Yes, Ashok. Shanti would want you to look after your foot. You can't help her if you can't walk my friend."

"Thank you, Doctor. I will do as you say." Ashok's hand lifted to swipe at his eyes.

As Phillip strapped the ankle, he thought of the disappointment ahead for Ashok. He may never find his sister, and if he did, what condition would she be in?

~~~

For the first time Phillip felt lonely. Surrounded by many, yet alone. His thoughts drifted to his friends back home; many of them had married and had a baby or two. For an instant he felt regret. He'd turned down an offer in a solid medical practice, for what? An empty apartment and empty arms.

A thick lump swelled in his throat as his eyes met those of a small child. Her face split in a huge grin as she saw him look at her.

Hadn't he told the Lord he would forsake everything for the call? Rubbing his hand over his hair, he sighed. Charlotte had unsettled him. In the few days of knowing her, he'd pictured them together, working with and loving the fatherless. He was a fool—she'd never given any indication she was coming back.

His mouth curved slightly. A man was allowed to dream. He'd liked her, seen something in her that resonated within him. Maybe she would come back.

"Dr. Phillip, may I speak with you?" Ashok asked.

"Sure thing. How's the ankle?" Phillip's hand ruffed Ashok's hair in affection. In the week the boy had been here, Phillip had managed to have a few conversations with him. The lad had a strong faith, a belief that God would come through for him.

"My foot is much better now, see." Ashok tilted his ankle up and down.

"That's good. Remember it may be a bit weak, so go easy on it. No running or football until you're sure it's strong." As he said this, Phillip knew full well that this young boy wasn't intending to pursue games or football as many other boys did.

Ashok nodded. He reached out and touched the sleeve of Phillip's shirt. "Dr. Phillip, you know how you told me that people pray for each other? Could you pray for my sister, Shanti? I know God must listen to a great man like you."

Phillip eyed Ashok with sympathy. Squatting down beside him, he cupped Ashok's thin shoulders in his hands. "I will pray for her every day. Can I pray now?"

A tear squeezed out the side of Ashok's eye, and he nodded.

"Lord Jesus, you see this young man who loves you. Look after Shanti for us. Bring someone to help Ashok find her, Lord. What seems impossible to us is possible to you. Thank you for letting me meet Ashok; he's a fine young man, and I believe you have a great plan for his life. Amen."

Spontaneously Phillip pulled Ashok into a bear hug. The boy sobbed and Phillip rubbed his back. These were his children.

"Come back anytime, lad." A commotion at the gate disturbed their conversation. Both Phillip and Ashok watched as a taxi pulled up.

A tall, blond man stepped out of the car and looked around. He looked vaguely familiar to Phillip, and he tried to place where he'd met him. Ashok stepped back slightly as the man approached.

"Hello, I'm Eli Turner. I'm looking for Dr. Phillip Mangan."

"That would be me," Phillip answered.

Eli extended his hand and Phillip automatically placed his in it.

"I'm Charlotte's brother. I believe she spent some days volunteering here with you."

Phillip's skin crawled; he couldn't help the feeling that something was wrong. Surely Eli would have talked with his sister about her time here? Eli's resemblance to Charlotte was incredible. "Yes, she did. I see the family resemblance, now I know you're her brother."

Eli's lips twitched slightly. "Can we talk?" he asked.

Phillip glanced at Ashok and smiled. Ashok returned the smile and started to move away. He stopped suddenly and turned. "Dr. Phillip, I thank God for you," Ashok said as he moved off.

"Who is that?" Eli asked.

"A very special young man. Follow me. I can offer you terrible coffee or a bottle of warm water."

~~~

Eli's eyes followed the skinny Indian boy as he walked across the compound. He frowned at the feeling he was missing something significant. Pushing the thought away, he turned and accompanied Phillip into the clinic. Charlotte had talked highly of this man, and Eli needed someone he could trust as a contact here.

"So, what's it to be? Coffee or water?"

"Water, thanks."

Phillip handed him a warm bottle of water and sat down in one of the two chairs in the room. He indicated with his hand to the other chair and opened his own bottle of water.

"How's Charlotte? I know she was only here a short time, but she made a big impact on us all."

Eli's gaze dropped. He'd assumed Philip knew what had happened. He squared his shoulders. "Charlie never made it home. She was abducted from her hotel room six days ago."

The color drained from Phillip's face and Eli's mouth tightened. His heart pounded against his rib cage as he watched the guys open display of grief.

Phillip's shoulders slumped, and he bent over and cupped his face in his hands. "No, no—please God, no," he utter despairingly.

Eli lifted the water bottled and took a deep swig. He noticed his hand was shaking slightly and he tightened his grip on the bottle.

Phillip stood up and moved across the room. He grabbed a towel and wiped his face before he settled back in the chair.

"I'm sorry. Charlotte is such a special person, and the thought of her—" He coughed as he cleared his throat.

"I'm here to find her and bring her home. There are no leads, or if anyone did see anything, no one is talking. The general consensus is that she's been gone too long and has probably been taken out of the country."

"I can't believe that," Phillip exclaimed.

"The police are involved, but their resources are limited. I would appreciate any help you can give me."

"We must find her. What have you got so far?"

"The hotel manager is apologetic, said no one heard anything. I find that hard to believe, as I heard the noise they made breaking into the room through my phone. It would have woken a deaf man. Charlotte also said her room was unlocked the day before and that the manager of the hotel said it was a mistake, that the maid probably forgot to lock it."

Phillip lunged out of his chair. "Wait here," he called, racing from the room.

Walking to the door, Eli leaned his shoulder on the doorjamb. He watched Phillip run out the gate and down the street. His eyebrows rose as he pondered Phillip's action. He took another swig from his bottle and turned to look at the children gathered around the compound. He took in their shabby clothes and dirty faces. They were of all ages, and there seemed to be some order in the way they milled. These were the children Charlie had talked about, sang to.

He smiled, lifted his hand, and waved to them. Slowly one person after another lifted their hand in response. Eli could see how their faces had pulled at Charlotte's heart.

Phillip walked slowly back towards him, shaking his head. "Sorry about that. Remember Ashok, the young boy I introduced to you?"

"Yeah."

"His sister was taken from him about ten days ago. He's looking for her."

"Taken, you mean the same as Charlie?" Eli slammed his hand on the doorframe, causing dust particles to take flight. He'd felt led to talk to the boy but had ignored the inner prompting.

"Careful there, Eli. You could have the whole building down on us. Ashok told me about what happened to his sister; she's only eight years old. He tried to stop the two men from taking her, and they hurled him into a wall. He landed awkwardly, spraining his ankle. That's what brought him to me. He knows what the men look like and plans to find them and rescue his sister. Big call for a small lad."

Eli moved back into the shack, collapsed into his chair, and stretched out his legs. A little girl—could it be the same people? He shuddered to think of such a young child being forced into sexual labor. He sighed heavily and his mouth twisted in disgust.

Visions of Charlie as a child flew through his mind. He remembered pushing her on a swing and her laughing and telling him she was flying. His stomach knotted as unwanted images of his sister being used and abused made him feel ill. He clenched his fists, took a deep breath, and tried to concentrate on what Phillip was saying.

"I prayed with Ashok just before you arrived. I asked God to send someone to help him. Maybe that someone is you. You're both on the same quest. You could help each other."

"I agree it would be good to talk to Ashok, see what information he can give me. I know that one of the men who took Charlie had a scar on his face. Did Ashok mention anything like that to you?"

"No, we didn't get into details. Ashok is a good kid. It would mean a lot to him to be able to travel with you."

"He would only slow me down. I need to move with as much speed as possible, not babysit some ten-year-old kid, hobbling around in circles."

"I think you'd be surprised by Ashok. He may be only a boy, but he's street smart. You could do a lot worse for a guide," Phillip stated.

Shaking his head, Eli was adamant that Ashok would only get in the way; what could a boy that age do to help him? He felt for him, of course, and he would try and find his sister as well, but he couldn't make any promises.

"I have a spare bedroom, you're welcome to it. We can use my place as a base," Phillip offered.

Surprised and pleased by the offer, Eli smiled. "Yeah, that would be great. How long have you lived here, Phillip?"

"Three years. This is home for six months of the year, then I head home to work for six months to fund my time here."

Eli's mouth twitched. He'd put money on Phillip being an American. "Where's home?"

"States. I've got some money saved up, so if you get short of funds, let me know."

"Thanks, I appreciate the offer."

"I have some contacts on the street and will put the word out. Have you got photos?"

"Yes, I'll get you some."

The sound of the shuffling feet at the door ended their conversation. Phillip moved quickly to help an injured boy into the room. Blood soaked the motley yellow T-shirt he wore, and he clutched his stomach in an attempt to stem the blood flow.

"What happened this time, lad? Weren't you in here a couple of weeks ago with a knife wound to your arm?"

"Can I help, Phillip?" Eli's stomach turned at the sight of blood, but if his new friend needed him.

"No. You go. Ask around outside for where you might find Ashok. His friend Bashaar lives on Masjid Road. He'll be able to help you." Phillip ripped the T-shirt off his patient, and his whole attention was now on the boy on the table.

Eli listened to the calm tone of voice Phillip used to reassure the boy and didn't want to interrupt him. "What number Masjid Road?" he asked backing towards the door.

"No number, he lives on the pavement." Phillip looked up and gave him a smile. "I'm here until 6:00 p.m., call back then and I'll give you a key to the apartment and my phone number."

As Eli left the clinic, it felt like his eyes were opened for the first time. He knew of the hardship of poverty but had never allowed the truth of how it affected individual people to penetrate his small, secure world. Children lived on the streets. No warm bed, no cozy home, no food in the fridge for midnight snacks. His steps moved with new purpose. If he could find Ashok, maybe he could make a difference in one child's life.

Chapter 17

Shanti's smile had died the day they took her from Ashok. She lay on a woven mat, staring at the ceiling. Black spots where flies had defecated were scattered across the surface. My life is like that, she thought, dirty. She imagined her blood turning black, like the pox disease she'd seen spread over some of the children who worked the dump. Everyone who saw her would know she was rotten. Shanti screwed up her face. Even the worms she'd seen on some people's skin wouldn't want to live on her body. She'd stopped counting the times she'd been taken to the boss. The first time had been the worst. Now her mind shut down completely and she went into a mental void while he used her.

Padma had told her that eventually the boss would tire of her and hand her over to Scarface. Padma was the only person Shanti talked to, and then only in response to a direct question.

Her words had disappeared with her smile. The other girls had stopped trying to get her into conversation. Their talk was meaningless, and she stared blankly at them, as if she had no language. They called her stupid to her face and she didn't care.

Shanti tried not to think about Ashok. She missed him so much, yet she didn't know whether she wanted him to find her and see what she'd become. She wasn't his little sister anymore; she wasn't the girl who saw good in everyone and everything. She hated life. A soul-destroying hatred grew deep within her for the boss and even Padma. Padma could have helped her escape but chose to ignore her pleas.

She heard two girls fighting and tilted her head to watch. The other girls squabbled constantly. No one was happy; everyone dealt with her captivity as best she could. Fighting was a way of escape for them, distracting them from the reality of their prison.

Her escape was thoughts of dying. She sucked in a long, deep breath, closed her mouth, and stopped breathing. Her mind counted—one, two, three, four, five, six, seven, eight—she frowned as she tried to remember what number came after eight. Ashok had tried to teach her the numbers, but she hadn't been interested. Expelling her breath, she sighed. If she were to die, what would they do with her body? Would Ashok ever stop looking for her if he didn't know she was dead? Closing her eyes, she tried to picture his face, and his words haunted her. *Jesus knows your name, Shanti.*

She sat up and hugged her knees to her chest. She didn't believe that anymore. There was no God. Ashok had been the one who looked after her, and now she had to survive by herself. If there was a God, then where was he? He certainly didn't care for her, or anyone it seemed.

Her attention was caught by the conversation two girls were having next to her.

"I saw her again last night. Scarface is making her walk the hall, naked. They must be preparing her. She's beautiful and she walks with her head held high, like a princess."

"Wait until she knows her lot, she'll soon realize there ain't no princesses here." The other girl smirked.

Shanti shuddered at the thought of being made to walk naked. She knew she'd eventually be like the others. Servicing, as they called it, many men. She hated the boss, but at least it was only him she had to be with. It didn't hurt so much now when he took her. The fear that gripped her stomach every time Scarface came for her was not the sex, but the evil she saw on the boss's face. It was like some monster took control of him. The way he looked at her sent shivers down her spine. He sneered as he performed vicious, cruel acts on her body. He mumbled a type of chant and his face contorted strangely.

Looking down at the cigarette burns on her arm, she shuddered. She blinked several times to stop from crying. Tears were wasted emotion; Padma had drilled this into her.

Sometimes, as she tried to get to sleep at night, she dreamed of the boss killing her. He would run the blade of his knife across her neck, opening the skin and exposing the filth hidden there. She could feel the warmth of her blood seeping down her chest, and the feeling often lulled her to sleep.

Death filled her mind, day and night.

Chapter 18

Macy squinted at her friend. She'd agreed to meet for coffee and now she regretted it. She'd known Anne for thirty years; their families had grown up together. Anne talked nonstop about her daughter's wedding plans.

Nodding as if she were listening, Macy's hand tightened on the arm of the chair. Anger pulsed within her and her heart pummeled her chest. How could life carry on as if nothing were wrong? She didn't have the energy to be interested in Anne's dilemma of not being able to find the right dress.

Placing her cup carefully down on Anne's highly polished table Macy stood to her feet. Her hand swept through her short wavy hair, and she avoided her friend's eyes.

Anne stopped talking mid-sentence and gazed at her.

Macy reached for her handbag. "I'm sorry, Anne, but I need to go," she stated firmly.

"Sit down, Macy. I know I've been rattling on, but I don't know what to say to you. Talk to me, let me help."

Lowering herself back into the chair, Macy closed her eyes. She clasped her fingers together and wondered what to say.

Anne touched her hand. "I thought maybe if I rattled on, it might give you a break from thinking about Charlotte. I can't imagine what it's like for you."

The caring tone in her friend's voice brought tears to Macy's eyes. Her shoulders slumped, and she sighed. Looking up, she gave a watery smile. "I'm sorry, Anne," she said softly.

"Please don't apologize. Tell me, how is Bill?"

"He's coming along well, physically. But he's lost something. It's like he's given up hope. No matter what I say to him, he just gives a weak smile and doesn't reply." Macy shifted her gaze around the room, and she shrugged. "I get so angry with him. I try to be patient, but really, he's being so selfish. It's not only him who's lost a daughter."

"Have you spoken to the doctor about this? Maybe depression is a side effect from the surgery, and Charlie going missing has accelerated the process."

Giving a faint nod, Macy felt her face heat. "Yes. It can be a symptom. I know I'm being hard on him. But Anne, he's been the one I've always leaned on. He's meant to be my rock, and now I have to make every decision. I saw a red-back spider the other day and realized we hadn't had our placed sprayed for the summer. Bill usually takes care of these things. I asked him whom he usually calls, and he said he couldn't remember. I spent half an hour going through last year's checkbook until I found the name. It's all too much."

Anne reached across the table and took her hand. "Macy, you're not alone, we love you. You need to let us help."

Macy had never felt so vulnerable, so needy. She pressed Anne's hand and pulled away. "I feel so helpless. It's like everyone I love—has—left me." Macy cupped her face in her hands and wept.

She felt Anne's arm go around her, and she turned into her embrace. Macy allowed her friend's love to comfort her. Slowly she moved away and gave her first genuine smile in days. Somehow the touch of her friend had strengthened her. Macy pulled out a tissue and noisily blew her nose while Anne clucked over her.

"I'm going to talk to that stubborn husband of mine," Anne declared. "He thinks Bill needs time to get well, and because of this he's stayed away. I think what Bill needs is his friends around him— we're family, after all."

"I think you're right. Having some of his friends round to pray and talk with him could help snap him out of it. I need him to believe we'll get Charlotte back. If he thinks she's gone, it makes it difficult for me to hold onto hope."

"Have you heard from Eli in the last couple of days?" Anne inquired.

"Yes. Eli's been amazing. He calls me all the time to let me know how he is. He's keeping in close touch with the Missing Persons Bureau over there. They're actively passing out photos, using media— you know—newspapers, radio and Charlotte's photo has been on the television. Because we know Charlie's been abducted, it helps in a way, because the police can't just say she disappeared."

"Oh, Macy. This is just unbelievable."

"I know. It feels like I'm talking about someone else, not my precious daughter. The scary thing is the police are saying that the window of time to find her is closing." Macy licked her lips and drew a quick breath. She couldn't cope with the thought of not finding Charlotte. Shaking her head adamantly, she clasped her hands together and continued. Talking helped, she decided.

"Although the police here haven't been able to help over there, they have assigned us a case worker. She's been very helpful with connecting us with an organization that supports families in these situations. They can arrange free flights, funding, and they have experience with other people going through the same heartbreak."

"I have an idea," Anne said. "How about you and I meet every day for an hour and pray specifically for things that we feel need to happen."

"I'd like that." Macy smiled her thanks. "Starting now?"

~~~

The smile stayed on Macy's face as she drove home, and even when she entered the house, she felt uplifted. Placing her keys on the bench, she went to find Bill. She'd love him more, show him that nothing would stop her from believing in him, or in Eli finding Charlotte.

As she entered the room, she stopped. Bill was sitting in the lounge, gazing into space. How long had he sat there?

Shaking her head slightly, she moved across the room and flung her arms around him and gave him a smacking big kiss on his lips.

"Hello, darling. It's a bit warm in here. Mind if I open a window?" Macy snapped open the window and then sat across from him. She grinned at his emotionless face and saw his eyes flicker slightly. His way of coping was about to change, whether he liked it or not.

"I've got a few friends coming over for dinner tonight, any preference on what we eat?"

Bill sat up slightly and his lips tightened. "I don't think that's a good idea," he snapped.

Her smile widened. She believed in him even when he didn't believe in himself. She would be patient with him because love was patient and kind. If that meant pushing him slightly to get up and moving—then that's exactly what she'd do. "I think it's a great idea," she answered sweetly.

Chapter 19

The sound of the door locking as Scarface left the room caused Charlotte to release her breath. She would never get used to being naked, exposed to uncaring eyes. A shiver ran down her back as she frantically searched the new room. A big bed filled most of the space. Charlotte tried not to think about the significance of the bed. There was a cupboard in the corner, and she moved over to investigate. Her eyes widened as she noted her clothes. Her backpack was at the bottom of the cupboard, and Charlotte pulled it out. Dropping to her knees, she searched for underwear. Her lips compressed as she realized they'd removed it. Charlotte's hands shook slightly as she pulled on a T-shirt.

How many days had the man with the scar made her walk around naked? When she refused to do as he told her, she'd paid the consequence. He was a dangerous person and enjoyed inflicting pain.

The cane he used to punish her with was slender and tortured her skin. Charlotte longed to snap the beastly thing in two. Her body felt alien to her. Every inch ached and was sensitive to touch. The deep bruising covered large areas. He seemed to have a formula for hitting her, waiting ten or twenty seconds between slashes so the pain from each strike was separate and grueling. He tormented her, telling her she would spend the rest of her life here, and the sooner she accepted her lot the easier it would be. The boss had wealthy clients lined up for her; it was her pale skin and blonde hair that drew the big dollars. Of course she'd never see any of it—she was their slave, to be used as they saw fit.

Charlotte dug through her clothes; they'd taken her jeans, so she had no option but to put on a skirt. She closed her eyes and tried to concentrate. Her body felt weak from lack of food. She longed for a shower, her scalp itched, and she felt a scream building within her.

Pulling back her hair from her face, she went to wind it in a bun when she heard the door open. Charlotte spun around, her eyes widening at the woman who stood there.

"I am Padma. Come with me and I will help you bath."

Charging across the room Charlotte grabbed the woman's top. "You must help me. Please, I need to get out of here."

Padma stared at Charlotte, her eyes showing no emotion. Charlotte shook Padma until the woman pushed her away.

"Come with me, Padma, this is the pit of hell and we need to go, now!" Desperation laced Charlotte's voice.

"There is no way out of here. Do you think I haven't tried? Come." Spinning on her heels, Padma threw open the door and marched down the hall.

Charlotte froze. Tears streamed down her face. *God, where are you? You promised to look after me, protect me. Since I was a child I have loved you, followed you—why have you abandoned me?*

Padma returned. She stood in the doorway and scowled at Charlotte. "I said come. It is time for you to get cleaned up. Or do you want me to get Scarface?" she threatened chillingly.

Wiping away the moisture on her face Charlotte raised her chin and moved to stand directly in front of Padma.

The two women stared at each other. Padma was the first to avert her eyes.

"Since you won't help me, tell me what to expect," Charlotte

115

demanded in a firm voice.

Padma shrugged and turned away. Charlotte screamed and grabbed hold of Padma's arm, twisting it.

"Tell me," Charlotte demanded.

"All right. Let me go."

Releasing Padma, Charlotte stepped back. Her stomach fluttered with nerves as she waited for Padma to speak.

"The boss sold first rights to you, to a rich businessman who likes them fresh. You will be with him until he tires of you. After that you will service other men. You should be hoping that the rich man will not tire of you."

Charlotte felt the shiver deep in her spine. Her lips trembled and her eyes welled up.

"I'm sorry," Padma said softly.

"Thank you." Charlotte followed Padma down the hall; her feet felt as if they were made of concrete, and each step she took was a step closer to her destruction.

As she soaked in the tub, Charlotte's eyes closed. Padma sponged her back and gently massaged oil into her skin. A rich, woody aroma made Charlotte sniff. She sat up straight, and water overflowed onto the floor.

Padma brushed water off her sari in annoyance.

"Padma, what would happen if the man with a scar on his face . . . messed my face up, or bruised me badly? Would the boss put off my meeting the man?"

"That would depend on the mood he's in. He could also decide to throw you to the pack instead of waiting longer," Padma answered dully.

Charlotte licked her lips. "It's worth a try, don't you think?"

Shrugging Padma moved away from the tub. She motioned for Charlotte to get out of the water. Charlotte's chin dropped to her chest. Her wet, straggly hair surrounded her face like the branches of a willow tree shielding their trunk. She longed to stay in the lukewarm water; to get out meant to get ready for what lay ahead.

"You get Scarface angry enough to go against the boss's instructions, you court danger. He may kill you," Padma whispered.

Charlotte's head snapped up as a small glimmer of hope inched its way to the surface of her mind. She grabbed the towel, stepped out of the tub, and curved her lips in a confident smile.

The instant Padma left Charlotte dropped to her knees. The walls themselves seemed to glare at her, mocking her very existence. *Lord, I would rather die than be subjected to a stranger's lust. What good can come of this? Why won't you answer me?* She crawled along the floor to the door and clambered up. Her fists pounded the door over and over again.

"Let me out of here," she screamed. "I will—not—do—as—you—want."

The door opened just as Charlotte had thrown both arms at it. She fell through the doorway to the floor. She looked at the boots that filled her field of vision, and fear churned her stomach. Now that he stood in front of her, her resolve weakened.

Scarface took a step towards her, and Charlotte scrambled to her feet and moved away from him.

"You waste my time, girl, with your useless cries." Scarface scowled and turned to leave her.

Charlotte picked up the water jug and threw it at him. It bounced off his shoulder and shattered on the floor.

He stood completely still. The air in the room thickened. He slowly turned, his hands fisted at his sides. The fury in his eyes burned her skin. Charlotte pursed her lips in anticipation.

"You are nothing but a dog, wagging your tail, following after your master. You have no mind of your own," she mocked.

Scarface sneered as he moved towards her.

Laughing Charlotte drew back into the room. Her heart pounded. "You don't even have a name! Scarface is no name. I'm going to call you Saul. How does that sound?"

He caught her by the hair and yanked her to an inch from his face. Tears smarted in her eyes, and she blinked furiously to stop them falling. His putrid breath fanned her cheeks, and she noticed there was a tiny scar under his left eye.

His face tightened. Charlotte could see his struggle for control. She spat in his face and watched, fascinated, as his eyes widened in surprise. A deep guttural sound came from his mouth as his fist thrust forward, slamming into her chin. Her head flung back with a snap. His other hand wound her hair tighter, and he tossed her across the room.

Charlotte ignored the throbbing in her chin and scrambled to her feet. She fought the urge to back off. She took two tentative steps towards him, hands on hips. "Is that the best you can do?"

Scarface's lips pressed together and he hissed as he lunged at her. She cried out as his clenched fist smacked into her eye. Her body buckled over in pain. Time stretched out and to Charlotte it seemed as if things moved in slow motion. Each time he lifted his hand she could hear the swooshing sound of his fist coming towards her and the thud of his knuckles connecting with her body. Her breath caught in her throat and tried to strangle her.

He dropped her to the floor and stepped back.

Charlotte touched her face, and her fingers came away sticky with blood. Her mind cleared and she looked up at him. She reached out to him in a gesture, beckoned him close. He bent towards her, and Charlotte tried to lift herself up. Her voice was raw, and blood oozed from a split in her lip.

"I'm sorry, it's not your fault—forgive me."

Scarface frowned. He raked his hand through his hair as the consequence of his actions suddenly hit him. Charlotte flopped back and closed her eyes.

Chapter 20

Striding down the street, Eli lifted his hand to cover his nose. The putrid smell of rotting food turned his stomach. India had a real problem with rubbish, he thought. Mumbai's population was around eighteen million, compared to Australia's total population of twenty-odd million. He stopped and watched birds scavenge from the filth. People moved along the street, as if not seeing the garbage. It was part of the environment and had been piled high in one place, like the community hoped a truck would come along and take it away.

He longed for the wide-open spaces of home. Never again would he complain when driving from Sydney to Brisbane. The last time he'd driven the ten-hour stretch, Charlie had gone with him. They had laughed the hours away, what with her singing "Waltzing Matilda" over and over again until he gave up and joined in.

Frowning, he felt his face tighten at the thought of never seeing her again. He'd been asking questions of local vendors, showing Charlie's photo around, and inquiring of a man with a scar on his face. Today was the first lead he had. He was to meet a wiry little man who'd told him to come to the end of this street at 6:00 p.m. Eli had tried to get him to talk to him then, but the man was adamant they were being watched. He'd looked scared and scurried off after making the arrangement.

The light was dimming, and Eli was glad he'd phoned Phillip to tell him where he was going. He glanced behind him at the sound of footsteps but shrugged when nothing seemed out of place. Eli pushed the uneasy feeling away and chided himself for being paranoid. He rounded the corner. The street seemed unusually quiet, like everyone had at that moment stopped talking. Eli spun around and felt the hair on his skin rise. He searched out the shadows, and his heart rate quickened.

Two men stepped out of the darkness and walked towards him. Eli squared his shoulders and put his hand in his pocket to finger his phone.

The smack on the back of his head came as a complete surprise, and he stumbled and fell to the ground. Sticky warmth oozed across his scalp as he tried to get up. His eyes blurred and he collapsed, his head falling heavily on the ground.

~~~

Ashok dared not breathe. He lay hidden from the street in the culvert and watched as the two men bent over the man he'd met at the clinic. He'd been following him all day, trying to get up the courage to talk to him. He inched forward to hear what was being said.

"What do you want to do with him?" the tall gangly man asked.

"Kill him, but not here. He's not going anywhere in a hurry, let's go get the van." The fatter man's face was in shadow, and Ashok squinted to see if it helped him see better. The man gave a cruel laugh, and the tone of his voice sent shivers down Ashok's spine. He wanted to scurry back into his hiding place and not care about the stranger, but something stopped him. The man on the ground needed his help. He watched the two men walk away, and once he was sure they were out of sight, he climbed up out of the drain.

Creeping over to the man, he touched his chest. The man moaned and moved slightly. Ashok twisted his head to look in the direction of the bad men and had a sense he needed to hurry. His arms circled the man's chest. He dragged his heavy body towards the drain, which was more of a ditch, really. Ashok thought that if he could get him balanced on the side, his body weight would do the rest. His back ached with the weight of the man, and sweat rolled from his forehead and dripped into his eyes. He breathed heavily and finally gave the man a shove over the edge of the ditch. Ashok watched as he rolled down the slope and then heard a thud as he stopped at the bottom. He looked back to see if there was any trail left behind on the ground that would give him away. There wasn't. His mouth lifted in a slight smile as he dusted his hands on his pants and jumped over the edge of the ditch. He gripped the man's feet and he dragged him farther along the narrow tunnel. Ashok puffed and panted, and his shoulders stung. Finally he collapsed beside the stranger and rested his head on a pillow of dirt. He listened for any noise that might alert him to being found out. His eyes drooped and the weight of them made it easy to go to sleep.

~~~

Eli turned his head slightly, and the movement caused him to moan. His hand lifted to the place where he'd been hit, and memory returned. His fingers came away sticky. Tentatively he sat up. His eyes narrowed as he took in the ditch. The boy sitting across from him hugged his knees, and his smile brought an instance response from Eli.

"Hi," Eli said simply.

"Hello," the boy replied. Eli recognized him as the boy Phillip had introduced him to. How had he ended up in this ditch with him? The putrid smell of stagnant water and something dead stole his breath. Eli attempted to stand, but he wobbled.

"Careful, saab, you have a bad cut on your head."

"You're Ashok, aren't you?" Eli asked.

The boy's eyes widened. "Yes. You remember me?"

"From the clinic. I met you with Dr. Phillip."

Ashok squinted in the gloomy light. He leaned forward and touched Eli's arm.

Eli closed his eyes briefly. He remembered meeting the two men in the street and the hit on the head. He caught hold of Ashok's and pulled the young boy towards him.

"How did I get here?"

"I dragged you, saab. The bad men were going to come back and kill you. I heard them."

"You—dragged me?" Eli looked at the skinny lad and tried to imagine how he would have been able to move his body weight.

Ashok grinned and nodded. "Yes, saab. Jesus gave me the strength of an elephant to move you."

"I see." Eli's mouth curved in a smile. "Thank you, Ashok. You saved my life."

"The two men came back for you, saab. I prayed they wouldn't come down here, and they didn't. A group of people came into the street when they returned, and maybe they were making so much noise that the men left."

He could have been dead if it hadn't been for this boy. Phillip had suggested he find Ashok and that together, they look for their sisters. Eli had huffed at the idea and hadn't wanted the boy slowing him down, yet here Ashok was, saving his life. Eli hung his head in shame.

"Looks like we have something in common, Ashok. My name is Eli and I'm looking for my sister too. Her name is Charlie. What's your sister's name?"

"Shanti. Did they take your sister from you, like they took Shanti?"

"Yes, lad. Let's get out of here and go back to Dr. Phillip's to get cleaned up?"

Chapter 21

The pain woke her. Charlotte opened her eyes and groaned. It felt like a hammer had smashed every inch of her body. Turning her head, she saw Padma sitting quietly, staring at her hands.

"Padma?" Charlotte whispered.

Standing Padma used a damp cloth to sponge Charlotte's forehead. The grim look on her face gave nothing away.

"Did it work, Padma? Have I more time to heal before—"

Padma's eyes rose to hers and watered. "No. You have until tonight. The boss said the client wouldn't care if you were messed up."

Charlotte sucked in a deep breath. An anguished sob escaped her mouth. Her hand fluttered to her face. She turned away from Padma, and tears streamed down her cheeks. The pain in her body was nothing compared to the torment in her soul.

Padma touched her arm.

Charlotte turned back to her, and their eyes locked. "Please help me up." Charlotte moved slowly and sucked in her bottom lip. Her face felt on fire, and she had to brace her hands on the side of the bed for support. With Padma's help she stood and wobbled on her feet. Padma's arm circled her shoulders and helped her gain balance.

"Thank you." Lifting her head, Charlotte took a small step away from the bed. She drew a steadying breath.

"It was worth a try." Charlotte gave Padma a sad smile and looked down at the blood on her top. "I need to—can I bath, Padma?"

~~~

Charlotte paced the room, her mind in turmoil. She had to hang on to what she believed; she couldn't let circumstance shake the foundation of her faith. "The Lord is my shepherd, I shall not be in want. He makes me lie down in green pastures, he leads me beside quiet waters, he restores my soul. He guides me in paths of righteousness for his name's sake. Even though I walk through the valley of the shadow of death, I will fear no evil, for you are with me, your rod and your staff, they comfort me." Her shoulders shook and her fingers twisted together.

"Lord, no matter what they do to my body, I will love you. I don't understand this, but I know you haven't deserted me." The noise at the door startled Charlotte. She spun around and backed further into the room.

Scarface beckoned her forward. Charlotte's eyes caught his, and she refused to look away, though a stranger stood beside him.

"Girl, this is an important client of ours." Scarface's voice was harsh. "You are to please him."

Charlotte felt the stranger's eyes bore into her. He was of medium height and his chin looked like it was made of steel. He wasn't big, but what there was of him was solid, unyielding. His eyes frightened Charlotte the most. They bulged out of their sockets, fixating on her as if she were prey. She crossed her arms protectively in front of her, lifted her head, and turned her back on them.

The stranger's laughter crawled along her skin, and she heard the door creak. She spun around to see Saul leave the room. The man took off his coat, and Charlotte's chin trembled. He wasn't a big man, but his presence seemed to take over the room.

"My name is Charlotte, please don't do this," she beseeched him. He stared back at her, his eyes moving slowly down her body. Charlotte shuddered at his look and cleared her throat. "I'm from Australia. I was on holiday when these monsters kidnapped me. Please, my family will pay you if you help me escape this place."

"Why do you think you are here, Charlotte?" he sneered as he moved towards her.

"Touch me and you'll be sorry. I'm a daughter of the Most High God, and you will not go unpunished for violating me." Charlotte moved across the room and kept the bed between them.

"I don't see your god here now, Charrllete! Just you and me. Come here now, or you will be the one who is sorry."

Charlotte's eyes became wild, and she lunged away as he circled the bed. Her heart pounded and she gasped as he yanked at her sari, trying to choke her with it. Her hand went to her throat and she pulled the material free. She spun to face him, and his hand caught the side of her face.

Something in Charlotte snapped, she screamed and tore at him. Her fingers raked down his face and she kicked at his shins, her legs and arms flying wildly. He pinned her down, his face contorted with anger. She shivered as she looked up into his gray eyes, and a sense of helplessness filled her. She would fight him, even if he killed her. Death would be better than complying to such a man.

The stranger let her go and stood up. He dusted down his pants with bony fingers and sat on the bed to take off his shoes. Charlotte felt toyed with, like a mouse in a cage. She scrambled up off the floor and backed away from him, racing to the door. She frantically tried the handle, hoping against hope that Scarface hadn't locked it. But he had. As she turned back towards the stranger, her heart pounded violently.

"The way I see it," he said, "you either do as I tell you, or I beat you to within an inch of your life and take you anyway."

Tears spilled freely down her face. "Have you a daughter, sir? Or a sister, a mother. Would you do such a thing to them? You are an animal to be in such a place, and you will destroy your own soul."

The light in the room flickered, and the man laughed. "I have no soul, I belong to the devil himself."

Chapter 22

Eli spread his hands out on the shower wall and allowed the water to rain down over his face. Charlie had been missing twenty-one days, and the only lead he had was a small boy who believed God would help them. Ashok's faith was built on a tattered card he carried in his pocket, yet he had an unshakable belief that they would find their sisters. Even if they did find them, what state would they be in? Eli's head dropped down between his outstretched arms. Would Charlie's eyes still be sparkling with enthusiasm? Would she be able to put what had happened behind her and return to normal life? Would any of them survive this? Shaking his head, he turned off the shower and grabbed a towel. After he dried off, he dressed and then stood looking at his reflection in the mirror.

Gone was the guy hungry for adventure and fun. In his place he saw a haggard man with dark smudges under his eyes. Ashok, who lived on the street, appeared healthier than he did. A smile tugged at his lips as he recalled the look on Ashok's face when Phillip put a burger and chips on his plate. Maybe taking the boy with him was a good idea. Together they could encourage each other to not to give up.

As he heard a text message come through on his mobile phone, he lifted his head. Eli's mouth tightened. It would be his mother; he hadn't contacted her for a couple of days, and she would be worried. Sighing, he glanced at the message and hit the redial button.

"Eli, are you all right?" The concern in her voice touched a spot in his heart, and his hand unconsciously went to the bump on his head.

"How's Dad?" he asked to avoid answering her question.

"He's coming along. Some of his friends from church have been calling in every couple of days, and he's starting to pick up. He's more like himself. This morning he wanted to know where you were. I told him you were in India looking for Charlotte. He cried, Eli. Bill told me to tell you to be careful, that he didn't want to lose his son as well as his daughter."

"Dad cried?" A lump rose in Eli's throat, and he swallowed. When had he ever seen his father cry? He had always been a tower of strength to them all.

"Yes, he did. It's a good thing, though. I feel like he's coming back to me. Does that make sense?"

"Sure, Mum," he said.

"Have you—I mean, is there any news on Charlotte?"

"No one's seen her. It's like she wasn't even here. I have a lead on some men who could be connected to the abduction of young girls." Eli told her about Ashok, leaving out the incident where he'd been attacked.

"Ashok and I are leaving for Vashi in the morning. I'm going to ask around to see if there's anywhere I can go to . . . meet with women." Eli's face heated as he told his mother this, and a gurgle of laughter split from his lips. "Hey, Mum. Bet you never thought you would be encouraging your son to visit women of the night."

"It's not funny, Eli. Not funny at all. You be careful, don't take any unnecessary risks."

"I'll do what I have to. Pray for me. Prayer cover is the best thing you can do right now, and pray for Ashok too."

~~~

Shanti feared sleep more each night. The dream revisited her time and time again, and her body ached with dread. It was late, almost morning. She'd been with the boss for hours, and now she had time to herself. She turned on her side and tried to keep her eyes open. The boss had screamed at her tonight, and she knew he was tiring of her. Part of her was pleased, but what would it mean? She scanned the room of sleeping girls, and tears threatened to spill. The girls laughed and made crude jokes about sex and the men they'd met. They had accepted this as their lot.

What was it the boss had said when he was cutting her arm tonight. "Prince of Darkness, take this blood as a sacrifice to you." Who was the Prince of Darkness? Why did he need her blood? The burning in her eyes caused her to blink, and slowly her lids shut, flickering as the nightmare invaded her mind.

Her feet felt heavy, like she had rocks in her shoes. She started to bend down to remove the stones, when she realized she had no shoes on. Vines held her ankles, and the dense jungle closed in around her. Shanti kicked and screamed until she loosed the jungle rope from her feet. She needed to get her bearings. If she could get to the river, she'd be safe; Ashok was on the other side of the river, waiting for her. Shanti's eyes snapped shut for a moment. She mumbled something and then started to move forward. Tears blurred her vision and she angrily swiped them away. The trees seemed to reach for her, scratching her skin and causing her to stumble. Her arms swung out, pushing at an invisible adversary. She scrambled to her feet and spun on her heels, heading in the other direction. She could hear the rustle of something following her, and her eyes darted frantically around. She lunged over a fallen log, breathing hard. Her eyes widened in fear; the *chaya* moved towards her, shapeless, powerful, alive. As it spread up her arm, the hair on her body rose. Her flailing arms hit out in protest, and sweat covered her body.

Shanti sat up, panting. The dream had seemed so real. Her skin glistened with sweat and her heart pounded. She glanced across the room and saw Padma watching her as if she knew. Their eyes locked and Padma frowned. Her lips tightened and she turned and left the room. Shanti decided that sleep wasn't something she wanted tonight. She got up and went to the bathroom. As she splashed water over her face, her hands became frantic. She scrubbed at her skin, trying to remove the invisible dirt that crawled over her. It felt like a thousand maggots from the rubbish dump were working their way up her body and into her hair. She felt caked in their filth and had to clean her body, even if it meant tearing off her skin.

~~~

Eli followed Ashok silently. The boy's ankle still caused him to limp slightly, and Eli thought of how God orchestrated divine appointments. He would never have meet Ashok if he hadn't come to Phillip's clinic. But then if Ashok hadn't sprained his ankle, Shanti might still be with him. Shaking his head at the thoughts that rambled through his mind, he caught up with Ashok, who had stopped.

They both looked across the road at the house where two men leaned against the door. Ashok squatted down and looked up at Eli with searching eyes.

"Are you sure you want to do this, Eli?" he whispered.

"What option do I have?" Eli shrugged and patted the boy's shoulder. He would pay to get into the place and take it from there. He pulled out a small bottle of whiskey and tipped some in his hands and then rubbed it on his neck and sprinkled some on his shirt. Then he ruffed up his hair with his hand and gave Ashok a smile. "What do you think, do I look like a bum?"

Ashok's eyes widened, and his lips disappeared into his mouth. "What should I do, Eli, if you don't come back?" His voice wobbled.

"Lad, I want you to go sit over there and pray for me. I will be back." Eli turned and walked across the street, stumbling once and laughing out loud. The two men straightened off the wall and turned towards him.

"Hello, hello," he slurred.

The hand on his shoulder stopped him from entering the house. Eli spun around, and his eyes met the heavily built man beside him. Eli lifted his hand and grinned.

"Hey, yah." He leaned in, his hand spread open on the man's chest. "Mister, you got any European girls? Pretty blondes? Hmm, yes sir—make me feel like I'm at home."

The man shoved him back and grinned. "We have whatever you want, boy. Pay up and go have a look."

Eli pulled out his wallet and dropped it to the ground. He fumbled for it and then hiccupped and stumbled as he scrunched up some notes and placed them in the man's hand. "That enough?"

"Sure, knock yourself out." The man stepped back and indicated with his arm for Eli to proceed.

If Charlotte and Shanti were here, how would he get them out? Ashok had given him a description of Shanti, but she could be any small child to Eli. He'd have to look for a scar on the child's knee.

He moved into the house. Dingy lighting cast a pallid glow over the front room. It had rails suspended from the walls; sheets hung from them, partitioning sections off like small rooms. Eli frowned. How degrading. These poor women had nothing but a sheet between them as they were used by paying creeps who violated their bodies. Anger simmered in his chest, and his fists clenched.

A woman came up to him. Her eyes seemed dead, void of all color. She touched his arm and beckoned him towards a room. He followed and remembered that he was meant to be intoxicated. He felt his stomach churn as he heard the murmur of other men already active in screened-off areas. Everything in him wanted to run from this place. Men had brought this upon these poor women, with their sexual lust and the money it made.

"What you waiting for, man? Go pick, hurry up, will you?"

"I want a English girl, blonde. You got any?"

"What matter the hair? Girl body all the same. Go pick one," she hissed.

"No, I want my money back, blonde or not at all!" He pretended to sway, and his voice got louder.

"Quiet. You disturb our guests. We have English girl. Come this way."

Eli's chest tightened, and he grimaced. "Has to be pretty. I like young ones too. Maybe I can have two?"

"In there, go look." She shoved him.

Lifting back the curtain, Eli jaw tightened. The girl lay on a mattress on the floor, and her dirty hair fell over her face. He squatted beside her and fingered her hair, moving it off her face. Tears welled up in his eyes, and he sucked in a breath. The girl stared back at him, her eyes dazed, obviously drugged.

Standing, he spun around and charged after the woman.

"No, no. Not her, someone else. Another girl, I don't like her." He grabbed the woman and twisted her around to face him. "I want someone else. I paid good money, come on, you got another pretty white girl for me?"

"It's her or you get the hell out of here," she sneered.

"What about a child, then, say ten years old? I like young girls, you help me out and I may have a little extra for you." Eli chuckled and pulled her up close. As he waited for her response, he swallowed, the bile rising up in his throat at the words he'd spoken. He wanted to be anywhere but here.

"Let go of me. We don't have children here. You get out of here." Her voice was menacing and rising.

"Calm down, will you. I just thought I'd ask. No other European girls or children? Okay, okay, I'll take that one. Take it easy, crazy woman."

Returning to the cubicle Eli pushed back the curtain and moved in with the drugged woman. He sat beside her, his eyes gaping at the state she was in. Someone's daughter. He pushed back the ache in his chest and helped her sit up. She tried to smile at him, but her head flopped back.

"It's okay, I won't hurt you," he whispered.

Taking out the photo of Charlotte, he showed it to her. "Have you seen this woman? Are there any other white women here?"

She shrugged and reached for his clothing. "I make you feel good, mister, please, they don't like it if the customers aren't satisfied."

Eli pulled her face close to his. "Have you seen her? Please look— she's my sister."

Tears welled in the woman's eyes. "I have a sister, two years younger than me. Used to look out for her—but now—" Her eyes dropped to the photo.

"No, I haven't seen her. I've been here for months." She rubbed her hand over the needle marks in her arm and sighed.

"What's your name?" Eli asked. His heart burned at the thought of leaving her here. But if he tried to take her with him, he could blow his cover. News would spread quickly about what he was doing, and he'd never have the chance to find Charlie. Hardening his heart, he turned away from her.

"You don't want to know my name, mister, call me whore. You want to do it now?" her voice held no emotion and mocked him. She opened her cape, exposing her chest, and Eli adverted his eyes. He pulled some money from his wallet and pushed it into her hand.

"I'm sorry. This might help you get out of here." He briefly cupped her face in his hand. "I'll come back if I can."

Eli stood and stumbled through the hall. He deliberately fell into the cubicles as though in a drunken stupor. Men yelled and shoved him away. Eli's mouth lifted slightly as he walked towards the door, and he pulled out his shirt and made a pretense of tucking it back in. The men outside didn't even acknowledge his departure. He slouched across the road, his head and shoulders bent and his heart heavy.

Ashok scrambled to his feet and raced after him. "Eli, stop, please,"

Ashok begged.

Stopping, Eli stared at the ground. His heart pounded and guilt tore at his soul. He'd left her there, some poor girl who didn't care enough to tell him her name. He looked around at Ashok. His brows drew together and his eyes smarted with unshed tears.

Ashok touched his arm. "Eli—are you all right?"

At the sound of his name on the boy's lips, shock rippled through his body. He yanked the boy into an embrace and held on tight.

His friends little arms spread around him, and one of his hands patted Eli's back in comfort.

Eli sucked in a breath and wiped his face. "I'm sorry, Ashok. I don't know what came over me. Thank you."

"Did you find them? Are they in there?"

Eli shook his head. No, their sisters weren't there, but many others were.

Chapter 23

There was something about Charlotte that confused Padma. Charlotte handled the beatings from Scarface with such dignity. When Charlotte's plan to put off the inevitable hadn't worked, Padma had been amazed at how she had verbally prayed for strength from her God.

She stood outside Charlotte's cell and steeled herself for what she would see. The man Charlotte had been with was known to be particularly brutal.

Padma reached out to open Charlotte's door, when she heard a shuffle behind her. Her hand dropped away and she angled her head to see Scarface standing in the shadows watching her. She turned and glared at him. What did he want? To gloat once again at the control he had over them?

He stepped out of the shadow and moved towards her, his hand reached behind her and pushed open the door.

She turned, and together they looked in the room. Her jaw locked at the sight of Charlotte lying prostrate on the floor, naked. Her long hair sprawled down her back, and her body was completely still. She looked—lifeless. There was an eerie stillness in the room, like the calm after a storm.

Scarface shoved her aside and hunched down beside Charlotte's body.

"Is she dead?" Padma whispered.

His fingers cupped Charlotte's throat, and he looked up and shook his head. Their eyes met and something flashed over his face; for a moment Padma thought it was concern. He turned Charlotte over and she moaned. There was a gash on her forehead, and her left eye was swollen beyond recognition.

"Clean her up, she has two days," he snarled and stormed out of the room.

Padma squatted beside Charlotte. She moved to brush the hair out of Charlotte's face, like a child's, but some of the strands had become sticky with blood and held fast to her skin like glue.

Biting her lower lip in disgust, Padma scowled. How long had she been doing this, cleaning up the damage done to beautiful young women by—animals? Why was this girl so different? What was it about Charlotte that pulled at her heart? A heart hardened to the things that went on here.

Moving to the basin, she prepared water. She glanced at the bed and saw the bloodstains on the bedding, telling their own story.

Closing her eyes, Padma remembered what it had been like the first time. Being unable to stop the abuse and knowing nobody would come for her. She'd been older than Charlotte, twenty-six. She'd been no stranger to sex, but when she'd wanted it, not when others made her submit to their strength and violence.

She'd clean Charlotte's wounds and get out of here before she woke up. The last thing she wanted was for the girl to wake up and want to talk. She gently went about cleaning the injuries over Charlotte's body. Next she tidied up the room, changed the sheets, and dressed Charlotte in a clean sari.

Charlotte's eyes flickered briefly, and her mouth moved as she tried to speak.

At the sound of Charlotte's voice, Padma froze. She looked at the door with longing and took a tentative step towards it.

"Why?" Charlotte asked, looking directly at Padma.

Padma's breath caught in her throat. Her eyes smarted and she shrugged.

Charlotte turned on her side, pulled her knees up, and hugged them with her arms. She gently rocked herself, tears streaming down her face. The sound of Charlotte humming startled Padma. She needed to get out of the room, away from the agony she saw on Charlotte's face, and distance herself from the question she had no answer to.

"Valley of shadows," Charlotte whispered.

"Shadows," Padma stated, her eyes narrowing. "The Hindi word for shadow is *chaya*, Charlotte. Yes, you're right—we are hidden from the world in the chaya!"

~~~

How long she lay on the filthy floor, rocking, Charlotte didn't know. The light in the room faded and her tears stilled. She screwed up her eyes, only to cry out in pain as her swollen eye protested the movement. Her index finger gently touched the puffy skin of her cheek, and she shuddered. The man had enjoyed hitting her.

She wanted to give up and die. All her life she'd dreamed that one day she'd marry and have a family. Now she was tainted, soiled, ruined. She'd thought Jesus would somehow rescue her. That the door would burst open, and it would all be a terrible mistake.

Voices ridiculed her, taunted her mind. What was the point of carrying on, it was useless.

Charlotte pulled at her clothes and screamed into the empty room. "You abandoned me," she wailed.

I never left you.

"How can you say that? Did you see what he did to me?"

She bit her lip, and the taste of blood silenced her accusations. How could she blame God for what happened? He wasn't the one who had abducted and abused her. Jesus had suffered. He knew the humiliation

137

of abuse, to the point of death.

Sighing, she slowly sat up. They may be able to damage her body, but they would not destroy her spirit. Hoisting herself up off the floor, Charlotte moved across the room to the door. She twisted the door handle and found it unlocked. Lifting her head, she walked out of the room and headed for the bathroom.

Surprise quickened her heartbeat as a door on the right of the hall opened. She stopped and looked up into Saul's eyes.

"Good evening, Saul." Charlotte nodded and continued to the bathroom.

Once inside, she leaned heavily against the door and sucked in a breath. *Lord Jesus, help me love my enemies. Open Saul's heart to your voice; help me to love him as you have loved me.*

She shuddered. She couldn't allow hate to enter her mind in this place of chaya, she thought. Evil lurked in the corners and festered in the deprived minds of the men who paid for the destruction of their souls. Charlotte knew she'd heard the word chaya before but couldn't remember in what context. As fast as she could, she relieved herself and slipped back into the hall.

Saul leaned against the wall, waiting for her, and Charlotte felt a moment of panic before she moved towards him.

Lifting her chin, she smiled and acted out the courage she longed to have. "Can you please get something for me? There is a game I play with stones. I throw them up in the air and catch them on the back of my hand. I need five small, smooth stones all the same size."

"You think I care about what you want? Your place is to serve, not be served," he mocked as he pushed off the wall. "And Charlotte, call me Saul one more time, and I promise you stones will be the last thing on your mind."

He grabbed her chin and pushed her to her knees.

Charlotte kept her eyes downcast and stayed quiet.

"It would do you good to remember your place, girl." He turned and strode off down the hall, leaving Charlotte on her hands and knees.

She sat back on her ankles and choked back her raw emotions.

Slowly a discomfort in her belly reminded her she needed food; there must be a kitchen somewhere in the house. She could hear women's voices and followed them to a doorway. Squaring her shoulders, she opened the door and entered the room. Many pairs of eyes turned in her direction, and it took all of Charlotte's willpower not to lift her hand to hide her eye.

"Hello," she said in a nervous smile.

The woman closest to her stood up and beckoned her into the room. Charlotte realized that this must be a sort of common room for the women. There were mats on the floor, and it looked like some of them must sleep here.

"My name is Charlotte." She spoke to the room of women, hopeful that someone would welcome her. Her gaze swept across the many faces staring at her.

No one spoke.

Lifting her shoulders slightly she shrugged and moved slowly to the centre of the room, where a table housed a large pot of steaming rice and bowls.

Were they all prisoners here?

~~~

As he packed up the equipment, Phillip prayed. His shoulders sagged, as if weighted down by a load of heavy rocks.

Lord, where is she? It's been a month and still no news. His mind ran over the things that happened to girls who were forced into the sex trade. How would she endure?

Lord, she's your daughter, you know where she is—help Eli find her. He slammed the bag shut and dropped the case to the floor. The waiting was killing him. Every avenue he'd tried to find her had come up blank. No one had heard anything. He needed to try something else, but what? He raked his hand through his hair and remembered Charlie telling him he needed a haircut. Had she really reached out and touched his hair at the time, or was it a wistful memory? Why was his heart so burdened for her? He had known her such a brief time; many of the children he treated, he knew longer—yet Charlotte's face haunted him.

Lord, I want to drop everything and scour the streets for her. Leave no stone unturned. Lord, I'm drawn to her, as no other woman I've ever met. She's in my dreams. My heart shudders in pain for what she's going through. Encourage her to hang on, Lord Jesus—be her strength.

Phillip wiped at the moisture on his cheeks, and he squared his shoulders and picked up the case. He moved outside, locked the building, and moved to his van. He felt sure he could smell Charlotte's perfume in the van, and he sniffed deeply.

As he drove past a group of people loitering on the street, an idea formed in his mind. It could just work; it might lead him to her. The sides of his mouth lifted in a slight smile, and his hands loosened on the steering wheel. Doing nothing led to hopelessness, defeat.

Making plans led to action, purpose, and direction.

Chapter 24

Macy laced her fingers behind her head and rested her elbows on her knees. The agony of loss was too much. She sat on Charlotte's bed, longing to feel close to her daughter. Today she wanted to crawl into a ball and give up. She wanted to hold Charlotte one more time, to reassure her that Mummy loved her and that everything would be all right. Was that too much to ask?

Her friends had stopped asking about Charlotte and Eli, presuming it was too difficult to talk about. Bill was back at work and slowly improving. He prayed with her each night for the return of their children, but it seemed like he had distanced himself from the pain of it. How could he carry on as if things were all right? Nothing was all right; she would never be all right again. Her only daughter was lost, she could even be dead, in some godforsaken place. Buried in an unnamed grave where no one could mourn her loss.

Her throat locked in pain, and she pulled at her hair. A silent scream raked her body. Her daughter was dead. Hope shriveled up inside her, and she collapsed on the bed, staring blankly into space as if she would find refuge in the blankness of nothing. It would have been better had Charlotte never been born than to feel this pain now. The thought stabbed at Macy and she sat up. How could she think such a thing?

Forgive me, Lord Jesus. Thank you for my precious daughter. Give me strength to believe that we will find her.

The tears came softly now, slowly making a path down her cheeks.

Macy pictured Charlotte's precious face, excitement causing her eyes to sparkle as she talked about India. Charlotte had believed India was her future, that God would show her what he wanted her to do there. Little did any of them know that India would become Charlotte's prison.

She'd had such hopes for Charlotte. She would marry a nice Christian man, have children—her grandchildren—and live close to her so that she could visit her often. They would be best friends and share everything. Now Macy's only desire was that Charlotte might survive the nightmare she was living through.

Lord Jesus, Charlotte's yours. I'm desperate for her return, her safety. Lord, I'm sorry if as a mother I've held onto Charlotte, as if she belonged to me. But please, I beg you, hear a mother's cry. Release my little girl from the dungeon that holds her. Help me not lose hope, pick me up, Lord. I need your arms around me—I can't make it on my own.

Her chin dropped to her chest and she breathed in deeply. She closed her eyes and summoned up the faith to hold onto Jesus one more time.

"Macy, phone, it's Pamela Benton." Bill called up the stairs.

Pulling a tissue out of her pocket she wiped her face and moved down the stairs. She gave Bill a small smile and took the phone out of his hand.

Macy gripped the phone tighter. Charlie admired and loved Pamela. She remembered Charlie saying that Pamela inspired her never to stop serving God. Even though Pamela was getting on in age, the young people in youth group still loved the gentle, godly woman.

"Hello, Pamela. How are you?"

"Taking one day at a time these days, Macy. The reason I've called is to see if you would be interested in speaking at youth group. Since

Charlotte went missing, the young people seem to have lost hope. I thought if you could come and share how you and your family are trusting God, and leaning on him at this difficult time—then maybe it will help the young people not to give up on their faith."

How could Pamela ask such a thing? There was no way she could stand in front of a group of young people and talk about Charlotte without breaking down.

"I don't know, Pamela."

"Don't give me your answer now, Macy, pray about it. I believe we will get Charlotte back, dear. God is faithful, don't lose hope."

"I'm trying not to. I'll let you know my decision in a few days, is that okay?"

"Yes, of course. I'll look forward to your call."

Macy heard Bill shuffle behind her and turned to look at him. The weekends were so quiet without Eli or Charlotte here.

Bill's eyes sought hers, and she blinked several times to stop the tears from escaping her lids. How could she explain to him that she was terrified of losing him as well?

He moved towards her and pulled her into his arms. His head rested on her cheek and she felt him kiss her face. Her arms tightened around his waist and she burrowed her head into his shoulder.

"Macy, sweetheart. You have enough to worry about without taking on more. I think you should say no to Pamela."

Pushing away, Macy frowned. Why couldn't he just hold her and not give his opinion? "It's not about us, Bill. Maybe I should do it. Maybe God wants me to."

~~~

Eli was unprepared for how he felt as he watched Ashok trot across the road towards the woman buying bread. They'd heard she came to the market every day and bought far too much bread for an ordinary family. Who was she feeding, how many? Ashok planned to bump into her and offer to carry her shopping home as an apology. The boy tilted his head and looked back at him. Eli nodded and smiled. The boy was full of courage.

The boy's simple faith challenged him. Had his faith ever been as strong as Ashok's? How can you have faith without trials? If faith isn't tested, then is it really faith?

He shrugged, settled back against the wall, and pulled his hat farther down over his eyes. He watched the scene play out before him. Ashok knocked into the woman, sending her shopping flying. The boy threw his hands in the air and looked around him in confusion.

"Many apologies, *memsaab*. Please, I will help you." He scrambled on his hands and knees, picking up the scattered items.

Eli sat up straighter to see if she would engage in conversation with Ashok.

"Here, give that to me," she scowled.

"I am the most clumsy of boys. It would be my delight to help you home with your goods, memsaab," Ashok nodded and bowed before her again and again.

"Stop that, boy. Yes, you can help me." She shoved a bag into his arms and turned away.

Ashok stood still, with his mouth open wide.

Eli couldn't help but grin at the look on his face. It had worked.

"Are you coming?" the woman asked.

"Yes, yes, certainly, memsaab." Ashok sped after her without even a glance in his direction.

Eli gave Ashok and the woman a few moments' head start and then followed. He scanned the street for any signs of danger, any shadows lurking that could leap out and trap them. They had visited four brothels and still no sign of either Charlotte or Shanti. It was getting harder to walk inside the dens of inequity and see the women's empty faces. Each time it was harder to walk away and leave the girls there.

The world as he knew it was fading further and further away. He could no longer pretend that the world was a good, safe place, when he saw injustice everywhere he looked.

His eyes burned as he took in Ashok's slight limp. A child without parents to love and look after him. Where was the justice in that? Every child deserved love and security.

Would he be able to walk away from Ashok when all this was finished? His mouth tightened and he dropped his head. He sauntered to the other side of the road as he noticed the woman stop and look back at him. Eli kept walking watching them from his peripheral vision.

The woman continued walking and indicated for Ashok to hurry after her. Eli turned the corner and waited, his heart rate increasing as he counted to fifty. Slowly, he peered around the corner and saw them turn into a street to the right. He waited until they were out of sight, then he rushed after them, stopping only when he got to the corner of the ally.

The dark street seemed overly quiet, and the hair on the back of his neck rose. He squinted and crept behind them, careful not to make a sound. Ashok coughed as a signal that they were stopping.

Eli ducked behind a pile of old furniture abandoned on the side of the street. He watched as the woman took out a key and opened a red door, beckoning Ashok in after her. Eli hadn't planned on the boy entering the house. He glanced down the street to see if anybody had seen him hide. His jaw tightened as he noticed a man standing at the corner, watching him.

The man took a step towards him, and Eli was momentarily unsure what to do. Penetrating dark eyes locked on his, and something stopped Eli from moving. The man stopped inches from Eli and frowned. He grabbed Eli's elbow.

Eli pushed the man's hand away. He stepped into the street and walked beside him towards the same red door that Ashok had entered. Eli thought of how the Israelites had painted blood on their doors to stop the spirit of death visiting their homes—would this door signify hope or destruction? His fingers fisted in anger. He should be home, working, falling in love, unaffected by what he now knew happened to the innocent.

The man pulled out a key and pushed the door open, then glanced towards Eli before he stepped ahead of him into the house.

There was no one forcing Eli to enter the house, yet he felt compelled to follow the stranger. He looked quickly behind him to the silent street, then stepped through the red door.

Chapter 25

The taste of blood on her tongue made Shanti touch her lip with her finger. She hugged her knees and tried to hide within herself. The chatter of the girls was not helping her thumping head. Closing her eyes tight, she tried to think of something good.

Jesus knows your name, Shanti. She wished the words Ashok had told her were true.

If you know my name, Jesus, why haven't you sent someone to rescue me? Do you hate me? Am I a bad girl?

The boss said she was a bad, bad girl. She shuddered as she thought of the look in his eye as he said it. She rubbed up and down her arms as if trying to warm herself or rub off some growing disease.

It was the silence in the room that caused Shanti to open her eyes. The white lady stood by the door. Shanti crossed her legs and gently licked her swollen lip. Someone new always caused a stir, and she'd heard the talk of a white lady walking the halls. Shanti didn't care who she was; what did it matter? She watched dully as the woman moved towards the food table. She told the girls her name was Charlotte. Shanti thought the name sounded pretty. The woman's face was beaten up, and Shanti wondered if she'd spent time with the boss.

All eyes watched as Charlotte took a bowl of rice and turned around for somewhere to sit. No one spoke or made room for her. Shanti felt an urge to call her over but looked down and twisted her hands together.

"You think you can be top girl here?" Gargi barked in broken English. "You are nothing but a whore like the rest of us." She scowled and pushed Charlotte, knocking her bowl of rice from her hand.

Shanti cringed as Gargi spoke. Gargi was nasty. She got whatever she wanted and didn't care who she hurt to get it. Shanti's eyes swung back to Charlotte to see what she would do.

Charlotte stood completely still, looking from the spilled rice to the intimidating woman in front of her. It seemed that everyone in the room held her breath in anticipation of a fight.

"I have no wish to be top girl. My definition of a whore is a woman who sells her body for money. Who here has received money for being assaulted time and time again?" Charlotte asked gently.

"You mock me, girl?" Gargi slapped Charlotte's face, and Shanti slipped further back on her mat.

Charlotte's hand cupped her reddening cheek, and she straightened her shoulders. She turned her back on Gargi and picked up another bowl and began spooning rice into it.

Gargi moved towards her with her hands lifted.

"Stop!" Padma ordered in a steely tone.

Gargi spun around and glared at Padma.

Shanti's lips twitched slightly; Gargi hated being told what to do. If she didn't obey, Padma could increase her hours in service. They all knew the power Padma had with Scarface. Gargi stormed across the room and out the door.

The room exploded with whispers, and Padma told someone to clean the rice off the floor. Shanti watched as Padma moved to Charlotte and laid a hand on her arm, indicating for Charlotte to follow her. As Shanti looked up, Charlotte winked at her with her good eye.

Shanti's mouth gaped in surprise. A glimmer of a smile lifted her lips, and a giggle escaped her mouth.

At the sound of her own laughter, a sound not heard since she'd entered the house, tears filled Shanti's eyes.

~~~

The child on the mat had shocked Charlotte. How old was she? What was she doing in a place like this? As soon as she was in Padma's private room, she sat down on her bed without asking and looked down at the bowl of rice in her hands.

"Make yourself at home, won't you," Padma said sarcastically.

"Padma, you and I are going to be friends, so get off your high horse. Who is that child? She can't be more than six years old." Charlotte's eyes bore into Padma's for answers.

"I have no friends here." Bitterness filled Padma's voice. "The sooner you learn you're on your own, the better."

"The child? Tell me."

"Her name is Shanti. I'm not sure of her age."

"Surely she's not—she doesn't—she isn't put with men, is she?"

"What does it matter to you? You will soon stop caring about what happens to other people. But don't annoy Gargi, she's not a person you want for an enemy."

"Thank you, Padma, for the warning, but I think it's a little too late. I will pray for her."

She looked down at the rice, knowing she needed to refuel her body. Her stomach churned with nerves and she felt nauseated. She hadn't handled Gargi well. She'd wanted to hit her back.

Lord, forgive me. Jesus, help me reach out to Gargi and please protect me from her anger.

She looked up and the stern expression on Padma's face made her smile. The woman held herself with such iron control that Charlotte couldn't help but want to hug her.

As she crossed her leg, pain shot down her thigh. She moved carefully to another position. "How often will I be forced to be with that animal, Padma?"

"As often as he wants you. It's up to the boss. Once he tires of you, you will go to other men. This is your life now, you must adjust or you will not survive."

"I will never accept that it's all right to be treated like a piece of meat. I may be a prisoner here, and they may have control over my body, but my mind is free and my spirit will soar!"

"We will see. Eat," Padma commanded.

Charlotte spooned the rice up with her fingers and chewed slowly. The bland taste drew a frown to her forehead, and she closed her eyes as she imagined some of the rice dishes her mother had cooked.

Lord, forgive me for not being more thankful for the food you've provided. Bless the hands that cooked this rice, Jesus. Help me to survive here, give me purpose, help me to—trust you.

"The door to the room I'm in, wasn't locked. Does that mean I can now leave when I want to?"

"Yes, except when you're working. There is an outside area I will show you. The room we just came from is the main sleeping and common room for everyone. You will move there eventually."

Charlotte thought about that. The only reason she had a room to herself was because she was wanted by the rich, brutal man she was 'servicing'. She shuddered at the terrible word they all used. She would call it like it was—she was being abused, not servicing, never servicing. She hated the room, the bed. How could she sleep there knowing what was to come?

"I want to move into the common room now. I would prefer to be with the other women."

"Don't be a fool, you will have to sleep on the floor."

"The floor is better than a bed soiled in abuse."

Charlotte placed her half-eaten bowl of rice down and stood to face Padma. "Please."

Padma shrugged. "As you wish."

"Thank you." Charlotte moved, picked up Padma's hand, and

pulled her towards the bed. The shock on Padma's face was comical. Charlotte smiled and squeezed her hand before letting it go.

"Padma, if I cooperate with the man, will he stop hitting me so much?"

"You could try not fighting him, Charlotte. But from my experience, a man like him must enjoy hurting girls."

~~~

Phillip squinted as he walked towards the man he'd been told may be a contact. He'd heard men were seen entering and leaving the place throughout the night. Phillip shoved his hands in his pockets and slouched. Now that he was acting on his idea, doubts jammed his mind. He said a quick prayer for wisdom and continued to walk towards the large muscled man, who seemed taller than him by at least two inches.

"May I have a word with you, please," Phillip asked.

The man's stare was stony, and he didn't speak.

Ignoring his nerves, Phillip grinned. "I'm hoping you can help me. I've a need to earn some extra cash."

The man's eyebrows rose slightly, showing some interest in what Phillip was saying. Still he didn't speak.

"You see, I'm a doctor. I work at the Mission Clinic for free and need to support myself."

"In what way do you think I would be interested in hiring you?" the man asked.

"I don't know, sometimes people need a doctor who will keep his mouth shut, you know what I'm saying?" Phillip looked around him, as if seeing if anyone was listening, then leaned forward and whispered. "If any of the girls you work with were sick or hurt—" He made himself chuckle.

"Get out of here, I don't know what you're talking about." The man shoved him away.

"Okay, man, don't get upset. I'm just saying I'm available. You know where to find me—at the free clinic." Phillip scowled at the man and shrugged as he turned away and moved off down the street. He could feel the man's eyes boring into his back, and he stopped himself from turning to look. He straightened his shoulders. It had been a risky move, but worth the chance of finding Charlotte.

He'd told some of the boys he'd treated to get the word out, that he was interested in offering his services to the brothels in the area. His heart felt heavy. Charlotte could be well out of the area, but he had to do something. Eli had phoned him two days ago, but no word about where he was, or any sighting of Charlotte.

Lord, it's in your hands, I trust you. Be with Charlotte today. Help her to see your hand in the little things, help her not to lose faith, Father.

~~~

"Dr. Phillip, Dr. Phillip." The boy yelled, running towards him. Phillip frowned and tried to place the lad.

"Please, saab, there's been an accident by the train station. My friend is hurt, blood everywhere, you must come now." The boy pulled on Phillip's arm.

Phillip was frustrated that demands on his time kept interfering with his focus on finding Charlotte. Puffing, he followed the skinny lad up the stairs to the platform. People milled around, pushing each other to get a closer look.

"Let us through, Dr. Phillip is here," the boy demanded.

They reached the injured boy, and Phillip squatted down, taking in the swollen head of a boy of around fifteen years of age. The boy's eyes were closed and Phillip automatically lifted the lad's arm to feel for a pulse. He closed his eyes and laid his head on the boy's chest.

Nothing. Slowly he began to pump the chest, counting as he did it. He didn't know how long the lad had been lying here, and maybe it was too late, but he had to try.

After five minutes he stopped. The boy was dead. Phillip clenched his hands in anger. Another unnamed boy dies on the streets of Mumbai. Who would mourn his death?

Phillip scanned the crowd of spectators for the boy who had pulled him along. He was nowhere to be seen. Phillip pushed a hand through his hair and stood up. He turned around expecting to see the lad, to be able to offer some words of comfort, but he'd gone.

Wearily Phillip moved away. Someone would come and move the body. He wondered what the boy's name had been and what was the purpose of his life. Who would have given him such a serious head wound? As he moved away from the crowd, his eyes welled up. Such a waste. All he wanted to do was get home and have a shower to wash away the filth of the street and the premature death of a young man. His head was starting to pound and his steps quickened.

Two men blocked his path. The one on the left nodded solemnly. The other turned and beckoned for him to follow.

His first instinct was to run in the opposite direction. These men looked like they had stepped out of the underworld. No one knew where he was, and he could easily disappear into the night without a trace. His chin jutted out and he squared his shoulders. Was he crazy? But what choice did he have? His feet took him in the direction of the man in front of him. He knew the other man followed behind him, and he felt sandwiched between them. Where were they taking him? They turned a corner and Phillip scanned the street for a familiar face. His heart pounded in his chest and he tried to control his breathing. A car pulled up in front of them, and the man he'd followed opened the door and glared at him.

Phillip didn't need to be told to get in. He shuffled along the seat to the other side and waited. He wouldn't be the one to break the silence; he'd wait and see what played out. He squeezed his right hand as a reminder that he wasn't alone; Jesus was a close as his right hand. A heartbeat away.

Chapter 26

The room was dimly lit, and Eli's eyes took a moment to adjust to the change of light. He scanned the faces of at least twenty people, crammed into the small space. No one spoke, and they all watched him as he followed the man to the back of the house.

Eli heard the muffled sound of the whispers coming from the people they'd passed. A frown settled on his brow.

What was this place? Nothing here resembled the other brothels he'd visited. There was an unexplained peace here. He reached out and grabbed the man he followed.

"What is this place? Who are all those people?" he asked.

The man gave a brief smile and opened a door leading to the kitchen. A woman knelt beside a large cooking pot, which sat on a small portable cooker. Ashok sat beside her, eating a piece of bread and smiling, his head turned towards them, as he heard them enter the room.

"Eli, hello," he said with his mouth full of bread.

There was no threat here, only welcome. Eli smiled and held out his hand to the man behind him.

"I'm Eli. Thank you for feeding my young friend, here. Forgive me for the intrusion."

The man grasped his hand tightly and shook it. "I'm Tanvir Gupta. I pastor these people, and we have church here every day. We saw you watching the house and were concerned. Ashok heard our conversation and said you were his friend. You are welcome here. Please eat."

Looking at the amount of food cooking, Eli cringed. There were so many people to feed, and by the look of it, not much food. He glanced at Ashok, and the boy's grin grew. Sauce of some sort dripped down his chin, and he looked relaxed and at home.

"Thank you, but I ate earlier. You're very kind. I didn't realize this was a home church." Although Eli was excited to meet these people, he felt disappointed at another dead end. Would they ever find Charlie?

"Eli, I hope you don't mind my curiosity, but I can see sadness on your face. How can I help my new friend?"

Shrugging his shoulders, Eli avoided Tanvir's eyes. Was his pain so evident that a complete stranger could read him? As he was trying to decide what to say, he heard the voices in the other room rise up in song.

"Stand and listen Eli," Tanvir suggested.

Bowing his head, Eli closed his eyes and listened. The words touched his soul, and he wondered what they meant. Shivers ran down his spine as Tanvir led him back to the room. The voices of men and women singing in Hindi touched Eli in such a way that he wanted to drop to his knees. He didn't understand the words, but he felt the tangible presence of God, as if he were standing directly in front of him.

Ashok's small hand took hold of his and Eli squeezed it gently. He gave in to the need to be on his knees and dropped to the ground, bending over until his head touched the floor.

As he listened to the words of the song, he knew they were for him and he wondered at their meaning. Pastor Tanvir began to sing in English and others joined in, as if this was the most natural thing in the world.

"Your grace is sufficient for me, my power is made perfect in weakness." Over and over they sang the words. Eli knew the verse and mouthed the words silently. "My grace is sufficient for you, for my power is made perfect in weakness. Therefore I will boast all the more gladly about my weaknesses, so that Christ's power may rest on me."

He'd been trying to find Charlie in his own strength. When something was broken, he was the man to fix it. It was his job to rescue his little sister—hadn't he always been the one to look out for her? Pride had taken the place of prayer.

His shoulders shook as he realized his helplessness. He couldn't find her; he'd tried, and every avenue he took led to a dead end. His chest hurt with the pressure of containing his emotion.

Release Charlotte to me.

He clenched his fists and grunted. His eyes welled up at the thought of letting Charlie go. What if he never saw her again?

Lord, she needs me to find her.

Eli waited for God's response, and he shuddered to think he was arguing with God. Tears flowed down his cheeks, and his shoulders shook. Ashok's arm circled his back and his head rested against Eli's shoulder. The boy sniffed loudly and patted Eli's hand.

Lord, I thought I'd come over here and within a week I'd find Charlie and take her home. I can't stand not knowing where she is and what's happening to her. Why aren't you helping me? Anger pumped blood into his veins, and he swiped away the tears. *Where were you when Charlie was being abducted?* How could he accept that God was telling him to release Charlie? What did that mean?

"Eli, may I comfort you?" Tanvir asked gently.

Ashok had sat back and was hugging his knees; he gave Eli a watery smile and nodded. The boy closed his eyes, and Eli stood to follow Tanvir out of the room.

Tanvir sat down on an old chair and indicated for Eli to sit.

Eli felt cornered and wanted to be anywhere but here. He noticed the pastor looked relaxed and in no hurry to question him. Heat spread across Eli's cheeks, and he felt condemned. His head drooped in shame.

"It helps to talk, my friend," the softly spoken words prompted.

The words spilled out of Eli, like water released from a dam. He spoke of the loss of his sister, his sense of helplessness in not being able to find her, and his anger at God for not intervening. All the time he talked, Tanvir nodded solemnly.

"Yes, yes, Eli. I can understand why you are upset. You are angry because God has not done what you long for him to do. It is difficult to trust Jesus when you feel your prayers are not answered. This is the hardest thing about faith, my friend."

"Tanvir, why would God tell me to release Charlotte to him? What does he mean?"

"What frightens you the most about releasing Charlotte to him, Eli?" Tanvir's gentle eyes showed no sign of judgment, and Eli gave a weak smile.

"If I release her to him, does that mean I won't see her again in this lifetime? Does it mean I go back to Australia without her?" He slumped, defeated.

"I don't know, but if it did, would you do it?"

Everything in him wanted to scream no. How could God want him to abandon his sister, abandon Ashok? He felt the blood drain out of his face and his breath caught in his chest.

He could do nothing more, he'd exhausted all his options. He had to get to the end of himself, to let God take control. Why was this so difficult?

He raised his eyes to meet Tanvir's and nodded. The act of obedience didn't make him feel better immediately, but he slowly unclenched his fists. He would trust God to do what only he could do. If he never saw his sister again, he had to believe that God was in control. He'd always hated the saying 'Let go and let God', but now that was exactly what he had to do.

~~~

Ashok tried to slow his heart from thumping in his chest. He took big breaths and sucked in his lips. He didn't want to cry; he didn't want Eli to know his heart was shattering into little pieces inside him.

Eli was going away—he'd told him that he needed to go back to Australia to see his parents.

Ashok wished he had parents to go to, to lean into and leave the burden of failure with them.

He would never stop looking for Shanti; he would search until he was an old man, if he had to. Hadn't he promised her this? A promise was something you kept. If he stopped looking for her, didn't that say she was no longer important to him?

Shaking his head, he watched Eli from under his lashes. He loved this man. For the first time in his life he felt valued by an older man, and now he was leaving. His heart felt like it was being ripped out all over again.

Hadn't they become a team on a quest to save their sisters? Should he ask him to stay?

His hands began to shake, and he tried not to think about being alone again. Jesus would never leave him, he reminded himself. Eli had taught him many things that Jesus had said, and he had given him a little Bible. Even though Ashok couldn't read the words, he liked to run his finger over them, knowing they were important. A priceless treasure.

"Ashok, come here." Eli beckoned him over and patted the side of the bed.

He wanted to drag his feet, avoid the pain of good-bye. He wanted to scream and shout. Didn't Eli understand how hurt he felt? How could he abandon him and their sisters? He sat beside Eli and his shoulders slumped.

"Come on, mate, it's not that bad. I'll be back. I've explained to you I have to go home and check on my parents. I've been here two

158

months, and what we've been doing isn't leading us any closer to Shanti and Charlie."

Ashok felt a tear slip down his cheek and he wanted to run out of the room. He admired Eli so much and didn't want him to think he was a silly boy for crying.

Shock ripped through his body as Eli pulled him roughly to his chest. Eli held him tightly in his arms, and Ashok gulped when he heard Eli's sob.

He lifted his head slightly to see Eli's face. Eli's eyes were shut and tears streamed down his cheeks. He didn't seem ashamed of crying.

Ashok buried his head in Eli's shoulder and gripped his shirt in desperation. He allowed the pressure to rise from his chest, and he cried. Sobs raked through his body and in some strange way brought him comfort. Slowly he relaxed and allowed his body to slump against Eli. He wanted to sleep.

Eli's rough thumb ran across Ashok's face, removing the moisture of his tears.

"Ashok, I love you. You're a mighty little man. I will be back, I promise."

Something in Ashok snapped, and he pulled back. "I promised my Shanti I would find her. I will never stop looking for her. Never! You may go back to your Australia, but I will keep looking. I continue to believe that Shanti and your sister, Charlie, are in the next place I look."

Eli sighed, and Ashok moved away from the bed. He straightened his back and tensed. This was good-bye. His lips trembled, and his eyes filled with water. Ashok blinked several times, trying to stop the overflow of tears.

Eli came towards him and took his hand. "Ashok, I do not lie. I will be back. I believe the Lord wants me to go home for a time. I have to obey."

Ashok looked at his toes, and nodded.

Eli turned Ashok's hand over, so the palm faced upwards. Ashok felt something placed in his palm, and his head snapped up. It was Eli's ring. He'd noticed it the first time he'd seen Eli. Eli had told him how special it was to him. The ring had belonged to Eli's *baap* and now was his. Ashok's eyes widened at the significance of the ring sitting in his hand.

"I want you to hold onto this for me, Ashok. You know how important it is to me, but you mean more to me than this ring does." Eli spoke softly, and his other hand rested on Ashok's shoulder.

"No, no. This is your baap's ring, you must not leave it with me," Ashok begged.

"It's a symbol of love, my friend. My father loves me and wanted me to have it, and I want you to have it, so you know that I will come back to you and that I love you."

Eli pulled out a thin leather strap and slipped the ring onto it, he then tied the strap around Ashok's neck.

"This is my promise to you, Ashok, I will come back and get my ring from you. In the meantime, I want you to stay in touch with Dr. Phillip. He will tell me how you are, where you are."

He lifted his head and his heart filled with happiness. Eli would be back; he was giving him his most prized possession to look after.

"If you think you have a lead to the girls, I want you to promise me you'll go to Dr. Phillip and tell him. Do not try to get them out on your own. Will you promise me this?"

Ashok had visited many dangerous places with Eli and he knew the sense of being careful. He was no help to Shanti if he were dead. Nodding solemnly, he agreed.

"Good. Dr. Phillip has said you can stay here until I get back. I have left some money with him to help with food, so make this your base, okay?"

"Thank you." Impulsively Ashok threw his arms around his friend and hugged him tightly. He stepped away and walked backwards to the door. "Good-bye, Eli. I have love for you, bursting in my heart." He spun around and raced out of the door. He could not bear to stay a moment longer and look at Eli's face.

Chapter 27

All the girls knew Gargi was pregnant. She was trying to hide the fact from Scarface by binding her stomach in cloth to make it appear smaller. Gargi was unbearable to be around, snapping at everyone, and for a while Charlotte watched from a distance as other girls sniggered and mocked her.

No one liked Gargi, but Charlotte saw a hauntingly beautiful, frightened woman unable to cope with bouts of nausea and vomiting. She could see the exhaustion and stress on Gargi's face and longed to help her.

It was early afternoon, and there were only a few girls in the common room. Gargi lay on her mat with her back to the room. Charlotte wanted to show her that she was special and not alone. A small smile touched her lips and she hurried out of the room.

Walking carefully, Charlotte returned, balancing the bowl of warm water as it slurped from side to side in the bowl.

Sitting cross-legged on the floor beside Gargi, she reached out to touch Gargi's shoulder.

Gargi turned over and frowned at Charlotte. "What do you want?"

"Relax. I'm going to wash and massage your feet. My grandma

told me that when she was pregnant, this helped her relax. Then I'm going to brush your hair."

Gargi patted her tangled, unwashed hair. She sat up and scowled at Charlotte.

"Don't say I'm pregnant!" she cursed and scrambled to her knees.

Charlotte put her hand on Gargi's shoulder to stop her from rising. "You don't have to talk to me, but I am doing this, so quit moving."

Reaching over Charlotte picked up one of Gargi's feet. She gently stroked the top of the foot and then moved firmly over her ankle.

She could feel Gargi's eyes boring holes into her and smiled. Looking up, she raised an eyebrow. "Why don't you close your eyes, that way you won't have to see me," she said softly.

Gargi leaned back and Charlotte saw the wary look on her face before she quickly replaced it with her usual scowl. As Charlotte continued to massage the girl's feet, her thoughts wandered.

What would it be like to be pregnant in a place like this? Not knowing who the father was, trying to hide that she was pregnant instead of celebrating with friends, feeling totally alone without God's strength.

Lord Jesus, help me be Gargi's friend. Show me how to reach her in love.

She heard the deep sigh escape Gargi's lips and looked up.

Gargi pulled herself up on her elbows and tilted her head. She squinted before she sat completely up. "Don't think I'm going to thank you. I didn't ask you to do that."

Charlotte rinsed her hands in the water and dried them against her dress. Picking up the comb and brush, she started on the mass of knots in Gargi's hair.

"Maybe I should have done this first. By the time I've detangled this mess, you're sure to be tense again."

Her back ached from sitting unsupported, and her hands felt like they'd been working the brush for an hour. She dropped the brush and ran her fingers through the loosed strands of hair.

163

"There," she stated with triumph in her voice, "you look beautiful. I'll wash your hair for you in the morning and tie it up."

Gargi's eyes widened and welled up with emotion, and she blinked several times. She hoisted herself up and walked away.

Charlotte cranked her neck and moved her shoulders to relieve the tension. She felt weary, but good.

~~~

Following the others wearily down the hall, Charlotte tried to prepare herself for the night ahead. She hated the room where her abuse happened, night after night. Something tightened inside her chest, knotting and twisting until she could hardly breathe.

Padma told her not to fight, to let him have his way and get it over with. She'd told her to let her mind escape to another place, then it would be easier on her. Charlotte tried that, but the reality of what was happening always brought tears to her eyes.

Tonight she was determined to be dignified and talk to the creep about Jesus. He wasn't beyond saving; no one was.

She stopped in the hall and closed her eyes. Taking long breaths, she inhaled air deep into her lungs. If she could slow down her heart rate, she'd be in control.

She sensed someone watching her and quickly opened her eyes.

Saul stood directly in front of her, scowling.

Charlotte's gaze locked with his. What did he want? She was on the way, wasn't she?

Saul extended his hand towards her and opened his fist. Inside the palm of his hand were five small, smooth stones.

"You got the stones for me," she said softy, her mouth tilting in a genuine smile.

Saul grunted and closed his fingers.

Charlotte's eyes darkened with confusion, and she tentatively touched his arm.

He grunted. "You can have them to play your stupid game, if you survive the night," he stated, avoiding eye contact. "Get going."

Her mouth went dry, and her eyes widened. Why would Saul say such a thing and offer her an incentive to get through the night?

Her feet felt glued to the floor and fear pulsed through her veins. She licked her lips and gripped his arm. "What do you mean?" Her voice trembled.

"Take your hand off me!" he snarled. "You're stronger than you think, Charlotte, go prove it to yourself."

He seized her arm and dragged her along the hall. Opening the door, Saul paused and pulled her to within an inch of his face.

"Make me proud, angel girl." His voice was edged with sarcasm.

Charlotte listened as he locked the door and the sound of the key clicking echoed in the empty room, heightening her nerves.

Falling to her knees, she prayed, her lips moving with words of desperation. *Lord, rescue me from this prison. When I say my foot is slipping, your love, O Lord, supports me. When anxiety is so great within me, your arms console me.*

The door opened. Wide-eyed, Charlotte scrambled to her feet.

Three men entered the room.

Her tormenter leered. "I've brought my friends to meet you, Charlotte. I've told them how obliging you are to me. Come here, my pet."

~~~

She couldn't stay in this room a moment longer. Gritting her teeth, Charlotte groaned as she pulled herself up to sit on the edge of the bed. How could this be happening to her? She tentatively lifted her arm and sucked in a breath as pain pulsed through her back. Her head dropped to her chest in defeat. What was the point of fighting? God had abandoned her.

The door flew open, and Charlotte glanced towards it.

Saul entered the room, stopped in front of her, and crossed his arms. Charlotte knew she should reach for her sari to cover herself, but the distance seemed too far.

"Did you survive, girl?" he sneered, "or are you going to sit there like a broken doll?"

"Arrrrrrgh," Charlotte screamed as she lunged at him.

Saul swatted her aside like a bothersome fly. She crumpled to the floor, exhausted, broken, and depleted. Tears spilled out of her eyes and streamed down her cheeks.

"Stand up, get dressed, and I will give you your precious stones." He clanked them in his hand.

Charlotte tilted her head to one side and she sniffed as she looked at him. For a moment she thought she saw a softening in his eyes, but shook her head at the notion.

Crawling across the room on her hands and knees, she reached her sari, then slung it over her and shakily stood.

"Give me the stones," she said as she raised her chin and squared her shoulders.

Nodding, Saul placed them into her outstretched hand and left the room.

Charlotte sucked in her bottom lip to stop it from trembling. She followed him out of the room, her legs shaking as she carefully placed one foot in front of the other. It felt like she'd been turned inside out. Everything ached.

As she stepped into the common room, she breathed a sigh of relief. She needed some purpose to keep going, and Saul had given it to her.

She looked across the room and saw Shanti huddled in a ball on her mat, and her heart melted. This little girl had no friends, no one to encourage and love her.

Charlotte's body throbbed in places she hadn't known existed, and she rubbed at her back. She bent over and picked up the end of her mat and dragged it over to where Shanti lay. She pushed the edge of her mat closer to Shanti's with her foot and groaned as she lowered her body to the thin pad.

Shanti turned and looked at her. Charlotte winked and closed her eyes. She could feel Shanti staring but didn't have the energy to move.

"Hope you don't mind if I sleep here from now on, Shanti," she whispered, expecting no response. Shanti hadn't uttered a word since Charlotte had met her. "I could use a friend about now. Good night, sweetheart." Charlotte allowed her shoulders to go limp and breathed out heavily.

She was drifting off to sleep when she felt the small hand take hold of hers, and she smiled.

~~~

How long had she stared at Charlotte in the dim light before sleep captured her? Shanti gave a tiny sigh. She'd never had a friend before, only Ashok, and he didn't count because he was her brother. She pulled back further against the wall.

Charlotte stretched her arms above her head and groaned.

Shanti wondered if she'd change her mind about sleeping next to her, now it was morning. She ducked her head between her knees and hid her face.

Her hair smelled of flowers, and she hated the smell. Padma kept it clean for the boss, but she wished it smelt like dust and rubbish to make him not want her.

"Morning, Shanti," Charlotte murmured sleepily.

Rubbing her arms, Shanti watched as Charlotte swung her legs up under her and hugged her knees. The smile on her face confused Shanti.

When Charlotte's fingers touched her shoulder Shanti gasped at the show of affection, and tears surfaced in her eyes.

"I'm going to the bathroom to clean up and then come back and teach you how to play knuckle bones." Charlotte reached under the end of her mat and pulled out five small stones. She bent towards Shanti and held out the stones. "Can you look after these for me, Shanti?" she whispered.

Shanti nodded solemnly and reached out to take them, and a small smile twitched her lips.

Charlotte moaned as she tried to stand and closed her eyes.

Jumping to her feet Shanti gently took her new friend's arm. She'd seen the bloodstains on Charlotte's sari last night, and she looked down to avoid Charlotte's eyes. This was a bad place. She hated the men who came here, and she hated the boss.

"Thank you, sweetheart. Do you want to come and have a wash too?"

Shaking her head, Shanti sat down on her mat, and crossed her legs. She moved the stones from hand to hand and only looked up after Charlotte had gone.

She gingerly touched the healing cut on the inside of her thigh. Why did the boss have to cut her? He kept chanting, 'It's in the blood'. He was creepy, and Shanti hated thinking about him.

She closed her eyes and tried to picture Ashok's face. What would he be doing today? Was he still trying to find her?

Jesus, if you're listening to me, Ashok said you were my friend. Can you look after my brother for me? Help him to forget me and be happy. I'm sorry I've been bad. Thank you for Charlotte wanting to be my friend.

Other women began to wake up, and Shanti liked the sound. The soft murmurs and shuffling reassured her that she was safe.

Most days she lay back down and drifted back to sleep; there was nothing else to do but wait for the evening to approach and the evil to start all over again.

The boss called her every night. Sometimes he made her stand naked in one place all night, while he slept. These were the hardest nights because if she made a sound or moved and he woke, he would get so angry, and his anger terrified her.

Once she sat down because her body ached with the strain of standing completely still. She'd thought he wouldn't know, but he'd woken and seen her. He'd forced her sit in the fire, and her skin was still tender from the blisters.

She'd bitten her lip so many times to stop from screaming, that a ridge was forming on the inside of her mouth. She licked the surface as a reminder of the consequences of disobeying the boss.

"Shanti," Charlotte called from the door, "Come here."

Scurrying across the room Shanti followed Charlotte to the outside courtyard. She hadn't been there since they'd first brought her in.

She cranked her head back to look at the sky and squinted at the sun.

As a light breeze fanned her cheeks, she opened her mouth. Her gaze swept the small area, and she ran her hand over the bark of the tree.

The rough surface caught at her fingers, but she didn't care. Warmth filled her and she felt a sob catch in her throat.

Charlotte sat on the dry, dusty dirt and patted the ground beside her. Shanti watched as Charlotte smoothed the dirt in front of her with the palm of her hand, not caring about the dust floating around them.

Shanti plopped down and clapped her hands in excitement.

Charlotte smiled and began tossing the stones up and capturing them on the back of her hand. Shanti's eyes widened in surprise as she watched Charlotte demonstrate the game.

"Okay, let me tell you what to do, then you can have a go."

"I can't do that, Miss. Charlotte," Shanti said breathlessly, her voice creaking like a door that hadn't been used in a long time. Her words brought a huge grin to Charlotte's face.

"Yes you can, it will just take practice. We will play every day. Now let me show you. You hold all five stones in your hand, like this. Then you throw them up, quickly turn your hand over, and catch as many as you can on the back of your hand. Here, you have a go."

Shanti copied Charlotte and giggled as the stones went in all different directions.

Laughing, Charlotte picked up the stones. "It's easier to catch them if you spread your fingers a little bit. Try again."

Shanti loved the game. But when Charlotte said it was time to have lunch and then a nap because they needed their energy for later, Shanti felt all her happiness fade from her heart.

She dragged her feet back to the common room and walked past the food on the table to her mat. She lay down with her back to the room.

She heard Charlotte sit down and wanted to turn to her, but tears flooded her eyes. What would her new friend think of her? She should be used to the routine by now, not crying over what she could not change.

"Shanti, you must eat, sweetheart. Then I want to tell you a story. Do you like stories?"

She shrugged and then turned over. Her eyes filled with tears again, and she sucked in her bottom lip with her teeth.

Charlotte's hands captured hers and she leaned in close to Shanti's face.

"Shanti, do you believe in God?" she whispered.

Shanti shrugged. She couldn't get the words out of her mouth. Her throat felt swollen and tight.

"He believes in you, sweetheart. He loves you."

Pulling her hands free, Shanti sat up and frowned. "Then why doesn't he help me?"

Charlotte ran her hand over Shanti's head and pulled her into her arms. "This place is so full of darkness, Shanti. We need to pray together, so God can hear us. It says in the Bible that if two people agree about anything they ask for, it will be given to them by their Father in heaven. That Jesus will be with them." Charlotte sighed and sat back. "Will you pray with me every day?"

Shanti nodded. She wanted to believe. She really did.

Charlotte cupped Shanti's hands in both of hers, and Shanti's eyes widened as she saw Charlotte's eyes brighten.

"Lord Jesus, we know you're here with us. Lord this is a dark, evil place. We cannot survive without your help. Please give Shanti strength to endure what happens to her. Help her feel your presence, when she is taken where she doesn't want to go. Lord Jesus, please help us to hold onto the hope of rescue, to trust that you will lift us out of this prison and restore us stronger and better than before. Amen."

"Amen," Shanti echoed.

Chapter 28

The shove on his shoulder woke him. Phillip rubbed his eyes and shuffled out of the car. He stretched his arms above his head and yawned. He wanted them to think he was relaxed and in control. He'd never experienced fear before, but the thumping in his chest certainly had his attention.

As he ran his hand through his hair, he wished he'd told someone what he'd done. He could disappear, and no one would know where to start looking.

"Hurry up, follow me," the man in front of him ordered.

Phillip scanned the street for any familiar signs. The house was fenced off, and there seemed to be only one entrance.

He hurried after the man and noticed the other guy was following close behind him. He thought about his next move and decided to act annoyed.

"Slow down, will you. First you hustle me into your car with no explanation of where we're going." Phillip slapped the side of his leg and stopped walking. "Then you expect me to do as you command without any discussion of what you expect of me."

The man in front of him stopped, turned towards him, and snarled.

Phillip shrugged his shoulders and raised the corners of his lips slightly.

Guy Two grabbed his arms from behind. He stumbled and was forcibly yanked along.

Indignant, he pulled his arm free. "All right, all right. I'm coming. Take it easy."

The inside of the house smelled of perfume, many different types mixed together to make a sickly aroma. He was pulled down a hallway, and he noticed doors leading in all directions.

Was Charlotte behind one of these doors? His breath caught at the thought.

They entered a courtyard that housed one lonely, dried-up tree and he looked up at the small window of sky, framed by the buildings. They reentered the building through another door and continued through the house.

He glanced to the right as they passed an open door. Women filled the room, confirming he was in a brothel. Angling his head back he tried to scan the room, but a shove from behind made him continue walking.

His "employers" led him into a room where a woman lay sprawled on a bed. Sweat glistened on her forehead and the bed linen was rumpled, as if she'd tossed and turned many times.

Phillip moved forward and took her wrist, laying two fingers across it. Her pulse was erratic, and her skin burned with fever. Everything in him wanted to help her, but he made himself step away from the bed and cross his arms. He lifted his eyebrows and gave a careless grin.

"Gentlemen, we need to come to an arrangement for payment—before I look at our patient."

"Twenty thousand rupe," the man snapped.

"Thirty thousand, and a girl before I leave." Phillip counted to ten before the man gave a mocking laugh.

"Done. She miscarried and needs medicine or something to get her back on her feet." He turned and walked out of the room.

Phillip was very aware of the other man leaning against the wall, looking bored. He approached the girl and scanned her face. The smell of sickness rose from her body, and he sucked in a shallow breath.

Her face was pale under her brown skin. Phillip couldn't imagine what she'd lived through to get in this state.

Removing the sheet from her, he gently palpated her abdomen.

"Can you get me some water and clean cloths?" he asked over his shoulder. "And next time you pick me up, it might be a good idea to warn me I'll be needing my medical bag."

The man shrugged and left without speaking.

Carefully examining the girl he discover she hadn't miscarried; she'd had an abortion. He'd seen blotched abortions before, and this one was really bad.

They'd used a sharp object to break the amniotic sac inside her womb and obviously had to cut her to get the baby out.

He shuddered as he realized she must have been well on in her pregnancy and whoever had performed the operation hadn't cared about the poor girl. He needed to get her fever down or she could die.

He noticed the vaginal warts, a gift from her many clients.

A shadow crossed his spirit as he compared her to the prostitutes who came to the clinic. A niggling doubt entered his mind about the way he'd judged them, and his jaw tightened as he pushed the thought away. He had no time to think about such things now.

Lord Jesus, help me. What should I do? You know this girl's name, you love her—heal her, Father, please, as a special favor to me.

The man arrived back with water and rags, and Phillip went about cleaning her up the best he could. She would never carry another child, and he grieved for her.

"She has an infection caused by the abortion. Her temperature is soaring and without medication and proper care she'll die," Phillip snapped. He heard the tension in his voice and breathed in deeply to calm his nerves. "Let me take her to the clinic and care for her there."

The man glared at him and shrugged. Phillip's hands fisted, and he wanted to scream at the lack of compassion in the man's face. "Go, ask your boss. Now!"

~~~

Charlotte hadn't seen Gargi for days and was worried. The last time she'd sat brushing Gargi's hair, the girl had shared her excitement about having a baby. She longed to hold her child and her hand had cupped her swollen stomach lovingly.

Gargi had whispered her plan of escape to Charlotte, and asked her to pray. Charlotte sucked in her bottom lip, and her eyes smarted with unshed tears.

There was tension among the girls. No one was talking and everyone seemed to be avoiding eye contact.

Charlotte had to know. She quietly left the room in search of Padma.

The door to Padma's room was open, and Charlotte stood silently waiting to be seen.

Saul held Padma's arm in a vice like grip, and Padma glared at him.

"I will not do it. Get one of the other girls," Padma declared bravely.

Saul pushed his face closer to Padma's, and Charlotte gasped, not wanting to see her friend hurt.

"Excuse me for interrupting. Can I help?" she asked meekly, her eyes downcast.

Shoving Padma away Saul strode over to Charlotte. He gripped her upper arms, pulling her into the room. His foot flicked out, kicking the door shut.

"What are you doing sneaking around, listening to conversations that don't concern you?"

Charlotte's arms burned where his fingers dug in. She inhaled deeply to calm her nerves. "I'm sorry, Saul. I was coming to ask Padma a question and overheard you talking."

He let her go, and his eyes narrowed in speculation. A crooked smile lifted the corner of his mouth. "You think you can care for everyone, angel girl? Let's see how much energy you have looking

175

after Gargi and working as well."

"Scarface, if Charlotte is to care for Gargi, she needs to be excused from duties for a time," Padma demanded.

"No. She is too valuable, she will do both. Get her what she needs and bring her to me." He spun on his heels and went to leave. Padma raced across the room and grabbed his arm.

"Forgive me, Scarface. I will come with you and take care of Gargi. Charlotte, leave us."

"Ahh, you think you can tell me what to do," he spat. "You will learn your place, Padma. Charlotte will do it."

Saul left the room, and Charlotte sunk onto the bed.

Padma looked furious and paced around, with her hands fisted by her side. "When will you learn to keep your mouth shut, you stupid girl?"

"I thought he was going to hit you. I'm sorry." Charlotte looked at her hands and felt a sob rise from her chest. Had they hurt Gargi so much that she needed someone to care for her?

She looked up, "The baby?"

"Gone. Do not talk of it again. Come, I will take you to her."

~~~

Phillip stared at the young woman on the bed and lifted her hand in his. He gently squeezed her hand in an attempt to encourage her to fight. Why didn't they protect the girls from getting pregnant?

Lord, as much as I pray for this young woman, I can't help but hope Charlie isn't in a place like this. It's inhuman what they've done to this girl. Did they even use an anesthetic?

A noise at the door caused him to drop her arm and turn around.

"It's time to go. A girl is coming to look after her. Boss said you bring drugs back and make her better."

Nodding solemnly, Phillip glanced at the girl's face, turned and left the room. As he followed the man down the hall he remembered his request to have a girl as part payment.

Right now the thought of staying here a moment longer disgusted him.

Softly spoken words alerted him to the presence of women in the hallway. A shiver ran down his spine and he spun around, sure he'd heard Charlie's voice.

The door to the room he'd left was open. A beautiful Indian woman stood in the hallway instructing another woman, who stood inside the room, just out of view.

His heart rate increased and he wanted to call out Charlotte's name. Could it be her? What would happen if he ran back to see?

"Wait," he called to the man in front of him.

Chapter 29

It seemed surreal to be back in Australia, and part of him wanted to be anywhere but outside his parent's house. Eli scratched the two-day growth on his chin and stepped out of the car.

He hoped he'd made the right decision in not telling them he was coming. He couldn't tell them over the phone that he'd felt led to take a break and tidy up some things back here. He had to resign from his job, arrange financial support to keep looking for Charlie, and explain the difficult situation to his parents.

Eli chided himself for being a coward; not only had he not parked in their driveway, he'd parked across the street to give him more time to pull his nerves together.

The hum of a lawn mower and the serenity of the quiet cul-de-sac brought tears to his eyes. The air smelt fresh, and there were no hungry children lying on the footpath. What a contrast to the streets of India.

Closing his eyes, he asked for wisdom on how to talk to his parents. He hesitated and looked at his shoes. Normally he would have knocked and gone straight in, knowing the door would be unlocked. They would be surprised to see him, but upset to have him back without Charlie.

That was the problem; he'd let them down. He wanted to turn

around and walk away, sort out his affairs, and go back to India without them being any the wiser. But he shook his head at the notion, his lips twitching. His parents loved him, they would understand—not blame him. He had to stop taking responsibility for something that was out of his control.

The door opened, and his head snapped up. His father stood stock-still, smiling at him.

"Hi, Dad." He gave a lopsided smile.

"Eli, Son—you surprised me." Bill tilted his head to look behind Eli.

His father's expression change as he realized Charlotte wasn't with him, and the haunted look in his father's eyes caused a physical pain to Eli's chest.

Eli slowly shook his head and watched helplessly as Bill's shoulders sagged.

"Can I come in, Dad?"

"Of course." Bill's arms went around Eli in a bear hug, and Eli felt his shoulders relax. He realized he'd been holding his breath.

Although his mother had told him his father was much better, the last time he'd seen him, he'd looked like a walking shadow.

Eli allowed his father's embrace to pump warmth into his frozen heart.

"Is Mum home?"

"No," his father answered. "Maybe that's a good thing, gives you and me a chance to talk."

Tears filled Eli's eyes as he told his father about his frustration at not being able to find Charlie. He lowered his head and cleared his throat.

"Eli, it's not your fault. We have to trust God with Charlie, we have to hold onto hope, Son."

The inside of his stomach churned over with nerves, and he felt the peace he'd been trying to hold onto slip out of his reach.

How could he explain to his parents what it was like over there?

The places he'd seen and people he'd met. How he had pretended to be a customer visiting brothels, to try and locate Charlie. The women he'd talked to, so lost, so bound. What about them? Who would help them escape their captivity?

Shaking his head, he tried to focus on what his father was saying.

"When we hadn't heard from you in a week, we were beginning to worry."

"Mmm. Any chance of a coffee, Dad?"

"Of course, come through to the kitchen."

Eli looked around at the house he'd grown up in. Some things never changed. His mother had a love for indoor pot plants and photos. She artistically placed them together, drawing the eye to both.

He stopped and picked up a photo of Charlie on a swing, when she was about twelve. His mouth tightened as he placed it down and followed his father into the kitchen.

Both men turned toward the kitchen door as Macy walked in carrying two bags of groceries.

Her mouth gaped open at the sight of Eli.

Bill rushed over and took the groceries from her. Macy flew across the room and flung her arms around his waist.

"Oh my goodness, Eli." Hugging tight, she laughed. "Where's Charlie, is she upstairs?" Macy released him and turned to leave the room.

"Mum, wait!" Eli yelled, his hand clutching his stomach. It felt like a dagger was being twisted inside him.

Macy stopped and slowly turned back to him.

Eli watched the color drain from his mother's perfectly made-up face. He clenched his fists by his sides; there was nothing he could do to make it easier for her.

"What are you doing here—without Charlotte?" she asked accusingly.

"Mum, I—"

"Macy, Eli's only been here ten minutes. I'm about to make coffee, do you want a cup?"

"No. What I want to know is, where—is—my—daughter? Eli, you promised you would bring her ack. Have you given up on her, is that why you're here?"

"No, I haven't given up on finding Charlie. I just needed to come home for a couple of weeks to organize—"

"Two weeks! You would leave her there, alone, for two weeks. What are you thinking?" she screeched.

Macy paced back and forth, then stopped and slapped her hands down on the kitchen bench. "What kind of brother are you, to do such a thing?" Her shoulders slumped and she burst into tears.

Bill looked at Eli, and mouthed the word *sorry*.

Eli shrugged, his eyes narrowing in pain at his mother's words.

"Son, why don't you go to your apartment, get cleaned up, and come back here for dinner. Then you can tell us your plans." Bill's voice was tight with stress, and Eli hated that he'd caused his father further pain.

He nodded, looked at his mother, and felt his heart tear in two. Had he lost his mother's love, as well as his sister?

As he left the house he couldn't help but think how his life had changed in the last three and a half months.

The ripple effect of what had happened to Charlie had changed all their lives. He'd always been his mother's hero, and now she could hardly stand the sight of him. She didn't care about what it was like for him.

How could she understand the fear he lived with? Fear of not finding Charlie, and, of finding Charlie. What would she be like, having lived through such a nightmare?

Had his mother once asked if he was okay? Did she even realize the danger Ashok and he put themselves in every time they entered the dark, shadowed areas where Charlie could be hidden?

He blinked twice as tears stung his eyes. His heart yearned to give in to self-pity and anger.

Forgive your mother, as I have forgiven you.

Eli pulled the car over to the curb and switched off the engine. He gripped the steering wheel and rested his forehead on his hands; his knuckles were white. What was Charlie doing right now? Did she have the luxury of wallowing in self-pity?

Sighing, he lifted his head and started the car. He had to get a grip. He knew his mother loved him; she was beside herself with worry, and he was the closest target. He had to let the words go. Once he explained how difficult it was and that every lead he'd gotten hadn't panned out, she would understand his frustration.

Chapter 30

Rain streamed down Ashok's face as he ran. His clothes clung to him like a second skin and the sound of thunder echoed around him, mocking his helplessness. He ran like one possessed.

Throwing his head back, he screamed into the night. Rain filled his open mouth and he swallowed.

The dank, dusty taste caused him to cough, and he sneezed into his hand. The rain was so heavy it was like a curtain in front of him, blurring his vision.

He'd been asking everyone he saw if they'd seen Shanti. He rubbed Eli's ring and closed his eyes tight, wishing his friend were here.

His shoulders slumped as he staggered to a stop. Panting, he bent in half and tried to slow his breathing.

Anyone with any sense would be taking shelter, not out in this storm. He'd go to Dr. Phillip's. He didn't want to be a burden and presume he was welcome, but at least having a destination would give him hope.

His hair was plastered to his face. Ashok hugged his jacket closer to his chest, thankful he still had it. He thought of the shoes he'd lost, and his mouth tightened. Why did bad things keep happening to him?

His feet splashed through the water, and his thoughts wandered to Shanti. He missed her so much. It felt like a part of him had been torn violently out of him, and his life was in tatters.

He tried to picture her beautiful round face, and a sob broke free from his mouth. "Shanti—" His shoulders dropped further and a part of him wanted to lie on the street and give up.

A car sped past. Water surged from its tires like a wave. Ashok jumped aside to avoid being hit, but a body of water soaked him further.

Stamping his foot he kicked at the stream of water pooling at his feet. He ducked his head into his jacket and ran the rest of the distance to the apartments.

He looked around, hoping no one would see him or accuse him of trespassing. If he couldn't stay here, he would crawl into a ball and die. The night was too long, too dark, and too cold.

Walking close to the building, he edged his way to Dr. Phillip's front door and knocked. His chin drooped to his chest, and it felt like his body belonged to someone else. The thought of being alone one more night closed in around him.

He hammered the door, longing to magically cause it to open. When there was no response, Ashok slipped to the ground and leaned his back against the unrelenting wood.

Tears dripped down his water-drenched cheeks. He circled his arms around his drawn-up legs and dropped his forehead to rest on his knees. His shoulders shook as sobs of despair raked his body.

He was shrinking to the size of a speck of dust, invisible to the naked eye and ignored because of his unimportance. Ashok caught his breath and wrung his hands together as he tried to pray.

"Jesus," he sobbed, "help me."

He curled into a ball and lay on the doorstep. Eli had told him that Jesus would never leave him, nor forsake him. Did that mean Jesus was here with him, on this step? He took out his soaked card, held it to his chest, and closed his eyes.

Tucking his head into his arms, he allowed his heart to be warmed. "Jesus," he whispered, "I'm so tired. Bring Dr. Phillip home and please tell Shanti I love her."

~~~

Phillip stood looking down at Ashok. His mouth tightened, and a frown furrowed his forehead. He quietly reached over him and opened the door, then stooped and picked the boy up.

Carrying him to the spare bedroom, he placed him on the bed. He felt the heat radiating off Ashok's skin and sighed. The boy had a fever.

Ashok did not wake as he lifted first one arm then the other out of his jacket. He heard Ashok mumble Shanti's name and some words that he couldn't distinguish.

Running a hand through his hair, Phillip sighed. All he wanted to do was collapse into bed and catch a few hours' sleep before he had to be back at the clinic.

What a night. A silent, angry trip home with unresponsive men and a filthy blindfold tied tightly over his eyes.

He pulled the blanket up to Ashok's chin and gently touched his young face. Phillip hunched by the bed and softly prayed for the boy. "Lord Jesus, touch Ashok, heal his fever, and encourage him not to give up hope of finding his sister."

Standing, he stretched and went to find his own bed.

~~~~

Macy sat with her hands in her lap. She had to apologies to Eli, but the words stuck in her throat. He'd looked so hurt when she'd accused him of giving up on Charlotte.

"Mum, Dad. The police told me I'm wasting my time continuing to look for Charlie. They believe the window of time to recover a person abducted is ten days, tops. She could be anywhere by now."

A vice seemed to twist tighter and tighter in Macy's chest as she listened to Eli. Ten days? It had been months. Was her baby lost

185

forever? She stared blankly at Eli and blinked, not seeing him.

"I've visited numerous brothels around where she was taken, and nothing. There have been no sightings of her anywhere. I've offered a reward for any information or sighting, but it's like she never existed." Eli released a breath.

"What do the police suggest we do now?" Bill asked.

"They aren't interested. They suggested I accept that she's gone and move on."

Macy felt the heat in her face intensify as she shook her head violently. "Never!" she yelled. "I'll never stop believing we'll find Charlotte. Never!" She folded her arms protectively across her chest and glared at Eli, as if he'd seconded the police's opinion.

Eli's eyes flickered between his parents. "I agree, Mum. My plan is to settle things up here. Resign my job, put my apartment on the market, and get as much cash together as I can."

"You're going back?" Macy gulped.

"Of course. I don't know whether I'll find her, but I'll keep looking until the Lord tells me there's no hope."

Macy nodded and covered her hot cheeks with her hands. She'd accused him of abandoning Charlotte, yet here he was, prepared to give up everything.

Heart breaking, she stood and squatted beside Eli's chair. "I'm sorry for what I said to you, Eli. I hope you can forgive me. I love you, it's not your fault that this is happening."

Shrugging Eli gave a fleeting smile. His eyes watered and she reached out to grasp his arm. "We can't let this destroy our family. How can I help?"

"If it wasn't for God's grace and mercy, I would have given up by now. There was a time in India when all I wanted to do was wallow in self-pity. I blamed myself for Charlie being in this situation."

Macy cupped his face in her hand and gently smoothed the frown between his eyes. She thought back to when he was a little boy and how she used to comfort him when he was hurt.

"No, Son, it's never been your fault." Macy wrapped her arms around Eli and rubbed his back, trying to ease some of his tension. She wanted to cover him and keep him safe like a mother hen protects her chicks.

Eli pulled away from her and wiped his cheek. "Charlie begged me to go with her. If I'd considered how important this trip was to her and given up two or three weeks of my life—" He gave a deep sigh.

"She asked me to go with her too, Eli," Bill stated softly. "We cannot continue to go over the what-ifs. It's totally unproductive."

"That's just what I'm saying, Dad. I've forgiven myself. I felt God telling me to release Charlie to him. I had to come to the place of helplessness and recognize my sin. I believed that I could find her, that I didn't need God to help me. I held something back from God. Believing in Jesus, yes, but not really believing that I needed him that much. What you would call a self-made man."

His words shocked Macy. She narrowed her eyes and leaned on his shoulder, to help her stand.

Moving back to her chair, she sat down heavily. What sort of mother was she? Everything in her wanted to deny what he was saying and encourage him, tell him she was proud of all he'd achieved, that he was amazing.

How many times had she told him what she thought he wanted to hear? Smoothing away opportunities for him to grow closer to God. She'd gotten in God's way too many times, tried to fix what she'd perceived was broken, rescuing her son from unpleasant feelings— from truth.

She sucked in her lips and closed her eyes. *Forgive me, Jesus.*

"I'm coming with you, Eli," Bill stated firmly. "I think its time we involved the media and put some pressure on the police to continue their search for Charlotte."

"Dad, the people who have Charlie don't care about the police. The people who visit brothels, if that's where she is, would not help the police with their search."

187

"What if we placed a large reward? I've been thinking about this, and I think I can put together $100,000."

Macy gasped and turned to Bill. "Why haven't you talked to me about this? Where will we get that amount of money?"

"I've arranged to cash in some of our shares, and if need be, we can mortgage the house."

Her neck burned with shame; how could she have become so self-focused that she'd stopped caring about her husband and his feelings? She'd been treating him like a child since his heart attack, not giving him credence for having an active brain.

I'm sorry, Lord. I seem to be doing nothing right.

~~~

Talking to his parents about how he was feeling helped. A relaxed smile lifted the corners of his mouth, and he felt better.

The shrilling of a phone interrupted Eli's thoughts, and he looked across at his mother before pulling out his mobile phone and holding it to his ear.

"Eli, it's Ted. We met me on the plane to India about three months ago."

"Yes, I remember. I'm sorry I never got the chance to look you up. I'm back in Australia for a couple of weeks, then returning to India to continue looking for my sister." Eli squinted as he tried to recall his conversation with the Ted on the plane.

"It would be good to see you, Eli. Look, I won't waste your time, I overhead some guys talking in the hotel lobby last night." Ted cleared his throat.

Eli sat straighter in his chair, and looked over at his parents. "Go on, what did you hear?" His voice sounded gruff to his own ears, and he tried to ignore the thumping of his heart. Hope started to bubble inside him.

"They were bragging about a great night they'd had, and I heard one of them mention the name Charlotte."

The thought of Charlie being part of what Ted said sent chills down Eli's spine. "Do you know who they were? What made you think they could be talking about my sister?"

"They were talking in—um, sexual tones, crude language and sly innuendoes. I'm sorry, Eli, but I thought it could be a lead. One of the men is a regular here, and I thought you could approach him and ask if he knew where you could go to have a good time with a—you know what I'm saying," he finished abruptly.

"Yes. How long do you think he'll be staying at the hotel?" He squeezed his eyes shut and roughly rubbed his forehead.

If he were still in India, it would have taken him minutes to get to the hotel.

His mind raced, trying to work out a way to handle the situation. "The minute I'm back in India, I'll come see you." He sighed heavily, his fingers opening and closing, tightly.

"If it was my sister, I'd want someone to act if they thought they had a lead. I know you're a praying man, Eli, so maybe you will find Charlotte."

"To be honest with you, Ted, I was struggling to hold onto hope before your call."

"Don't do that. There is always hope, my friend."

"I don't want to lose this lead. Can I give your phone number to a friend in India to see if he can follow it up for me?"

"Of course, give me his details so I can expect his call."

189

Chapter 31

The chaya was getting heavier, thicker. As the denseness of the air coated her throat, Shanti could hardly breathe, for gagging. She knew she needed to get up off the damp jungle floor and try to find her way to the river, but her thoughts scrambled to remember why she needed to get to the river.

The chaya was becoming something she accepted. At first she'd fought with intensity as it spread up her body, but now she lay still as its gooey substance overtook her.

The foul smell of decaying flesh made her gag. In pain, she clutched her stomach. She'd felt pain before, but this was different, centered on turning her inside out.

She pulled herself up and listened. A faraway sound urged her forward. The river.

Angling her head she listened, and the sound of gurgling water became clearer. Shanti licked her lips and took a deep breath.

If she could get to the river, she could drink. Ashok! How could she have forgotten him? He was waiting for her, she needed to try.

"Shanti, honey, wake up." Charlotte gently pulled Shanti into her arms and rocked her.

Opening her eyes, Shanti felt dazed and tried to return from another reality. She sighed and tried to smile at Charlotte.

Her lips seemed glued together, refusing to open to allow her to breathe air into her lungs. Panic widened her eyes, and she thrashed her hands at Charlotte.

"Hush, Shanti. You're safe now." Charlotte continued to rock her, whispering words she didn't understand, strange words, soft, beautiful words.

Shanti closed her eyes, trying to shut her mind to the jungle. She gasped when her lips opened and she sucked in a deep, long breath of clear air.

Charlotte gently released her, and Shanti's eyes snapped open. "Don't leave me, Charlie, please," she begged.

"I won't. I'm going to tell you a story to help you relax. Okay?"

Nodding, Shanti allowed Charlotte's presence to calm her. Charlotte lay down beside her and twirled her fingers through Shanti's hair.

"There once was a stripy green-and-yellow caterpillar who spent her days slithering over the ground looking for something to eat and wishing she could get out of the forest. Her name was Milky, because she like to eat the leaves of the milkweed that grew up from the forest floor." Charlotte smiled and paused.

Shanti thought about asking for a different story, one that wasn't in a forest.

"Charlie, what is milkweed? Could I drink milk from it like a cow?"

"No, sweetheart. Milkweed is a plant that grows tall with a bush of small-petalled flowers on it, and caterpillars love to eat it." Charlie smiled. "As I was saying, Milky would use her sticky feet to climb up the branches of the milkweed and nibble on the leaves until she was full. Often she would look up and see sunlight flicking through the canopy of trees, and her mouth would open wide in longing. She'd watch as beautiful creatures, with wings of silk and eye-catching colors, floated effortless through the air. If only she could fly, she thought. Milky would look at her fat, worm-like body and wish things

191

could be different."

Shanti licked her lips. She felt like Milky. She hated who she was and wished she could fly away from the boss forever. What did Milky have to live for, except to eat and get fat?

"One day as Milky was munching, she felt very tired and decided to have a sleep. She couldn't be bothered climbing down the tree, so she curled her chubby body into a half circle, hanging suspended from the branch. Milky breathed deeply and went into a frenzy, spinning a cocoon to sleep in. The more she spun, the more tired she became. Finally Milky sighed deeply and slept. She slept for twelve long days."

Charlotte reached over and rubbed Shanti's arm before continuing. "Milky had to work really hard to open her eyes, they seemed heavy and glued to her face, but she knew she had to. When she finally opened them and discovered she was in a dark cocoon, she panicked and twisted her body to try and break free. Her body felt different, and she desperately wanted to escape her prison. As she struggled, she grew weary, and part of her said, 'What's the point, I'm just an ugly caterpillar whose life means nothing, and I will always crawl around the ground with dirt on my feet. I should just stay here and die.'"

"Charlie, she can't die, she needs to fight to get out." Shanti gripped Charlotte's shirt and twisted the material in her fingers.

"I agree, Shanti. It's important not to give up. Do you want to know what Milky does?" Charlotte asked.

Leaning forward Shanti nodded.

"Milky twists around in her tight prison, gasping for breath. The cocoon feels airless, and she knows she needs to take a grip of her emotions. She stretches and bends violently from side to side. She jerks her body and pushes with everything she has, to her breaking point. Finally there's a small tear in the skin of the cocoon, and a gush of fresh air pushes through. Something is feeling strange to Milky. As she stretches, she feels like she has wings—and she pushes with all her might, and the cocoon snaps open. She opens her eyes and hangs upside down off the branch. Her energy is sapped, but in one final enormous effort, she wiggles her body free. Do you know what happens then, Shanti?"

"No, no, what happens?" Shanti sat up, clapping her hands.

Charlotte twisted her head to look across at the sleeping women. She held her finger to her mouth and pointed.

"We need to whisper, we don't want to wake anyone."

"Please, Charlie, tell me what happens," Shanti begged.

Charlotte moved her shoulders and changed her position to sit on Shanti's mat. She leaned back against the wall with her arm around Shanti.

"As Milky moves her body, she realizes something has happened. Her body has changed, and she looks down at the crumpled fabric wrapped around her body and is confused. Oh dear, poor Milky feels something terrible has happened to her and that her body is now worse than before. Milky is so stunned; she hangs upside down for some time. She is no longer a slithering caterpillar that lives on the ground, but what is she? She starts to move and stretch, and the fabric wrapped around her spreads out. Milky gasps as she realizes she has beautiful wings the colors of a rainbow, attached to her body. It's a miracle, she thinks, how can this be?"

"Was it in the struggle that she'd grown wings that would make her soar in the sky like the other creatures she'd seen? Was it in the stretching and bending to break free of her prison that she'd become strong enough to fight for her freedom? Milky stretched her wings and flapped. The soft noise of her wings moving, encouraged her to let go of the branch. She took off, flying, twirling, and dancing in the gentle breeze. She was beautiful, free, loved—there was a creator who had a bigger plan for her, bigger than she could ever imagine. She soared and longed to tell others of her transformation. It became her life's goal to help others break free from living on the forest floor, when all along they had been destined to fly in the sky."

Tears streamed down Shanti's face and she gulped. Could God have a plan to make her into a beautiful butterfly like Milky?

She turned her head into Charlotte's shoulder and snuggled close, embracing her friend. She felt warm all over.

Tentatively she looked up and smiled. "That story is about us, isn't it, Charlie? We're not to give up, and we need to fight like Milky."

"Yes, sweetheart. It's not about giving up, but about not giving in to the evil that is here. Our job is to hold onto our faith, pray, and not let our minds become infected with hopelessness or death. I know the boss does terrible things to you, I wish I could stop him. He can only destroy you if you let him get hold of your mind and heart. Does that make sense?"

"I think so. But how do I—" Shanti paused and then decided she trusted Charlie enough to share the truth with her.

She moved back a fraction and pulled up her top to show Charlotte the cuts on her stomach.

Charlotte gasped at the sight of many slivers of crusting cuts across the expanse of Shanti's skin. "Oh, Shanti. I'm so sorry, I never knew. Does he always cut you?"

She'd shown Charlie the cuts, and Charlie hadn't said she was bad.

Shanti nodded and smiled. "I think I know what to do now, I will simply tell Jesus to help me be strong and grow me into a beautiful butterfly. I will imagine myself flying like Milky."

Charlotte touched Shanti's face. "That's the way. Do you think you can go back to sleep now?"

Shanti nodded but felt to excited to sleep. She lay down and let Charlotte move.

"I'm going to check on Gargi. Come and knock on the door if you need me, okay?"

"Thank you, Charlie. I love you." She threw her arms around Charlotte's neck and clung on tight.

"I love you too, Shanti. Very much. We'll get out of here, you just wait and see."

~~~

She'd been looking after Gargi for two days. Charlotte's tension eased as she felt Gargi's forehead. She wasn't as hot. She gently touched her friend's arm, and her eyes welled with tears as she thought of the ordeal Gargi had lived through. Her mouth moved silently as she prayed.

Lord, thank you that Gargi seems to be getting better. Help her come to grips with losing her child. Please give me the words to comfort her.

Charlotte stood and moved away from the bed, her mind awhirl. So much had happened since she'd arrived in India.

Sighing, she glanced back at Gargi and wondered what her life had been like before she became a sex slave. Charlotte's mouth tightened as she pondered. Were all prostitutes slaves? Did any woman willingly sell her body for money? She doubted it. Some may pretend it was what they wanted to do, but surely deep down in their hearts, a part of them must die each time they were subjected to a stranger's lust.

Charlotte's hands began to shake, and she gripped them to her chest. What if she got pregnant? Dropping to her knees, she closed her eyes and tried to push the thoughts out of her mind.

Lord, Paul said he'd learned to be content in every circumstance, he claimed he could do everything in your strength. I hate what happens here, everything in me wants out! Help me to believe you're here with me. You are here, aren't you, Lord? I talk to Shanti about you as if I'm certain, yet I feel so weak.

"Charlie?" Gargi's voice was husky and small.

Clambering up off her knees, Charlotte bent over her Gargi. "Hello, welcome back, my friend. Can you sit up? I'll help you drink." Charlotte reached over and placed her arm around Gargi's back and brought a cup of water to her lips.

Gargi swallowed slowly and nodded she'd had enough.

Charlotte fussed around, smoothing her bed sheet and tidying the bed. When Gargi reached out and grabbed her arm, she stopped. Her mouth tightened at the look in Gargi's eyes.

"I'm sorry, Gargi, your baby didn't make it." She watched helplessly as tears streamed from Gargi's eyes. Charlotte licked her dry lips and continued. "Your child is now in the arms of Jesus. He will hold her until you join him."

"They killed my baby?" Gargi's knuckles turned white as she grasped Charlotte's arm in a tight grip.

"I'm sorry." Charlotte bowed her head.

Gargi's hands went to her flat stomach as she searched in vain for her child. "My baby," she shrieked.

The naked pain in her scream pieced Charlotte's heart like an arrow inflicting a physical wound.

Gargi struggled to pull herself up, and Charlotte quickly went to her aid.

"You must rest, Gargi. Get your strength back," Charlotte soothed.

"Why? What have I to live for now?" Her head hung down in defeat, and her shoulders shook as sobs racked her thin body.

Charlotte didn't try to stop her tears; she clasped Gargi's hands and allowed herself to grieve with her friend. Moments went by and neither of them spoke.

Charlotte drew a breath. "There are others here who need your love, Gargi. What about Shanti? She has no one, except us—we need to be her family." Charlotte freed Gargi's hand and rubbed at the pulse thumping in her neck. "I need you Gargi. I love you, please help me survive this place," she whispered.

Gargi stared blankly into space, her hands limp by her sides. All life seemed to drain from her, and Charlotte panicked.

Wrapping her hands around Gargi's shoulders, she shook her firmly. "Don't you do this, Gargi. Do you hear me? You will not leave me!" Her voice wobbled with emotion and her arms tightened.

Gargi turned her face away and closed her eyes. Slowly she circled her hands around Charlotte's waist. She rested her head on Charlotte's shoulder and allowed her body to be gently rocked like a child.

~~~

Phillip tapped his foot in a harsh beat as he waited for Eli to answer the phone. He'd left calling as long as possible to allow for the time difference between India and Australia, but he couldn't wait any longer.

"Hello," Eli answered groggily.

"Eli, it's Phillip. I think I've found her, well, I'm not sure exactly, but I think I heard her voice. I tried to go back and see if it was her but got hustled out of the place."

"Are you serious? Where, when?" Phillip heard Eli shuffle and imagined him sitting up in bed.

"I was taken in a car at night, about two hours' drive from here. I don't want to get your hopes up, but can you organize to get back here, as soon as possible, and get us as much prayer cover as you can." The line crackled, and Phillip moved across the room, closer to the window.

"Phillip, I don't know what you've been doing to be in a place where Charlie might be, and I don't care. Man, if it's her, I'll owe you big-time."

"Thing is, I don't know when they'll come for me again."

"I've already booked my flight. Unbelievable, I just get here and then I get two leads. You're sure, Phillip?"

"No, not at all. Look, stay there if you like, I can get someone else to trail me in a car. Not sure how to get her out, if it is her. Leave it a couple of days, and I'll see if they contact me and call you back."

"I need to tell you about a call I got yesterday." Eli explained Ted's call to Phillip, and Phillip swallowed as a thick lump rose in his throat. He tried not to imagine Charlie with three men.

"If I go to these guys, Eli, and end up at the same place where I think I heard Charlie, they will recognize me and blow my chances of getting to her," Phillip explained.

"You're right. Today's Wednesday, I'll be back by Monday next week. I'll phone Ted and ask him if he could talk to these guys? Pretend interest."

Phillip leaned his weight on his hand as he looked out the window. He listened to Eli tell him about how his parents were and his decision to stop them from travelling to India. He explained that he didn't want to worry about them, as well as whatever else happened.

"Where's Ashok?" Eli asked.

"He's here. I found him asleep on my doorstep the night I got back from the brothel. The boy's bone weary and has a chill. He misses you."

"I can't wait to see him." Eli cleared his throat. "I miss the little guy."

Something about the way Eli said the words lifted Phillip's spirits. The children here had a way of capturing your heart. Their big chocolate eyes and courageous spirits.

He thought of the care he'd seen between Ashok and Bashaar, both boys making the most of what life had dealt them. Phillip knew India was in his blood, he wondered if Eli would be able to walk away once all this was over.

Chapter 32

The sound of people arriving set Macy's heart pounding. How had she been talked into this? Not only had Bill convinced her they needed to let Eli return to India on his own, here she was ready to talk to one hundred teenagers about trusting in God.

Her eyes widened as she watched the girls file into the hall, followed by many adults. Macy sucked in a deep breath as her eyes sought Pamela's.

Pamela smiled and moved to stand beside her. "I'm sorry, Macy. Word got out that you're sharing tonight, and it looks like you've drawn a crowd." Pamela patted her shoulder and leaned forward to whisper a quick prayer for Macy to relax and trust God.

What a joke. Here she was about to speak about trusting God, and fear strangled her, threatening to take all her carefully prepared words from her.

She watched spellbound as Pamela welcomed everyone and thanked them all for coming. There must be at least three hundred people. All looking expectantly at her for some inspired word.

Macy gripped her hands together and inhaled deeply. She wanted to run to the bathroom and vomit.

A verse she'd memorized with Charlotte came to mind, and she whispered the words softly. "I can do everything through him who gives me strength." She could hear Charlie singing the words, over and over again.

Charlie had always been memorizing Scripture. Macy bowed her head as the precious memory touched her heart.

Squaring her shoulders, she looked up and imagined her daughter standing at the back of the hall. She'd be honest and share the difficulty she had trusting in Jesus. She'd explain how she had to get to the end of herself and rely totally on the word of God.

Jesus promised to never leave her or forsake her; he waited patiently for her to lean into him. She truly believed God would get her through anything—give her what she needed to handle every situation.

She believed Jesus was with Charlotte, empowering her to survive.

When life presses in, when pain becomes unbearable, that's when you need to tell yourself God is with you and has a plan.

You may not see it, you may feel everything is out of control—but you have to take captive every thought and believe that God is bigger, and true to his promises.

She'd tell them to hold onto Second Corinthians four, verse eighteen, 'Therefore we do not lose heart. Though outwardly we are wasting away, yet inwardly we are being renewed day by day. For our light and momentary troubles are achieving for us an eternal glory that far outweighs them all. So we fix our eyes not on what is seen, but on what is unseen. For what is seen is temporary, but what is unseen is eternal.'

Macy stepped forward to the sound of clapping and smiled confidently.

~~~

"How'd it go?" Bill asked. He'd been anxious for Macy to get home.

"Better than I expected. The hall was packed."

"You're kidding. You mean, I could have come?"

Macy's eyes twinkled as she dropped down into a lounge chair, leaning her head back.

Bill smiled at the picture she made. He loved her. Always had, always would.

He closed his eyes to relax in the peaceful silence that often surrounded them. That's one of the things he loved most about Macy, she didn't need to fill every space with words.

"Bill, what would it be like if Charlie didn't come—home?"

"Don't say that, honey. We need to believe God will return her to us." He couldn't visualize his life without Charlie in it. How could he get up each day knowing he'd never see her again?

"I think we need to release her totally to God. He is God, after all. As I was speaking tonight, I thought about how my prayers for her have been conditional. More or less, me demanding God return her to me."

"What's wrong with that? God understands that we want her back home, safe with us. What parent wouldn't pray such a prayer?" Bill sat up, no longer relaxed, his jaw tightening.

"All I'm saying is, I always look at the now, not the big picture. You know we've always believed God has a special plan for Charlie."

Bill clapped his hand down on his knee, the noise causing Macy to jump.

"You can't believe that being missing, maybe in a brothel, is God's plan for Charlie. No way, Macy. I won't believe that for a minute!" He sounded tense and irritable to his own ears. Bill sucked in a breath and tried to relax.

"Of course not. I'm not saying it's God's fault that she's missing. We live in a fallen world and bad things happen. I know our little girl is making a difference wherever she is. Even if she . . . dies—and we have to prepare ourselves for that, Bill." Macy massaged a spot on her forehead. "Even if we never see her again, we have to hold onto the truth that we will embrace her again in heaven."

"I won't listen to you talking like this, Macy. You may need to prepare yourself for Charlie to be dead, but I refuse to." Bill jumped to his feet and stormed out of the room.

~~~

She couldn't get Gargi to eat. Charlotte chewed on the inside of her lip, and a frown furrowed her forehead. Her friend needed a doctor. She couldn't stand by and watch her die, even if it meant begging Saul to show compassion.

Charlotte lifted her chin and charged down the hall in search of the giant man, who puzzled her with his contrasting behavior.

She saw him with two other men leaving through the compound doors.

"Saul," she shouted, "wait, please." She ran to catch up with him.

He turned at the sound of her voice, nodded, and motioned for his companions to continue without him. Then he crossed his arms over his chest and stood waiting.

"Gargi needs a doctor. Her temperature is going up, and she's not eating. She needs to be on medication to stop the infection," Charlotte told him urgently.

Saul shrugged and turned to go.

Charlotte grabbed his arm. "No, you need to listen to me. If you don't get her help, she'll die, and her blood will be on your hands."

"You think that worries me, angel girl? I will get the doctor back, but not because you tell me to, because she is money to us." His eyes darkened as he looked down at her hand clutching his arm.

Stepping back Charlotte removed her hand. "Thank you, Saul."

He yanked her off her feet and pulled her face close to his face. She could taste the staleness of his breath, and wiggled to get free. Funny, she thought, he no longer frightened her.

"Stop calling me that! The next time I hear that word coming out of your mouth, I will make you swallow your tongue—hear me good, Charlotte," he sneered.

"Why? Does the name remind you of a time when you had hope

in your heart?"

He threw her to the floor and hissed at her. "Get back to Gargi. You have another hour before your customers arrive. When you've finished with them, return to Gargi, and the doctor should be there."

"Thank you—Saul," she said as she spun on her heels and dashed down the hall, a gurgle of laughter escaping her lips.

She turned before entering Gargi's room and looked back at him. The slight twitching of Saul's lips caused hope to bubbled inside her. She lifted her hand and waved at him, her eyes misting with tears at all God could do in a man like Saul.

~~~

She'd never get used to this. Charlotte's shivered as she thought of the night she'd had. She'd tried to engage some of the men in conversations, but they didn't want to hear her voice, they just wanted to use her body.

Charlotte frowned as she thought of their blank faces. Each man, blending into the other. Nameless, walking shadows, claiming what wasn't theirs.

Tonight there'd been twenty men. She wanted to shrivel up inside at what they'd done to her. How could anyone survive without the strength of the Lord?

Closing her eyes, she leaned against the wall outside Gargi's room. Her mind searched for reassurance, something to hold onto as her body begged for escape.

She'd heard a girl moaning in the bathroom yesterday as she urinated. Charlotte had studied sexually transmitted disease in depth back home and wasn't blind to the symptoms she saw around her. How long before she too contracted chlamydia or herpes? Her skin crawled and itched at the thought of crabs on her body.

Her eyes snapped open and she pushed away from the wall. A Bible verse pushed through the images trying to discourage her. Her lips moved silently as she spoke the words to her soul. *You intended to harm me, but God intended it for good to accomplish what is now being done, the saving of many lives.*

She marveled at the words and clutched her hands together. Could God use her here, to save many lives? Is that what he wanted from her?

She wearily opened Gargi's door and moved to the bed.

Her friend's forehead was on fire. Charlotte pulled the sheet off her and gasped at the sight of blood seeping through Gargi's gown.

Gargi's eyes opened and locked with Charlotte's. She hastily looked away, averting her head to the wall.

"Gargi, what have you done to yourself?" Charlotte asked. She gently lifted the gown from Gargi's stomach and she gasped at what she saw.

Claw like marks lined her skin. It looked like she'd been attacked by a large cat. Could Gargi have done this to herself?

Charlotte's hand gently cupped Gargi's cheek and turned her face. "It's okay, I'm here. Please don't do this to yourself, you need to fight, your life matters."

"Only to you, Charlie. No one else has ever cared for me. My parents sold me to this place, when I was twelve. The money they received was more important to them than their youngest daughter."

"You have another Father, Gargi. One who knew you before you were born, he wove you together in a hidden place. Jesus loves you, wants to give you a new life."

"I don't understand what you're saying and I don't care. I'm better off dead. If this is my lot—" She sobbed.

Charlotte brushed a tear from her own cheek. "It's not, Gargi. Believe me, God has a plan for your life, and it's a good plan. You have to give yourself to him, my friend. Trust him. Can you do that?" she whispered.

"I'm scared to. If I believe what you say and give my useless life to him—what if he lets me down, like everyone else I've ever loved? How will I survive that?" Gargi's eyes widened.

"He won't let you down. God is faithful to his promises."

"How can you say that when you're a slave in a brothel?" Gargi mocked.

"I may be here physically, but my mind and spirit belong to Jesus. No one can take that from me. You may see me weary, abused, and beaten—but no one can defeat me. This life is harsh and unfair, but one day I'll have eternal life and spend eternity with Jesus. The decisions you make today impact how you spend eternity." Charlotte smiled and her heart lightened.

She gave a heavy sigh and her shoulders relaxed. Gargi had to make her own decision; all Charlotte had to do was love her, and God would do the rest.

She got busy washing her friend and finally sat back to close her eyes.

Her stomach rumbled, but she felt too tired to move. Food would have to come later.

At the sound of a soft knock, she turned her head toward the door. "Come in," Charlotte called.

Gargi turned her head to watch as Shanti walked in.

Shanti lowered her head and slipped to Charlotte's side. Her eyes warily moved to Gargi on the bed, and her hands fluttered nervously before she clasped them in front of her.

"Hello, sweetheart. Have you come to say hello to Gargi?" Charlotte asked.

Shanti nodded her head and tried to smile. "Hello, Gargi," she murmured.

Gargi stared at Shanti with blank eyes.

Charlotte pulled Shanti onto her lap and hugged her.

"The doctor is coming to see Gargi soon, Shanti, so I'll be staying here."

Shanti nodded again, and tears threatened to spill from her eyes. She ducked her head into Charlotte's shoulder, and Charlotte felt her shiver.

Pulling away slightly, Charlotte frowned. "What is it, Shanti?"

"I came to ask you and Gargi to pray for me. Boss called for me. I'm frightened he will cut me again. Please, Charlie, can't you stop him?"

Gargi struggled to sit up. "What do you mean, cut you?"

Shanti glanced at Charlotte and waited for her encouraging nod. She pulled up her sari and showed Gargi her scars, some fresh and others healing.

Gargi clasped her hand over her mouth and she cried out, "Come to me, child." She beckoned with outstretched arms.

Shanti's eyes widened at the invitation. She climbed down off Charlotte's knee and joined Gargi on the bed.

Tears filled Charlotte's eyes at the scene they made. Gargi looked like the mother she longed to be—embracing her child. Charlotte blinked several times to control her tears. She approached the bed, placed one hand on each of their shoulders, and bowed her head to pray.

"Lord Jesus, protect Shanti. Can you please give her strength and confidence to know you're with her. One more thing Lord, help us to escape this horrible place, amen."

"Amen." Shanti gave a shy smile. "Thanks, Charlie." She sprung to her feet and headed for the door. "See you in the morning," she said, closing the door softly behind her.

As Charlotte thought of the young girl's courage she felt her heart melt with love for her, Gargi eased herself down on the bed and stared at the ceiling.

Charlotte's eyes burned as she watched Gargi slip into an unsettled sleep. Slowly she too gave into the need to sleep and closed her eyes.

A noise in the hallway woke her, and she stood hastily as the door burst open.

Saul strode across to her, and she lowered her head to hide her sleepiness. She heard another man enter the room behind Saul, and kept her head low.

There was a shuffle and gasp as the other man dropped something. And then he spoke.

Heat burned Charlotte's body and it felt like her heart stopped beating. She felt frozen in time, and she covered her heart with her hand. Her mouth gaped open at the sound of his familiar voice, and she stared wide-eyed as Phillip's eyes met hers briefly.

He yawned and looked around the room with a bored expression on his face.

She watched, mouth agape, as he turned back to Saul.

Shock melted away from Charlotte as everything in the room returned to normal. Phillip was actually in the room with her, and a bubble of excitement entered her heart. She looked down to keep from exposing her hope.

"It's going to cost you more this time. I have medicine, and you interrupted my sleep."

Saul sneered at him and pointed to Charlotte. "The girl will get me when you're ready to leave. I'm sure a pocket full of fresh cash will help wake you up." Saul left them, and Charlotte stood dumbfounded as Phillip turned to her.

His eyes welled up, and his arms surrounded her in an urgent embrace.

"Charlie," he whispered. He gently touched her face and he kissed her forehead softly.

"Phillip, oh my gosh, Phillip—it's really you!"

He set her away from him, tears spilling down his face. He swiped at the moisture on his cheeks and sucked in a loud breath. He glanced at the bed and Charlotte saw a shadow of concern flash across his face.

"Hello," he said wearily. "I hear you aren't doing so well."

Gargi squinted and looked from Phillip to Charlotte, her eyebrows rising.

"I've brought you some medicine to help get the fever down." He reached over and opened his bag. As he examined Gargi his gaze kept swinging towards Charlotte and heat scorched her cheeks in response.

He placed a bottle of pills beside Gargi and smiled. "These should help."

Charlotte's eyes blurred as she watched him. Her heart pounded crazily in her chest, and she longed to ask him a thousand questions.

"Charlie, I don't have much time. Can we talk, over there?" He pointed to the corner of the room.

Smiling Charlotte joined him, and rested her hand on his arm. It seemed unbelievable that he was here. Hope fluttered in her heart at the thought of escape.

"Charlie, I have enough money to buy you out of this place. I've made an arrangement with one of the guards, but we have to go now, before that big dude comes back." He caught her hand and pulled her toward the door.

Charlotte tugged back and dug her heels into the floor. Everything in her wanted to go with him, to run and never look back, but her heart opposed her. So many things held her to this prison.

"Wait, Phillip. I can't leave," she said, her voice rising in pitch.

"What? Are you crazy?" He stammered, dropping her hand.

"I can't leave without Shanti, Gargi, and Padma." Her eyes pleaded with him to understand. Her heart pounded loudly in her ears, and she wished she could take his hand and run from here, never to return.

"Shanti's here?" His head dropped, and he raked a hand through his already tousled hair.

"You know her?" Charlotte asked in surprise.

"Yes. Her brother, Ashok, is staying with me. He's been helping Eli look for the both of you."

"Eli? He's here too?" Charlotte's shoulders shook, and she sucked in a sob.

"You're coming with me, Charlotte. Once I get you safe, we'll try and get the others." His voice was stern, as if talking to a child.

Shaking her head Charlotte looked across at Gargi. Her friend had swung her legs over the side of the bed. She beckoned her over.

"Gargi, be careful, you're not strong enough to get up."

"You must go with him, Charlie," she stated dully.

Charlotte's eyes blurred again, and she reached over and patted Gargi's hand. "Phillip, you must take Gargi. She's sick, and you have to help her."

"No. I won't leave you here," he exclaimed.

"You don't have a choice. I'm not leaving Shanti. She's only little, and I have to help her."

Phillip cupped her face with both his hands. His eyes pleaded with her, and something moved in Charlotte's heart.

"I promise you, Charlie. I'll come back for Shanti, Gargi, and your other friend. But right now I have to take you with me." He gently kissed her cheek, and his arms circled her body, drawing her close to his chest.

Charlotte's face heated and she felt dizzy with emotion. Her gaze locked with his, and the love she saw reflected there caused her breath to catch.

She blinked and tried to think, but her mind felt befuddled.

Slowly, she pulled out of his embrace. She tilted her head slightly and backed away.

Everything in her wanted to go with him, to get out now before the opportunity disappeared. Her eyes swam with tears, and dread weighed heavily on her shoulders.

"I'm sorry," she whispered. "I have to stay."

Phillip's face paled. "Charlie, think of your family. How can you do this?"

"I believe you'll come back for us, Phillip." She closed her eyes briefly before lifting her chin. "I'll help Gargi get ready."

"Where's Shanti now? Can you go and get her? Maybe we can take her with us, and then come back for Gargi and—

"No. Shanti's with the boss. You have to take Gargi. Maybe you could tell them you fear for her life and that unless she's hospitalized, she'll die or something," Charlotte said as she moved to Gargi.

Gargi grabbed Charlotte's hand, and tears welled up in her eyes.

"Charlie, you can't mean to stay here when you have an opportunity to get out," she stammered.

Charlotte squeezed Gargi's hand gently. "I love you, Gargi. Just promise me you'll think about how much Jesus loves you." Charlotte gave her a watery smile and glanced over her shoulder to Phillip, who hadn't moved.

"Please forgive me, Phillip," she uttered softly, her hand outstretched to him.

Phillip nodded and moved to her side. His forehead rested on hers, and he briefly closed his eyes. "Charlie, I want to tie you up and drag you out of here, but that won't work if you're going to fight me."

He took out his mobile phone and handed it to her. "It's fully charged, but keep it turned off to save the battery. It's on silent, and I'll only communicate through texts, that way no one will see you talking on it."

Charlotte gazed at the phone and the connection it gave her to him—and through him, to her family. Her hand shook, and she fought the desire to throw herself at him and beg him not to leave her.

She lowered her eyes to keep them from telling of her inner turmoil. She slipped the phone into her underwear as the door burst open and Scarface and another man entered.

Phillip reacted quickly and pushed Charlotte away and laughed. "Nice merchandise you have here, guys. Shame about this one though." He pointed at Gargi. "I'm taking her with me, she needs to be hospitalized if she's to live. Her fever's too high for medication to control, she needs to be on a intravenous pump."

"No, she stays," Scarface replied.

"Come on, man. The girl's going to die if you don't let me take her. It's one thing to earn dirty money, it's another to watch a person die."

"You need to harden up, Doctor. Think of her as an expendable chattel. People die every day."

"I'm a doctor. I can't let that happen." Phillip clenched his fists at his sides.

The other man laughed, clamping his hand on Phillip's arm in a vice like grip. "Time to go, Doctor. You want to save lives, go back to your mission clinic."

Phillip snarled and glared at Scarface. "All right, I'll buy her from you—or better still, not charge you for this visit or the next two times you need me to come out here. What do you say? She's not going to earn you any more money, and you would have to pay to get rid of her body. If I can get her well, she could become my own—" Phillip clapped his hands together in glee and laughed.

Charlotte shivered at Phillip's unspoken words. Even as a means to an end, she hated what they signified. That men could think this way disgusted her. The way Saul looked at her and Gargi as if they were nothing more than sexual toys angered her.

Scarface looked at the other man and shrugged. He moved to the bed and looked down at Gargi, who had her eyes closed and was breathing heavily. "Charlotte." He beckoned her, pointing to Gargi's sari. "What's this blood?"

Charlotte wanted to smile at Gargi's quick thinking. She moved towards her friend and bowed her head to Saul. "I've tried to stop the bleeding, Saul, but as you can see it's started up again."

He grunted and pushed Charlotte towards the door. "Get out. Don't come back to this room."

Stumbling Charlotte pulled herself up. She wanted to take one last look at Phillip but kept her eyes averted as she left the room.

Charlotte ran down the hall, needing to get as far away from her friends as possible before she broke down and cried.

She reached her mat and sunk to her knees, her shoulders heavy with pain. Fearful thoughts raced through her brain, bringing more anguish to her heart.

What if Phillip couldn't come back? What if she had to spend the rest of her life here? What if he didn't text, would that mean he hadn't been able to get away with Gargi?

She buried her head in her hands and tried to control the stream of questions that bombarded her mind.

Lord, help me think of other things.

The tingle that had become so familiar washed over her skin. *Whatever is true, whatever is noble, whatever is right, whatever is pure, whatever is lovely, whatever is admirable—if anything is excellent or praiseworthy—think about such things.*

Jesus, thank you for sending Phillip to look for me and to help Gargi get out of here. Silent tears drenched her hands, and her hair shielded her face. *Lord Jesus, I told him I wouldn't leave without Shanti and Padma, but what of the others? It's not fair that anyone is subjected to such a life.*

She blinked and sniffed as she turned over. She wiped her hand down her side and closed her eyes.

How many other girls were held captive in places like this? A foul taste filled her mouth at the cruelty of greed. Her soul ached as she pictured vulnerable young women being abducted and trafficked for money.

Chapter 33

The bustle of people in the noisy reception area of the hotel exacerbated Eli's headache. He sat watching people come and go, trying not to clench his jaw in frustration.

He glanced at his watch and stood to walk over to the window. Ted had said he'd meet him here an hour ago and still the guy hadn't shown up. He'd already tried his phone twice.

Maybe he should grab a room and leave a message at reception for Ted to call when he arrived. He'd come straight from the airport, and jet lag was setting in. He wearily rubbed his hand over his eyes and yawned.

"Eli, I'm sorry to keep you waiting."

Turning towards Ted, Eli's mouth twitched as he saw Ted's outstretched hand. With a slight pause, he remembered the last time he'd ignored Ted's hand.

You never know whom God places in your path. Shaking his head, he went with his gut instinct and grabbed the guy in a hard, brief hug.

Ted's surprise at the show of affection was visible on his face, and Eli smiled. "I was just about to put up camp in your reception area and have myself a little nap. Good to see you again, Ted."

"Come to my office, I'll get us some coffee." Ted picked up Eli's suitcase, turned, and led the way through the lobby to an office large enough to house a small family.

"Have you found out anything, Ted?"

"By the time I got your call, they'd all checked out. However, the chap who was bragging the most is a regular here. Seems he books in at least once a month, and the staff say he spends up large in the bar and frequents the local houses."

Eli wanted to slam his fist into something. They needed this lead to turn up something.

A pulse moved in his temple as he thought of the men who made brothels possible. Where was their dignity, respect? Anger swelled in his chest as he thought of Charlotte's name being tossed around like a dirty, used rag.

Where was his sister? *Lord, help me,* he screamed silently, seeing nothing but his hopelessness.

"He'll be back, Eli. We just have to be ready for him," Ted stated confidently.

"So what, we have three weeks to wait! I have to be honest with you, Ted, the waiting is—killing me." He swatted at a fly and screwed up his face in distaste.

"Yes, well—I can understand that. You look like a good sleep would do you the world of good. How about I arrange a room for you, and then you can crash?"

"I planned to bunk down at Phillip's apartment, but he's not answering his phone." Eli covered his mouth as another yawn escaped. "I'll leave him a message and take you up on that for tonight. Thanks."

~~~

Ashok played with the ring, twirling it round and round. He pulled his legs up under him on Dr. Phillip's couch, and a small smile twitched his lips. That the kind doctor would let him stay here on his own, trusting him with his things, made Ashok feel valued. The way he valued Shanti.

Did she still believe he'd find her? What would Shanti think of Dr. Phillip? Would she look at him through her long, dark lashes and smile?

A tear dribbled down his nose, and he sniffed. He wanted to hold her, kiss her face, and tell her he loved her more than anything else in the whole world.

Jesus, will I see her again? Will I be able to tell her one more time that I love her most?

Ashok bowed his head in shame. He thought of the times he heard of some person going missing on the street and how he'd told himself it was the way things were. Why was it that until it happened to you, you didn't feel sad for someone else's situation? You cared, but separated yourself from their misery.

Jesus, I'm sorry. Help me to feel for other people who are sad.

He sniffed again and stood up and moved around the room. He spotted a book sitting on a small table and went to look at it. It looked like the Bible Eli had shown him, but had a different color cover.

Carefully he picked it up and cradled it to his chest. Eli said God spoke to him through the Bible.

Ashok held it up to his ear and listened. He wished he could read, then maybe God would say something to him.

He sat cross-legged on the floor with the Bible resting on his knees. With hesitant fingers he opened the cover and touched the thin paper. It ruffled in his hand and he breathed in deep at the sight of so many words covering the pages.

Did God write them all? He leaned forward and sniffed the paper, liking the musty smell. He pulled out his old card and looked at it. The paper was stained and rubbed with much use.

He looked at the creases where he'd folded it numerous times. He couldn't read the words, but he knew Jesus loved him.

Tears flowed steadily down his cheeks and he squeezed his eyes closed tight. His shoulders shook and his lips trembled. If all he had was Jesus, would that be enough?

Nodding, Ashok's lips lifted in the beginning of a smile. "Jesus," he whispered in awe.

He lay on his side, hugging the Bible and his card. His knees came up, and he rocked.

Ashok was sure he could feel Jesus picking him up. He closed his eyes and allowed his mind to go with Jesus.

Jesus held his hand and led him to a raging river. They stood together and Ashok looked at the beauty of the water.

There were silver fish jumping at the edge closest to him, and the sun reflected their scales.

Ashok laughed.

Jesus's hand pointed across the large expand of water, to a girl running towards them.

Her hand waved joyfully in the air. Her face was split by the biggest smile, and her musical voice lifted in the breeze and floated across the river to him.

Shanti. He could see her, she looked different somehow, but beautiful. It was like her feet flew through the air towards them.

Ashok looked up at Jesus, and it was like he didn't need words.

Jesus loved him, loved Shanti.

He felt warmth invade his body, pushing out all the pain and fear, leaving in its place a promise. Joy bubbled inside him, tingling through his hands and feet.

He wanted to jump, skip, and dance. He laughed a deep, belly-shaking laugh and saw that Jesus was laughing too.

"Ashok, time for bed, boy."

Ashok's eyes snapped open, and he had to blink several times to see that it was Dr. Phillip who had picked him up.

"I—." His mind was still caught up with Jesus and he didn't want to leave the river, he wanted to wait there for Shanti to join them.

Sighing, he pushed his head into Dr. Phillip's chest and relaxed as he carried him to the bedroom. Dr. Phillip laid him on the bed, placed the Bible beside him, and pulled up the sheet to his face.

Ashok's eyes widened when the doctor leaned in and kissed his face.

"Sleep tight, we have a lot to talk about in the morning," Phillip ruffled his hair and left the room.

His heart beat steadily, and as his eyes eased closed he felt close to Shanti.

"Soon Shanti, soon," he whispered.

~~~

His apartment had only two bedrooms. He had a child in one room and a sick woman in the other.

Phillip ran a hand through his hair and rubbed his forehead wearily.

When Eli arrived, he could share the main bedroom with Ashok, and Phillip decided he'd sleep on the couch until they decided what to do with Gargi.

How had this happened? All his plans had been turned around on him, and now he had Gargi here and not Charlie.

Compassion for Gargi filled his heart. She'd not stopped crying since he lifted her and carried her to the car. Her eyes, pools of uncertainty and shock.

He didn't know what to do with her, he supposed he'd need to take her to hospital to authenticate his words, but he knew with proper care, food, and love she'd heal.

His mind slipped to Charlotte, and his mouth felt dry. How could he not have seen the truth earlier? What had blinded him to think women in the sex trade had a choice?

His jaw clenched as if the pain they experienced were his own. He'd believed he was better than them, and judged them as being stupid and foolish. He'd looked down on them and grouped them as hopeless.

He bit back a groan and lowered his head. "Jesus, forgive me. Help me to see all people through your eyes. Give me a chance to make it up to the women I've offended."

He pictured Charlotte as she'd asked him to forgive her. How could her face remain so open and trusting, after all she'd experienced?

If someone asked him what type of woman he wanted to marry, he'd say a woman who loved God. A woman who lived this love every day by caring for others.

Charlie had certainly demonstrated this tonight. She'd given up the chance of freedom for Gargi. Would he have been so generous, if it'd been him?

He could see the blinking light on the phone telling him he had a message. He pressed the button to hear Eli's voice saying he'd arrived and would be around in the morning.

Phillip grimaced at what he'd have to tell him. He still didn't know where Charlie was. The trip back had been the same as before; both he and Gargi had been blindfolded and squashed into the backseat between two men.

Gargi had collapsed into him, and he'd tried to support her body and act like he was okay with the way things had played out.

Now, in his apartment, he could see the darkness lifting through the blind and decided to grab a few hours' sleep while he could.

Shuffling around in his bedroom drawers, he found what he was looking for—a spare mobile phone. He plugged it into the power socket and slipped in a sim card.

As soon as the battery showed it had a bar of power, his finger went busy texting Charlie.

Gargi's safe. Eli's here, we'll get u out, hang on. His finger stopped for a moment and he frowned. *I won't stop until ur free. Charlie, I love you.* Phillip stared down at the words *Charlie, I love you,* and slowly deleted them.

As much as he longed to tell her, it was too soon. He didn't believe in love at first sight, or first fight. He smiled as he remembered her disdain at his rude attitude to her.

It was her Christ like spirit that drew him; even in the midst of uncertainly she leaned into Jesus and gave herself up for others.

His heart pounded at the confusion and deep despair he'd felt leaving her there. It was like ripping out his heart and tossing it to the dogs. Her eyes broke him.

Chapter 34

The soft bed was pure luxury. Gargi touched the fluffy pillow and longed to stay asleep. But too much had happened. She couldn't avoid thinking about Charlie any longer. She'd never met anyone like her. Even when she'd been nasty and continually ridiculing her, Charlie had demonstrated love.

It had been when Charlie's hands massaged her back and feet as her pregnancy progressed that things had begun to change for Gargi.

Charlie's touch had begun to soften her heart. No one had ever shown her what it was like to be cared for.

Gargi licked her lips and longed for a glass of water; her thirst made her restless.

Most of her life had been about survival, doing what she had to, to get by. She'd developed a hard, bitter mindset and didn't care who she hurt, as long as she was okay.

But the thing was, she wasn't okay and never had been. Her hand went to her heart, and she pressed the ache inside her chest.

Charlie had told her about Jesus, but she found it too incredible to believe. She'd seen families sacrifice their children for monetary gain, but Charlie told her God loved the world so much that he gave his one and only Son, Jesus, to pay the penalty for her sin. That he died in her place.

Gargi pounded her fist into her pillow, her thoughts tormenting her.

She'd never had faith in anything. She remembered her mother talking about a state of being free from suffering and the continuing cycle of birth, life, and rebirth. Gargi had loved her mother as only a child could. She'd trusted her and tried to please her.

She bent over in pain as a deep sob rose from her soul. Had her mother never loved her? Tears streamed down her face unchecked. Gargi hugged her body and she rocked, trying to find comfort from the anguish in her heart.

She tried to picture her mother's face and longed for a time to surface in her mind when there was a good memory. A tremor moved through her body, and she stopped rocking.

No one had ever cared for her, not until Charlie. Gargi pulled her hair as she realized she'd become just like her mother: uncaring, hard, and selfish. She felt lost, caught up in all the bad things that had happened to her, and unable to find a way out of the darkness in her mind.

Gargi chewed her lower lip, trying to remember what Charlie had said about being lost. Her eyes widened as she recalled Charlie's words.

God didn't want anyone to be lost and spend an eternity separated from him. That's why, Charlie said, anyone who believes in Jesus can have eternal life. A life that lives forever.

Sitting up slowly Gargi let her legs dangle over the side of the bed. Her heart raced and her head thumped with a headache. She'd cried so much last night that her eyes felt beyond recognition.

She'd loved her baby and hadn't even got to hold it. If she'd loved the little life that grew inside her that much, how much more must God love her?

A deep frown creased her brow. How could he let his Son die like that?

Her heavy sigh broke the silence in the room, and she wished Charlie were there to help her understand.

She braced herself and stood, leaning on the bed. As blood pumped through her body, she wobbled on her feet. Moving a hand through her hair, she tried to smooth the thick, dark mass to some semblance of order.

Her mouth formed an *O* as she pictured Charlie's eyes boring into her soul.

Charlie could have escaped the brothel—but she'd made Dr. Phillip take her instead. She'd chosen to stay, in her place.

The truth struck her like a slap across the face. Charlie was copying what Jesus had taught her. She was prepared to give up her freedom for my release, Gargi thought in disbelief.

An anguished sob slipped through her lips, and she fell to her knees.

Jesus, your Father didn't make you die, did he? You chose to, to save me. You love me—that much. Oh, God—I'm so sorry for being so selfish, for all the people I've hated and hurt. Help me love you like Charlie does. I give you my—my—life, I want to live for you too. You released me from prison, but it's the prison inside my mind I want freedom from. Help me to know the truth and to trust in you.

An alluring smell made her stomach rumble, and she felt hungry for the first time in days. It felt like the physical bands across her chest had been removed and the tightness had gone.

She released a breath she hadn't known she'd been holding and felt like laughing.

With tentative steps she moved to the door and slipped out of the room. She found Dr. Phillip and a small boy busy cooking in a tiny kitchen.

Gargi felt speechless. She'd never spoken to a man in any context, except sex. She wanted to go and hide.

Phillip started placing plates of cooked food on the table. "Morning, Gargi. You're just in time for breakfast. This is Ashok. I told him we had a guest staying with us."

Her eyes widened at the sight of Shanti's brother, and she wanted to span the distance between them and hug him.

Such an alien feeling, this loving. She lowered her eyes to hide her emotion.

Phillip pulled out a chair. "Come, join us."

"Thank you," she murmured softly, her skin heating at his kindness.

She could feel Ashok looking at her, and her eyes watered as they locked on his.

The shape of his eyes and nose were the same as little Shanti's. She stared at him openly, taking in his gentle face and large grin.

If Ashok felt uncomfortable by her scrutiny, he didn't show it. He dove into his food with full concentration and seemed to savor every mouthful.

A shadow flicked over her heart as she thought about her own lost child. Would she be able to carry another child? Was her body so damaged by the murder of her baby that no child would survive in her womb?

She'd have to gather the courage to ask Dr. Phillip. A pulse beat in her neck at the thought of never being able to be a mother, and her eyes greedily returned to Ashok.

Phillip wiped his mouth and smiled at her. "You look much better this morning, Gargi. I thought we'd wait to have a chat about what's happened until my friend arrives. Tuck in."

"Tuck in?" Her eyes widened in question

"That means eat." Ashok giggled and took another bite.

Phillip laughed at the face Ashok made and reached over to pick up a piece of toast from the plate in the middle of the table.

When they'd all cleared away the dishes, Gargi felt her strength ebbing. She looked around for somewhere to sit, before she fell down.

A hand took her arm and gently pulled her towards another room. "Miss. Gargi, please come and rest. You sit for a while." Ashok's face showed concern, and she tried to smile.

"Thank you, Ashok." Gargi gave him a quick hug before she slid into a large chair.

Phillip followed them into the lounge and sat across from her; he looked at his watch and glanced at the front door.

Gargi wondered whom he was expecting. She leaned back wearily, thankful she could just sit here without any demands on her. It was like she could feel the strength being drained from her body.

A loud banging on the door made her jump, and she sat to attention, scanning the room for an escape route.

"Ashok, I think the door is for you," Phillip stated lazily, spreading his legs out before him and crossing his ankles.

Ashok sprung up, raced to the door, and flung it open.

He stood transfixed. His mouth gaped open, and his arms hung floppy by his sides.

Gargi twisted in her seat to see who was there, and the sight of the tall, blond man startled her. He had to be Charlie's brother; the coloring was the same, yet that's where the familiarity stopped. He was masculine and commanded attention.

She sat further back in her seat and chewed her bottom lip. What would he say when he knew Phillip had saved her and left Charlie? Fear chiseled her chest, and she had difficulty breathing.

"Eli!" Ashok's arms moved quickly, and he jumped up and down.

Laughing Eli pulled Ashok into his arms, and swung him around in a secure grip. Gargi watched in surprise as the big man swallowed the little boy in an embrace, and her heart softened towards him.

"How have you been, my little friend?" Eli asked, his eyes sparkling with unshed tears.

Gargi wondered at a man who showed emotions so readily. She looked across at Dr. Phillip, who now stood and watched the scene play out with a smile on his face.

Eli put Ashok down, pulled his suitcase behind him, and looked across the room.

Gargi watched as his eyes widened slightly when he spotted her. She struggled to stand and swayed with a moment of dizziness.

Eli reached out to steady her, and the concern she saw reflected in his eyes made her shake.

"Hello," he said gently. "Are you okay?"

She glanced at Dr. Phillip to see what he would say, and nodded solemnly.

"Eli," Dr. Phillip said, "welcome back, my friend. This is Gargi, she's staying here for a few days. Come and sit down, and we'll tell you and Ashok what we've been up to."

Gargi glanced up at Eli and allowed him to help her back into the chair. He seemed to realize she was unwell, and his body language assured her she was safe here. Her heart thudded, and she wished she could be anywhere but here when he heard the news.

"Well, boys, Gargi and I have some good news," Phillip said, sounding excited.

Ashok moved to sit by Eli, and his hand got lost in Eli's large one.

Gargi wondered what it would be like to have a large hand like that hold hers in encouragement. She looked up and saw Eli gazing at her. Her lips curved slightly and lowered her head.

"Gargi is Charlie's friend. Last night I was called back to the place I told you about, and saw Charlie."

"You actually saw her? She's alive?" Tears of relief spilled down Eli's cheeks.

"Yes, I spoke to her. You'd be very proud of her, Eli. She refused to come with me because she couldn't get to Shanti. We only had a small window of time, so she helped me get Gargi out," Phillip explained.

"My sister is with your Charlie, Eli!" Ashok uttered through his tears. "Praise to Jesus for looking after my Shanti."

Gargi's lips tightened as she tried to hide her distress at Ashok's words. Charlotte was unable to protect Shanti from the boss. Gargi shuddered as she thought of Shanti's cuts and burns.

Eli wiped his face and moved to hunch in front of Gargi's chair. "You were with her? Are you all right?" His hand rested softly on her arm, and Gargi sucked in a breath.

His eyes bore into hers with questions, and she felt heat rise up her neck at the thought of being interrogated by him.

How could she tell them that they may never get Charlie out? She tried to speak, but her voice sounded gruff to her ears. She stopped and shook her head. It was all too much, and she looked across at Dr. Phillip in desperation.

"Gargi's been unwell. I think she's had enough excitement for now."

"Yes, of course." Eli stood and offered her a hand. "We can talk later. You don't know how good it makes me feel to see you. To know that Phillip was able to help you escape. God will help us rescue Charlie and Shanti too."

Gargi felt suffocated by the hope she saw in his eyes. She wanted to believe in Jesus, she really did. But hadn't Charlie believed all this time and still had to endure the abuse?

Doubt of ever seeing her friend again brought tears to her eyes.

~~~

"Ashok, can you go to the market and get us some bread?" Phillip asked with a smile. He pulled out some notes and placed them into Ashok's outstretched hand. "Be sure to buy yourself something with the change, okay?"

"Thank you, Dr. Phillip. Maybe I can find something nice for Shanti." His grin was so wide, Eli could see all his teeth.

"In that case, you might need some more money. Here." Eli scrunched up a few notes and pushed them into Ashok's hand.

Ashok threw his arms around Eli's neck and clung to him. Laughing, the boy pulled away and dashed across the room and out the door.

The two men stood silently as the door closed behind Ashok.

Eli turned to his friend and frowned, his gut churned with tension. Seeing Gargi's condition made him more conscious of the need to get to Charlie. How could they wait three weeks in the hope that the lead from the hotel would pan out?

"I think you'd better bring me up-to-date. How about you make me some of that terrible coffee of yours, and we can spend some time praying and planning."

Eli's heart ached as he heard of Charlie's concern for her friends. He still saw her as his little sister who needed rescuing. Yet she'd sacrificed her chance of freedom for Gargi. She wasn't a child anymore, but a woman who made her own decisions.

Had she always been more mature in her faith than he'd thought? He remembered laughing at her when she was thirteen, telling her she was being too reflective.

She'd been standing looking out the rain-splattered lounge window as a storm rolled in. Her face had always been so expressive, and he'd asked her what she was thinking.

"Life changes constantly, seasons come and go, and we can do nothing about it. I think God wants us to learn from the seasons, don't you, Eli?"

"Sure, Bud. You put on a coat in winter and swimmers in the summer," he'd answered.

"I mean on the inside of us." She'd frowned. "No matter what happens in my life, I want to remember that it's not about me. Like when Grandpa died. I was sad until I remembered he was now home with Jesus."

Eli eyes smarted and he rubbed them. Clearing his throat, he straightened his shoulders and focused on Phillip. "Good thinking about giving Charlie the phone, mate. Can I text her?"

"Of course. Maybe you could get your parents to as well. It would encourage her to know we're all believing that she'll be free soon," Phillip answered.

"Mmm. I'll give Dad a call and pass on the number. They have to realize though, that she may not be able to text them back. If she gets caught with the phone, we could lose all hope of getting her out."

Eli scratched his neck as he felt heat burn his skin. He wanted to phone Charlie and tell her he was sorry, sorry he'd let her down.

He scowled at the thought. He'd dealt with his guilt for not going to India with her. Jesus had forgiven him, and he'd thought he'd forgiven himself.

Obviously it was something that the devil wanted to use to attack him. He'd have to be more diligent in what he allowed himself to think. He was no good to Charlie wallowing in self-pity and forgiven guilt.

"So, as I see it Eli, we now have two ways of finding her. One, your friend Ted's going to call as soon as our guy makes a reservation, or two, we wait for them to contact me again."

"Do we involve the police, or do you think they'll sabotage the whole thing?" Eli gripped his knees as he leaned forward. The thought of other women, like Gargi, being in the same situation as Charlie concerned him. "How can we get Charlie and Shanti out and leave others behind?"

"I know what you mean. I wanted to force Charlie to come with me. Even Gargi was encouraging Charlie to listen to me and escape while she could."

"Gargi's eyes are so vulnerable. What they did to her was inhuman. Do you think she's going to be all right, Phillip?" Eli's shoulders burned with tension as he thought of Charlie going through a similar nightmare.

Could his beautiful, innocent sister be pregnant? What if they didn't find her and she got sick?

The vision of Charlie being attacked with a knife caused him to squeeze his eyes shut and suck in a deep breath.

Phillip's voice pulled him out of the horror of his thoughts.

"Gargi will recover physically, but the poor girl will never have another child. Only Jesus can heal her from such trauma. She'll need support to work through what's happened. Charlie will too."

Eli's gaze locked with Phillip's, and they stared at each other. Eli gritted his teeth and broke eye contact. He looked down at his hands and sighed. Getting the girls out was just the beginning; they would need support to—to what? Forgive.

His heart rate increased at the thought of Gargi's innocent baby being sacrificed to the knife, by uncaring hands.

They weren't the only ones who would have to work through forgiveness. His mouth tightened, and he felt an ache in his stomach.

His precious sister, his little Bud. What scars would she be carrying? If he could get his hands on anyone who'd hurt her, he knew he'd need God's strength to stop him from retaliating with violence.

"We have to work out a way to get in, get Charlie and Shanti to safety, and have the police raid the place," Phillip stated.

Eli nodded. He had a foul taste in his mouth, and his heart darkened at the danger they were stepping into.

Chapter 35

Blood oozed steadily from her wrist. Shanti stared at the pool of red gooey substance seeping onto the boss's floor and thought of moving her finger through it.

She felt disconnected from the pain and separate from her body as if flying high above the mountains on wings of silk. She could look down on herself and wondered if today was the day all her blood would drain from her body and she'd die.

She closed her eyes and tried to think about flying away, never to return. Even though she was lying on the floor it felt like her body was swaying slightly.

The kick in her back snapped her eyes open.

"Get up, go to Padma," the boss ordered.

Shanti stared at him. She didn't have the energy to move, and part of her wanted to see what he'd do if she ignored him.

She buckled over as his foot connected again with her back, and she pulled herself up on her knees.

Glancing at him through her lashes she watched as he moved away from her. As she noticed the knife he'd left on the floor, within reach of her fingers, she squinted.

He spun around and watched her, a wide, evil smile on his face, as if he wanted her to pick it up.

Slowly she stood and staggered from the room. She wouldn't go to Padma, she'd go and lie on her mat; and if she died, then Ashok would understand that she couldn't hold on any longer.

Her legs felt weak and Shanti had to concentrate on each step. She staggered into the common room.

Shanti heard the murmurs of concern some of the girls offered, but she couldn't make out their words.

Collapsing into a ball on her mat, she closed her eyes and sighed. *Jesus, could you come get me? I'm tired; I don't want to stay here anymore—please.*

"Shanti, can you show us how to play the game you play with the stones?" a girl asked.

Rolling over Shanti opened her eyes. She blinked as she saw three girls hunched down beside her. There was a time when she didn't want anything to do with the other girls here. She'd believed the only way to get through another day was to hide within herself and not talk, but Charlie had taught her how much they needed each other.

A glimmer of a smile lifted her lips as she looked at them.

"Oh, look at her arms. Come, let us help you, Shanti."

~~~

Charlie hunched down beside the toilet and pulled out the phone. Her heart sped up as she saw she had four texts. She scanned the words of the first text from her mother.

Charlie, I love you. The whole church is praying for your release. We will see you again soon! Take heart sweetheart, xxx Mum.

Squeezing her eyes tight she held the phone to her chest—Mum. Her shoulders shook as she silently cried. Tears streamed down her cheeks, wetting her neck. Taking a deep breath, she checked the next text.

Bud, I'm with Phillip. Smile out loud! God's on our side, we will get you out. Believe. Eli.

Her lips twitched slightly as she remembered the standing joke between them. *Smile out loud* was his way of saying laugh often. Hope gurgled in her throat and she chuckled. The next text was from her father.

Charlie, he can see you, believing for a miracle sweetheart. Love you—Dad.

Her lips widened as her father's voice hummed in her head. *"Charlotte Rose, he can see you. Reach out to him, sweet pea, and let his love surround you."* Her father's gentle words had echoed through her childhood, encouraging her, challenging her, and prompting her to believe.

Jesus, I know you're here with me. Hold me. I do believe, I do.

The shuffling noise at the door caused her to quickly hide the phone in her sari and scurry to her feet. She wiped her face with her hand, opened the door, and startled the woman entering the toilet.

"Sorry," she said as she hurried towards the common room. She'd try and read the last text under her blanket later.

Her lips twitched at how excited she felt. Mentally she made a plan on what she had to do to help the escape go smoothly. She'd have to tell Padma about Phillip and the plans she had made with him to escape.

She hesitated when she entered the room; something was wrong. The silence sent a chill down her spine.

Two girls squatted beside Shanti's mat, and one of them held Shanti's hand.

Charlotte raced across the room and peered into Shanti's pale face.

"What's happened?" she whispered.

"The boss cut her wrists. Charlie, she's lost a lot of blood," the young girl cried.

Charlotte's fingers feathered Shanti's face and she glanced at the rough, bloodstained bandages.

Her face heated in anger and her mouth tightened. "She's still bleeding. Who saw to her?"

The girls shrugged and looked across the room. Charlotte turned and saw Padma watching her. Charlotte motioned for Padma to come over.

Padma turned and left the room.

Charlotte's mouth dropped open in surprise, and tears welled up in her eyes.

"Come, girls. Pray with me," Charlotte commanded. She grabbed their hands and squeezed tightly. "Lord Jesus, Shanti needs your help. She's only little, please stop the bleeding and seal up her cuts, in Jesus's name, I pray." Her eyes snapped open and she released the girls' hands.

She smiled her encouragement and gently picked up one of Shanti's hands. As she unwrapped the soiled cloth, she frowned. Usually Padma was so kind and careful in how she looked after the girls.

Why had Padma not seen to Shanti's wounds herself? The deep cut stretched almost two inches and was still gaping open. She needed stitches.

"Go wash your hands, girls, and get back here quickly for me," Charlotte said calmly.

She lifted both Shanti's hands and held them elevated. She scanned Shanti's face, but the child didn't open her eyes.

Charlotte began to hum softly the words of the song she'd taught Shanti last week, hoping the sound of her voice would help her friend.

"What do you want us to do, Charlie?" the first girl back asked.

"Hold her hands gently up, like this, until I get back. Then you can help me with her. I'm going to get some things off Padma to stitch the cuts." She shuffled to her feet and darted out of the room.

Charlotte entered Padma's room without knocking and saw Padma sitting on her bed, hunched over.

She didn't acknowledge Charlotte but keep staring at her hands.

"Why haven't you stitched Shanti's wrists?" Charlotte asked, wanting to demand Padma's help.

"What's the point, the boss will only cut her again. The child's going to die, why put off the inevitable," Padma stated in a dull voice.

"No! She will not die. I'm taking what I need, Padma. I haven't time to talk to you about this now. But we will talk—."

Padma rose and stood in front of Charlotte, blocking her path. "Get out of my room, Charlotte." She crossed her arms and her eyes turned icy.

Charlotte hated confrontation, but she needed to help Shanti. Would she have to physically fight Padma to get to the medical supplies? Her shoulders drooped and her eyes welled up. She reached out her hands, palms up, and dropped to her knees.

"Please, I beg you. Don't let this place steal your compassion and hope."

"Hope," Padma screamed. "There is no hope here. Accept it—we're already dead."

"No, Padma, you're wrong. God has seen us, he will rescue us from this place," Charlotte said firmly. She took hold of Padma's sari. "Let me try to help Shanti, please."

Padma shrugged and turned away. She moved back to her bed and lay down.

Hurrying to the cupboard Charlotte took what she needed. She stopped by the bed and reached out to her friend.

"I have a plan to get out of here. I want you to come with me, Padma." Charlotte spoke quickly.

"I can never leave. Charlie, go and see to Shanti." She turned on her side and closed her eyes.

As Charlotte raced down the hall, she had an empty feeling in her stomach. Had she made a mistake in trusting Padma with her plan to escape?

~~~

Shanti lay completely still, and Charlotte's heart raced in her chest.

Could her little friend have died? She pressed her ear over Shanti's

234

heart, and when she heard the soft beat, breathed a sigh of relief.

Her hands quickly went to work. She threaded the cotton through the needle. Her eyes smarted, and she took a deep breath.

Padma made this look so simple, but Charlotte wished Phillip were here.

She sterilized the equipment in the solution of Clorox and hot water, scrubbing her hands until they were red.

Carefully she pulled Shanti's torn skin together with her fingers and looped the needle through, lacing the rip together with the cotton thread.

Shanti moaned and Charlotte's gaze snapped to her face. How brave the little girl was. Shanti never complained but soldiered on, talking continually of her brother and believing Jesus would one day make her into a beautiful butterfly.

Charlotte's neck ached and she licked her lips. She knotted and snipped off the end of cotton. She gently lay Shanti's wrist down and picked up the other hand.

As she finished, she nodded her thanks to the two girls and secured the bandage with a small clip.

Standing Charlotte stretched her shoulders, turned slightly, and noticed that everyone in the room watched her.

These women had become so important to her. Their lives mattered, and they had no idea how much God loved them. She'd spent hours praying that God would give them all strength and save them.

Her heart filled with joy as she saw the concern on their faces. She smiled and lifted her hands to God.

"Thank you, Jesus, for helping me. Thank you for my family here. Heal Shanti, please."

She dropped to her mat and gently took Shanti in her arms and began to sing.

"Jesus loves me this I know, for the Bible tells me so; little ones to him belong, they are weak but he is strong. Yes, Jesus loves me! Yes, Jesus loves me! Yes, Jesus loves me, the Bible tells me so."

Other voices joined in, and Charlotte stopped singing and listened. A number of women sang the words with her; others hummed.

They'd heard her sing the song numerous times, and she marveled that they had picked up the words.

She looked down and saw Shanti staring up at her. Charlotte smiled, and her heart felt ready to burst with joy.

Her voice rose in volume once more as she claimed the words over Shanti's life.

"Jesus loves me! He who died, heaven's gates to open wide; he will wash away my sin, let his little child come in. Yes, Jesus loves me! Yes, Jesus loves me, yes, Jesus loves me, the Bible tells me so." Charlotte closed her eyes and listened to the humming that echoed around the room, driving out darkness and replacing it with love.

She sensed someone staring at her, someone other than the women. She turned her head and saw Saul standing in the doorway, a frown furrowed deep into his forehead, and she wanted to laugh.

She smiled at him and continued singing. "Jesus loves me, loves me still, when I'm weak and ill, from his shining throne on high, comes to watch me where I lie. Yes, Jesus loves me! Yes, Jesus loves me! Yes, Jesus loves me! The Bible tells me so."

"Stop!" Scarface's voice thundered, and he stomped across the room towards Charlotte. His fists were clenched tightly and his face was murderous.

Charlotte eased Shanti out of her arms and stood to face him. Her chin rose, and her heart felt light. "Saul, we will stop singing, but only with our mouths. God's presence is here, can you feel him?"

His hand flew out, and the *crack* of his palm contacting with her face stopped all singing. Charlotte staggered backward and lifted her hand to her cheek. Her skin burned and her mouth tightened.

She wanted to hit back at him for interrupting a sacred moment of worship to God.

Daughter, a gentle answer turns away wrath, but a harsh word stirs up anger.

Slowly she ducked her head in submission and backed away.

Scarface spun around and snarled at the other women before he left the room.

Charlotte jumped to her feet the moment the door closed. She spun around in a circle and laughed. God was in this place.

~~~

The waiting was killing Eli. How much longer before something happened? He paced the small room and longed for some fresh air.

Phillip had left and taken Ashok with him on a clinic run. Eli was waiting for Gargi to leave her bedroom to see if she wanted to take a walk. He heard a shuffle behind him and turned to see her standing timidly in the open door.

"Good morning, Gargi." He beckoned her into the room.

Gargi sucked in her lips and nodded. "Good morning," she said hesitantly.

She looked tired, as if she hadn't slept. What must it be like for her to be here with strangers? He wanted to reassure her she'd be all right, that he'd look after her. His heart caught at the thought, and he frowned. How could he look after her, when he was yet to rescue his own sister?

"Mr. Eli, I need to talk to Dr. Phillip. When will he be back?" Her voice was soft and sounded worried.

"He'll be gone most of the day, I'm afraid. Can I help you?" he asked gently.

Gargi looked down at her hands, and he saw her lips tremble. This girl must be only a few years older than Charlie. "Do you have family, Gargi?"

She looked up at him in surprise. "I did once, but—they are not interested in me."

"Surely once they know you're free, they'll be excited to see you? We must find them for you," he stated firmly.

"No," she answered, her gaze moving restlessly around the room.

"Gargi, I'm Charlotte's brother and I can't wait to see her. Your family will celebrate your return to them, you wait and see."

Her eyes looked like large pools of swirling turmoil. "My family is not like yours. My family sold me to the brothel when I was twelve."

He had to lean forward to catch her words, and his stomach clenched as the meaning of them sunk into his brain.

Had she ever known love? His heart yearned to make it right for her, but how?

Gargi sat on the edge of her seat and fidgeted with the material on her knee.

Eli recognized she wore the sari she had on yesterday. She needed clothes, money. How stupid of him not to realize.

"I'm sorry your family abandoned you. Charlie cares about you and so do I. Phillip wouldn't have you in his home if he didn't want to help you. I know it takes time to build trust, but please let us help you."

Gargi's eyes locked on his and she nodded. "I don't know what to do, Mr. Eli. I go over and over in my head, trying to think of a way to survive, to make money to live on. I have no skills, I can hardly read—the only thing I know is prostitution and I can't—I won't go back to that, I won't!" She put her head in her hands and burst into tears.

Eli blinked in surprise. The sobbing woman stunned him. What should he do? If it was Charlie he'd gather her in his arms and comfort her, but this wasn't his sister.

Would she take it the wrong way if he held her, maybe think he wanted more from her? His heart hammered in his chest as he watched her.

He'd never felt more helpless.

Chapter 36

Shanti spread her legs out in front of her and leaned against the wall. Everyone else was working, and she had the common room to herself. Charlie had somehow convinced Scarface that she needed to rest.

A thick lump swelled in her throat at the thought of the boss, and her heart squeezed tight in her chest.

He hated her. His eyes reflected shadowy shapes, and she shuddered to think of returning to his room.

Could she survive long enough to be rescued? Charlie had told her how everyone had sung their song, and how God was healing her.

Her head felt like it was swaying, and she closed her eyes against the dizziness. Her eyes grew heavy and she slid down and snuggled into her blanket. She felt so tired and sleepy.

Charlie had told her she'd lost a lot of blood and that she needed to give her body time to make some more.

If she had a sister, she'd want her to be just like Charlie. Shanti knew Ashok would like her friend, and she couldn't wait to teach Ashok the song about Jesus loving them.

~~~

Charlotte's steps lagged. She longed for relief from the thoughts in her head.

One moment she was seeing God's hand in everything, and the next she felt ready to lose heart.

So many men tonight. Her body felt bruised and dirty. Even an hour in a bath wouldn't wash away what they'd done to her.

She knew Jesus's blood could make her clean as snow, but her shoulders stooped lower and her steps halted.

She was changed forever; there was no way she could emerge from this experience the same person. She had to take control of her mind, submit it to Jesus.

Lord, my body feels heavy. To take one more step—seems impossible. Her lips moved as she mumbled John sixteen, verse thirty-three. "I have told you these things, so that in me you may have peace. In this world you will have trouble. But take heart! I have overcome the world."

Jesus, forgive my stubborn heart. I want you to rescue me now, I know you lived through so much more, but I look around and see darkness and your light disappears from my eyes. When, oh Lord, when will you rescue me—when?

She tipped her head to one side and sighed heavily. God must be sick of her whining. If she had to be here, then she needed to get busy.

Straightening her back, she went to find Padma.

She entered her friend's room and sat on the bed to wait for her. An apple rolled out from under the pillow, and Charlotte picked it up. Her mouth watered at the thought of taking a bite and she swallowed. Surely it would be all right to take a small bite: why should Padma have an apple and not her?

Lifting the apple to her mouth she could almost taste the sweet, juicy texture.

Would she succumb to greed for a fleeting pleasure? Her hand dropped and she gazed down at the apple in disgust. Placing the apple back under the pillow, she stood.

"Take it, Charlie. It was a gift, but I want you to have it." Padma pulled the apple out and extended her hand.

Charlotte didn't hesitate; she took the apple and smiled. "Thank you. I'll share it with Shanti." She wanted to ask where the apple had come from but stopped herself. What did it matter?

"Padma, I want to talk to you about something, is now a good time?"

"Yes."

Charlotte never saw Padma amongst the girls who worked around her, and she wondered what she did while they serviced the men. Dare she ask?

"I want to thank you for arranging for Shanti to rest today. Is it possible for her to have another day?"

"I cannot say, it depends on the boss. I think he's away for the rest of the week, so your little friend may be left alone."

This was good news and Charlotte smiled. "Padma, what would you say if there was a way of out here?" she asked quietly.

"I would say you need to face reality and accept that this is your lot. Others have tried to escape and lived to regret it. The sooner you give up these thoughts, the sooner you will adjust to life here." Padma's lips lifted slightly. "Look at what's in your hand, Charlie. Good things do come to those who wait."

Charlotte looked at the apple and frowned. An apple couldn't substitute freedom.

"Padma, answer my question. Would you come with me if I had a way out of here?"

"You waste my time with idle talk. You want to live in illusion, fine. But I live in reality. Leave me," she snapped with a mocking scowl.

"Listen to me, Padma. I need your help if this is going to work. Remember the doctor who came to see Gargi?"

Padma's eyes narrowed. "Yes, what of him?"

"I know him. The next time he comes here, he is going to help us escape. I told him I wouldn't leave without Shanti and you."

Charlotte saw something flash in Padma's dark eyes and hesitated.

Padma's eyes bore into hers, and Charlotte dropped her eyes briefly. What was it she'd seen in her friend's eyes? Was it hope—or anger?

"You mean you knew him before you met him here?" Padma asked.

"Yes. If there's a chance of escape, it will be through him. We have to convince Saul that Shanti may die if she doesn't see the doctor. This is where you come in."

Padma moved around the room, her hands tightly clenched. She stopped and glared at Charlotte, her eyes troubled. "It's too risky."

"Any more risky than staying here?" Charlotte challenged.

"You want me to get Scarface to call your doctor friend and he helps us to escape, how exactly?"

"I don't know, but at least it's part of a plan. Can you think about it, Padma, please?"

"Don't let yourself hope, Charlie. These things have been tried before and failed. I'll talk to Scarface and see what happens," she shrugged her shoulders with indifference.

Charlotte moistened her lips and nodded. Padma puzzled her. One minute she was friendly and the next she was like an icy stranger.

Something stopped her from mentioning the mobile phone, and she trusted her instinct. Why get Padma into trouble if things didn't work out?

Excitement bubbled inside her as she thought of Shanti's reaction to Ashok's text. As soon as she was alone, she scanned the message, smiling as she pictured Eli typing the words for Ashok. "I'm coming for you Shanti, hold on. I love you, Ashok."

His simple words would surely encourage her to get well.

God, you're so amazing; not only am I with little Shanti, Eli's with Ashok. Two brothers and two sisters. Lord, reunite us all soon, please.

~~~

Ashok woke with a start. His jaw tightened and he gripped the bedding.

What was wrong? He shuffled out of bed and tip toed to Eli's room.

His friend was asleep, and Ashok stared down at him. What did Jesus want him to do?

He squatted beside Eli and whispered his name. If Eli woke up, he'd ask him to pray with him for their sisters, if he didn't wake, then he'd pray alone.

"Ashok," Eli mumbled sleepily.

"I'm sorry to wake you, Eli. We need to pray for our sisters. Something bad is going to happen, I can feel it here." He thumped his chest.

Eli leaned on his elbow and pushed the hair out of his eyes. He reached over and switched on the bed light and motioned for Ashok to join him.

Scrambling up beside Eli, Ashok put his hands together, and closed his eyes.

"Jesus, I know you woke me to pray for Shanti and Charlie," Ashok said. "I don't know why, but you do. Please help them."

Ashok shivered and leaned into Eli's arm. He blinked and tried hard not to cry. His sister needed him and he couldn't help her.

He turned his head into Eli's shoulder, and a shudder ripped through his body.

As Eli started to pray, Ashok visualized Jesus in the room.

"Lord Jesus, you're with Shanti and Charlie right now. Whatever is happening there, please give them your protection and give Charlie wisdom to know how to handle it." Eli stopped and patted Ashok's arm.

Ashok looked at him and nodded he understood.

"Jesus, you're my best friend. You helped Shanti and me. Helping us find food, keeping us from getting too sick. I told Shanti I would find her; please help me keep my promise. I think something bad is happening and only you can help. Thank you for being our friend, thank you for loving me and listening right now. Amen."

Relaxing his hands, Ashok sighed. He felt better, as if he'd done something important to help his sister.

"Are you okay, mate?" Eli asked, his hand ruffling through Ashok's hair.

"Yes, Jesus was here, Eli. He's there with them too, isn't he?" His voice shook with emotion.

"That's right. Do you think you can sleep now, or should we sneak to the kitchen for a midnight snack?"

"Can we?" Ashok asked excitedly.

"Come on, let's do it."

~~~

Charlotte lovingly brushed Shanti's hair and smiled over her head. Some things brought so much pleasure. "Shanti, I love you," she murmured.

"You do?" Shanti spun around to look at her.

"Yes, sweetheart. When we get out of here, I want to take care of you always."

"Ashok too?"

"Of course. Won't we have fun together? I feel like I already love Ashok, even though I've not met him."

"Ashok will love you, Charlie. He's a bit bossy sometimes, but he tries hard to look after me. The last thing he said to me was 'I will find you', and look, he found your brother and now they'll both find us."

Charlotte circled Shanti with her arms and pulled her close, her eyes watering with unshed tears at the favor of God. This child meant so much to her, and if she had her way, she'd never let her go.

"Charlotte, Padma wants to see you in her room," one of the girls called out from across the room.

Releasing Shanti, Charlotte stood and brushed a thick strand of black hair from Shanti's forehead. "Why don't you lie down again and rest. Remember Shanti, that you have to act really sick if Saul comes in. We need him to believe he has to get the doctor to come and see you."

Shanti nodded and grabbed Charlotte's hand. "I like Padma, Charlie. I'm glad she's coming with us."

"Me too, sweetheart." Charlotte watched from the door as Shanti lay on her mat. She was such a beautiful, loving child.

Charlotte chewed her lower lip; she'd have to work out a way to stop the boss from taking Shanti again.

Sighing, she hurried down the hall to Padma's room. The door was open, so she went in and smiled at her friend.

"Hi, Padma. How are you?"

Padma twisted her hands together and lifted her chin. "I've talked to Scarface about your doctor."

Charlotte frowned at the tense, edgy tone of Padma's voice. She'd need to encourage her that everything would work out, that God was on their side.

She moved across the room. "Did you convince Saul that Shanti needs a doctor?"

"I didn't try to convince him." Padma gave a bored shrug.

"What do you mean? You said you talked to him."

"You misunderstand me, Charlotte. I've told Scarface about your plans of escape. You see, there's something you don't know about me," she said in a cruel voice.

A chill went down Charlotte's spine at the look on Padma's face, and she folded her arms protectively.

"I thought I could trust you, Padma. Why did you tell him?"

"Why wouldn't I tell him? He is, after all, my husband." Padma's gaze left Charlotte's face and travelled over her shoulder.

Charlotte heard the door close softly behind her and spun around to see Saul grinning at her.

"Hey, angel face. Looks like your god messed this one up. Do you know what I do to girls who try and escape me?" He stepped into the room and loomed over Charlotte.

There was no place to run. Charlotte glanced at Padma and felt the pain of betrayal. Her eyes opened, and she saw Padma for what she was.

Charlotte's heart caught at the expression on the woman's face. She had no hope, no relationship with Jesus, and a cruel, controlling husband.

"I forgive you, Padma," she said simply and turned back to Saul.

His hand flew out and grabbed her hair. He yanked her towards him and pushed her down on her knees. "By the time I've finished with you, girl, you'll be renouncing that god of yours and saying, 'Scarface is my God'."

"Never," Charlotte spat out. She clutched at his fingers, trying to release her hair.

He pulled her close to his chest and ripped the sari off her shoulders, his mouth taking hers and kissing her roughly.

Gagging Charlotte moved her head from side to side, trying to avoid his foul-smelling mouth, but she couldn't escape his strength.

She heard Padma gasp as Saul continued to assault her mouth.

Surely he wouldn't rape her. He'd had many opportunities to do so in the past but hadn't touched her—why now?

"I'm the one who controls your life, girl. Just like I control Padma's. My loyal wife is going to watch me take you and enjoy it. Aren't you, Padma?" Scarface threw back his head and laughed. His hand snaked out and gripped Padma's arm.

She tried to pull away from him, but he easily overpowered her and secured her beside him.

"Please Scarface, let me go," Padma begged.

"You think I care about you, woman? I care about no one." His fist smashed into Padma's face with the sickening crunch of bone.

Blood seeped from her nostril and into her raised hand. Padma cowered in fear and hunched into a ball on the floor.

"Don't think you have any allies here, Charlotte. I've waited long enough for you and now you serve me." Saul rammed her to the floor and knelt over her, licking his lips.

Chapter 37

He'd been back in India two weeks, and still no news from Ted. Eli pulled on his shoes and stretched his legs. He needed to run out some of his frustration before he exploded.

It felt like his life was on hold, that he was in a time capsule waiting for someone to open the lid so he could breathe.

His feet slammed the road as he moved through the streets. He concentrated on his breathing in an attempt to release the pressure that had steadily built up over the last week.

He needed action, results. This was the hardest part of walking with the Lord, the waiting.

He thought of all the people doing life hard, with no knowledge of their Creator's love and help.

His muscles tightened, but he pushed on, enjoying the release of endorphins. His breathing came easily now and Eli felt he could do another half an hour. He took in the scene around him and realized that somewhere along the way he'd grown to love India.

He slowed his pace as he approached a crossroad. His eyes crinkled slightly at the sight of the cow relaxing in the middle of the road. Eli laughed as a yellow bus swerved around the cow, which seemed totally oblivious to the noise and chaos.

As Eli crossed the road, he passed a two-wheeled wooden cart being pulled by a man, and he marveled at the strength it would take to haul such a load.

The smell of burning oil made Eli hold his breath as he passed a stopped diesel truck with its engine running.

The mixture of smells assailed him and he tried to name them as he ran. Rubbish, urine, oil, and spices blended together with a damp earth odor.

Eli decided the smell wasn't too bad, and that he was getting used to it.

Ashok was a big part of who India was. The resilience of the boy touched Eli's heart. How many others had been born to extreme poverty where survival was difficult?

There was no way he'd be able to say good-bye to Ashok once Charlie was safe.

He stopped running and braced his hands on his knees. He'd adopt both Ashok and Shanti. The idea stunned him, but it brought a smile to his face.

He pulled his foot up behind him and stretched his quads. How do you adopt a child who has no identity? Would anyone even know Ashok had been born? How could he get him out of the country without a passport?

An eager smile spread over Eli's lips. There'd be a way, he thought. He'd wait to tell Ashok until after he'd found out more about the process.

Turning, he headed back. He'd make the most of the day and spend time with Ashok and Gargi, take them shopping. Gargi needed reassurance that she wasn't alone.

He frowned as he thought of her longing to know more about Jesus. The fact that she couldn't read astounded him.

How many children were robbed of the right to education because of captivity and poverty?

248

He'd make sure Gargi got the education she desired and would be able to read the Bible to her children. His heart pounded as he remembered her abuse, and his eyes welled up with tears for her loss.

She loved Ashok, he could see it in the way she continually rested her hand on his shoulder or gently touched his hair as she walked passed him.

If his plan came together to raise money to establish a home for abandoned children in India, then Gargi would be the perfect person to mother them.

She'd shyly told him about her conversation with Jesus and how Charlie had demonstrated God's love to her.

He found himself wanting to protect her from further heartache. He worked hard to make her smile, and when she did, his heart skipped.

Slowing to a jog, he tried to evaluate his feelings for her; surely anyone would feel compassion for someone who had experienced so much?

Phillip spent days looking out for the children of India because he loved them; were his own growing feelings for Gargi the same as Phillip's feelings for the children he treated?

Eli's feet slowed further as he strolled towards the apartment. Whatever came of their friendship, he would assure Gargi that he wouldn't abandon her, but support her to become a woman of influence in whatever area she chose.

As he entered the apartment Eli smiled at the laughter he heard coming out of the kitchen.

Ashok was covered in flour and Gargi was no better. Phillip sat at the table wiping moisture from his eyes as laughter bounced around the room.

Gargi turned towards him with such joy on her face that Eli caught his breath.

He'd never felt this way about Tina, and he'd only known Gargi for two weeks. Avoiding her eyes, he joined Phillip at the table and smiled at his friend.

"Looks like we're going out for breakfast," he said as he slapped Phillip on the shoulder.

"Yes, these two clowns got into a flour fight, and I was the innocent bystander. I hope they don't expect me to clean up the mess," Phillip answered lightly.

"Dr. Phillip, please forgive me." Gargi dropped to the floor and started to scoop up the flour with her hands.

Eli saw her cringe as Phillip squatted beside her and frowned at the haunted, fearful look in her eyes.

"Gargi." Phillip spoke gently as he smiled into her eyes. "I helped make this mess, so I'll clean up the kitchen while you and Ashok go and have a wash. Then Eli will buy us breakfast, won't you, my friend?"

"Sounds good to me. Then we're going shopping. Gargi needs some clothes, brushes for her hair, and other stuff."

Her eyes darkened at his words, and his face heated.

Did she think he'd want something in return for the money he spent? How could they reassure her she was safe with them? That the life she'd lived was over and that she deserved good things.

~~~

Today was Mother's day, and Macy couldn't stomach the thought of going to church and watching her friends with their children.

Bill had gone down to make breakfast for her, and she lay in bed, staring at the ceiling.

It was just wrong to celebrate Mother's day without either of her children here with her. Eli had called last night to talk to her, and she didn't expect him to phone again today.

She'd have to put on a brave face and pretend she had it all together, when in fact she wanted to break down and cry.

Last year Charlie had arranged a picnic lunch at the beach for her. She'd arrived to find the picnic shelter covered in pink and white balloons, and cutout butterflies fluttered all over the white plastic tablecloth.

Charlie had always loved butterflies. Eli and Charlie had made the day about celebrating the generations and had picked up their Nan and made sure the whole family had come. It had been a great day.

Sighing, Macy got out of bed. She needed to honor her mother; she too would be feeling the agony of Charlie not being here.

As she went downstairs, she plastered a smile on her face and joined Bill in the kitchen. Fresh flowers were arranged in her favorite vase and placed in the centre of the table.

A genuine smile surfaced, and she went to hug him.

"You ready for breakfast, darling?" He patted her back.

"Yes please."

"You sit down while I dish up. I think you got a message on your phone, I heard it beep," Bill turned to lift something out of the oven.

Macy didn't feel like a big breakfast, but she smiled as she thought of all the trouble he'd gone to. She picked up her phone and opened the text.

Mum, luv you, ur the greatest—Charlie xxx

"Bill, it's from Charlie. Oh, my," she sobbed, handing him the phone.

He read the message and nodded solemnly.

Dropping into a chair Macy allowed herself the luxury of a good cry. Her precious girl must have seen the date on Phillip's mobile phone.

Wiping her eyes, she gave a watery smile. She'd celebrate the honor of having such great children and thank Jesus every step of the way.

"Macy, I have a gift for you too. Can I give it to you now, before we eat?" Bill asked excitedly.

"I'd like that, thank you." She smiled, wiping her cheeks with a tissue.

Bill hurried out of the room and came back to hand her a flat oblong box.

Macy opened the package, puzzled by its shape.

She gasped at what she found and looked up to see Bill's handsome face grinning down at her.

"I thought it was time we joined our children," he stated simply.

Macy flung her arms around his neck and held on tight.

They were going to India.

Chapter 38

Macy smiled at the beautiful young Indian woman sitting across from her in the hotel. Eli had explained why Gargi was with them, and Macy was glad she'd suggested Gargi stay with Bill and her while they were in India.

She wiped her hand over her forehead and sighed. The heat was getting to her, and there was so much here that she hadn't expected.

At the airport she'd watched wide-eyed as women were separated from men to go through the security section. Tourists had another line, and Macy frowned as she thought of the differences to home.

The drive from the airport had been an eye-opener; seeing the poverty people lived in, Macy had looked down at the rings on her fingers and felt the weight of her wealth. She couldn't imagine living in a corrugated iron shack near a busy road.

Gargi sat with her hands folded in her lap, and Macy wondered about her life.

"Gargi, can you tell me about how you came to be in the brothel?" she asked softly.

Gargi shyly dropped her eyes, and Macy's heart softened.

"I can hardly remember. It seems like my whole life has been locked up there," she said wearily.

"I don't mean to be nosy. You've been through so much, my dear. I know talking helps me work through things, and I want to offer you a listening ear if you do want to talk," Macy explained.

"Thank you. Charlie said something similar to me. I owe Charlie so much, Mrs. Turner."

"Please, dear, call me Macy. Charlotte would be so happy seeing us sitting here together. Let's hope one day soon she can join us." Her voice caught slightly, and she dabbed her mouth with her handkerchief.

"I've never talked about my family," Gargi stated. "No one really cared enough to ask before. I can't picture my father's face, but I remember he was always angry, screaming at me to work harder and bring in more money."

She lifted her hands and gazed at her fingernails. "I remember biting my nails all the time because he scared me so much. I used to go out on the streets begging people for money, pulling at their clothes and trying to get something, anything I could take back to him. If I came back with nothing, he would beat me.

My mother was a quiet woman, never talking. The only thing she ever said to me was just before they sold me to the brothel. She told me that it was for the best and that my father wouldn't be able to beat me anymore."

Macy reached out and lightly touched Gargi's hand. Gargi turned her hand over and clasped Macy's fingers tightly.

"I've watched the way you and Mr. Turner greet Eli every time you see him with a kiss and embrace. My parents never touched me the way you touch Eli. I see the love you have for your son on your faces."

"You're mother missed out on so much, Gargi. I'm sorry she didn't know how to love you. You deserved so much more." Macy's eyes misted over and her stomach dropped.

A child needs a mother's love, she thought. How could you survive pain if you felt no one loved you? If no one touched you or cared enough to ask you how you were?

Gargi's lips parted in the beginning of a smile. "Charlie was the first person to touch me in a way that wasn't menacing or sexual. When I was pregnant, Charlie would massage my feet and brush my hair."

The thought of her daughter doing such a thing brought fresh tears to her eyes. Macy sat up straighter in her seat and told herself to breathe.

Gargi looked over at Macy and her mouth dropped open, tears rolling freely down her cheeks.

Macy sucked in a breath and moved from her seat and sat on the couch next to Gargi.

"May I hold you?" she asked carefully.

Gargi gnawed her bottom lip and nodded. As Macy's arms circled Gargi, her thoughts went to her daughter. If Charlie loved this girl enough to let her take her place in escaping, then she'd love her as well.

She closed her eyes and imagined holding Charlie.

Gargi sobbed into her shoulder, and Macy soothingly patted her back. Macy's chest tightened and her chin wobbled. Wave after wave of emotion pummeled her heart. "It's okay, sweetheart," Macy whispered. "You have a good cry. We girls need to cry sometimes, and you've been through so much, it's okay."

Slowly Gargi pulled away from her, and Macy's heart wrenched at the look on the young woman's face.

"They took my baby from me, before it even had a chance to live," she whispered. "My arms ache with emptiness."

Tears slipped down Macy's cheeks, but she ignored them. What must it be like to lose a child in this way? Her throat felt thick with emotion; she breathed in deeply. Her arms felt heavy like lead.

She too wanted to hold her baby.

Gargi hiccupped. "I—I can't have any more children. Dr. Phillip explained what they did to me, and I'll never again feel the miracle of my child growing inside me."

"I'm sorry, Gargi," Macy said softly.

"You're right, it has helped to speak of this. I cannot change what happened, and I am grateful that my loss has brought me to Jesus. I can only believe that one day I will be able to serve him in some way, to make my life worthwhile."

~~~

Eli hated the pretense and frowned as he lifted the glass of beer to his mouth. He leaned heavily against the bar and glanced across at Ted, who nodded slightly to indicate the man next to him.

Knowing he had only one chance at this, Eli prayed God would go before him and help him play the sleazy businessman.

"Hey, Ted, how'd you get on with my request, mate?" he asked loudly enough for his words to be heard easily by the man next to him.

"Lower your voice, will you?" Ted commanded, looking around and giving a sheepish grin to their target.

Eli turned his head and stared blankly at the man beside him.

Rage boiled inside him at the thought of this man touching his sister. Pushing it down, he gave a lopsided smile and extended his hand in greeting. "Name's Geoff. Didn't mean to intrude on your space, mate."

"No problem, nice to have a bit of company, name's Tony Gladstone," he said as he shook Eli's hand.

"I was saying the same thing to me old mate here. I have a need for some company, but bit partial to the female type—if you know what I mean. It's been a while." Eli downed his beer and indicated with his finger for another. "My little lady back home is getting a bit predictable these days and I—uh, forget it, sorry mate, I'm jabbering on." Eli sat back and closed his eyes briefly before turning to Ted.

"Ted and I go way back, used to play the town when we were younger, now he's a serious businessman and all work and no play, isn't that right, Ted?"

"Sure, sure, Geoff. I think you've had enough to drink for one night. Why don't you go to your room and call your wife, talk to your kids?" Standing, he slapped Eli on the back. "I'll see you tomorrow. I'm off home."

Eli spun on his stool and watched him move away. He turned back to Tony and shrugged. "Looks like I'm on my own tonight," he muttered.

Tony leaned back in his chair and grinned. "Not necessarily. How long you here for?"

"A few days, always swing an extra night on these trips," Eli answered in a bored tone.

"Maybe I could help you out. I know the town well, have connections—could set you up," he suggested cunningly.

Eli leaned towards him, mustering a surprised look on his face. "You serious?"

"Sure, it's up to you. What's your fantasy?"

Eli's jaw tightened with the pressure of not grabbing the guy by the neck.

He shrugged his shoulders and gazed into his beer. "Mmm, I'd be embarrassed to tell you," he slurred.

"If a man can't take what he needs, make it happen, then the world is a very sad place," Tony commented.

"Yeah, I suppose you're right. You tell me your fantasy, and I'll think about sharing mine," Eli challenged.

"Thing is, Geoff, I've lived my fantasy many times over. I can guarantee you will too, for a price, of course," he said brazenly.

"Hey, money is no problem, I'm loaded." He took another sip of beer and glanced at Tony.

His stomach churned in disgust at the words he was about to say. "I have a sister, cute wee thing she is. Always wondered what it'd be like to do it with her. Suppose you think I'm one sick pervert now." Eli slumped over the bar.

"Not at all, sounds like fun. What about a sister look-alike?" Tony suggested.

"Yeah, that could work. She's pretty, blonde, petite—the same

257

complexion as me—I suppose something close to that could work, I've got a pretty vivid imagination."

Tony chuckled. "Just so happens I know the perfect girl. If you're serious, I'll see if I can set it up for tomorrow night. One condition though, I get to watch. What do you say?"

"You want to watch?" Beads of sweat formed on Eli's forehead. He clenched his fists in an effort not to take the guy down. He took a gulp of his drink, swirled it around in his mouth, and nodded. Clearing his throat, he threw his head back. "Hey man, that's some turn-on, sure, why not."

Tony leaned in close to Eli, invading his personal space. His booming voice drew attention to them, and Eli wanted to shove him back but gritted his teeth.

An attractive woman arrived beside Tony and waved to get the barman's attention.

Tony's hand snaked out and rubbed up her arm. He ogled her in such a disgusting way that Eli felt like screaming at him.

"Hey peaches, you want a good time tonight?" he purred, not seeming to care that he was loud and brash. The woman moved away and didn't bother to reply.

Eli pulled himself up in his chair. He'd had enough, he wanted this done and dusted. "How much will this sting me?"

Tony swiveled in his chair as if he had all the time in the world. "Not so fast, friend. You think I'd take just anyone to this little number?"

"Come on, Tony. You've got my senses wired talking about it. You can't flick me off now." Eli slurred his voice and reached out to touch the guy's arm.

"Mmm. Well, you seem like a guy who likes a good time—"

Was he stalling? Eli dropped his head into his hands and rested his elbows on the bar. A shadow crossed his spirit, and his stomach knotted. If the deal didn't happen soon, he'd blow it.

"Two hundred dollars, plus a hundred bucks for me as a finder's fee." Tony smirked.

Eli whistled. "I don't know, that's an awful lot of cash."

"Your choice, but this girl could be your twin." Tony sat back and folded his arms, a smug smile on his face.

Eli coughed into his hand. "Let's do it. Under no circumstances is Ted to know; his saintly values could get me burned. As I've said, he's forgotten what the word *fun* means."

"Sure Geoff, it'll be our little secret. I'll meet you here tomorrow at 6:00 p.m. You'll need cash up front buddy, but take my word for it; this little lady is feisty, well worth the money. Maybe I'll take a turn with her myself, when you've finished." He laughed and swallowed the remaining scotch in his glass, stood, and left.

Eli's eyes glazed over. His muscles locked in his shoulders and up his neck. The intensity of his sorrow made him want to weep.

Charlie, his mind screamed, forgive me for talking about you like this.

Oh, Lord, the corruptness of our world. How can I ever make it up to her? How can I look into her eyes, knowing what this man and others did to her?

His head dropped to rest on his folded arms.

"Are you all right Eli?" Ted asked, coming around the bar and sitting on the chair Tony had vacated.

Eli lifted his head and stared at his new friend. Would he ever get over this? He longed to hold Charlie yet feared his heart could not cope with what he'd find.

Sighing heavily, he pushed himself up and glanced around the bar. The smell of alcohol and smoke choked him; he needed fresh air before he threw up.

His gaze met Ted's and he nodded. "It's on for tomorrow night."

~~~

Macy stepped aside to let Eli enter the hotel room. His face looked different to her. Chiseled with tension and sadness. New lines had appeared around his eyes. Her boy was aging, and there was nothing she could do about it. How could this be happening to her family?

Anger rushed up to join her sorrow. It wasn't fair. She reached over and kissed his cheek. Her heart caught at how she so often took him for granted, and she remembered Gargi's comments.

She hugged Eli and kissed him again.

"Hey, Mum. Where are Dad and Gargi?"

"Your father's gone to the police station again. He's determined to make his presence felt. That way, when the time comes for them to act on your lead, they may act quickly," Macy answered.

"His being there is only going to antagonize them. I don't want him drawing attention to us until the time's right. Can you talk to him for me, Mum?"

"Yes, yes. But he needs to be doing something. The waiting is agonizing."

"Tell me about it. Where's Gargi?" Eli asked.

"Here she is." Macy indicated to Gargi as she entered the room. Macy moistened her lips, concern stinging her eyes as she watched her son rush over to Gargi's side to greet the young woman.

"Come and sit down, Gargi. How are you?" he asked gently.

Macy knew her son well, and the way he was responding to Gargi frightened her. Surely he couldn't have feelings for the girl, she thought.

Her heart rate increased as she stared at the two young people talking about their day. Macy bit her lower lip. What if Eli did want something more than friendship from Gargi? Did she want her son marrying a woman who had so much to work through and who couldn't give him children? What about the cultural difference?

As her mind battled with these questions, Macy realized she could be talking about her own daughter.

She caught her breath and excused herself as she rushed to her room.

Closing the door quietly behind her, Macy collapsed on the bed. What sort of woman was she? One minute she was saying she was

260

going to love Gargi, and then she was thinking she wasn't good enough for her son.

Her face heated with shame and her fingers cupped her cheeks. Macy closed her eyes, and her lips moved as she spoke softly to Jesus.

Lord Jesus, forgive me. My world is upside down and I keep stumbling over my own feet. Don't let anything I do cause Gargi further pain. If Eli does fall in love with her, I promise to be joyful and love her as my daughter.

Sighing, Macy kicked off her shoes and relaxed on the bed. A tear trickled down her cheek, and she smoothed it into her skin.

A small smile lifted her lips, and she let her shoulders sink into the mattress. Eli had always been a compassionate man, she mused. He would naturally want to make sure Gargi was okay too.

She wouldn't go ahead of herself, she decided, just wait and see what happened.

She heard a soft knock and turned towards the door. Sitting, she swung her legs over the side of the bed and crossed the room.

"Mum, are you okay?" The frown on his forehead showed his concern, and Macy's heart lightened.

"Yes, darling. I get a bit emotional these days, and watching you and Gargi set me off. Is your father home yet?"

"He just walked in. What do you mean, watching me and Gargi?" His frown deepened.

"She's a lovely young woman, and I was touched by—by how kind you are to her. I love you so much and am so proud of the man you are. I haven't told you that enough, Eli." She gently touched his face, and blinked several times to stop her tears spilling.

Eli's large arms pulled her close and hugged her. Macy sighed, and her heart felt warmed by her son's embrace.

"I love you too, Mum," he said as he released her, bending low to kiss her cheek.

"Can you tell me how it went at the hotel? I want all the details."

"No you don't." A deep frown grooved his forehead. "He fell for it.

We're a go for tomorrow."

Chapter 39

Ashok scratched a face in the dirt with the stick. His frown deepened. He blinked back the tears threatening to fall and breathed heavily.

He missed Shanti so much. Every day seemed longer without her.

He'd crept into the hall last night and listened to Eli and Dr. Phillip talking about Gargi and the horrible things she'd lived through.

Ashok's heart still hammered in his chest when he thought of his Shanti going through bad stuff like that. He'd seen Gargi's eyes fill with water when she thought no one was watching.

Why did bad things happen to good people?

The stick in his hand scribbled over his picture and he slammed it hard into the ground, time and time again until it snapped.

If he were bigger, he'd make someone pay for hurting Shanti.

His face burned with anger and his jaw tightened. He jumped to his feet and kicked at the dirt.

Ashok coughed as dust particles caught in his throat. He threw back his head and glared at the sky.

Jesus, you said you were my friend. Where are you? What about my sister? I can't wait anymore, I need her, now!

His hands balled into fists and his eyes darted around him. His breath came quickly as a prickly feeling ran down his spine.

He spun around and searched the shadows.

His skin crawled, like something was out to get him. Something dark and dangerous. He needed to find Eli, he'd know what to do.

He stumbled as he scurried back to the apartment. Panting, he heaved open the door and raced to the kitchen. His face felt heated and sweat dripped down his back.

"Ashok, what's the matter?" Eli asked, quickly coming to his side.

"I don't know," Ashok hollered and burst into tears.

"Son, it's all right," Eli soothed as he picked Ashok up and hugged him to his chest.

Ashok tried to stop crying, but the more he tried, the tighter his chest became. Giving into the security he felt in Eli's arms, he let his head flop onto Eli's chest and his tears soaked Eli's T-shirt.

"I don't know if this is the right time to tell you, Ashok. I wanted to wait until we had Shanti here with us, but I want you both to stay with me—forever," Eli said in a gentle voice, his hand rubbing Ashok's back.

Ashok lifted his head, and his mouth dropped open. Fresh tears stung his eyes, and he blinked in astonishment. "You want us?" he murmured weakly.

"I do, very much. What do you say?" Eli's eyes sparkled, and his mouth lifted at the corners in an excited smile.

"Yes—yes—yes," Ashok screamed. "Eli, I'll tell Shanti everything you've done for us, and she'll love you too.' He threw his arms around Eli's neck and clung on tight.

Ashok heard a noise behind him and turned to see Eli's mother watching them.

He watched spellbound as her eyes narrowed and her mouth dropped open.

Eli turned and motioned for her to join them.

Ashok's stomach flipped in fear. Had she heard them? Would she make Eli change his mind about wanting him and Shanti? His heart thumped as she approached, and he moved out of Eli's arms.

"Mum, Ashok's agreed to let me adopt him. As soon as Charlie and Shanti are free, I'm going to begin the process," he said firmly.

Ashok's eyes widened. He didn't know what *adopt* meant, but it sounded important.

Mrs. Turner's face had paled, and her eyes darted to his face. Ashok wanted to hide behind the couch. Would she be angry?

"You're sure about this, Eli? It's a huge decision, not one to be made lightly," she said gently.

"I've been praying about it, and it feels right. I love Ashok, and I want to take care of him and Shanti." Eli squatted down in front of Ashok and placed his hands on Ashok's shoulders.

"Ashok, the word *adopt* means that I become your father and you become my son. We have to get permission for this to happen, but I promise you I'll do everything in my power to make it happen."

Mrs. Turner cleared her throat and gave a deep sigh.

He watched her from under his lashes. She sat silently in a chair, and her forehead was creased in a frown. Ashok licked his lips as she closed her eyes. What was she thinking? She must hate him, he thought with sadness.

Bowing his head, he wondered if he should disappear once he had Shanti with him. He didn't want to make Mrs. Turner angry with Eli.

"Can you come here Ashok, please," Mrs. Turner asked.

Ashok stepped back and would have continued out the room if Eli's hand hadn't stopped him.

Eli nodded and gave him a slight push towards Mrs. Turner.

Lifting his chin, he inched over to stand in front of her.

"I'm very proud of the way you've been helping Eli look for Charlotte and your sister. Obviously Eli has grown to love you very much; he wants to be your father. Do you know what it'll mean if he does become your father?" she asked in a soft voice.

Ashok looked at the floor and remained silent. He could feel his stomach shaking and wondered if she could see his trembling.

Her finger lifted his chin until he had to look at her. He didn't want to let Eli down, so he squared his shoulders and stared into her eyes.

"If Eli is your father, Ashok, then I'll be your grandmother," she said with a watery smile.

His jaw dropped down in surprise. His grandmother? Tears flooded his eyes as he looked at her.

Mrs. Turner opened her arms to him, and he hesitated for a moment before throwing himself at her.

She held him close to her heart. Ashok had never felt such warmth. Gargi had touched his hair and shoulders, but he'd never had a hug like this from a woman before.

His arms spread around her spongy waist, and the shaking inside his stomach increased until he was sobbing in her arms. God must love him very much to give him a father and grandmother on the same day.

Now all he needed was his sister.

~~~

She couldn't sleep. Charlotte turned her head and stared at Shanti's sleeping form. She'd tried to pretend nothing was the matter, but the young girl had known there was something wrong.

A hope deferred makes the heart sick, but a longing fulfilled is a tree of life.

Charlotte turned on her side, away from Shanti.

Lord Jesus, my hope for freedom is slipping away from me, and my eyes are growing dim.

I can't see a way out, Lord. I long in the depth of my heart to be released from this evil place, but time and time again I am overshadowed by darkness.

How can I protect Shanti if I can't even protect myself?

Pain shot through her shoulder, and Charlotte groaned. Sitting up, she sighed and gave up on sleeping. She looked across the room at the huddled bodies of her friends.

Rage began to boil inside her and she wanted to scream at them to wake up and fight.

Her gaze was drawn to the opposite corner, and she could swear she could feel something looking at her.

Charlotte shuddered and pushed to her feet. She would not crawl into a hole and go quietly, she would fight for these women.

She stepped over mats until she stood in the middle of the room. Throwing her head back, she lifted her arms in the air.

"Almighty God, you are the Creator of the heavens, you stretched them out, you spread out the earth with all that springs from it, you give breath to its people, and life to those who walk on it: You, Lord, have called me in righteousness, you take hold of my hand. You keep me and make me a light for the Gentiles, to open eyes that are blind, to free captives from prison and to release from the dungeon those who sit in darkness."

Charlotte caught her breath as the verse from the book of Isaiah echoed around the quiet room. Her arms dropped and she wearily glanced around.

She ducked and laughed as a shoe narrowly missed her head.

These women were blind and captive. Her chin lifted in determination. Whether she got out of here or not, Charlotte decided, she'd spend the rest of her life seeking to set the captive free.

As this settled in her heart, Charlotte felt the ties of imprisonment slip from her; she was free.

"Come," she called. "Let me tell you a story of a great King who died so his people could live."

"Charlie, you fool. You will bring Scarface down upon us. Go back to bed."

Chapter 40

Ashok grabbed Eli's shirt. "I need to be there for Shanti. Please let me come, Eli, please," he begged.

"I don't want you getting hurt. This isn't a game we're playing, son," Eli replied firmly.'

Ashok dropped his hands from Eli's shirt. His heart twisted at the thought of being left behind, and a thick lump swelled in his throat.

He had to make Eli understand. "I promised Shanti I'd find her—you would have me break my promise to my sister?" He stared boldly into Eli's eyes.

The silence thickened between them. Ashok refused to look away, and the question hung in the air, challenging Eli to answer it.

"You do exactly as Phillip tells you, and you don't put yourself in any danger—do you hear me?"

Ashok flashed a triumphant smile and clapped his hands. "Oh, yes. Thank you, Eli. I'll see Shanti soon, I feel it here." He tapped his hand over his heart.

"Listen carefully, Ashok. Phillip and Ted will be parked outside the hotel; you must wait with them in the car. Ted's arranged for someone to phone Phillip the minute he sees me leave with Tony. Then you will follow us by car to wherever our destination is. Once you arrive at the brothel, Phillip will call Dad with the address."

Ashok rubbed his forehead and frowned. "Why is he calling Mr. Turner?" Surely Mr. Turner could not help them.

"Dad's been making a nuisance of himself at the police station. They know he means business, and he'll be at the police station when he receives Phillip's call. He plans to push them into making a raid on the place." The edge of Eli's mouth curved slightly. "Dad's going to politely suggest they do as he says, or the media will be arriving at the brothel in their place. Nothing like a little coercion to get some cooperation."

Ashok didn't hold any hope in the police helping and he didn't know what media or coercion meant, and he didn't care.

All he wanted was to see Shanti and feel his arms around her. He felt his stomach bubble with excitement. Finally they were doing something.

~~~

The paper had been a gift from one of her customers, and Charlotte almost smiled as she remembered his red, embarrassed face as he offered it to her.

She sat cross-legged on the floor and showed the girls how to make paper flowers. They giggled like schoolgirls as their hands folded the paper as she instructed.

Charlotte watched as they concentrated and leaned towards each other. The crinkling sound of paper folding brought softness to the room, something alien to the harsh nothingness that usually filled the space.

Friendships developed slowly in this place, and Charlotte felt hopeful that things were changing, that they were starting to care about each other.

"Charlotte, come with me. I need to talk to you," Padma demanded from the door. Charlotte took in Padma's frozen stance; the set of her chin brooked no discussion.

The girls stopped talking, and Charlotte gave them a reassuring smile. "I'll be excited to see how many flowers you've made by the time I get back," she said as she handed the flower she was working on to Shanti and patted her shoulder.

As she walked behind Padma, Charlotte's mouth moved as she uttered a silent prayer. She stood stiffly inside Padma's room and waited.

"Please, sit down." Padma indicated to the bed.

"No, thank you," Charlotte replied as she loosely laced her fingers together and shifted her weight from one foot to the other.

Her eyes boldly locked on Padma's, and she lifted an eyebrow in enquiry.

Padma ran her tongue over her lips and waved her hand. "You said you forgave me, Charlie. Surely forgiveness means we can still be— friends?"

Charlotte couldn't believe her ears. "I don't trust you."

The powerful smell of Padma's jasmine perfume sickened her. It would always remind her of sex, she thought. Padma had told her she used it to open the senses to new experiences. She hated it and what it signified in this place.

Padma lowered her eyes and nodded. "I had no choice, Charlie. My husband would kill me if I kept anything from him. You've had firsthand experience of what he can do; surely you understand the position you put me in."

"You made a choice Padma, and that's the end of it." She didn't want to be having this discussion. Everything in this room sickened her. The sight of the rumpled bed triggered pictures of Saul and she gasped.

"I had no choice. You wouldn't have been successful in escaping." Padma sighed. "Your friend would have been killed, and others would have been injured. You're a fool if you think your plan would have worked."

"We'll never know, will we?" Charlotte stated dryly, inching towards the door.

Padma's face flushed under her dark skin. She sat heavily on the bed. Her head dropped, and Charlotte was amazed to see tears glistening on her cheeks.

Charlotte's heart contracted. She took a tentative step towards the bed and stopped. What if she opened her heart to Padma again and she stomped all over it? Where was the wisdom in that?

"I'm so sorry," Padma whispered. "I don't know why I keep trying to make him love me. He's so evil. A part of me believes he cares for me, and I can't leave him."

Charlotte nibbled on her lower lip for a moment, then moved to crouch beside Padma, being careful not to touch the bed.

"You deserve better, my friend," Charlotte exclaimed. "He raped me and made you watch. He takes pleasure in ridiculing us, treating us like animals. He forces me to lick his toes. It's degrading! I've prayed and prayed for his heart to change. I've tried to see him as a man God loves; yet my heart goes cold when I think of him. I have to be honest and say I think he's made his choice, and that's between him and God."

"He's my husband," Padma said in a weak voice.

"A husband loves his wife, he doesn't hit and abuse her. I'm sorry, but what he does is wrong and he *is* answerable for it. He will pay, Padma, and if you're not careful, he'll take you down with him."

"There is nothing I can do." Padma clawed at the bedding with her fingers, and her voice faded in hopelessness.

"Yes, there is! You can surrender your life to Jesus Christ and begin to tell yourself the truth. We may never get out of here, but that doesn't mean we have to bow down to lies."

"What do you mean?" Padma's face was laced with uncertainty.

"If you accept this as your lot, then you'll stop fighting for justice, stop believing freedom is possible. You must fight, even if you only fight in your heart and mind," Charlotte exclaimed.

Padma's mouth fell open, and she clutched at Charlotte. "Do you think your God can forgive me?" she asked breathlessly.

"Jesus Christ loves you, Padma. If you ask him to forgive you, he will. Will you ask him now?" Charlotte asked, her shoulders tensing in hope.

"I—I need time to think, to get things right first." She hesitated and moistened her lips.

"'The thief comes only to steal and kill and destroy; I have come that they may have life, and have it to the full.' Jesus said that, Padma. Don't let the truth be stolen from you. Tomorrow may be too late," Charlotte begged.

A tentative knock caused Padma to jump off the bed and wipe away her tears. A woman stood meekly in the doorway, a paper flower dangling from her fingers. "I'm sorry to interrupt you, Padma. Charlie, can I speak to you, please?"

Charlotte glanced at Padma before she moved across the room to her friend. "What is it?"

The girl moved close to Charlotte, keeping a speculative watch on Padma the whole time.

Charlotte marveled at the relationships that were developing in the girls. They were becoming family. Her heart warmed at the thought.

"Charlie, the boss has called for Shanti. She's run to the toilets to hide."

Charlotte's heart gripped tight in her chest, and her eyes snapped to Padma. "I can't let him take her. Will you help me?"

"It's impossible. There's no place to hide her where he won't find her," Padma stated harshly.

"I have to try." Charlotte rushed out of the room.

If she could convince the boss to use her instead of Shanti, if she could beg him to leave the child alone, maybe she'd have a chance.

She rushed to the toilets and scanned the room. Shanti wasn't there. She pressed against the racing pulse in her throat and hurried towards the boss's room.

Outside his door she hesitated, and whispered a prayer before flinging the door open.

Shanti was huddled in the corner of the room, seemingly ignored by the man idly flicking through a newspaper.

Charlotte's skin prickled as she took in his appearance. His face seemed empty, devoid of all emotion, as if he could turn his thoughts off and on as he chose.

Shanti scrambled to her feet as Charlotte stepped further into the room.

The boss's gaze lifted, and he gave a slight inclination of his head.

Charlotte thought his eyes seemed to darken, if that were possible. She'd never seen such black eyes. A nervous tic moved at her temple.

Shanti raced over to Charlotte and stood behind her.

The boss gave her a calculating smile.

"Well, well, the angel girl. Scarface has spoken highly of you." He spoke in a smooth, educated voice, and Charlotte frowned in surprise. She'd only met him once and presumed he would be an animal like Saul.

"Sir, I've come to beg you to leave Shanti alone," she said clearly, her chin rising slightly, and she straightened her shoulders.

"And why should I do that? She belongs to me, and I will do what I want with her." His mouth twisted as he stood to face her, and she noticed his teeth were unnaturally white.

"She's just a child. Surely a man like you—an educated, intelligent man— would prefer a woman whom you can have a conversation with? A woman who will challenge your mind as well as your body? Let me take Shanti's place?"

The trembling started deep in her stomach; the thought of him touching her with his soft, manicured hands terrified her.

"An interesting thought." He moved towards her.

Charlotte wanted to back away but stood her ground. She had to appear fearless if this was going to work.

The boss ran a long fingernail down her cheek, and Charlotte

273

shuddered as the sharp edge scratched her skin. He bared his teeth like a hungry dog ready to devour a piece of fresh meat.

Pushing Shanti further behind her, Charlotte stepped towards the boss.

His fingers bit into her arms as he pulled her close. He leaned forward until his mouth was by her ear. She could feel his hot breath on her neck and shuddered.

"You think you can bargain with me? I can have you anytime I like and still take the child. You are nothing, do you hear me?" he snarled.

His fist slammed into the side of Charlotte's head.

She staggered and fell to her knees. The ringing in her ears caused her to feel faint, and she closed her eyes.

Shanti pushed at her, begging her to get up. Shaking her head to clear her mind, she stood and once again faced the boss.

"We are leaving. Come on, Shanti." Charlotte grabbed Shanti's arm and spun towards the door.

Scarface stood in front of her, blocking the way, his face expressionless.

Charlotte's throat locked in terror, and her arms spread around Shanti protectively.

"Remove her from my presence," the boss uttered in a bored tone. He walked over to his newspaper and resumed reading.

Scarface smirked and advanced towards Charlotte. Charlotte locked her fingers tighter around Shanti and set her chin. She wouldn't let go without a fight; she couldn't leave Shanti with that animal. She had to try and reason with Saul.

"Please, Saul. Shanti's only little, surely you can help her? A man like you has power. Why do you bow down to him like a slave?"

Scarface laughed and spat at her. "Let me show you my power, angel girl." He grabbed her fingers and began to bend them back one by one.

She heard the snap of her index finger an instant before she screamed as pain shot up her hand and into her wrist.

He flicked her hand away and she stepped back. She focused on Shanti and tried to push the pain away.

Pulling Shanti with her, she shuffled from side to side, trying to avoid Saul.

He was playing with her like a cat teasing a mouse. She knew it, but she couldn't let Shanti go. Tears flowed freely down her face as she struggled to keep her hold.

Scarface yanked Shanti out of her arms and hurled her across the floor towards the boss.

"Noooooo!" Charlotte screamed, chasing after her.

Scarface lifted his foot as Charlotte moved past him, and she lurched over it, falling face first. Her hands came out to save her, and tears flooded her eyes as sharp pain coursed through the top of her hand.

Pushing up with her other hand, she cradled her injured fingers and tried to regain control. She glanced at Shanti, who stood meekly in the middle of the room. The look of quiet acceptance etched on Shanti's face tore at Charlotte's heart. This pain was more excruciating than the snapping of her finger.

"Enough with the games. Get her out of here. Now!" The boss's face contorted in anger.

Scarface nodded. His hands clawed into Charlotte's arms as he hoisted her over his shoulder.

The dull pain in her stomach as his shoulder slammed into it caused her to gasp.

Charlotte screamed, pummeling at Scarface's back, heedless of her injury, watching helplessly as Shanti turned towards the boss.

As the door closed, hiding Shanti from view, Charlotte stopped struggling and drew a deep breath to try and calm her nerves.

Her clothing shifted, and she could feel Saul's hand creeping up her leg. She tried to pull down her sari, and he laughed at her struggle. Heat spread up her neck and her face burned at the position she was in.

Scarface strode down the hall, flung open the door to one of the workrooms, and dropped her.

Charlotte scurried out of his way and watched him warily. He stood before her with a smirk on his face and his arms crossed.

Her eyes flashed and anger spread through her like streams of molten lava. She sprung to her feet and walked towards him. She pushed at his solid chest and stomped her foot.

"I've had enough of you pushing me around! Back off!" she screamed, her hands on her hips.

Scarface threw back his head and laughed.

Charlotte felt on fire. She raised her arms, and her voice held an authority that wasn't her own.

"My God upholds me with his right hand. You will not touch me." Charlotte glared at him and her chin lifted in faith.

Scarface clenched his fists and lunged towards her. His hands flapped out in panic as his legs gave way and he slumped to the ground. His mouth opened in shock as he scrambled to his feet.

Charlotte's eyes widened and she hurried to the door.

Scarface cursed, spun around and threw his body at her. His legs wobbled and buckled at the knees. He collapsed in front of her. Bracing himself up on his hands, he crawled towards her. His eyes bore into hers and he cursed.

"Having trouble standing, Saul?" she asked sweetly.

"What have you done to me? Why can't I stand?" he hollered, fear paling his face.

Charlotte felt lightheaded, as if she'd just been for a long run. Her eyes welled up and she tilted her face. "God loves you, Saul. Perhaps you should think about that as you lie there."

Charlotte slipped out of the room, before compassion for the man had her on her knees before him.

Shanti needed her. Her heart fluttered as hope bubbled inside her. She had to believe that the power of God she'd just witnessed would help her get Shanti away from the boss.

The door to the boss's rooms was locked, and Charlotte frantically twisted the door handle. She banged on the wooden panel and yelled out to Shanti.

The thud of her hand on the wood echoed back at her, and she pressed her ear to the roughly painted door and listened.

It was eerily quiet. She nibbled her lip, uncertain what to do.

Could Shanti have been sent back to the common room? She forced herself to inhale a breath, spun around, and charged down the hall. The waning light caused shadows to press in around her, and Charlotte felt the air thicken.

She stood on the threshold of the common room. Her eyes pricked with tears, and fear gnawed at her stomach. Shanti wasn't here.

Chapter 41

The car sped along the street, and Eli wondered if he'd ever get used to the traffic in India. Cars vied for prominence, and the three lanes of traffic could be mistaken for six.

He glanced down into the car's side mirror. The headlights of the car following them blinked back at him, giving him a sense of security. Eli hoped it was Phillip's car.

So far things had gone to plan.

The way Tony kept talking about the girls at the brothel was making it difficult for Eli to play his part.

"You got your money ready, Geoff? They don't let you in unless you pay up front." Tony glanced his way, and Eli nodded and pulled a wad of notes from his shirt pocket.

He waved the money in front of Tony and grinned. "Should be enough for a good night, I reckon." Eli laughed and stuffed the money back into his pocket.

"You owe me for setting this up. How about you buy me a drink when we get back to the hotel?"

"It's a deal. Are we just about there?" Eli shifted in his seat, his senses heightening and adrenaline pumping through his veins. He needed action.

As Tony parked the car and turned off the engine, everything in Eli screamed to throw open the door and race into the house to find his sister. Making himself sit back, he looked around, seemingly in no hurry.

Ever since Charlie had gone missing, he'd visualized this moment. What if she wasn't here? What if the girl Tony was bringing him to meet wasn't Charlie?

Panic and fear pulled at his gut. His stomach rolled and he steeled himself. He became like a machine. Forcing feelings down and moving automatically.

As he stepped into the street, he assessed the house Tony was pointing at. One entry through a wooden gate and no visible windows.

Tony slapped him on the back and ambled across the street. His laugh grated on Eli's nerves and he forced himself to breathe. His footsteps crunched on the loose gravel, the sound unnerving him. His heartbeat accelerated as they stepped inside the compound.

A thickset man stepped out of the shadows and blocked their path. He nodded at Eli and greeted Tony by name. Eli waited, holding tightly to the steely amour that held him together. He forced himself to respond jovially to the pimp as he handed over his money.

~~~

Shanti squatted on the floor, not sure what to do. The room he'd taken her to was hidden behind a huge curtain, and she wondered if anyone would ever find her here.

She sniffed and crinkled her nose, not liking the musty smell. There were no windows, and the only light came from the flickering of the candles placed on a round table in the corner.

The table had a black cloth over it and a big cup with a strange pattern engraved into the metal. Shanti watched spellbound as light bounced off the cup. She shivered as she imagined it being alive.

The stillness in the room caused Shanti to look at the boss. Why was he standing so still? He seemed to not blink, and his eyes were fixed on her face. He'd not said a word since Scarface had taken Charlie away.

Shanti had been scared before and trembled at the things the boss had done to her, but this time the fear that scratched at her heart was freezing her to numbness.

It would be better, she thought, if he hit her. His stare was like the lash of icy spears pricking her skin. Her eyes darted around the empty room, and she longed for a way to escape. She wanted to move further away from him, but his eyes controlled her.

No Shanti, her mind whispered, stay still, don't make him angry. Her eyes widened as he brought his hands forward and she saw the knife. It was like nothing she'd ever seen before, and her stomach clenched in reaction to it.

The blade was huge and the handle was curled with an evil face on it. She licked her lips, trying to break the spell he had over her. She twisted her hands together and wanted to cry.

"Come here," he ordered, his eyes bulging as he looked at her.

Jesus, help me, her mind screamed.

Shanti shook her head and inched back. Her eyes caught his, and she knew it was time to speak. "You are a bad, bad man. Jesus is not happy with you." Her voice sounded shaky to her ears, but then she noticed she'd stopped trembling. "I feel sorry for you, Mr. Boss. Ashok told me that people like you are sad, and dying inside."

She slowly unbent her knees and stood. She wouldn't stay here another minute. Shanti smiled and imagined Jesus taking her hand, leading her out of the danger of the jungle.

Her body jerked as she was grabbed by her arm and yanked across the room.

The boss hissed at her, and she uttered a gasp of disbelief. She'd been so sure Jesus was with her, that she'd be able to walk out of the room.

Her heart fluttered and her hands clenched into fists. The boss scooped her up and carried her across the room. She could feel the edge of the knife against her back and tried to stay still; she didn't want him to slip and cut her.

The boss dropped the knife to the floor and laid her on a narrow table. His large hand pressed down on her chest and his other hand pulled a tie up over her body.

Shanti pulled her legs up to her stomach in panic. The pressure of his hand hurt, and she knew she had to stop him from tying her to the table.

"Relax child, this is what you were born for. You are a sacrifice to my god, Baalin. A great honor."

Heat flooded Shanti's face. Her breath came quickly and her chest struggled to take in air. Her eyes flooded with tears and she knew there was nothing she could do.

He lowered his face and his lips grazed hers.

She pushed her head back against the table, trying to avoid him. The hard surface was unrelenting, and Shanti thrashed her head from side to side.

Please, Jesus. I want to see Ashok one more time. I want to tell him I love him. I don't want to die.

The ropes tightened as she tried to move her feet.

"Arggghh." Shanti screamed with everything in her. The sound bounced off the walls and mocked her.

The boss threw back his head and laughed. His face contorted and Shanti's eyes widened in fear. His skin bagged and his face seemed sharper, as if something was taking over his body.

"Jesus," she whispered, her voice disappearing.

He pulled a rag across her mouth and knotted it, yanking the material tight across her face.

Shanti pushed at the rag with her tongue, hating the dryness in her mouth. She could taste dust and desperately wanted to lick her lips.

The boss started to chant strange words, and Shanti tried to close her ears to the sound of his voice. He laid the knife on her stomach, its

281

blade cold against her skin, and his fingers fanned her cheeks.

Shanti's eyes snapped open. She wanted to block from her mind everything that was happening but couldn't. Her eyes dried up and she couldn't even blink. All her energy was channeled into trying to control the beating of her heart against her chest. It felt like it was going to burst through her skin and drop to the floor.

He moved the knife and flicked the razor-sharp tip under her chin. Shanti felt a warm trickle of blood make a path down her neck.

He lifted the knife above her chest and closed his eyes.

~~~

"Has anyone seen Shanti?" Charlotte asked. The women in the room shook their heads and told her Shanti hadn't returned.

Charlotte could see they were getting ready to go to work and were distracted. She knew they needed to distance themselves from everything around them to prepare for the night ahead.

A sense of urgency rushed through her. Scarface was out of action for now, so she had a window of time to find her friend. She needed something to help her break into the boss's room.

Her head throbbed with tension, and she spun around and raced towards Padma's room. Soon the house would be filled with men, and her chance of getting Shanti away from the boss would diminish.

Padma sat on the bed as if nothing were wrong. Charlotte wanted to hit her in anger. "Padma, help me. I need something to break the lock on the boss's door."

Padma stared at her as if she'd lost her mind. This made Charlotte seethe. "Don't just sit there, get up and help me!" she screamed.

"Charlie, are you mad? You can't break down the boss's door. He'll kill you." Padma sprung to her feet and glared at Charlotte.

"No, he won't, because I'm getting out of here." She charged across the room to Padma's cupboards and started to rummage around until she found a screwdriver.

"Your friend isn't coming, Charlie. Remember, I ruined your plan of escape. There is no hope." Padma blocked the doorway and stood with both hands on her hips.

"There is always hope, always! God is more powerful than any plan of man. I intend to get Shanti and walk out the front door, and no one is going to stop me. Now either get out of my way or come with me. Make your choice."

Charlotte moved towards the door and wanted to cry as Padma moved aside to let her pass. She looked back to see if her friend would follow, but Padma had resumed her posture of hopelessness on the bed.

Charlotte gritted her teeth, wanting to shake Padma. She turned on her heels and took off down the hall.

Chapter 42

The house was stale, and smelt of darkness. Eli followed Tony down a dingy hall and into a dark, empty room. The dim light unnerved Eli, and the stench of sickly perfume made him want to throw up.

His chest tightened when he saw the bed with a single stained sheet covering the mattress.

What if this didn't work and he failed Charlie after coming so close? His gaze snapped back to Tony, and his hands balled into fists. He couldn't stand here like a turkey awaiting slaughter.

His jaw jutted in determination and he stepped towards Tony and scowled. How many girls had this man used? His hand snapped out and he grabbed the material of Tony's shirt.

"Where is she? When will they bring her?"

"Let go of me! What do you think you're doing? Relax, Geoff." Tony screwed up his face and pulled at Eli's hand.

Eli gritted his teeth and let go of Tony. He stepped back and exhaled. He wanted to wipe the smug look off Tony's face. "Sorry, mate. The excitement got to me."

"We're here now, they will—um—bring the girl to us. I didn't tell you before, but it's not the girl I told you about. She's not available.

Still, what does it matter when the lights go out?" He laughed.

Not Charlie? Eli stood motionless. His mind wanted to deny the possibility of things going wrong. He blew out a breath and ran a hand through his hair. If she was in this place, failure wasn't an option.

"You disgust me. You'll go down for bringing people here to exploit innocent women." Eli glared at Tony. "The police are on their way, and they know all about you. If you want to get any leniency, I suggest you stay in this room. I'm going to find my sister."

"Your sister? So you're playing the hero, come to rescue the little beauty," Tony mocked. "Do you want me to tell you how good she was in the sack?"

Eli lunged at him, toppling them both to the ground.

Tony grabbed Eli's shoulders and twisted, unbalancing Eli's hold. Tony scrambled to his feet and crouched, ready to attack.

Adrenaline pumped through Eli, and his jaw tightened. He had to silence Tony before he called the alarm.

"I'll enjoy this, boy." Tony leered. "Just like I enjoyed taking your sister."

Eli rushed at him, blocking a swing aimed at his head. Oxygen saturated his muscles and the squalor jumped into vivid detail.

His leg swung out and cut Tony's legs from underneath him.

Something snapped in Eli; he wanted to hurt the man for touching Charlie. His fist smashed into Tony's face and he heard the crunch of impact. He swung his arm back to hit again.

"Argggh," Tony yelled and rammed his head into Eli's stomach, pushing him across the room.

Eli slammed against the wall, the loud *thud* mocking his need to keep quiet. He sucked in a breath and began pummeling Tony's sides.

Tony pushed away, panting.

"Enough," Eli shouted, charging after Tony.

Using the full force of his body he slammed his fists into Tony again and again.

Tony slid to the floor like a deflated balloon, and Eli stood over him, blood dripping from his fists. His chest rose and fell raggedly as he tried to regain his breath.

Dropping to one knee, Eli pulled a roll of duct tape from his pocket and slapped a length of it over Tony's bloodied mouth. Quickly Eli wound tape around his wrists and ankles.

Eli flexed his fingers and wiped his hands on Tony's shirt.

Slipping quietly out of the room, Eli moved with purpose down the hall and opened each door he came to. Each room showed a scene that would forever be etched on Eli's mind.

Women beckoning him in, with lost eyes and scanty clothing. His heart contracted and he shook his head. "I'm looking for my sister, Charlotte. Is she here?"

Silence greeted his question and he moved on.

She had to be here. His heart raced, and desperation made his steps quicken.

A woman moved towards him like she owned the place; she walked with authority and stared straight at him.

Eli grabbed her arms in a vice like grip. He narrowed his eyes, wanting to shake her. "My sister, Charlotte, where is she?" He saw the shock on her face, and her shoulders stiffened.

"Charlie's brother?" she asked, stunned.

"Yes, Charlie. Quick, tell me where she is," he demanded, his heart pounding at her recognition of Charlie's name.

The sound of sirens brought people out of the rooms, and the woman paled and tried to pull away.

"Move, take me to her—now!" His voice snapped, and he shoved her down the hall.

"You don't understand, my husband—"

"Woman, I don't have time for this." He charged down the hall, dragging her with him.

They pushed past young women who moved as if sleepwalking in the opposite direction. He searched their faces for Charlie, longing to see her.

286

Eli stopped and twisted around to face the woman.

Tears streamed unchecked down her face, and she lifted her chin slightly. Her eyes locked on his, and he saw her brokenness reflected back at him.

"Which way?" he asked softly.

"This way. I'm Padma, Charlie's friend," she said and hurried ahead of him. They turned down a narrow hall and went through several doors. He could hear a banging noise and ran ahead to see if Charlotte was there.

He saw her. His feet halted and tears flooded his eyes.

"Charlie," he called.

She spun around, and her eyes widened at the sight of him.

Charlotte dropped whatever it was she was holding and ran to him. His arms opened and then he was holding her.

Eli couldn't breathe. He'd dreamed of this moment and now it was here.

The sound of screaming floated down the hallway, and Eli tensed. He needed to find Shanti and get out of here.

Charlotte pulled back, and he saw the tears spilling down her face, her beautiful face.

He brushed his fingers against them and her eyes softened. His lips trembled and his eyes welled up.

"You're safe now, Bud. It's over."

Charlotte tensed and she glanced behind her. She grabbed his hand and pulled him towards the door.

"Eli, Shanti must be in this room. We have to get her out."

He heard the desperation in her voice and tried the handle. Everything in him wanted to bundle Charlie up and get her to safety. The longer they stayed, the greater the risk of her being hurt.

"Shanti," Charlotte screamed, banging the door.

Eli felt the blood leave his face. Shanti was Ashok's sister and the daughter he himself longed for.

Eli gritted his teeth and he moved Charlotte aside. He'd break down the door with his bare hands if he had to.

Both Charlotte and Eli froze as they heard a muffled scream come from behind the door.

~~~

Police cars lined the street, and Ashok breathed a sigh of relief. His breath fogged the car window, and he lifted his hand to wipe the moisture so he could see.

Dr. Phillip had told him to stay in the car, but his heart was screaming out to Shanti, and he desperately wanted to go to her.

He watched as policemen ran everywhere. Women started emerging from the gate, and Ashok scanned the crowd for anyone Shanti's age.

He wiped his hand over the window in frustration. His hands slapped down on the back of the car seat; he couldn't wait a minute longer. He'd promised Shanti he'd find her. Sitting here like a lame dog wasn't going to keep his promise.

Ashok opened the door and slipped into the shadows. He didn't want some policeman, or Dr. Phillip, stopping him.

His eyes adjusted to the dark and he saw the entrance to the compound. He waited a moment, then sprinted to the gate and slipped in. He could feel Shanti in this place, she was close, he knew it.

His heart thumped wildly in his chest and his hands moved along the wall beside him.

A woman jumped out in front of him, and he opened his mouth to scream—he hadn't seen her there—she placed a hand on his shoulder.

He closed his mouth and shrugged her off and moved on.

Calm down, he told himself. He had to trust Jesus. Jesus would help him find Shanti.

A small smile of confidence lifted his lips, and he moved down the hallway, no longer caring who saw him.

~~~

The air in the room seemed filled with flapping noises. Shanti wondered if she was imagining it or if her fear was making her hear things.

She stared up at the boss, and fresh tears seeped out the corner of her eyes, dampening her hair. She sniffed.

Shanti tried to move her right leg to relieve the cramping. She flexed her foot and screamed out as pain tightened her muscle.

The boss glanced at her and it seemed to Shanti as if he didn't see her. His eyes glazed over with a film and she shuddered.

He moved over to the round table, carefully placed the knife on the cloth, and picked up the cup. Shanti followed him with her eyes as he lifted the cup to his mouth and kissed the symbol carved into the side.

She couldn't stop the rumble that started in her stomach, moved up her chest, and tightened and locked her throat. Panic gripped her and she struggled to breathe.

"Child, this knife will make you a love offering to Baalin." His lips pressed down and spread over the flat, smooth blade. She squeezed her eyes tight at the terrifying sight of him caressing the blade. She heard a whoosh as he waved it through the air, a terrible, scary sound that echoed around the room.

The banging in the other room stopped the boss's movements.

Shanti's eyes flew open and she saw the boss's face take on a deathly stillness. He turned and moved to the door, checking the lock. Then he returned.

Her heart flipped. Would whoever was there get to her in time? She blinked to clear her eyes of tears and stared at the boss as he lifted the knife above her.

Jesus, are you here? I'm scared.

Her eyes widened as she saw the knife lower to her stomach and the tip of the blade touched her bare skin, stinging her.

Sucking in a deep breath, Shanti pulled her stomach in tight. He lifted the knife again and held it above his head. Closing his eyes, he chanted, and Shanti screamed into the gag.

Didn't he know she was only a little girl who wanted to see her brother? She shivered and closed her eyes tight.

Shanti, I have come that you may have life, and have it to the full.

She let out a deep breath. The light in the room seemed brighter, clearer, and she was sure she could hear the sound of the river. She raised her head to look at the boss.

Who else was in the room? There was someone behind him, she was sure of it.

The boss's voice mocked her. "Your humble servant gives you this child, Baalin. My god, I pour out her blood for you. Look favorably upon me and give me wealth and power," the boss chanted as he waved the knife over her body.

Jesus was in the room with her, she could sense him. He was going to save her. Shanti's lips twitched under the tie and she wanted to laugh.

"Argggggh," the boss screamed as he lifted the knife higher above his head and then plunged it down towards her.

Shanti knew Jesus would save her, she wasn't afraid of any old knife.

The blade glinted and sparkles danced off it as it descended towards her.

Her body jumped as the blade sliced through her skin and pushed deep into her stomach. He twisted the handle, and pain screamed through every part of her. She tried to take a deep breath but all the air in her chest had been sucked out.

Her eyes gazed in disbelief as he pulled the bloodied knife from her to lift it above his head again. Her mouth moved as she tried to break free.

"Nooooooooooo," she screamed into the filthy rag.

Shanti heard the crash as if from a distance. Was someone screaming out her name? She tried to listen, to think, but her mind was all woozy and she wanted to close her eyes.

Someone touched her face, and warmth spread through her.

She forced her eyes open and blinked to see who was bending over her. The light was so bright behind the person that she had to blink several times to adjust her vision.

"Shanti, don't be afraid, I am with you. I will never leave you or forsake you. You are mine."

Shanti's heart felt like it was going to burst. Jesus was standing over her.

She stared into the light and his features began to take form; she wanted to reach out and touch him, tell him how much she loved him.

The door burst open and Shanti glanced away from Jesus for a moment. Charlie and a man had raced into the room.

The boss cursed and slammed the knife into her chest.

Her body twitched, and a scream started in her that echoed through her mind and found escape through the soggy material gagging her mouth.

~~~

Charlotte flung herself across the room towards the table. Out of the corner of her eye she saw Eli slam into the boss and hurl him to the floor.

Her hands fluttered over Shanti's chest, but she didn't know what to do. Blood poured out of her tiny body, and Charlotte stood immobilized in fear. She reached down and gently removed the gag from Shanti's mouth.

Shanti's head tilted towards her, and Charlotte brushed her fingers through Shanti's hair.

"Shanti, hang on sweetheart. Help is coming. Can you hear me, listen to my voice, Shanti. The police are here, you're safe now."

Charlotte quickly untied the straps holding poor little Shanti prisoner. She wanted to pull out the knife that was buried deep within the child, but wisdom told her to leave it. Her fingers spread across the other wound, trying to still the blood flow. "Eli, help me," she screamed.

Eli pushed the man to the ground and stood puffing beside her. "Phillip will know what to do, we need to get her to him."

He lifted Shanti in his arms, being careful not to dislodge the knife.

Looking at the blood on her hands, Charlotte shuddered. She ran after Eli, and her heart contracted as she saw her friend's lifeless body in Eli's arms. They came to the hallway and Charlotte grabbed Eli's arm.

"Take her in there and bring Phillip to her."

Eli placed Shanti gently on the bed and raced out of the room, screaming Phillip's name.

"Charlie, press down on the wound to try and stop the bleeding," Padma suggested.

Charlotte hadn't known Padma had joined her, and she nodded. She pushed the middle of Shanti's stomach and tried not to think about how much this would be hurting the little girl.

The more she pressed, down the more the other wound seemed to bleed. She screamed, "Jesus, please help me."

~~~

Ashok's skin prickled and his heart beat wildly. He ran one way, then the other. He searched out the shadows as he hunched down.

Police moved through the house, making a lot of noise, but seemed uninterested in him. Ashok hated this place, hated that Shanti had been locked up here by bad men.

He heard someone scream out to Jesus. Quickly he turned and raced in the direction of the voice. Hope fluttered in his heart.

He came to a room with the door slightly opened and he pushed it with his fingertips. He saw two women bending over someone on the bed. His eyes widened and he charged across the room.

"Shanti," he whispered. His heart screamed in his chest as he saw the blood pouring from her stomach and the knife still attached to her.

He touched her, and his stomach dropped at the lack of color in her face. "Shanti, I'm here. It's Ashok," he stated firmly. He'd found her and everything had to be all right.

The woman moved back to give him room, and her hand rested

briefly on his shoulder. "Shanti, wake up!" he screamed in a tormented voice. "It's Ashok, I'm here now so you need to open your eyes."

Her eyelids flickered and he leaned in close to her face. He kissed her cheek and his tears mingled with hers.

Dr. Phillip moved in beside him and his hands began to move over Shanti's body. Ashok ignored him and kept his eyes on his sister's face. Dr. Phillip would fix her up, and he'd tell her that they were going to live with Eli forever. His lips trembled and he felt his jaw lock.

"I'm sorry, there's nothing I can do." Phillip's voice trembled. "I don't think she's going to make it. She's lost too much blood and—"

Ashok turned to look at him; the words he'd heard confused him.

It wasn't too late. They'd found Shanti and she would live. Jesus would make certain of that.

Shaking his head, he climbed up on the bed and pulled her into his arms. Her body sagged against him, and he could feel her breath on his face. She was alive and he was going to make sure she didn't die.

"Shanti, I love you. Do you hear me? I love you. You can't die, I need you," he sobbed.

"Ashok?" Shanti's eyes opened, and her voice was just above a whisper. "You found me, I knew you would."

Shanti's skin looked like all the color had been rubbed out and a dirty brown-grey remained. Her eyelids were swollen from crying, and there was blood coating her everywhere.

Ashok expelled a big breath and sucked air into his lungs. "I promised I'd find you, Shanti. You know I always keep my promises. I'm sorry I lost you, but it's okay now 'cause we're back together."

Swallowing past the lump in his throat Ashok's chin shook. Fear gripped his insides and he hung onto a thread of hope as he leaned over her.

"Can you see Jesus, Ashok?" Shanti asked. Her eyes left his face and she looked behind him.

Ashok turned to see what she was looking at. No one was there.

"No, I can't see him, but I know he loves us." Ashok thought of the card in his pocket and wanted to get it out to show her. But he didn't want to let his sister go.

"I can see him, he's smiling at me. The river Ashok, oh the river," Shanti said, lifting her hand slightly.

Ashok slumped. What did it mean if Shanti could see Jesus?

He looked around the room and panic gripped him. "Stay with me, you're my sister and I need you."

Shanti moved her head and gazed up at him.

He could hardly breathe with watching her. His throat felt clogged with unshed tears, and his heart was in agony. Part of him wanted to run away; he couldn't bear to see her in such pain.

Ashok lay her down and cupped her face with his hands. Her blood soaked his clothes, and he longed to get her out of here.

He could hear someone crying softly behind him and tried to block the sound out.

"Remember how you got better after the dog bit you? You will get better now too. It may take longer, but don't give up, Shanti."

"Don't be afraid, Ashok. Jesus will look after me. I love you," she said, her voice fading.

"Stay with me, I need you, pleeeeease," he screamed.

Ashok knew when she left him; he felt her body go heavy in his arms. His head dropped to her shoulder and he lay beside her. Her arm flopped onto the bed, and he picked it up and flung it over his shoulder.

She couldn't be dead, what good would that do? Her arm fell off him, and his shoulders shook.

Jesus had taken his Shanti.

"Why, Jesus? I don't understand. Why?" He wept, despair carving its way through his body.

He felt hands on his back and shrugged to stop Eli from touching him. He didn't want to talk to anyone or to move. Maybe Jesus would breathe air back into Shanti and she would be okay.

Can you, Jesus? For me, his mind screamed. He didn't want to live if she was dead. What purpose would his life have if he didn't have his little sister to look after?

"Ashok, I'm sorry, son. She's gone." Eli's voice sounded distant, far away.

When Eli picked him up, Ashok let him. He didn't struggle, and as he looked up at his friend, his eyes blurred.

Death would be better than this feeling of emptiness that seeped into his heart.

Couldn't Jesus be trusted? Hadn't Jesus promised to take care of him and Shanti?

Ashok closed his eyes tightly, and anger pushed away faith in his heart.

Chapter 43

The grey cloud that covered the sky seemed appropriate to Macy. She looked out the window of Phillip's apartment, her arms crossed protectively over her stomach.

She knew Charlotte was safe, but Ashok's little sister had died.

Relief bubbled up inside her that it hadn't been Charlie, and her cheeks burned in shame at her selfish thought. No one should have died. It wasn't fair at all.

She pushed her hair back off her face and glanced over to see Bill pacing and looking at his watch. Phillip had called to tell them Eli was staying with Ashok, who wanted to stay outside the house until the police took Shanti's body away.

Phillip was bringing Charlotte to them. Tears of relief flooded her eyes, and she blinked several times to stop their flow.

Her baby girl, safe.

Macy closed her eyes and pictured Charlie home in Australia and tucked up in her bedroom. She wanted to do all the things mothers did with their daughters; going out to lunch, shopping, and planning Charlotte's wedding.

Sighing she shook her head as the picture faded. What Charlotte needed most from her was love and protection. Her poor daughter needed looking after, sheltering from the big ugly world. Yes, the sooner they got her home the better. She'd talk to Bill about it and book flights in the morning.

The sound of the key in the lock caused her heart to speed up. She looked across at Bill, and their eyes locked for a moment.

Macy moved across the room to stand beside him, and he grabbed her hand and squeezed.

The sight of her daughter's lank hair and bloodstained clothes chipped another piece of Macy's heart.

She'd expected Charlotte to run straight into her arms, but she stood inside the door staring at them. Bill stepped forward and opened his arms and Macy watched, confused, as Charlotte slowly stepped into his embrace.

Macy sucked in her lower lip and moved to join them. Her arms circled the both of them, and Charlotte shifted slightly to include her.

The vice like control Macy had held over her emotions snapped. Her eyes welled up and her throat locked with the effort to stop her tears.

Charlotte lifted sad eyes to her.

The pain Macy saw mirrored an awareness of things she could only guess at. A deep, gut-wrenching sob came out of Macy's mouth.

Charlotte turned to comfort her and patted her shoulder. Her daughter's smile stemmed her flow of tears, and Macy shook herself.

It was Charlotte who needed help, not her.

Phillip held out a box of tissues. She gave him a watery smile and grabbed a handful.

"I'm sorry, sweetheart. It's just so wonderful to see you," she murmured. She saw the shadow of grief on her daughter's face and swallowed back her words. The little girl must have meant a lot to her daughter.

"It's good to see you too, Mum. Thanks for being here for me, for not giving up on finding me." Her voice sounded flat to Macy's ears, and she didn't know what to do to make things better.

Phillip moved towards Charlotte and laid a hand on her shoulder. "Charlie, I'd like you to lie down, get some sleep. Will you take half a sleeping pill for me?" he asked gently.

Macy blinked several times as she saw Charlotte's eyes flood with tears.

"Phil, I can't believe she's gone. I loved her so much," Charlotte stated, her voice choked with grief.

Macy's chest tightened as Charlotte stepped into Phillips arms and sobbed. She licked her lips and her mouth felt suddenly dry. Was there more to Charlotte's relationship with Phillip than she knew?

She watched her daughter pull away and rub a hand over her eyes. Getting her to bed was a good idea.

"Which room can she take, Phillip?" Macy asked, taking control.

"The back room. There are clean towels in the hall cupboard, Mrs. Turner. I'll get Charlie something to change into after her shower."

"Thank you. Come on Charlie, I'll help you. We have plenty of time to talk tomorrow." With a heavy heart, Macy led her daughter out of the room. Charlotte had been through so much. She'd changed; her sweet, innocent daughter was gone forever and replaced by a woman who had lived through the most horrendous nightmare.

Grief at the tragedy of it all pulled at Macy, and she wanted to tear her clothes apart and weep. There was nothing she could say that would make this right.

~~~

Eli cleared his throat and rested his hand on Ashok's shoulder. He refused to let the boy push him away. He'd seen the lad turn as stiff as a stone as the police carried Shanti out of the house.

Ashok's mouth had taken on a hard line, and Eli longed to reassure him that everything would be all right. But would it? How do you explain such a cruel death?

Eli gave a deep sob and closed his eyes briefly. His head pounded and he longed for respite from the ache behind his eyes. He wiped at the sweat on his forehead and repositioned his feet.

Too much had happened tonight. He should be celebrating that he'd found Charlie, yet grief twisted his stomach and he wanted to fast-track time to when things would feel better.

Seeing Ashok's pain seemed worse than anything he'd ever experienced. *Lord Jesus, help me know what to say.*

"Ashok. Shanti saw Jesus. You heard her say that, didn't you?"

"So what, it doesn't bring her back to me, does it." Ashok yanked away from Eli's hand. A vein pulsed madly at his temple, and his chin jutted out.

Eli winced at the boy's words and shook his head. "She's not in pain anymore, Ashok. Jesus rescued her, took her home to heaven," he said patiently.

"I want her here with me. I hate Jesus! He promised me he'd look after her." His voice was sharp and his eyes blazed with anger.

Ashok pulled out the card in his pocket and ripped it in two and tossed it to the ground.

Eli cleared his throat as emotion choked him. "I don't understand why she had to die, son. One day when you're with her again you can ask her what it was like taking Jesus's hand and feeling no pain."

Ashok didn't answer. He dropped his head and stared blankly at the torn card.

"Are you ready to go?" Eli asked. His gaze locked onto Ashok's face.

The boy nodded and moved towards the door. Eli wanted to pick him up and carry him close to his heart, but refrained. The boy had aged before his eyes tonight, and he didn't want to push affection on him.

He stooped down, picked up the pieces of the ripped card, dusted them, and put them in his pocket.

They walked out of the compound, and Eli spotted Ted leaning against his car. The police had given him half an hour before they expected him to show up at the police station to make a report. It was going to be a long night.

He turned and squatted down beside Ashok, gently massaging the boy's shoulders. "Ashok, I know you don't understand why Jesus didn't save Shanti's life. I don't either, son. But what I do know is, her life mattered, and one day we'll look back and see the significance of it."

Ashok's eyes shifted slightly and he stared at Eli's chin, avoiding his eyes. His mouth trembled and Eli could feel the shiver that went through him.

"You still have a sister, she just lives with Jesus. She's still here, son." He gently touched Ashok's chest and then pulled Ashok into his arms and stood.

"I love you. You're my boy, my son. Jesus didn't want you to be alone once he took Shanti home, so he gave you me." Eli smiled and rubbed his hand over Ashok's hair.

"Ted's going to take us back to Phillip's, then I have to go to the police station to make out a report. You'll be safe at Phillip's, and I'll be back by the time you wake up. Okay?"

Ashok's big brown eyes closed with weariness, and he nodded into Eli's chest.

Chapter 44

The first rays of daylight snuck through the blind, and Charlotte turned her head. It had been months since she'd had a window to gaze through, and now she lay on the bed too despondent to get up and look.

Shanti was gone.

Her sweet smile lost to her forever. She turned on her side and tucked her legs up. The soft texture of the mattress seemed foreign to her after sleeping on a hard floor for so long.

She could hear the sound of voices and knew she should get up and see her parents. The sadness she saw reflected in her parents' eyes brought her pain. She wasn't the same person who had crept out of the house six months ago, believing the world was a safe place.

Could she go back to her old life? From a few things her mother had said last night, this was exactly what she expected her to do.

How could she forget Shanti and all she'd suffered and lost, her young life brutally stolen from her? Who would speak up for other children like Shanti? The injustice and cruelty of forcing women and children into sexual servitude needed to be addressed.

Her skin crawled as she pictured some of the men she'd been with, and she sat up and flung away the covers.

It wasn't right. What about all the girls that had come out of the brothel? What would happen to them? Who would provide them with food and shelter until they got work?

If she went back to safety in Australia, with her parents, would that be fair?

Her heart fluttered and she closed her eyes. *Lord, I don't know what to do. I don't feel like I'm Mum and Dad's little girl anymore.*

Tears spilled down her face, and she pictured how different things would have been if Shanti had lived. She'd be excitedly telling her about Australia and kangaroos, building up a picture for the young girl.

Her mother knocked and entered the room. Charlotte hastily wiped away her tears and turned towards her. She noticed the pile of clothes in her mother's hand.

"Morning Charlie," Macy said as she joined Charlotte on the bed. "Did you manage to get some sleep?"

Charlotte nodded, pulled up her knee, and looked at her mother. There were new lines on her mother's face that she hadn't noticed last night. She must have been so worried, Charlotte thought.

"Yes, I did. Mum, are you okay? I know this must have been a horrible time for you."

"Having you safe is all that matters." Macy reached over and hugged Charlotte close. "Do you want to get dressed and come and have some breakfast? Your father's making pancakes, and Gargi is here to see you."

Charlotte's mouth parted in a smile and she stood. Yes, she wanted to see Gargi—she had missed her friend and longed to hear how she was.

"Give me a few minute and I'll be out. Thanks for the clothes, Mum."

As Charlotte stepped into the lounge area, her eyes widened. Not only were her parents here, but she also saw Eli, Phillip, Ashok, and Gargi. Gargi stepped towards her, and the confident look on her face surprised Charlotte.

"Charlie, my sister. I have something to tell you." Gargi took Charlotte's hands. "I have met Jesus! Thank you for leading me to him. My life is now his," she blurted out.

A deep, bubbling joy burst from Charlotte's mouth, and she laughed. Her eyes watered as she realized Gargi was truly her sister now.

She flung her arms around Gargi and hugged her tight, weeping and laughing at the same time.

Her brother walked towards her and lifted his hand to cup her cheek. He looked exhausted, and Charlotte went into his arms. There was an unspoken understanding between them. He knew that nothing would be the same.

As she stepped back, she noticed his eyes moved to Gargi and softened.

Charlotte licked her lips and wondered at the look she'd seen pass between them. A small smile tugged at her mouth as she contemplated the thought of Eli falling for her friend.

"Where are these pancakes I smell?" she asked, and everyone laughed.

Plates and food were passed around, and as Charlotte was about to lift her fork to her mouth, she noticed Ashok sitting on the floor in the corner.

She glanced at Eli and lifted her eyebrows in question. He placed his hand over his heart and shrugged.

Picking up another fork, Charlotte moved to sit on the floor beside Ashok.

"Hi. Shanti told me all about you, Ashok. She loved you so much and was so proud of you."

The boy's head drooped some more, and Charlotte prayed for the right words. "I told Shanti about my Dad's pancakes, and she said you'd probably like them." Charlotte forked a piece of doughy mixture, covered it with syrup, and offered it to him.

Ashok's mouth trembled as he took the fork from her and ate the pancake.

She watched as he savored the flavor. "Was she right? Do you like them?"

"Yes." He nodded. "Very much."

"Good. Share my plate with me, and I'll tell you some of the things I love about Shanti. She is the bravest person I've ever met."

Once the meal was finished, Ashok asked Eli if he could go outside for a while, and Charlotte watched the boy leave.

She'd told Shanti she wanted to provide a home for her and Ashok. Her mouth tightened in determination. She didn't know how that would look, but she couldn't abandon Ashok—she'd make sure he had a family.

"About Ashok," she started. "I promised Shanti he could stay with me. I can't abandon the boy just because Shanti didn't make it."

"Ashok's staying with me, Charlie. I love him and I've already told him that he's my son," Eli stated firmly. "Sorry, Sis, but how does the role of aunt fit?"

Her eyes widened as she looked at her brother. Pride at the man he'd become filled her, and she smiled. "Fits perfectly, just let me help, okay?"

"I expect you to," he answered cockily and grinned. Her mother chose that moment to move across the room to perch on the chair beside her.

"I've arranged tickets for our flight home on Wednesday morning," Macy informed her.

Charlotte felt the blood leave her face. She felt dizzy. Wednesday? What day was it today, she wondered.

Her eyes flickered across the room and locked onto Phillip. He stared back and she wondered what he was thinking.

Could she just pack up, leave, and never look back? She cleared her throat and twisted her hands.

"Mum, I not sure I'm ready to go back home yet," she said.

"Honey, I know you must be feeling dreadful. Your father and I will look after everything," Macy stated firmly.

Charlotte tilted her head and saw her mother as if for the first time. A sigh escaped her lips and she looked down at her hands. In the past she'd let her mother make decisions for her because it was easier than conflict.

Why was that, Charlotte asked herself. Was it because she didn't really care about the outcome or because she thought her mother wouldn't love her if she disagreed with her?

How often had she seen her father do the same thing? She ran a hand through her hair, liking the feel of the silken softness through her fingers.

She glanced at her father, and he smiled and shrugged.

"Could you give me a few days to decide what I want to do? I need to know God wants me to leave India. I can't walk away from everything that's happened and pretend it hasn't affected my life." Her eyes watered and Charlotte blinked to stem her tears.

"Dear, I know you need time to process everything, but you can do that at home. You have no idea how hard it's been for us. I want to hold you, tuck you up in your bed, and get our lives back to normal."

Charlotte hated arguing with her mother, especially in front of everyone. She couldn't expect her mother to understand how much she'd grown to love the sad, lonely girls in the brothel.

Her head rose as calmness spread through her body. That was it! She loved them; as simple as that sounded, it meant she couldn't leave them.

"Mum, I know you don't want to hear this, but I'm staying."

"That's ridiculous!" Macy's face puckered. "You're only eighteen and you're coming back to Australia with us."

Charlotte shook her head and braced herself. Was she really only eighteen? Her body felt much older. What she'd lived through had taken all evidence of youth from her.

She shuddered as she thought of Shanti dying before her eyes and her being unable to protect her. She stared into space, seeing things she could not speak of.

Macy cleared her throat and moved to stand beside Bill.

Charlotte's heart warmed at the love she saw on their faces. They would always be her parents, but they couldn't live her life for her.

A part of her wished that they could, that she could be like a puppet protected from further pain, but another part of her needed to fight against cruelty.

"My heart is here, and I want to help girls like me, like Gargi and Shanti. I don't know what that will look like, but with God's help I'll work it out." Charlotte set her shoulders back and looked directly into her mother's eyes.

Macy grabbed Bill's arm. "Bill, don't just stand there, talk some sense into her," she demanded.

Charlotte glanced at her father and saw a moment of indecision flash across his face.

"Charlie, you have to understand that your mother and I are frightened to leave you here."

She wanted to rush to her father, hug and reassure him that God would protect her. She rubbed the back of her neck, and a shooting pain shot up her hand, reminding her that her finger was broken.

Looking down she saw the swelling and bruising around her knuckles and sighed. There were a lot of things she didn't understand, but she did know that God hadn't abandoned her.

"Dad, I understand your fear. I'm sorry I can't tell you that nothing bad will happen to me, because truthfully I don't know."

Macy started to cry and Charlotte sucked in her lips. Tension spiraled through her as she watched her father put his arms around her mother. She sped across the room to embrace them, tears streaming down her face.

"I'm sorry," she whispered.

As her father stepped back, Charlotte looked into his eyes and caught her breath at the sorrow she saw reflected there.

He gave her a watery smile and nodded. She tilted her head to look at her mother.

Macy threw her arms around her, pulling her so close that nothing separated them. Charlotte's throat locked, making it hard to breathe. It was as if her mother were saying good-bye for the last time.

After her parents had gone, Charlotte collapsed into the chair and stared at the closed door. She felt drained. She'd had to steel herself not to run after them, wanting to make everything right for them. They'd been through so much because of her, and it tore at her heart.

She could feel the tension in the room and wondered who'd be the first to speak. She looked across at Eli, who stared into space with a frown grooving his forehead. She wondered when he'd last eaten.

Gargi shuffled her feet. She perched on the edge of her seat, looking down at her hands. How different her friend seemed, almost meek.

"That's a first, seeing you stand up to Mum like that," Eli pointed out with a smile.

"Are you serious, Charlie?" Gargi asked, her eyes sparkling with excitement. Charlotte grinned at her and nodded. Now that she'd spoken the words out loud, it felt right.

She glanced at Phillip, and the direct look he gave her caused her cheeks to heat. She couldn't think about how she felt about him. She needed to focus on how she was going to stay in India and where to start.

"Can I throw some ideas around that are taking shape in my mind? I want to establish a home for girls coming out of captivity, a place where they can be supported to create a new life for themselves. A place to restore hope and demonstrate God's love."

"I want the same thing." Gargi jumped up and clapped her hands. "I've been praying to Jesus to help me know what I can do. I have no skills to support myself, and there are many others like me. How do you begin again when you don't have the strength of Jesus in you? I wanted to kill myself when I was in the brothel. I had no hope and no desire to live. Yes, Charlie—I must be a part of this."

307

Phillip pushed away from the wall he'd been leaning on and moved across the room to stand beside Charlotte.

"I'm in. I think that's a great idea. The first step would be to get some financial backers. You need to put down on paper exactly what you plan to do and sell the idea to others." He reached out and gently touched Charlotte's cheek. "I'm glad you're not leaving, Charlie." He grinned and stepped back at the sound of Eli clearing his throat loudly.

Charlotte's heart gave a small flutter. She could still feel the impression of Phillip's fingers on her cheek.

"I think the first step is the name," Charlotte said softly. "Shanti's Rest." Joy filled her heart at the legacy Shanti's life was leaving behind.

"Do you know the meaning of the name Shanti, Charlie?" Gargi asked, her face alight with joy.

"No, but I can tell by your face that you do," Charlotte replied with a laugh.

"Shanti means—calm, peace! I think that's beautiful, just like our little Shanti. Shanti's Rest, a place where girls can come and find peace."

Tears glimmered in Charlotte's eyes as she blinked. Sadness pulled at her heart as she pictured Shanti's little face, wide-eyed and laughing as she played knucklebones.

Charlotte lifted her chin in determination and nodded. "Can I talk to you for a moment in private, Eli?" She glanced at her friends apologetically, and they both nodded and left the room.

"Come here, Bud." He lifted his arm and Charlotte stepped into his embrace.

He'd never given up on finding her; the cost to him must have been enormous. She lifted her head and locked eyes with him; she opened her mouth in surprise as she saw his eyes flood. Her hand splayed over his chest, and she stood on her toes to kiss his cheek.

"Thank you, Eli. I knew you wouldn't give up until you found me. I love you." She stopped as emotion clogged her throat.

Eli sighed. His eyes closed and he tightened his arms.

Words weren't needed between them; he was her brother. Charlotte let the tears fall unchecked down her cheeks.

There was another boy who should have been hugging his sister right now, but instead he was outside somewhere, lost within himself.

Charlotte pulled away and tried to compose herself. "What comes next for you, Eli?"

"One day at a time, Charlie. I have to set the ball in motion towards adopting Ashok. This isn't going to be easy, as the boy has no identity. You and I both have tourist visas, which we need to sort out." He glanced towards the closed door, and his mouth lifted slightly.

"Charlie, I know I haven't known Gargi long, but I'm drawn to her. I think I could easily fall in love with her."

Charlotte felt her stomach roll. She already loved Gargi like a sister and wanted nothing more than to see her happy.

What made her hesitate? Eli was a kind, gentle man, but was he patient enough to wait however long it took—maybe years—for Gargi to heal from the scars of her abuse?

"What are you thinking, Sis?"

Charlotte's heart twisted as she looked at Eli's open face. The last thing she wanted to do was hurt or discourage him.

"Any girl you fall in love with will be blessed, Eli. Just don't expect too much from Gargi. She needs a friend right now more than she needs a boyfriend. It could take her years to get to the place where she's ready. Are you prepared to wait?"

"I think I am. Friend it is. Don't worry Bud, I'm not going to put any pressure on her, ever." He smoothed her hair off her face. "I'm sorry Charlie. I wish I could make things right for you."

Slipping her arms around him she rested her head on his chest.

Oh, the hug of a brother, she thought. Safe, undemanding, and gentle.

Chapter 45

Ashok's fingers tensed as he held the card, and his eyes narrowed. The faded picture of Jesus holding the lamb in his arms stared back at him.

It seemed like Jesus's eyes shined in the picture. He rubbed his finger over the tape that Eli had used to join the tear and felt his chest tighten.

He'd told Shanti over and over again that the card said Jesus would keep you in happiness if you trusted him.

Fear fluttered in his chest and he sucked in a deep breath. He'd told Jesus he didn't trust him. His shoulders hunched and his body felt heavy with pain.

Was he being mean, wanting Shanti here with him?

Shanti had looked happy when she'd told him Jesus was smiling at her. She'd been hurt bad and lost lots of blood.

He shuddered as he remembered Eli showering him in his clothes and seeing Shanti's blood wash down the drain.

Would it have been too hard for her to get better from the knife wounds?

What was she doing right now, he wondered. Would she be missing him as well? He longed to talk to her, to hear her voice one more time.

310

He'd tell her he was sorry that it took him so long to find her.

A big tear plopped on his hand, and Ashok sniffed. Would the ache inside him ever go away? Who would need him now, the way Shanti had?

He knew Eli loved him, and his heart pumped inside his chest at the thought: Eli wanted to be his father.

Jesus, I'm sorry I got angry at you. I hate what happened, but I do trust you. Help me to be a good boy, help me to laugh again.

"Hello, Ashok." Gargi sat down on the step beside him. "May I see your card?"

Ashok glanced at her and nodded. He handed over the card and watched as her eyes skimmed the picture.

"What does it say, can you tell me?" she asked gently. "I can't read."

Ashok peered at the words and nodded solemnly. "Eli taught me to read the words. I used to think it said Jesus will keep you in happiness if you trust him."

His chin wobbled as he stretched out his hand for the card. Gargi gave it to him and leaned over to see the picture.

Ashok ran his tongue over his lips and peered at the words. He pointed to the first word, then the next as he began to read.

"'I am the good shepherd, I know my own sheep, and they know me.' Do you believe that, Gargi?"

"Yes, I do." She took his hand and laced their fingers together. "I'm sorry Shanti died. Do you think Jesus carried her in his arms like he's carrying the lamb?" she asked with a tender smile.

Ashok couldn't answer. Love squeezed at his chest, and his face burned. He pictured his Shanti safe in Jesus's arms, and happiness spread through his body. His eyes closed, and he was sure he could hear Shanti's giggle.

"When I was ready to give up, your sister's strength reached out to me. I will never forget her and the impact she had on my life. She knew you'd find her, and you did. Well done, Ashok."

"I found her too late," he stated sadly, his eyes downcast.

"I don't think so. Look at all that's happened. I'm free, the brothel's closed down, and Shanti's happy with Jesus and doesn't feel any more pain."

What Gargi said was true, Ashok thought. He straightened his shoulders and looked down at their joined hands.

Gargi squeezed his hand until he looked up at her. "Ashok, do you think we could be friends? Charlie was my first friend ever, and I think you and I could be special friends."

"Yes," he said and twisted towards her.

She released his hand, and Ashok shuffled his bottom on the step until he was close enough to wind his arms around her waist.

As he burrowed into her embrace, he didn't feel so lonely.

~~~

She wanted to slam the door shut, but years of control took over and Macy clicked the door quietly behind her.

She had to get Bill to listen to her. His condescending look in the taxi had angered her. She was not the one in the wrong here. A deep frown furrowed her brow, and she could feel the beginning of a headache tapping behind her eyes.

"She doesn't belong to you, you have to release her to God," Bill stated as he came to stand in front of her.

Macy avoided his eyes. How dare he sound so righteous when she knew Charlotte belonged to God?

"Have you forgotten already that this is India? That this is where the nightmare began, where we lost our baby girl." She hated the biting tone she heard in her voice.

"It's not only in India that evil lurks. People get abducted everywhere. The world's a mess, but there is hope. Things will change if people stand up to what's wrong and call loudly for justice. This is what Charlie wants to do, and I for one want to help her."

Macy's eyes twitched, and her stomach churned. She collapsed into a chair and wanted to cry.

The picture of getting Charlie home and looking after her began to fade in her mind. It wasn't going to happen.

"They both want to stay here, Bill," she murmured weakly.

"I know, darling," he replied gently, and she looked up. Bill dabbed at his eyes and Macy sprung up and ran over to embrace him.

"I don't know what to do or think now she's safe. I can't imagine going home without her."

"I've been thinking about that. I think you'd be great at spreading the word about what Charlotte wants to do. You know, raising awareness and sponsorship for the programmes that Charlie and Gargi come up with."

She knew what he was trying to do, and her heart filled with love for him. He too would miss their children, but knew better than to try and hold on to what wasn't theirs.

They'd been through so much together; his health was still a fragile thing and yet he'd spent every day hammering the police to take action.

Admiration for her husband beat in her chest, and she lifted her hand and lovingly squeezed his shoulder.

Stepping back from Bill, Macy sat heavily in a chair. She leaned her head back wearily and closed her eyes. A picture of Charlotte as a child popped into her mind.

Her lips lifted slightly at the memory. Charlie was holding Muffin, a kitten they'd had, in a strangling hold, and Macy remembered coaxing her child's fingers from around the frightened cat's neck. Charlie didn't want Muffin to go outside because she was frightened the cat would get lost.

Macy sucked in a deep breath as she remembered explaining to Charlotte that cats were born to climb trees and explore and that she had to let her go.

Looking down she saw her hands were clasped tightly together. She flexed her fingers, unlocking them. Her heart pounded, and she felt heat infuse her body. She finally understood. She swallowed and cleared her throat.

"I'm sorry, Bill. When I feel things slipping out of my control, I panic and try and force my way through."

Bill looked across at her, and she lifted a hand to stop him from saying anything. She needed to speak the words. "If this is what Charlotte wants to do, or should I say, what God wants her to do, then I'll support her."

Bill drew her close and she marveled again at how well she fit under his shoulder. She smiled as she thought of the way Phillip looked at Charlie. Maybe God had bigger plans than even Charlotte knew.

She sighed heavily and felt her shoulders relax. It was like she'd dropped a huge boulder she'd been trying to carry on her own.

For now, Macy decided, she had things to organize. There were plane tickets to cancel and a daughter to take shopping, two daughters one day if Eli had his way.

Laughter bubbled up within her, and she felt her shoulders relax. Two daughters and a grandson! She threw back her head and surprised Bill by her laugh.

He kissed the top of her head and pulled back to look at her.

She shrugged, gave a cheeky smile, and asked him for the credit card.

Chapter 46

The sun shone down on Charlotte's back, warming her, and she lifted her hand to shade her eyes as she scanned the large building in front of her which was to become the home of Shanti's Rest.

It needed painting and some new windows, but the rest of the outside was structurally sound.

She marveled at how Ted had been excited about their plans and thrown a cocktail party at his hotel, inviting two hundred wealthy guests. Money had not stopped pouring in, and now the dream had become a reality.

The architect hadn't charged them for the plans, another demonstration of God's faithfulness.

It was exciting to visualize the finished picture of lounges, bedrooms, and offices. There would be a classroom where the girls could be taught to read and start a journey towards education, but most importantly a small chapel where they could spend time worshiping God.

She could hear the ear-splitting sound of electric saws and hammers and walked around the building to get away from the noise.

Her expression softened as she saw Eli and Pastor Tanvir deep in conversation with two other men from church.

The church with the red door already felt like home to her. The welcome she'd received, and the love, warmed her heart.

"Charlie," Ashok shouted, waving from the second-storey window.

Waving, she blew him a kiss. The young boy was growing in confidence. Eli took him to school every day, and he was a fast learner.

She still saw many moments of deep sadness in his eyes, which she understood only too well. Charlotte loved Ashok. He touched her heart with his simple faith and trusting dark eyes.

She wondered about herself. She saw the promise in Phillip's eyes and loved him for holding back on talking to her about how he felt.

She needed time to adjust to what had happened. The nightmare of her abuse often surfaced from the depths of her mind to haunt her. If she closed her eyes she could still see Saul's face mocking her and she found herself cringing at the oddest of times. She knew in her head she was safe but sometime even a man glancing in her direction could send a chill down her spine.

Phillip had suggested 'Shanti's Rest' employ a psychologist to help the girls work through the aftermath of their abuse. Her stomach churned at the thought of trying to put into words what she was feeling.

Shanti had been so very young, yet greed and lust had stolen her life. Trafficking was a lucrative business, she'd discovered.

The sun moved behind a cloud, and Charlotte shivered. Her mouth felt dry and she moistened her lips. This world really was a deep, sunless valley of shadows, she thought, wrapping her arms around herself protectively.

The cloud moved, the sun broke free, and a glimmer of a smile touched her lips. No, she challenged herself. The light of the Son's love dispels the darkness of this world.

Charlotte thought of the word *chaya*. Her search on the Internet had confirmed that she'd heard the word before. The word *chaya* had multiple meanings. It may mean shadow in Hindi, but in Hebrew it meant life.

She knew God was helping her work through what had happened, and Shanti's Rest gave her a purpose to hold on to.

When Charlotte told Gargi she was going to scour the neighborhood for the other girls who'd been freed by the police raid, she'd willingly offered to go with her.

Now, as Charlotte looked at the four girls sitting cross-legged on the road, her heart felt full.

She clutched her hands together and closed her eyes, blocking out all around her. She could feel a gentle breeze caressing her skin, as if the fingers of Jesus were stroking her face. Lightness filled her soul as her heart believed.

Yes, Lord. Even though I walk through the darkest valley, I will fear no evil, for you are with me; your rod and staff comfort me.

"Charlie, come play knucklebones," one of the girls beckoned her.

Turning towards her Charlotte smiled. She'd love nothing more than to sit on the hard, dusty road with them and throw up small rough stone into the air. Each time she played, she felt close to Shanti.

Charlotte sat between two girls and reached over to touch one of them on the shoulder. She smiled and watched as they tossed the stones up in the air.

As her gaze rose, she saw the figure of a woman in the distance.

The woman stopped, turned, and began to retreat. Charlotte watched her move further away and wondered who she was.

The woman stopped and lowered her head before she hesitantly turned around and started back toward her.

Charlotte scrambled to her feet, squinting in the glare of the noonday sun, and her hand came up to shield her eyes.

She took a tentative step forward, and as the distance shortened between them, a smile burst across her face and tears streamed down her cheeks.

Charlotte ran towards the woman, her arms open wide and her heart bursting with joy.

"Oh my Lord, my precious Lord—it's Padma."

Anchored

Successful business man, David O'Malley thought life would be simpler moving from Sydney to the picturesque seaside town of Blue Bay, known for it's stunning beaches and friendly locals. An unexpected brutal hit and run not only leaves David questioning his decision to move, but throws the sleepy town into a spin, with suspicions running high.

Mia Dawson had lived in Blue Bay her whole life and she'd never met anyone quite like David. Despite his obvious good looks and city charm her heart was guarded. A series of unexpected events threatens Mia's safety, but sadly she cannot run to the one man she needs the most - her father.

Overwhelmed by deceit and lies, Jonathan only has himself to blame. There's a bitter wedge between him and his only daughter, Mia, which haunts him day and night. Despite living under the same roof his family is falling apart.

Mystery, mistrust and betrayal run deep throughout Anchored. A story where relationships are important but not always as they seem.

View full details at
TraceyHoffmann.com

Made in the USA
San Bernardino, CA
11 December 2013